INTO THIN AIR

Visit us at www.boldstrokesbooks.com

By the Author

Threads of the Heart

Embracing the Dawn

Into Thin Air

INTO THIN AIR

by

Jeannie Levig

2017

INTO THIN AIR

ISBN 13: 978-1-62639-722-4

This Trade Paperback Original Is Published By
Bold Strokes Books, Inc.
P.O. Box 249
Valley Falls, NY 12185

First Edition: January 2017

CREDITS
EDITORS: Victoria Villasenor and Cindy Cresap
PRODUCTION DESIGN: Susan Ramundo
COVER DESIGN BY Sheri (GRAPHICARTIST2020@HOTMAIL.COM)
COVER PHOTO BY Erik Levig

Acknowledgments

Always in my list of blessings for which to be grateful are my amazing family, spiritual circle, and friends who give me their unwavering love and support in everything I do. I couldn't walk this path without each and every one of you. Thank you.

I am forever thankful for Jamie Patterson, my Ideal Reader and best friend, for her honest and trustworthy feedback, and on this book in particular, thank you for seeing me through it. This one was tough to write. Thank you for keeping me moving and always reminding me to trust what comes through.

Immeasurable appreciation and admiration for the amazing team at Bold Strokes Books. To Radclyffe for creating and tirelessly leading this publishing house that is so dedicated to making sure every book is of the highest quality and all of its authors are fully supported in their growth and development as writers. To Sandy Lowe for taking a chance on this book and believing in my ability to write it—as well as the million other things she does each day to help keep BSB running smoothly. To my editors extraordinaire, Victoria Villasenor and Cindy Cresap. Vic, thank you for your patience and extra support on this project and for your guidance and insights with these characters in particular. In general, thank you for the dedication and heart you put into your—and my—work and for making my stories stronger. And for always making the editing experience fun, interesting, and expanding. To Cindy, I am so grateful for your impeccable copy editing and everything else you do in the production of my books. And a huge thank you to all the behind the scenes people at BSB committed to excellence in publishing.

Finally, a heartfelt thank you to all the readers who buy my books. This is all for you. Thank you for sharing this experience with me. And always feel free to drop me a note and say hi.

CHAPTER ONE

A s Hannah Lewis ascended through the haze of sleep, she became aware of Jordan behind her. She was conscious of her own nakedness beneath her nightshirt and released a soft moan of morning desire. "Spoon me," she murmured.

Jordan moved in closer, her body molding to Hannah's.

Hannah reached back and grazed the seam of the cotton pants covering Jordan's thigh. She curled her toes, and the soles of her feet found the hardness of shoes through the thin jersey sheet. Another moan, this one of disappointment, vibrated in her throat. "You're dressed."

Jordan combed Hannah's hair off her cheek. "I am." Her moist breath caressed Hannah's ear. "I have a racquetball game, then I'm putting in some time at work. I'll be home by three-ish." Her soft voice held the stillness of wanting Hannah to go back to sleep. Hannah had taught Jordan early in their three years together never to leave without saying good-bye—*and no, a note doesn't count*—but she knew Jordan still hated waking her.

Hannah eased backward. The warmth of Jordan's legs pressed against the backs of her own, her pelvis against Hannah's ass, her breasts against her back, did nothing to encourage sleep. "Don't go."

Jordan's sigh feathered across the curve of Hannah's neck, and she slipped her arm around Hannah's waist and pulled her close. Her hand moved beneath the shirt to cup Hannah's breast, her thumb teasing the nipple into stiff arousal. She suckled Hannah's earlobe between her full lips.

Hannah's breath caught. Eyes still closed, she squeezed her thighs together. She was already wet, wanting release. She could climax right now under Jordan's practiced touch, the proverbial morning quickie, but she knew Jordan would give her all. She didn't scrimp where Hannah was concerned, whether with gifts or words, and certainly not in lovemaking. It was only Jordan's emotional economy that sometimes left Hannah wondering.

On the surface, evidenced by Christmas card photos, barbecues with friends, and even the private moments they shared, Jordan was the perfect girlfriend. There were the obvious physical benefits—ash-colored eyes that reached into Hannah's depths and caressed her very core; sleek, long, dark hair; the toned body of the athlete; even the nontraditional allure of her slightly crooked smile. Not a conventional beauty, but she drew stares that stroked Hannah's ego for having a lover everyone else desired.

Her attentiveness and consideration affected Hannah even more, though. She would stop at the deli on her way home from work for Hannah's favorite hummus and pita chips, if she knew the day had been long or hectic. She would pick up lox and bagels after her early— very early—morning run for them to share in bed when Hannah finally stirred. She made herself available, for listening, snuggling, or sex, even at times like this when she had other commitments. Hannah couldn't really say the same.

On another level, however, Jordan sometimes felt as far away and unreachable as if she were in Bali, and she had a knack for feeling removed even when wrapped completely around Hannah— like now.

Jordan flicked her tongue behind Hannah's ear, then kissed her neck. Her hand moved over Hannah's breasts, toying with both nipples simultaneously.

Hannah gasped. "Oh, Jory." She turned in Jordan's arms, easing onto her back.

Jordan shifted over her and gently claimed her mouth with soft lips.

Hannah opened to receive her tongue just as Jordan's skilled fingers closed around her hard nipple, squeezing and rolling it until Hannah's hips came up off the bed.

They kissed long and deep, moving with the orchestration of familiarity to extricate Hannah from her nightshirt.

Hannah sank back into the pillow, finally opening her eyes. She threaded her arms around Jordan's neck and gazed into veiled features. Yes, this was one of those times when Jordan was somewhere far away, but at the moment, Hannah didn't care.

As Jordan settled her length on top of her, the sateen finish of her button-up shirt caressed Hannah's bare and aching nipples, while the bulk of her pants and shoes through the sheet gave Hannah the tantalizing feeling of the bad-girl-being-ravished fantasy. She arched into Jordan.

Jordan dipped her head and bit Hannah's lower lip, then soothed the nip with her hot tongue.

Hannah released a deep groan. She pulled Jordan's mouth hard against her own.

They kissed for long seconds that turned into long minutes. Their bodies moved against one another. Jordan slipped her thigh between Hannah's, while Hannah ran her hands up Jordan's back, reveling in the play of taut muscles beneath the fabric.

Hannah thrust her hips, her breathing fast and shallow.

Jordan caught Hannah's lip between her teeth one last time before leaving her gasping for more. She moved down Hannah's body, grazing her teeth against stretched neck muscles, trailing kisses along Hannah's collarbone, sucking oh-so-deeply on her sensitized, engorged nipples, finally making her way over Hannah's shivering stomach toward the ultimate destination. When she reached it, Jordan looped her arms around Hannah's hips, opened her wide, and feasted.

Hannah cried out over and over with each slow, deliberate stroke of Jordan's tongue and with every purposeful pause just short of fulfillment.

At the very instant Hannah knew she couldn't take anymore, Jordan closed her lips around Hannah's throbbing need and sucked scream after scream of pleasure from her.

Finally, Hannah lay limp and drained.

Jordan crawled up beside her and tenderly nestled her into a snug embrace.

Eyes still closed, Hannah burrowed into her. "I want to do you," she whispered. At least, she thought she actually said it.

Jordan didn't respond. She pressed her lips to Hannah's hair.

Her body sated, her mind quieter than even at its first conscious thought of the day, Hannah felt the weight of sleep settling over her once again. She knew if she drifted off, Jordan would be gone when she woke again. Jordan did that, but after everything she had just done to her, how could Hannah be mad? She struggled to ward off her dimming awareness, but the final week of school and the anticipation of her summer away from the high school that served as her second home ten months out of each year combined to pull her into darkness on this first morning of luxury and, with her debilitating orgasm, even decadence. She surrendered once again to sleep.

Jordan Webber tossed her gym bag onto the backseat of her Chevy Equinox and climbed in behind the wheel. She read the text message that'd just come in.

From: Liz

Want 2 keep r game. Had car trouble. Can u pick me up at mechanics?

An address followed.

Jordan sent a quick *yep*, then dropped her phone onto the passenger's seat. She took a moment to program the location into Geraldine—she'd named her GPS Geraldine Penelope Sanders—and was glad she'd spent a little extra time with Hannah, more than she'd even intended. Otherwise, she'd already be heading in the opposite direction.

She'd learned early in their relationship to begin her exits sooner than was actually necessary for punctuality, but even then she sometimes found herself running a few minutes late. Hannah had a habit of wanting attention, usually sex, right when Jordan needed to be somewhere else. Maybe it was tied in with her issues around being given up for adoption, her fear of not being wanted. Maybe it was a way of establishing her importance in their relationship. Jordan wasn't sure. She just knew it was easier if she went ahead and took care of Hannah's needs than if she tried to explain she didn't have time or wasn't in the mood. Not that she minded making love to her. After all, if you truly minded making love to your girlfriend, chances were, she shouldn't be your girlfriend.

She actually loved sex with Hannah. It was easy, relatively uncomplicated, fun—all of which described their overall relationship as well. Hannah had a tendency toward self-absorption, but even that worked for Jordan. It allowed her to keep those parts of herself she didn't want to deal with tucked away in the nooks and crannies of her consciousness. There was the confused and frightened teenaged Jordan who'd learned to lie about her sexual feelings for—and sometimes explorations with—girls, as well as one particular older woman, after listening to Reverend Palmer's condemnations of homosexuality and warnings of a fiery afterlife. And there was the manipulative Jordan, who'd gone to law school on her father's checkbook, knowing all along she'd turn her back on his plans for her to join his corporate firm in exchange for a career as a civil rights attorney. And there was the restless, maverick Jordan who'd never been able to commit to one woman. Hannah's oblivious nature worked well, because Jordan simply didn't want to share those aspects of herself. Ever.

Jordan checked her watch. She and Liz would still be able to make their court time, even with the detour to the mechanic's shop. She stepped on the gas and eased the SUV into the flow of traffic.

She'd only known Liz for a month or so. She always played racquetball with her best friend, Nikki, but Nikki had broken her foot—jumping over a goat, of all things—and had been out of commission on the courts for over a month. Jordan had spent the first couple of weeks getting a game with anyone who happened to be available at the time, but then she'd met Liz, a newbie to the gym but not to the game. She gave Jordan a good workout.

Liz was in Los Angeles for a lengthy yet temporary job assignment, something to do with lighting for a new business complex going up somewhere in the Valley. Her company put her up at the Sheraton, she ate a lot of takeout, and she worked out at the gym. She didn't know very many people, didn't socialize with colleagues, and seemed to like it that way. She played racquetball with Jordan three times a week. That was pretty much all Jordan knew about her, and she felt no need to know anything more. Jordan liked her privacy and gave everyone else theirs.

"Turn left in six hundred feet," Geraldine said in her helpful yet mildly sexy tone.

Jordan obeyed. Geraldine was the one woman she *always* obeyed. The street was narrow, lined with small businesses still closed at this early hour on a Saturday. She wasn't entirely sure where she was.

"Continue for two hundred feet. Your destination will be on the right."

Jordan saw Liz get out of a car parked at the curb a short way down the street, her white shorts and T-shirt brilliant in the morning sunshine. Sunglasses hid her eyes. She waved to the spot behind hers.

Jordan killed the engine and opened her door. "Hey. What happened?" She closed the distance between them.

Liz smiled. "Thank you so much for this. My car was making a horrible noise. I called a guy I work with, and he sent me straight here." She motioned to a building boasting Fast 'n Fair Car Repair. "The shop's his brother's. They'll be here in a few minutes." She opened her back door and leaned inside. "Can you take these for me? I don't want to leave them." She handed Jordan a briefcase and a laptop.

"Sure." Jordan looped the strap to the canvas bag over a shoulder and gripped the handle of the attaché.

A white van made its way up the street toward her.

She moved closer to Liz's car to give the driver room. She heard the whoosh of the side panel sliding open. Curious, she started to turn.

A damp cloth covered her nose and mouth. A strong hand held it firmly in place. An arm snaked around her waist and yanked her backward.

Confusion gave way to fear—then panic. She dropped the briefcase. She tried to fight, but a pungent odor gagged her. Her last sight was Liz walking toward the Equinox as the tentacles of unconsciousness pulled her into darkness.

CHAPTER TWO

Hannah stared at the cordless phone lying on the kitchen table. She had lost count of how many times she'd called Jordan's cell over the past three hours. It had gone straight to voice mail every time. For the first hour, she just assumed Jordan was in a meeting. *Odd for a Saturday, but certainly possible.* Then she decided Jordan had forgotten to turn her phone back on following the assumed meeting, and after that, she imagined *the meeting* must have to do with some big case, important enough to call everyone in on a weekend and even more complicated than anyone originally knew. Once she started calling the main office, though, and got no answer, she had to admit she'd made up every possibility and something truly could be wrong.

What though? What would be considered *wrong* in a life as normal as theirs? Her thoughts drifted to all those TV shows that aired stories about somebody's loved one turning out to be the serial killer for which every law enforcement agency in three states has been searching for a decade, or someone waking up to find the person she lives with vanished into the night in a UFO or—equally as alien—the witness protection program.

Their lives weren't like that. Theirs was just an average one in Santa Monica, California, in which she, as a high school counselor, sometimes had the unfortunate task of breaking it to an otherwise intelligent teenaged girl that yes, you *really can* get pregnant the first time, and Jordan, as a civil liberties attorney, spent her days helping people realize their rights. It was a life in which two women spent Sunday mornings at the farmer's market, occasionally made love on the living room floor, and shared an appreciation for quirky movies like *Lars and the Real Girl.*

Hannah remembered a show she had watched once where a woman was abducted by a couple on her way home from a book club meeting and kept in the hollow pedestal of a waterbed for the next four years, let out only to be used as a sex slave by the husband and to help the wife clean the house. At the time, Hannah thought the woman kidnapped must have been into some weird stuff for that to have happened, but now she wondered. Could she have been a typical, middle class, thirty-something Flo Schmo who simply happened to be in the wrong place at the wrong time?

The doorbell rang.

Hannah jumped. *Jordan.* She leapt up, almost toppling her chair, and ran to answer it. She pulled open the door, relief washing away a fear she hadn't fully realized gripped her. Then she recognized her sister. Her heart tightened again. "Kate," she said, unable to hide her disappointment. "I thought you were Jory."

"Why would Jordan ring the bell?" Kate swept past her. "I take it she hasn't shown up yet."

Hannah eased the door closed. "No, not yet." She had forgotten she called Kate.

"Well, maybe if she's run off, you can get back to men. I still say you're not gay." Kate dropped onto the sofa. Her dark blue capris and sleeveless, pink cotton blouse bore the usual resemblance to what Hannah wore. It had always been that way. Without even talking, they would show up places wearing amazingly similar outfits. "We're identical twins," Kate said, as she often did. "And I'm not gay, so you can't be either." It was a position she had held since Hannah had come out ten years earlier.

Jordan always said there was nothing identical about them. She called Kate the crystallized version of Hannah—hard, sharp-edged, cold as the undead and just as creepy. Though Hannah and Kate were truly identical physically, Jordan could always tell them apart from any angle. Hannah believed that was the reason Kate had never liked her. Once, she had tried to fool Jordan, the way they had done with everyone when they were children, but Jordan had known instantly and rejected the kiss Kate was attempting to plant on her.

Hannah released an irritated sigh. "The last *man* I was with was Jimmy Robertson when we were eleven." She sat on the edge of the recliner across from Kate. "I'd get arrested if I went after eleven-year-olds now."

"I'm sure Jimmy Robertson isn't eleven anymore," Kate said. "And I remember him being pretty cute."

Hannah looked into her own clear green eyes, her own patrician features, recognizing her own relentless, dog-with-a-bone tendencies. "Why are you here?"

Kate flashed Hannah's bright smile and leaned back into the plush sofa cushion. She crossed her long legs. "To support you. To be with you while you're worried." She ran her fingers through her shoulder-length blond hair. "You're worried, aren't you? You sounded worried on the phone."

Hannah's thoughts returned to Jordan. "I think I'm starting to be," she said. "She was supposed to be home hours ago, and she's not answering her phone."

Kate shrugged. "So, she's late. It can't be the first time."

Late. Hannah allowed the word to wander the twists and turns of her neural pathways. First, Jordan had simply *been out.* Then, she *hadn't been home yet.* After another half hour or so, maybe she had been officially *late.* What was she now as the time was going on seven o'clock? At what point did someone become *missing*? "No," she said to Kate. "It's not the first time she's been late, but it's the first time she's been this late without calling." Jordan couldn't be *missing*, though. Not yet. Not, at least, until Hannah had contacted a few people she might be with.

"Have you tried that friend of hers?" Kate asked, reading Hannah's mind as she frequently did. "What's her name? Vickie? Mickey?"

"Nikki," Hannah said, tossing her an annoyed glance. Kate never remembered the names of people she considered superfluous. "And no, I haven't."

"Why not? I'd think she'd be the first person you'd try."

She should have been. Nikki had been Jordan's best friend since before Hannah had come into the picture, and for the first six months Hannah and Jordan were dating, Nikki had been around a lot. She and Hannah had started to become close, too. When Hannah had moved in with Jordan, though, something changed. Nikki had all but vanished. She still saw Jordan, still played racquetball and basketball with her and grabbed a beer or caught a movie several times a month, but she didn't do anything with *them* anymore.

Hannah had tried to fix whatever had happened; she'd extended invitations to Nikki, had asked if something was wrong, but that just seemed to make things awkward between them. Hannah had even asked Jordan about it, but Jordan had assured her everything was fine, that Nikki just got funny sometimes, and not to worry about it. It was that awkwardness that still lingered between them that had kept Hannah from calling Nikki earlier, but now, her reluctance stemmed from the question, if Jordan wasn't with Nikki, where the hell was she? "I haven't called anyone. I was still waiting."

"How long are you going to wait?" Kate's steady gaze held Hannah's.

Hannah sighed and went to get the phone. As she listened to the third ring on the other end of the line, she pictured Jordan and Nikki, kicked back on Nikki's ratty old couch, knocking back a few beers and watching whatever sized and shaped ball now in season bounce around the television screen. Irritation tightened her jaw.

"Hey, where you been?" Nikki asked when she picked up, her tone casual. "I've been calling you all afternoon."

Hannah's hope fell. Clearly, Nikki knew as little as she did about Jordan's whereabouts. "Nikki, it's Hannah. I was hoping Jordan was with you, but I guess not, huh?"

"Hannah? No, she's not with me." Nikki paused. "Is everything okay?"

Fear had been prowling the outskirts of Hannah's heart like a wild animal stalking its prey, but now, at the confirmation that the one other person who almost always knew where Jordan was had no idea either, Hannah felt its circle begin to tighten in her chest. "Oh, I'm sure everything's fine." She attempted a light air. "Jory's just late, and I haven't been able to reach her. I just thought she might be with you."

"How late is she?"

"She said she'd be home around three." A silence followed. Hannah envisioned Nikki checking her watch. Then she heard a muffled *no, thank you*. "Oh, I'm sorry. Are you out somewhere?"

"It's okay. I'm just—"

"I didn't mean to interrupt anything. I'm sure she'll be home soon."

"Well, I…" Nikki hesitated. "It's weird she's so late and hasn't called you. Will you let me know when she turns up?"

"Yes," Hannah said. There was no point in keeping Nikki on the phone since she didn't know anything either, but Hannah felt reluctant to let her go. This call was different from the one she made to Kate earlier, in which she voiced her irritation at Jordan's lack of consideration. This one had opened the door to the possibility that something might have happened to Jordan, and Nikki was a connection to her. "I'm sure she'll be home soon. Enjoy your evening."

Hannah ended the call and pursed her lips. She felt Kate's eyes on her. "Nikki doesn't know where she is." She heard the anxiety in her voice before she actually recognized its clench in her stomach.

"Well…hey…" Kate touched Hannah's shoulder. "Nikki's not her only friend, is she? Who else could she be with?"

Kate's atypical tenderness did more to heighten Hannah's apprehension than ease it. Hannah needed Kate to be flippant, dismissive, her usual annoying self, diminishing the situation and turning the topic back to her own latest drama. She needed her somehow to make this moment all about her, the way she always did. That would make it normal. It would mean everything was okay, that Jordan would walk through the front door any minute and Kate would give her the stink-eye.

Hannah tried to focus on the question. *Other friends?* Of course, Jordan had other friends, but who were they? They had friends together, couples they did things with, but those were Hannah's friends. Jordan wouldn't be with any of them without her. Jordan did do other things, though. She went to lunch with… *What's that guy's name? And there's Lexie…or Leslie…or Lucy…who cuts her hair.* Hadn't they gone to a WNBA game a few weeks ago? Hannah wished she had paid more attention. "I don't know." She shook her head. "I don't know her other friends." She blinked in surprised realization, the gap in her knowledge causing a sinking feeling in her stomach.

❖

Nikki Medina yanked the handle of the emergency brake into place and opened the car door. She swung her feet out in the way that was now habit after six weeks with her left foot in a cast and gripped the top of the door, then hoisted herself out. She'd be glad when the cast came off and her life could get back to normal. She grabbed her crutches from behind the driver's seat and slammed the car door.

After Hannah's call, Nikki had tried to go back to her dinner conversation with Cyndi, the cute blonde who'd been the maid of honor at her cousin's wedding two weeks earlier, but she hadn't been able to concentrate. All she'd been able to think about was Hannah sitting at home worrying and Jordan out God knows where, doing Christ knew what. Nikki did have to admit, though, it wasn't like her to just disappear for hours in such an obvious way. Cyndi had been understanding when Nikki cut their date inexcusably short—they hadn't even been served their appetizers yet—to go check the boat, the one place she knew to look for Jordan. When that'd proven unproductive, she'd headed over to their condo.

She hesitated, her fingertip lightly touching the button for the doorbell, and tried to quell her irritation. Jordan was her best friend and had been since they'd been assigned as doubles partners in a charity tennis tournament nine years earlier, but she could be an ass. She had someone like Hannah—no, not someone *like* Hannah. Hell, she had *Hannah* and took her for granted. Hannah was beautiful, smart, interesting, and wanted a full life with Jordan, and Jordan… *Jordan's an idiot.* When it came to women, Jordan was a phony, a liar, and Nikki resented the position Jordan had put her in. Normally, Nikki kept her distance from Hannah because she knew so much about Jordan, because she knew eventually she'd have to lie to Hannah, too—and because she hated how envious she felt watching the two of them together. Now, here she was, about to ring the doorbell, about to step into the role of comforting Hannah, and how could she do that without lying to her, or worse, without telling her the truth?

Nikki dropped her hand to the grip of her crutch. *I can't do this.* She hopped to turn and make her way back down the walk but lost her balance and fell against the jamb, one crutch clattering to the ground. She caught herself and straightened just as the door opened behind her. *So much for a stealthy getaway.* She glanced over her shoulder and saw the disappointment in Hannah's expression. "Sorry," she said as she leaned down to retrieve the crutch. "I'm still not very good with these things."

"Hi, Nikki." Hannah looked past her to the street.

"Still no Jordan?" Nikki asked, already knowing the answer.

Hannah opened the door wider, shaking her head. She gestured Nikki inside. "I'm glad you're here. You know Jory's other friends, don't you?"

Nikki ignored the pet name. Jordan disliked all nicknames, but despised that one in particular. Nikki knew the only reason she let Hannah use it was to avoid having to explain why she hated it so much. "I know some." She nodded to Kate on the couch.

"Did she mention having plans with any of them when you saw her this morning?" Hannah asked.

Nikki shifted her weight for a more solid stance. "I didn't see her this morning."

"She said she had a racquetball game." Hannah focused on Nikki for the first time.

Nikki warmed as she always did under Hannah's direct gaze. It didn't happen very often anymore, and she was surprised at the strength of her reaction. "It wasn't with me." She lifted her foot a few inches, indicating her cast. "I haven't been able to play since I broke my ankle."

Hannah glanced at it. "When was that?"

"About six weeks ago. Don't you remember? Jordan took me to the doctor to get it set." She studied Hannah for some flicker of recollection. "You were upset because she didn't get back in time for dinner with your friends?"

Hannah's eyes shifted. "Oh. Yes, I remember, now." She returned her attention to Nikki. "Who has she been playing with then?"

Nikki shrugged. "There are always people around the gym looking to pick up a game." How could Hannah not know Jordan hadn't been playing with Nikki? She'd been so mad that Jordan missed that dinner, how could she have forgotten? "The past three weeks or so she's been playing with a woman named Liz." Nikki moved to the recliner and eased into it.

"Who's Liz?"

"I don't know. Just someone who plays there. I only met her once, when I had lunch with Jordan after a game."

"She doesn't have a last name?" Hannah's tone sharpened.

Nikki felt a twinge of defensiveness. "I'm sure she does. I just don't know it. She was introduced to me as Liz."

"I'm sorry. I didn't mean to…" Hannah sighed. "I just don't know what to think right now." She sat on the sofa beside Kate.

"That's okay. I think we're both…all…" Nikki looked at Kate, who was examining her manicure. "I think we're all kind of anxious," she said, though Kate seemed a little bored. Nikki turned back to Hannah. "What do you know?"

Hannah shrugged. "She left this morning to go play racquetball, then go to her office to do some work. She said she'd be home around three."

"Have you talked to anyone from her office? Was it just her going in, or was there some kind of work thing going on?"

"I don't know," Hannah said, her voice quiet. "I called the main number a few times, and no one answered. I don't have the private numbers of anyone she works with."

Nikki was intrigued. How could someone's girlfriend know so little about her life? No wonder it was so easy for Jordan to do the things she did. "I have Dana's," she said, retrieving her cell phone from the back pocket of her jeans. "She might know."

Surprise flashed in Hannah's eyes. "Why do you have Dana's number?"

Why do you not? Nikki opened her contacts. "We go to concerts together sometimes." She scrolled down the list.

"You're dating Jordan's boss?"

"We're not dating. She's married to a stockbroker. We're both kind of eccentric in our music tastes." Nikki hesitated before tapping SEND. "Do you want to talk to her, or do you want me to?"

"I think I want to," Hannah said.

Nikki placed the call and handed her the phone.

After a moment, Hannah rose. "Hi, Dana, this is Hannah Lewis, Jordan Webber's girlfriend? We've met at a couple of your work functions…no, I'm just using Nikki's phone…" She strolled into the kitchen as she spoke.

Nikki turned to find Kate's cool gaze fixed on her. It was almost like having Hannah's eyes locked on her, only Kate's were sharper. She felt heat creep into her cheeks.

"Do you know where she is?" Kate whispered.

"No." Nikki laughed. "If I did, I'd go tell her to get her ass home."

Kate eyed her. "You do know some places she *could* be, though, don't you?"

There was no point in trying to pretend anything with *this* woman. If she was shrewd enough to be asking these questions, she suspected something, and if she hadn't said anything to Hannah before now, it wasn't likely she'd give anything away. "I already checked the one place I know. She wasn't there."

"You find her and get her home." Kate's voice held an uncompromising warning. "Nobody hurts my sister."

Then, Nikki saw it: the concern—not for Jordan, but for Hannah—the protectiveness, the love. Beneath that air of indifference, Kate would do anything for Hannah, or at least make sure someone else did. It was the same feeling, the same fixation, that'd begun to grow in Nikki during the first six months of Jordan's relationship with Hannah. She'd begun to want to protect her, to keep her safe from Jordan's demons, but she couldn't know the things she knew and still face Hannah over a dinner table, a game of pool, or TGIF pizza and beer. She couldn't protect Jordan *and* Hannah at the same time. She'd had to get some distance, and she'd had to keep it over the years.

And yet, Jordan wasn't evil. She wasn't mean or a bad person. She just didn't know how to quiet her soul, how to chase all the insecurities, all the doubts, all the self-recrimination from her depths. They all remained buried, eating away at her, perpetuating behaviors that either gave her a moment of respite from her emptiness or reinforced the belief that she was unlovable. Jordan needed a best friend, one who knew her and loved her just as she was. Nikki supposed everyone needed that, and even with Jordan's pitfalls, Nikki was still happy to be that kind of friend to her. She was glad Hannah had Kate. She pressed her lips together in a gentle smile and nodded.

Kate softened, and she leaned closer conspiratorially. "Can you stay with Hannah? I have a date."

Nikki startled at the abrupt change in subject. "What?"

Kate rolled her eyes. "Can you stay with Hannah until Jordan gets home? I have to go, and I'm afraid she'll freak out if she's alone. She has this abandonment thing."

"Oh. Yeah, sure."

"Dana's in San Francisco," Hannah said, returning to the living room. "She doesn't know of anything going on at the office. She said Jordan must have been working on something on her own." She stopped beside the couch and looked at them. "What are you two talking about?"

"I was just asking Nikki questions," Kate said, settling back into her seat. "Like they do on TV, to see if something came up she didn't know she knew."

Hannah pinned Nikki with an expectant look.

Nikki fidgeted. "I didn't come up with anything."

Hannah sighed. "So, we just wait, then?" She perched on the edge of the cushion beside Kate. The casualness of her words belied the tension in her features.

There had to be something they could do besides wait. Nikki let her thoughts begin to roam. This *was* unusual. Jordan was always good at being home when she said she would be to keep Hannah from asking questions or wondering about what she did. Hannah had been the one to push for monogamy, and although Jordan said she hadn't technically agreed to it, she'd let Hannah believe she had. Then, over the three years they'd been together, she'd become an expert juggler, continuing to sleep with other women while treating Hannah as though she'd never even look at anyone else. It was almost artful. So, why *this* all of a sudden? Why disappear in such a way that Hannah had no choice but to ask questions? Maybe something really had happened to Jordan. "Do you know if she actually got to her game this morning?" Nikki finally asked.

Hannah stared at her. "What do you mean?"

"You said she left for the gym and then she was going to the office. Did she make it to the gym?"

"I don't know. I just assumed—" Hannah paled. "You mean she could be missing since this morning? Oh, my God, that's over twelve hours."

"Sweetie, I'm sure that's not what she means," Kate said, slipping an arm around Hannah. She glared at Nikki.

"No, I'm not saying that." Nikki tried to backpedal. "I'm just thinking, maybe we should call the gym and see what time she left there." She gave a small shrug.

"Okay. You're probably right." Hannah folded her hands between her knees. "Will you do it?" she asked Nikki.

"Sure," Nikki said. She placed the call.

"LA Health and Fitness," a voice said on the other end of the line. "This is Ray. How can I help you?"

"Hi. My name's Nikki Medina, and I'm a member there."

"Yes, ma'am. What can I do for you?"

"My best friend is also a member, and she had a racquetball court reserved for this morning." Nikki kept her eyes down, avoiding Hannah's. "I was wondering if you could tell me if she kept her reservation."

"No, ma'am, I'm sorry. I can't give out any information about our members."

"I understand the whole privacy thing." Nikki shifted her phone to her other ear. "But this is important. No one's seen her since she left the house for the gym this morning, and we're just trying to find out if she made it there. Her name's Jordan Webber. If you could just check."

Ray paused. "Yeah, I'm sorry. I still don't think I can do that."

Nikki glanced at Hannah, taking in the taut set of her mouth, the rapid jiggle of her right foot. She wished she hadn't brought up the possibility that Jordan hadn't even made it to her first stop. "Is there someone else I can talk to…your supervisor? Or the manager, maybe?"

"I can leave a message for the manager and have her call you when she gets in on Monday." Ray was beginning to sound distracted.

"Monday?" Nikki's frustration escalated. "Look, I need to talk to someone before Monday. Something could've happened to my friend, and we need to know where to start looking." She regretted the words as soon as they passed her lips. She heard a sharp intake of breath. She looked at Hannah.

Hannah's eyes were wide.

Nikki forced a calmer tone. "Is there any way I could speak with your manager this evening to see if she can help?"

Another pause. "I could send her a text and see if she'll call you back. Would that help?"

Nikki sighed. "Yes. That would be great. Thank you." After leaving her number with Ray, she ended the call. "He's going to... well, you heard."

Hannah nodded.

Kate made eye contact with Nikki, then reached for her purse. "I'm going to cancel my date." She made a production of rummaging through its contents. "I don't want to leave you alone tonight."

"You don't need to do that. I'll be fine," Hannah said, a bit unconvincingly. "I'm sure Jory will be home soon." Her voice held a mild tremor.

"Actually," Nikki said, "I'd like to stay, if it's okay. I'd like to know when she gets home." That was the truth. If she did come home perfectly fine and nonchalant, Nikki wanted a word or two with her. If she didn't show up at all... Well, they'd count that dinosaur when it hatched.

Hannah looked at her, a hint of gratitude in her eyes. She nodded.

After Kate made a suitably concerned exit—checking and rechecking that Hannah would be all right, making her promise to call as soon as she heard anything, and assuring her everything would be fine—Nikki and Hannah were alone.

It was the first time in over two years. They'd been at social gatherings or games occasionally during that span, but always in groups. Nikki felt everything she'd left unsaid, everything she didn't want to say tonight, stretch between them like a deep chasm, the closeness that'd once begun to grow between them lost somewhere at the very bottom. Her stomach knotted at the awkwardness.

Hannah smoothed her palms over her thighs, glanced at Nikki, then away. "Can I get you something to drink?" She walked toward the kitchen. "Or, are you hungry?"

"Ice water would be good," Nikki said. She wanted something to do with her hands.

When Hannah returned with two glasses, she gave one to Nikki, then sat across from her. She took a long swallow of her drink, then smiled. "It's been a long time. How have you been?"

"Good." Nikki rested her elbows on her knees and turned her glass restlessly between her fingers. "Busy. You know, with the business and all."

"Yes, Jory's mentioned you've become quite the in-demand photographer," Hannah said, a hint of praise in her voice. "That has to feel good."

Satisfaction welled in Nikki as it always did when she thought about how much her studio had grown since that first wedding she'd shot for friends twelve years earlier at the starry-eyed age of twenty-two. She couldn't hold back a grin. "It does. I couldn't do it without Aleyda, though." She softened at the thought of her sister-in-law. "She's turned into more of a business partner than an assistant."

"How *is* Aleyda? And the kids?" Hannah shifted sideways on the couch and drew up her knees.

Nikki released an inner sigh of relief at the direction of the conversation. She leaned back and relaxed into the recliner. "They're all doing great."

"Is Tony still at UCLA?"

"Just finishing his sophomore year." Nikki was pleased Hannah remembered him by name, but then, that was the Hannah Nikki had been drawn to. When other things were going on, Hannah could be distracted and not even notice you, but when her attention was on you, it felt like no one else existed. "And Rob just graduated from high school. He's starting at UC Davis in the fall."

Hannah's eyes widened. "Seriously? That can't be."

Nikki chuckled. "Yup, he's grown up a lot in the past couple of years."

"What about your niece?" Hannah toyed absently with her painted toenails.

Nikki warmed at Hannah's interest in the people most important to her. She remembered the feeling from the times they'd spent together in the early months of Hannah and Jordan's relationship. "Cecelia's Cecelia." She laughed. "Directionless, but doing good." Part of their last real conversation flashed in the forefront of Nikki's mind. "What about you? The last time we talked, you said now that both of your adoptive parents had passed, you wanted to try to find your birth mom. Did you do that?" Nikki thought that if something that significant had happened, Jordan would have mentioned it, but she never knew with Jordan.

Hannah tilted her head. "No." Disappointment tempered her tone. "I tried to talk to Kate about it, but she's still adamant that she doesn't want anything to do with our birth mother. I thought after Dad's death, she might change her mind, but she didn't. And it doesn't seem right to do it without her."

Nikki listened, feeling more of the awkwardness fall away.

"I can't say I don't understand." Hannah stroked her thumb along the cuff of her capris. "Mom and Dad gave us a wonderful childhood and opportunities for amazing lives. They gave us so much love, and I don't ever mean to diminish that. I just want to know why our birth mother gave us up. I broached the subject with Dad once, and he said he thought that was normal." She paused. "You know, I don't think I ever thanked you for being there for me when my father died. You probably don't think it was a big deal, but it was to me. You were so thoughtful."

It was to me, too. It'd been a tantalizing taste of what being the person Hannah counted on would be like. Nikki remembered the day well.

Her phone had rung mid-afternoon, and she'd answered to Hannah's tearful plea for her to come to the hospital where Hannah's father had been taken following a heart attack. Jordan had been out of town on business, and Kate had been away at camp with her fifth grade class. Nikki had sat with Hannah in the surgery waiting room, and Hannah had collapsed into her arms when the doctors informed her that her father had died on the operating table. Nikki had stayed with her every minute until Jordan had gotten home the following day, helping Hannah with the paperwork, making sure she ate, putting her to bed, and sitting with her until she finally fell into a fitful sleep.

But the day of the funeral, it'd been Jordan who had stood beside Hannah and held her hand, and Jordan who had greeted friends and family with her at the reception. That night, however, when Jordan was on the phone into the late hours with her associates on the big case she was working, and Kate had fallen into an exhausted sleep on the sofa, it'd been Nikki who'd listened to Hannah's memories and childhood stories of her father, Nikki who'd explored with her the possibility of finding her birth mother, Nikki who'd held her while she grieved her loss. That was the night Nikki realized she was in too deep, that she needed some distance.

"I'm glad I could help," Nikki said. "That's what friends are for. Right?"

Hannah smiled. "You're a good friend," she said softly. "And I should have thanked you way before now. I'm sorry."

Nikki gave a single nod. "No problem." Her phone vibrated with an incoming text, and she checked the screen.

Hannah looked on with a hopeful expression.

"It's Dana, asking if we've heard from Jordan." Nikki sent a quick reply. She returned her attention to Hannah in time to see the unease pass through her eyes. Here she was again in the role of the one who was supposed to be offering Hannah comfort, but this time was different. She knew too much, and yet didn't know enough. She didn't know where Jordan was, but she knew what she could be doing. She didn't know if Jordan was okay, or if there was truly a reason to be worried. She didn't know what to say to fill the minutes, or maybe hours, of waiting. She just knew she had to come up with something.

Chapter Three

Jordan felt the gentle motion of the boat beneath her and the soft curves of a woman pressed against her. *Tina.* She didn't always know their names, but she remembered Tina. How odd, though. She remembered taking Tina back to her car when they had finished, and she thought it'd been several days ago. And yet, here they still were.

Tina's hand moved up Jordan's torso to her throat. She cupped Jordan's face and coaxed her lips to meet hers.

Jordan felt another stirring of awakening. "Mmm." She tried to open her eyes but couldn't.

The thrum of an engine vibrated through her with the kiss.

Another brain cell or two woke.

How can the engine be running when I'm below deck in the berth? She pulled back from Tina and tried to focus. She made another attempt to open her eyes. Her lids felt sewn shut. She shifted in the bed, but her limbs wouldn't move either.

"Shh," Tina soothed her, but she was no longer close. Her skin no longer warmed Jordan's.

With a final effort, Jordan felt her lids give. The dream fell away, and light stabbed her eyes. She squinted against the pain. A blurred figure moved over her.

"There you are. How do you feel?" The voice was familiar, feminine, comforting—but it wasn't Tina.

"Where am I?" The words rang clearly in her mind, but all she heard leave her throat was a garbled mutter. She coughed.

"Shh. Here, try some water." A hand slipped beneath her head and lifted her lips to a straw.

Jordan sucked cool liquid into her dry mouth. She moaned and swallowed deeply.

"Not so much at once," Not Tina said. "Take it slowly, or it'll come back up."

Jordan took a sip this time, then let Not Tina settle her head back onto the pillow. The bed shuddered beneath her. The engine continued a low hum.

This isn't right. Where am I? Confusion muddled her brain. Fear swelled in her gut, but before it could crest, her eyes fell closed again.

Hannah woke to the smell of coffee and the soft murmur of Nikki's voice, both from the kitchen. Nikki had been wonderful the night before. She had kept the conversation flowing with questions about what books Hannah had been reading or movies she had seen, and humorous stories of the most unusual weddings she had shot in the past months, keeping Hannah's mind from spiraling into the worst-case scenarios she could imagine about Jordan. It had worked for a while, but Hannah had finally broken down late in the night and cried herself to sleep. She remembered that taking place in Nikki's embrace, though. Now, she lay on the couch beneath the duvet from her and Jordan's bed.

Jordan! Was she home? Hannah sat up straight. Her eyes burned as she blinked against the morning sunlight streaming through the living room windows. *Is that who Nikki's talking to?* She strained to listen.

"Yes, I understand," Nikki said quietly. "We'll do that."

No one answered.

Hannah's hope crumbled like dry leaves. Jordan hadn't come home.

Hannah stepped into the kitchen as Nikki slipped her phone into her back pocket. "Who was that?" She walked to the coffeemaker and filled a mug already sitting beside it.

"The manager of the gym," Nikki said, opening the refrigerator and retrieving a pint of cream. She placed it in front of Hannah. "She wouldn't tell me if Jordan was there yesterday, but she said if we file a police report, she can release the information to them."

"The police?" Hannah's stomach churned. *That would mean Jordan's really gone.* She felt that old, familiar emptiness—something she had thought she unloaded in therapy years ago—try to take hold. "God, that's so..." She looked down into her cup.

"I know." Nikki leaned against the counter. "We should do something today, though. I could call Dana back and get the numbers of the rest of the people Jordan works with. And you should call your friends. But, you know, we can't really find out for sure how long she's been...actually...you know...until we know if she kept the reservation for the court."

Hannah sighed. She opened the carton of cream and poured some into her coffee. She watched the tendrils of white swirl into the black. It looked as though the world had slowed down. She could see each spiral movement as the two liquids blended. Her thoughts slowed to match it. She couldn't make a decision—what to do, who to call, whether to be mad at Jordan or afraid for her.

"Hannah?" Nikki's voice was gentle.

Hannah cleared her throat. "Yes. We should do something." She looked up into Nikki's dark brown eyes, so dark they were almost black, their texture seemingly that of luxuriant velvet. She remembered those eyes the night before, the years before, filled with laughter and affection. She realized she missed having Nikki around. What had happened?

"Okay," Nikki said. "I'll try Dana." She picked up her own mug, hobbled to the table, and sat down. "Do you have some paper and a pen?"

Once settled, each of them got to their calls.

Hannah's went as she would have predicted. "Hi, Marti... Janice...Stephanie... Have you seen or heard from Jordan, by any chance?"

"Jordan? No, why? Is something wrong?" all of them asked. The underlying question, however, was *Why would we have seen Jordan without you?* There was no reason Jordan would be with any of them. Hannah doubted she even knew how to reach them on her own— just like Hannah with Jordan's colleagues. Each conversation ended similarly, with questions asked and evaded to the best of Hannah's ability. She wasn't ready to go into any details, even if she'd had any. When all the calls were done, they only knew more places Jordan wasn't.

Hannah and Nikki sat in silence for a long moment, the air heavy between them. Hannah resisted looking up to meet Nikki's eyes, those patient, comforting eyes, because she knew once she did, it would be time to make that one call that would change everything.

Nikki just sat, waiting.

Finally, Hannah faced her and nodded.

Nikki dialed.

"Santa Monica Police Department," a woman's voice rang clearly through the phone's speaker. "This is Kristy."

"Hello," Hannah said. She hesitated, reluctant to say what had to follow. "I need to report someone missing." The words slid out. She had expected them to catch, in her throat, on her teeth, but they hadn't. They had just slipped right out.

"Yes, ma'am. Who is it that's missing?"

Hannah was grateful for the question, any question. Something she could simply answer. "My girlfriend."

"When was the last time anyone saw or spoke with her?" Kristy asked.

"Yesterday morning."

"Have you checked the hospitals?" Kristy's tone was matter-of-fact.

"The hospitals?" Hannah looked at Nikki. Images of car accidents, muggings, shootings flooded her mind. "Wouldn't someone have called me if she'd been admitted to a hospital?"

"If she didn't have any ID on her and couldn't tell them who to contact, they wouldn't know."

More pictures flashed—Jordan wheeled into an emergency room, unconscious on a gurney. She pondered the number of hospitals in the Los Angeles area and became overwhelmed. "I haven't," she said. "I wouldn't know where to start."

"What about the jail?" Kristy asked as though going down a checklist. "Could she have been arrested?"

Hannah huffed out a laugh. "Of course not." It was the first thing she had found funny in hours. "She's an attorney."

"What's her name? I'll go ahead and check real quick."

"Her name's Jordan Webber, but you don't need to—" Hannah cut herself off as she heard the tapping of computer keys. She listened to background voices and radio beeps.

"Okay, she hasn't been booked, so I'll enter a call to have an officer come out and take a report. In the meantime, go ahead and check the hospitals closest to her last known whereabouts and where she was supposed to be. You can get a list off the Internet. If you find her, please call back and let us know."

Kristy's efficiency rankled Hannah. It was as though all of this was nothing out of the ordinary, in fact, it was *so* ordinary it had a standard operating procedure. There was nothing ordinary about this. Jordan didn't simply *not come home*. She didn't get arrested in the middle of a Saturday or end up uncommunicative in a hospital somewhere. Hannah gave her address and contact information to Kristy in clipped answers and hung up with a very unsatisfying hard press of the *End Call* button. She remembered hanging up on Kate once on their grandmother's old kitchen wall phone, slamming the receiver down onto the hook. Now *that* had been satisfying.

Nikki gave her a mildly reproachful look. "It isn't her fault. She's just doing her job."

"I told her Jordan wouldn't have been arrested, and she still acted like she's some kind of criminal."

Nikki bit her lip. "People don't always know what their loved ones will do. My brother Jesse got arrested once for looking in some girl's window while he was jogging and was so embarrassed and afraid of his wife, he sat in jail for thirty-seven hours before he called anybody."

Hannah thought of Jordan's morning runs. What was Nikki saying? Did she know something Hannah didn't? Jordan was *her* girlfriend, not Nikki's. Surely, she knew her better. "Jordan isn't your brother."

"I'm just saying." Nikki shrugged.

"Well, she wasn't in jail." Hannah tried to hold onto the anger—it felt marginally better than fear—but her thoughts lingered on Nikki's brother. She had met him once, a shy, soft-spoken veterinarian's assistant who drove a VW bug. She couldn't imagine. "Jesse?" she asked. "Really?"

Nikki smiled and shrugged again. "He just happened to glance over while he was running past her house at the same minute she looked outside, but that was all it took." She bent and picked up her crutches. "It'll probably be a while before the police get here. If you want to grab a shower, I'll be here to get the door. And I can make the hospital calls while we wait."

More waiting. Any time she wasn't actively doing something like making phone calls, preparing her coffee, or putting away the dishes from the dishwasher, the reality of the situation crept in all around her. If she stopped at all, her anxiety felt like bony fingers tightening around her throat and beginning to squeeze. At the same time, she didn't want to be the one to check the hospitals. What if she found Jordan there? She couldn't bear even the thought of hearing, *yes, she was brought in this morning* and knowing what that could mean. "Thank you," she said, rubbing her hands over her face. "A shower will feel good."

After drying her hair and dressing in fresh clothes, Hannah stepped from the bedroom into the aroma of eggs and toast. Her stomach grumbled. She had forgotten she hadn't eaten the night before.

"Perfect timing," Nikki called from the kitchen. "Do you want more coffee or juice or both?"

The doorbell rang.

"I guess it doesn't matter." In that instant, Hannah realized she no longer thought it was Jordan at the door. What did that mean? Kate had been right—it hadn't made sense to think Jordan would do anything but let herself in.

Nikki came into the living room. "Want me to get it?"

"No," Hannah said, hearing her voice quaver ever so slightly.

The uniformed cop on the front stoop stood about six foot, and his ebony skin set off perfect white teeth when he smiled. "Good morning, I'm Officer Mullins. I'm looking for Hannah Lewis?"

"Yes, I'm Hannah. Please, come in." And so it began—the first moment Jordan would actually be considered missing.

As they all sat, Hannah and Nikki on the couch and Officer Mullins in the recliner, Hannah inhaled deeply.

Officer Mullins opened a small laptop on the coffee table in front of him. "Okay," he murmured as he began tapping the keys. "RP, Hannah Lewis. Address..." When he finished typing, he looked up. "What's the name of the person you want to report missing?"

Hannah's mouth went dry. "Jordan Webber," she said, her voice barely audible. She felt her world tilt with the absolute foreignness of the moment. She had never in her life done anything remotely like this.

"Does she have a middle name?" Mullins asked.

"Naomi."

"Date of birth?"

As the questions continued, Hannah relaxed a little. Height, weight, eye and hair color, kind of car, all came easily and seemed innocuous enough.

"And what's your relationship to her?" Mullins paused.

"She's my girlfriend," Hannah said automatically. Even though they lived together, they had never talked about being partners and they'd certainly never discussed marriage. Hannah had considered it from time to time, but for some reason hadn't felt comfortable bringing it up to Jordan.

"Okay. So, when was the last time you saw her?"

"Yesterday morning," Hannah said.

"About what time?"

Hannah hesitated. She thought back to waking to the feel of Jordan behind her, the morning sunlight in the room. "I don't know exactly. Early."

"Can you approximate?" Mullins asked. "It could be helpful if we at least have a ballpark figure." He watched Hannah.

"She was on her way to play racquetball," Nikki said. "And on Saturdays, she usually plays at seven. The manager of the gym said she could tell you whether or not she got there once the report's filed."

"Okay, that's good," Mullins said as he typed something into his laptop. He looked at Nikki. "And you are?"

"My name's Nikki Medina. I'm her best friend."

More tapping. "So, did either of you see her before she left?"

"I did," Hannah said, glad to have an answer. "So, that probably would have been around sixish, if her game was at seven."

"What was she wearing?"

Oh, God. Hannah recalled Jordan's eyes, her hands, her mouth, the weight of her body—and nothing else. "I don't know." She felt a hot blush creep into her face.

Mullins raised an eyebrow. "If you can remember anything…"

"Was she already dressed to play?" Nikki asked Hannah.

Hannah remembered the feel of Jordan's shirt against her breasts, the buttons. "No, she had on a dress shirt, sateen." *But what color?* She glimpsed it in her mind as she relived Jordan pulling her nightshirt over her head. "Pale yellow," she blurted.

"What else?" Mullins asked even as he entered the information. He seemed almost automated.

Hannah sighed. She doubted she could come up with anything else. She had barely opened her eyes. She shook her head.

"Pants? Skirt? Shorts?" Mullins waited, his hands poised above the keyboard.

Nikki chuckled. "Definitely not a skirt."

Hannah shifted her gaze to meet Nikki's. "No." She managed a weak smile. In that split second, she recalled the seam of Jordan's pants against her fingertips. *But which ones? What does she wear with that shirt?* "Cotton pants," she said, returning her attention to Mulllins. "But I don't know what color. I was mostly asleep when she left." God, what must he think of her—of her and Jordan's relationship? She didn't know what her girlfriend was wearing even though she had seen her. She knew what *she* would think, but he just kept asking questions in a bland, polite tone.

"Do you know what kind of shoes?"

Despondent, she gave a single shake of her head. She looked down at the coffee table. "Is this going to make it harder?"

"These are routine questions, Ms. Lewis. Just to get as much information as we can." Mullins spoke softly. "Would you like to take a break?"

Nikki slipped her hand over Hannah's on her thigh.

The shift in Mullins's monotone and Nikki's touch soothed her. She took in a breath. "No, I'm okay. Let's keep going." She refocused on Mullins but held on to Nikki.

"Okay." Mullins smiled. "Have you checked with her friends?"

Maybe Hannah did need a minute to regain her composure. With each question, she felt herself slide further beneath some invisible surface of normalcy, into darkness and out of the light of her life a mere two days earlier when she had turned in her school keys and headed into what she thought would be two months of summer break relaxation. She closed her eyes against a swell of emotion.

Nikki squeezed Hannah's fingers and began to explain the calls they had made. Her voice faded as Hannah searched her mind for something else to latch on to. She couldn't relive that series of disappointments.

Mullins leaned back, and the leather of his belt and holster creaked.

Hannah's eyes fluttered open and shifted to the sound. She thought of Batman's utility belt as she took in the little compartments positioned around the officer's narrow waist. Batman's belt, though, held crime-fighting necessities like batarangs and freeze grenades and a cryptographic sequencer, not mundane things like handcuffs and pepper spray and those gloves which, she knew from watching CSI, were used to handle corpses and unsavory evidence. No gun, though. Batman never used a gun because his parents were killed by one. She had learned a lot about Batman from a freshman boy she had been counseling the past several months, who lived and breathed all things Caped Crusader. She wondered how the first couple of days of *his* summer vacation were going.

"Hannah?" Nikki's voice touched her awareness, calling her back to the conversation.

"I'm sorry. What?" She looked between Nikki and Mullins.

"Officer Mullins asked about Jordan's family. I told him to my knowledge she hasn't talked to them for a long time. Do you know if they've been in contact recently?"

"Her family?" Hannah heard the incredulity in her own voice. Nikki had to know better than that. "You mean her parents? No. I've never even met them. She never talks to them."

"What about her brother?" Mullins asked.

"Brother?"

"Ms. Medina said she has a brother. David?"

Hannah blinked. "I...I don't know...anything about a brother." She looked at Nikki. "Jordan has a brother?"

"Well, yeah." Nikki blushed. "But I've never met him. She doesn't talk to him, either. That I know of."

Astonished, Hannah stared at Nikki. How could Nikki know that when she didn't? Sure, she hadn't known that Jordan was playing racquetball with a brand new person Hannah had never even heard of, and Nikki had. She hadn't known how to get in touch with Jordan's coworkers, and Nikki had. She'd had no idea what time she'd seen Jordan last, and Nikki had. But this...? Here was a relative, a brother, she hadn't had a clue existed—and Nikki had. "Well," Hannah said, her tone cool. "Clearly, you know far more than *I* do." A tremor vibrated through the foundation of everything else she thought she knew.

Mullins cleared his throat. "Okay, well...is your girlfriend involved with drugs in any way?"

"No." Hannah returned her attention to him. "Never."

"Did the two of you have a fight, or anything? Or has she been acting strange in any way?"

Hannah studied him, her anger rising as she comprehended his meaning. "She wouldn't just leave. Something must have happened to her." *What am I saying?* She didn't want to go there, but what he was suggesting was ridiculous.

"It's been known to take place." He scratched the underside of his chin. "People leave their lives behind way more than anyone realizes. Someone gets unhappy, wants a new start..." He shrugged.

The muscles in Hannah's neck tightened. She thought of her birth mother, the woman who had given her away, who had left *her* behind for a new start. Her old feelings of abandonment started oozing to the surface. "Jordan wouldn't do that. And she wasn't unhappy. I would have known if she was." She felt a twinge of embarrassment at her statement with everything she *hadn't* known. But this was different.

Mullins nodded. "She drives a Chevy. Does her car have OnStar? Maybe you could call and see if they can track it."

Hannah's temples began to throb. "It has an OnStar button."

"Check that out. Does she have an iPhone?"

"Yes." Hannah said, feeling a surge of hope without knowing why. Maybe it was just a thrill to actually know something about Jordan.

"You may be able to track it through the Apple Phone Finder," Mullins said as he closed his laptop.

"What are you doing?" Hannah asked, fear gripping her. "Is that all?"

Nikki tightened her grasp on Hannah's hand.

"It's all for now," Mullins said quietly. "I have all the basic information. I'll file the report and a detective will be in touch with you in the next day or two. We'll also flag her car as belonging to a missing person, so if it turns up, we'll be notified."

Hannah felt empty. She had expected more.

"What can we do?" Nikki asked.

Mullins rose. "Your best bet is to keep making calls to anyone you can think of that she knows and check out any favorite hangouts or vacation spots she might have. Things like that. And if you have numbers for her family, call them, even if you don't think she's been in touch with them. You never know. And the phone and car. See if you can track them."

"I thought that's what the police did," Hannah said, not even trying to keep the criticism out of her voice.

"Only on TV." Mullins gave a small smile that didn't reach his eyes. "Truth is, we can't really do much unless some sign of foul play surfaces. Right now, there's no evidence of that. It's not a crime just to be missing."

Nikki shook the officer's hand. "Thank you."

Hannah couldn't make herself move.

"If you do think of anything else, call me." He pulled a business card from his shirt pocket and gave it to Nikki.

Hannah watched as Nikki closed the door behind Mullins and turned. She studied Nikki, taking in every detail as though seeing her for the first time. Straight, dark brown hair that closely matched those rich eyes, fell just below her shoulders. A white, button-up shirt, sleeves rolled to her elbows highlighted bronze-colored skin, and black jeans hugged her narrow hips. Her trim frame and tight abs and thighs spoke to the workout schedule Hannah once knew she kept. She carried herself with the air of soft butch, just like Jordan. She looked as she always had, but suddenly she seemed like someone new, someone who knew more about Jordan than Hannah did.

"Are you okay?" Nikki asked.

"How do you know so much about Jordan?" Hannah's tone was sharp, but she didn't care.

Surprise flashed in Nikki's face, then softened into patience. "She's my best friend."

"She's *my girlfriend.*"

Nikki eased her weight onto the support of her crutches. "Yes, Hannah. I know. I didn't mean to overstep any boundaries. I just thought it was important to give the police as much information as we could."

"I'm not asking about boundaries. I'm asking how you know so much about her."

"We've spent a lot of time together. She's talked about things."

"She and I *live* together. We sleep together every night and wake up together every morning. We make love. We lie in each other's arms afterward and talk." Even as the words left her lips, Hannah wondered about their truth. Did they talk, or did *she* talk?

Nikki paused, searching Hannah's face. "What are you saying, really?"

Hannah remained silent. She didn't actually know.

"You think Jordan and I are having an affair?" Nikki's tone held amazement.

Hannah felt heat rise in her cheeks and her ears began to burn. She hadn't allowed herself to think it, but now that it had been said, she realized that *was* what she was implying. In the same moment, she realized how ludicrous it was.

Nikki laughed. "Hannah, I swear to you, Jordan and I are not having an affair. We've never…even back before you. We don't think of each other that way."

Slumping forward, Hannah buried her face in her hands. "Oh, God, Nikki. I know that. I'm sorry." She listened to Nikki close the distance between them and felt her ease onto the couch. Hannah shifted and leaned into her.

"It's okay," Nikki said, slipping an arm around Hannah's shoulder.

"I don't know what's wrong with me." Hannah's voice broke, and she began to cry.

Nikki hugged her. "Your girlfriend's missing. You're worried and scared. And you don't have any idea what to do. That's what's wrong." She stroked Hannah's back. "It's understandable."

A sob wrenched free from Hannah's throat.

Nikki pulled her closer. "Shh. It'll all be fine. Jordan will turn up, and she'll have some explanation, and everything will be okay."

Eventually, the tide of Hannah's emotions ebbed, and she lay quietly. Nikki's arms felt so good, so comforting, so safe. Hannah let herself absorb Nikki's full presence in their snug hold. She was so grateful not to be alone.

Nikki shifted, and she began to ease Hannah from her.

Hannah grasped the front of Nikki's shirt. "Don't go," she whispered.

Nikki relaxed again. "I thought you were asleep." She tightened her arms around Hannah. "I was just going to go make some fresh breakfast."

"No. Don't go," Hannah said. "Please. Just hold me." The longer she could stay right there, the longer she could not think about anything else.

CHAPTER FOUR

As Nikki cleaned up from the making of two breakfasts and loaded the dishwasher, she listened to the faint sounds of Hannah rummaging through the desk in the second bedroom that served as an office. She felt nauseous—and guilty. She should have told Mullins about the affairs or flings, or whatever they were, that Jordan had. How could she, though, with Hannah sitting right there? What if she'd revealed all and then Jordan showed up with some believable explanation for where she'd been all weekend?

On the other hand, what if one of the women she'd slept with had something to do with her disappearance? If Nikki kept silent, she'd be responsible for whatever could be happening to Jordan. How long could she keep the secrets she'd been entrusted with? And... how mad was Hannah going to be at her for not having *already* told her everything?

Hannah had been pissed because Nikki knew about David and she hadn't. For a second, she'd even thought Nikki and Jordan might have been having an affair. *How ridiculous is that?* Nikki might very well be the only woman Hannah *didn't* need to worry about in that sense. In fact, it was Hannah that Nikki had always had inappropriate thoughts and feelings about, not Jordan. She'd thought they'd subsided since she hadn't experienced them for quite some time, but it seemed now that'd only been because she'd kept her distance. Now, after not even a full twenty-four hours, they were, once again, surfacing.

Nikki rested her elbows on the counter and held her head in her hands. *Damn you, Jordan. Where the hell are you?*

"I couldn't find anything on OnStar from Jory's car paperwork," Hannah said, coming into the kitchen. "But there's a number I can call that I found online."

Nikki straightened but didn't turn around. "That's great." She drew a deep breath to compose herself.

Hannah dropped into one of the dinette chairs. "Is there any coffee left?"

"Yeah. I'll get it." Nikki grabbed a fresh cup and filled it. She heard a chime through the phone speaker, followed by *Welcome to OnStar.* The *para continuar en Español* and the *this call may be monitored* messages only vaguely registered in her awareness as she added cream to Hannah's drink. She sat down at the table and slid it across to her.

For emergencies, the automated voice continued, *roadside assistance, door unlocks, and stolen vehicles or missing persons, please press one. Please note that for vehicle thefts and missing persons, police involvement is required.*

Hannah punched a button, her mouth tight in a firm line.

"Emergency services. May I help you?" The words drifted across the line in an alto female voice.

Nikki listened as Hannah explained the situation.

"I'm not even sure if she has OnStar," Hannah said, finishing. "But I was hoping…"

"I'm sorry, ma'am. If you're not on the account, we can't release any information. And for the missing person, we'll need the case number of the police report."

"I don't have it yet, but I did file a report." Hannah's voice began to rise. "They said they couldn't do anything unless there was foul play involved, but she could be trapped in the car in some ravine somewhere." She slapped her hand down on the table.

"I'm sorry, ma'am. If you can get the police to—"

Hannah cut off the call. She dropped the phone and pressed her fingertips to her eyes, her breathing ragged.

Nikki remained silent. What could she say? If she'd told the police about Jordan's infidelities, would that be enough to bring the question of foul play into the conversation? She doubted it. In fact, if it did—if the TV dramas were accurate—it could make Hannah a suspect.

"I feel like a ghost in her life," Hannah said, her voice shaky. "I'm not really a part of anything—except sleeping in her bed every night."

Nikki studied Hannah's distraught expression, and watched her massage her temples. Her statement wasn't far from the truth, both parts of it. Nikki had never understood why Jordan had let Hannah move in with her, while she still maintained her sexual pursuits of other women. Clearly, Jordan felt there was *something* special about Hannah. After all, she'd never lived with a woman before—never even been in an actual relationship—and yet, she'd not only moved Hannah into her condo, but she'd maintained the living arrangement for over two years and the relationship for three. She never fully let Hannah into her life and heart, though. Nikki felt torn. Hannah really needed, deserved, to know the truth, but it wasn't Nikki's place to tell her. Maybe the only thing she could offer was comfort. She extended her hand across the table.

Hannah took it.

"I'm sorry," Nikki said softly.

The phone rang, and Hannah grabbed it. "Hello?"

Nikki waited, hopeful.

"Oh, hi, Kate...no...we filed a missing person's report. I don't really know what else to do."

Nikki sighed. She needed some time to think. She grabbed her crutches from their spot against the counter and moved toward the kitchen doorway.

"Where are you going?" Hannah asked, interrupting her call.

"I'm just going to run home to get cleaned up and change clothes. I'll be back."

Hannah covered the mouthpiece. "You can't go," she said, sounding almost frantic. "Please? I don't want to be alone."

"Maybe Kate can come over?" Nikki needed some space, a little air. She needed to clear her head and figure out what to do.

"Kate, I'll call you later," Hannah said and hung up. "Nikki, please. I don't want Kate here. She's too...I don't know... She gets crazy ideas. I need your...your calm."

Nikki stared into Hannah's clouded green eyes, remembering the softness of her hand, the feel of her against Nikki when she'd comforted her. If she held her again, felt Hannah's body meld into hers, had to think about where Jordan might be and what she might be doing one more time before she could regain some distance, she thought she'd scream.

"Please, Nikki," Hannah said again. "You could take a shower here."

Nikki shifted her weight. "I can't. I have this shower bag thing I have to use to cover my leg." She lifted her foot.

Hannah looked at the cast and frowned. "Well…" She faltered. "You could take a bath and just keep it up on the edge of the tub. And maybe change into some of Jory's workout clothes. Would that work?" She sounded so desperate.

Nikki winced inwardly. Would it? Maybe being alone in the bath would be enough. Maybe. If it were a long bath. Still a little reluctant, she nodded. "Okay."

Hannah released a deep sigh. "Thank you."

As Nikki resurfaced from soaking her hair, warm water sluiced over her bare skin and soothed her raw nerves. She poured shampoo into her palm and had already begun lathering it into her scalp before she realized her mistake. It was Hannah's shampoo. The spiced fruity scent swirled around her head, reminding her of Hannah's silky hair against her cheek as she'd held her. The memory, combined with the soft fragrance, stirred an old arousal in Nikki's abdomen. Her nipples tightened slightly. *Christ. Still?* She squeezed her eyes shut. *This* was why she'd had to get away from Hannah, but how could it still be so strong after all this time? She had to get a grip. This was so wrong—especially now.

She quickly rinsed her hair and glanced around the shower. She found another bottle of shampoo—Jordan's. Forcing her thoughts to what needed to be done when she was dressed, she rubbed the lather through her hair and over her body.

A knock sounded, and Nikki heard the door open on the other side of the shower curtain. She stiffened.

"Here are some clothes," Hannah said, her voice quiet in the damp air. "I'll leave them on the counter."

"Thanks," Nikki said. She remained motionless until she heard the door close. *Focus.* She had to stay focused.

She emerged from the bathroom in Jordan's navy blue running pants and a gray T-shirt from a half-marathon they'd done together in San Diego the previous year, and found Hannah sitting askew on the sofa with a laptop on the cushion beside her. "What're you doing?"

"I called Kate back, and she told me how to check that phone finder thingy the cop was talking about," Hannah said without looking up. "I found the site, but it needs a password."

Nikki looked over Hannah's shoulder to the screen. The curser blinked in an empty box beneath Jordan's email address. "Do you know it?"

"No," Hannah said, then sighed. "It's yet one more thing I don't know about my girlfriend." She shifted to look up at Nikki. "Do you?" There was an edge to her voice, but a softness in her gaze.

Nikki laughed. "No. I'm relieved to say I don't either."

A slight smile touched the corners of Hannah's mouth, and her eyes traveled down Nikki's body.

Something Nikki couldn't define passed through them. "What's the matter?" she asked.

Hannah pursed her lips. "It's just a little odd seeing you in Jory's clothes."

Nikki looked down at herself. "You want me to change back into my own?"

"No." Hannah returned her attention to Nikki's face. "It's okay." She pinched the fabric on Nikki's thigh and pulled it out from her skin. "I gave you the real stretchy pants so they'd fit over your cast more easily," she said, her tone lightening. She released the material, and it snapped back into place.

"Thanks," Nikki said, touched by the thoughtfulness. It was probably only Hannah's way of showing her gratitude for Nikki staying, but it still felt good. "Some people hide all their passwords in a file somewhere."

"What?"

"On the computer," Nikki said, pointing to the screen. "In a hidden file."

Hannah turned and lifted the laptop to her thighs. She closed the Apple log-in box.

"Try Documents," Nikki said.

Hannah touched the icon with her fingertip. Immediately, a password box came up. "Those are probably her work files."

"Hm." Nikki thought for a minute. "Okay, close that out and go into My Computer and into the C Drive."

Hannah did as directed.

Nikki scanned the list of files—AdwCleaner...Config.Msi... PerfLogs. She finished the list, noticing nothing that looked unusual, then skimmed back up. "Try Program Files." She slipped from the arm of the couch and onto the cushion beside Hannah.

Hannah opened the folder. "Do you know what you're looking for?"

"Not specifically," Nikki said. She was dimly aware of the warmth of Hannah's leg pressed gently against her own. "Just anything that catches—there. Try that." She pointed to a file.

"Alarter?" Hannah read aloud. "What's that?"

"Ali Larter," Nikki said.

Hannah stared at her.

"The actress? *Resident Evil*? *Heroes*?"

Hannah shook her head.

"Jordan thinks she's hot." Nikki shrugged.

Hannah's eyes narrowed.

"Sorry," Nikki said, turning back to the computer. She tapped the screen, and the file opened to reveal a list of websites and passwords, beginning with Amazon. Then American Express. The third was Apple iCloud, followed by *Password:Freedom1*.

Hannah cast a sideways glance at Nikki. "I'm impressed."

"It's not all that impressive." Nikki felt herself blushing under Hannah's praise. *Jeez, what a sap.* "A lot of people keep their passwords this way."

Hannah returned to iCloud.com and signed in to Jordan's account. She bypassed the *Mail*, *Contacts*, and other icons and went straight to *Find My Phone*. She tapped the big green button. On the next screen, she went immediately to *All Devices*.

Nikki felt Hannah's disappointment as her own eyes registered the *Offline* message beside *Jordan's iPhone*. She sighed. "Well, I guess we kind of knew that. All the calls were going straight to voice mail, right?" The words didn't comfort her, so she knew they wouldn't comfort Hannah either, but she didn't know what else to say.

"Isn't there a way to see where it was last?" Hannah asked.

Reaching across Hannah, Nikki moved the computer to her own lap and maneuvered around the site. "It doesn't look like it," she said, finally conceding defeat.

Hannah rested her head on Nikki's shoulder and released a deep breath.

The scent of the shampoo she'd gotten such a strong hit of in the bath gently caressed Nikki's senses. Its subtlety now was actually worse than being overwhelmed by it earlier. "We'll keep checking back, though." She gave the laptop back to Hannah and eased up from the couch. "You know, in case she turns it on again."

Hannah gazed up at her, eyes wide with evident concern. She simply nodded.

Nikki wanted so badly to be able to give her the reassurance that look was asking for, but her own fear was growing with each failed attempt at finding out *anything* about where the hell Jordan was. She felt useless.

❖

Jordan drifted back into consciousness to the smell of coffee and something sweet. Her stomach churned with both hunger and slight nausea. She heard the murmur of unintelligible voices, and the low tones of music playing. She remembered Tina again. *No, it wasn't Tina.* That was a dream, but the bed beneath her still vibrated, and now she could feel the mild sway of her surroundings. *Where the hell am I?* The rustle of someone shifting close beside her brought her to full attention. She opened her eyes and tried to sit.

Soft but strong restraints held her arms and legs in place.

Her heart began to pound as panic seized her. With sudden awareness, she remembered the van, the cloth over her mouth, the arm around her middle. Her gaze found Liz—not walking away this time, but sitting right beside the bed.

"Good morning," Liz said, her voice steady.

Jordan stared, waiting for something to make sense. At least Liz was someone she knew. Her anxiety eased a bit. "Where am I? Why am I tied down?" She tugged again on her bonds. "And what are you doing here?"

Liz closed the magazine on her lap and set it on the night table.

Jordan followed the movement. The room was small, like the sleeping berth of her boat. Or a motor home, maybe?

"You're safe," Liz said. She rose and adjusted the pillow beneath Jordan's head. "Do you want some water?"

Slowly, Jordan became aware of an ache in the muscles along her arms and legs and up her torso. "What I want," she said, her jaw tight, "is to know what the hell's going on. I want to be untied." She jerked on the restraints.

"I'm sorry. I can't do that. You might hurt yourself." Liz returned to her seat and smoothed the floral skirt she wore over her thighs and knees. "And I can't feed you, but I can get you some water."

Jordan studied her. She looked the same—dark blond hair framing slightly angular features, blue eyes that held intelligence—but still, she was different somehow. She wasn't the hard-edged, aloof businesswoman who kicked Jordan's ass at racquetball on a semi-regular basis. She seemed softer, like she should be more malleable, but she definitely had the upper hand here. Jordan felt her panic rising again. She had to stay calm. She had to be able to think. She had to get free. If she could convince Liz to untie her, maybe she could get a clearer picture of the situation. "I have to pee. I need a bathroom," she said.

A knowing smile shaped Liz's lips. "You have a catheter in. You can go any time you need to."

"What?" This was crazy. "You can't just tie someone down and catheterize them for no reason. That's illegal."

"I know you don't understand, but you will, soon. Everything will be explained." Liz sat still, clearly intent on staying with Jordan, but she offered nothing else.

"Look, I don't know what's going on," Jordan said, "but if you let me go right now, I won't press charges." It probably wasn't the truth, but it might work for the moment.

"Are you sure you don't want any water?" Liz's eyes warmed with…what was that? Sympathy? Pity?

Anger pumped through Jordan's veins like molten lead. Her voice rose with it. "No. I don't want any fucking water."

Liz pursed her lips into a thin line and averted her gaze. "We'll be at our destination by this evening. You'll be untied there."

"There? Where? Where are we going?"

Liz didn't answer.

A male voice sounded slightly above the music in another part of the motor home. "You want me to take over driving for a while after we stop?"

Jordan looked to the doorway.

"That would be great. Thanks," another one said.

"Who's that?" Jordan asked. "Who's out there?"

Liz stroked Jordan's arm. "No one you know. Just try to relax."

Jordan seethed. "I'm not going to relax until I know what the hell's happening and until I'm out of *these*." She yanked on the straps and tried to kick her feet. Her stomach turned, and bile rose in her throat. She moaned. "I'm going to be sick."

Liz moved quickly and took a wet washcloth from a pan. She pressed it to Jordan's forehead. "You need to calm down."

"Is everything okay back here?"

Jordan shot a look to the doorway again where a thirty-something man with a pasty complexion that contrasted a toned build leaned against the jamb. "Who are you?" she asked, her tone sharp. "And what's going on? Why did you kidnap me? What do you want?"

"She's just a little agitated," Liz said as though Jordan hadn't spoken. "She'll be okay."

"You'll need to sedate her." The man seemed completely indifferent to Jordan's presence. "We're stopping for gas soon."

Liz merely nodded.

The man turned and vanished from the doorway.

"Hey," Jordan yelled after him. "Get back here, you asshole. Let me go, or I'll make sure every one of you gets locked up for a very long time."

With no reaction, Liz tightened the restraint on Jordan's right arm.

For the first time, Jordan noticed an IV catheter in the underside of her forearm. She watched as Liz opened the drawer to the night table and took out a syringe. She began to thrash, but her arm was held completely still. "Liz, no. Please, don't do this."

"It's okay, I'm a nurse. I know what I'm doing," Liz said as she pushed the needle into the IV and pressed the plunger. "You're safe."

Jordan tried to fight, but within seconds, she spiraled back into unconsciousness, her only awareness the pounding of her heart.

Chapter Five

The rest of Sunday afternoon was filled with the ringing of the telephone as friends Hannah had spoken to earlier called to see if Jordan had been found. Each time she had to say, "No, she still hasn't come home," and, "We've filed a missing persons report, but..." she had to fight harder not to slip into complete despair. Finally, she stopped answering the phone and let the calls go to voice mail after caller ID had done its job.

At six o'clock, the doorbell rang.

Hannah started and glanced nervously at Nikki. She felt herself pale when she realized that rather than thinking it might be Jordan, she was terrified it was someone coming to tell her Jordan had been found dead. Slowly, she rose to answer the door. Relief flooded her when she saw Marti and Delia standing on the front step, one holding a covered casserole dish, the other their baby.

"Hi," Marti said, lifting the casserole. "We brought you some dinner." Marti and Hannah had been friends since college, but their lives had taken them in different directions from time to time over the years. They had reconnected several years earlier when they had found they were both heading into serious relationships and once again had more in common.

"Oh, you didn't need to do that," Hannah said, gesturing them inside. In truth, she was thrilled. Apparently, both she and Nikki had forgotten all about the body's need for food. Her stomach grumbled at the savory aroma wafting into the room.

"It helped us feel a little less useless," Delia said. She smiled at Nikki. "Hey, Nik. What's up?"

Nikki stood, and they hugged around the six-month-old boy in Delia's arms and thumped each other on the back.

"Hey, Ringo," Nikki said to the baby. Delia had insisted they call him that after her favorite Beatle. His real name was Christopher, after no one in particular, *in case,* Marti had said, *at some point he wants an identity of his own.* Nikki held his hand and gently slapped her palm to his.

Ringo giggled.

"You two know each other?" Hannah asked Delia and took the dish from Marti. She watched in surprise as Nikki gave Marti a quick kiss on the cheek.

Delia laughed. "Of course. We met here a couple of years ago. We've hit the courts together a few times since then with Jordan and whoever else we can scare up for a game, and Nikki and I do our own thing with the pool cues." She mimicked lining up a shot in the air.

Hannah couldn't recall when they had all done something together, but she was getting used to being the one who didn't know anything. Still, it felt a little unsettling to find out two of her closest friends seemed to know Nikki so well. She let the thought fall away, unable to take on anymore confusion. "This is huge," she said, indicating the casserole. "Can you two stay and help us eat it?"

"Ooooh, I was hoping you'd ask," Delia said. "It smelled so good when Marti was making it."

Marti frowned. "I swear, I've never been able to teach her any manners."

As Marti and Hannah threw together a quick salad, Nikki set the table.

"Oh, I forgot the wine in the car," Delia said in a rush. "Be right back." She shifted Ringo into her other arm.

"Let me take him," Nikki said, holding out her hands. "I haven't seen him in a while."

Hannah stared as Nikki adjusted the baby on her hip in a natural motion.

Ringo smiled and grabbed Nikki's nose.

"Ooow," Nikki wailed, pretending to struggle against his grip.

Ringo laughed hysterically. It was obviously a game they had played many times.

When they all sat down at the table, Marti opened a jar of baby food and reached for Ringo.

"Can I do it?" Nikki asked.

The arch of Marti's eyebrows mirrored that of Hannah's. Jordan had shown only polite interest in any of their friends' children.

"He just started on solids," Marti said. "It's not like giving him a bottle. Do you know how?"

"Hmm, let's see." Nikki studied Ringo. "I think it goes in this end." She pointed to his face.

Marti smirked. "Smartass."

The exchange was playful, familiar, easy. Hannah remembered such interaction between herself and Jordan and Nikki. A pang of... something...resonated in her chest, but with the thought of Jordan, it quickly gave way to worry again.

Nikki laughed and spooned some strained spinach into Ringo's open mouth. "I have all kinds of hidden talents. Not to mention, a whole bunch of nieces and nephews." She looked up and caught Hannah watching her. She flushed before feeding Ringo another bite.

Hannah wasn't sure if it was Nikki's ease with the baby or the cuteness of her blush, but the sight made her smile.

After dinner, Hannah brought Marti and Delia up to date on everything that had happened over the weekend. As she answered as many questions as she could, she felt calmed watching Nikki playing with Ringo on the floor and eventually settling into the recliner with him snuggled against her. The scene felt so right in some ways, but it should be Jordan there with her that brought up that feeling. Not Nikki. Then again, if it *were* Jordan there with them, it would be an entirely different tableau. It would be Delia or Marti entertaining the baby, the four adults would be discussing world events or sports scores, and the intimacy present in the room would be replaced by a much more casual connection. So why did this feel right when the other was what Hannah had chosen for her life? A disturbing ambiguity filled her.

"What are you going to do?" Delia asked, bringing Hannah back to the reality of the moment. "I mean, if Jordan doesn't show up pretty soon."

Hannah shook her head. "I don't know what to do," she whispered. She cleared her throat. "What do you do when someone just disappears into thin air?" Tears stung her eyes.

They exchanged glances, and Marti opened her arms to Hannah. As Hannah let herself be consoled, she looked at Nikki and Ringo. They were asleep, Ringo tucked securely in the fold of Nikki's body and Nikki's arm protectively around him. Hannah realized she had no idea where in the house Nikki had slept the previous night. Maybe right there in that chair, since Hannah had been on the couch. She didn't even know if Nikki had slept at all. She had to do better. Nikki had spent the night and waited with her. She had stayed that morning when she had wanted to go home. She had helped with all the phone calls and even taken charge of the ones Hannah was afraid to face. The least Hannah could do was make sure she had a comfortable place to sleep.

A little later, when Marti leaned down to pick up the sleeping baby so they could leave, Nikki startled awake and tightened her hold on him.

"Shh. It's okay," Marti whispered. "I've got him."

Nikki released him and rose to follow.

At the door, Hannah and Nikki watched the family walk down the steps. "See ya soon, Nik," Delia called. "Let's get together. When do you get that cast off?"

"Tomorrow." Nikki blinked sleepily.

"Call me."

Nikki nodded.

Hannah waved once more to her friends, then closed the door. "You get your cast off tomorrow?" It sounded foolish, since Nikki had just said that, but she felt that awkwardness between them again all of a sudden. She grasped for something to say.

"Yeah. At nine." Nikki rubbed her eyes, then scrubbed her hands over her face. "Sorry, I didn't mean to crash."

"It's okay. I'm exhausted, too. It's been a rough couple of days," Hannah said distractedly. She couldn't help feeling as though she should be doing something every minute to try to find Jordan, but she didn't know *what*. Nikki had checked the hospitals as the 911 dispatcher had said, and Officer Mullins had made some suggestions, but what were they? They had called any friends she knew of, they'd checked with the B&B in Shasta, where she and Jordan had stayed on a couple of getaways, and they were waiting for the police to contact the gym for more information. *What else did he say?* Hannah's brain was fried. She just wanted to go to sleep.

"What about Jordan's family?" Nikki said into the silence as though reading Hannah's mind. "Mullins said we should try to contact them even if we think she hasn't talked to them."

"Oh, yeah. That's the one I couldn't remember." Hannah walked to the couch and flopped onto it. "Do you know if her parents still live up north?"

"No," Nikki said, settling into the chair again. "I think her father has two law offices, one somewhere in northern California and one back East. New York, I think. But I'm not sure. Jordan only mentioned it briefly when she was talking about that case a few years ago, when she went up against her dad's firm."

"When was that? I remember they asked her about it in that interview she did, but other than that, she never said anything about it."

Nikki looked wary.

Hannah smiled. "Don't worry. I'm not going to bite your head off about what you know." She might still get irritated about what she didn't know, but she wouldn't take it out on Nikki. She had realized the problem coming up continuously wasn't with Jordan and Nikki's relationship, but rather with Jordan and hers.

Nikki nodded. "It was about a year before Jordan met you. Her father's a corporate lawyer and a senior partner in a big firm. They got slapped with a sexual harassment suit by a group of women who hired Jordan to represent them." She looked thoughtful as though processing something else.

Hannah remembered being fascinated with that aspect of Nikki when they had first become friends—how she could be in a conversation about something and not miss a beat of it while simultaneously thinking about three other things. She always somehow felt fully present, though.

"Maybe they're in her email addresses or contact list," Nikki said.

"The women?"

"Jordan's parents."

Oh. Right. She nodded, still unable to believe she didn't have the faintest idea how to contact her girlfriend's parents.

Nikki went into the office.

"We don't have her phone, though," Hannah called after her.

Nikki returned, carrying the laptop. "No, but there was an icon for both when we were in iCloud." She opened it and began tapping the screen, her expression hopeful. Within seconds, however, she frowned. "I guess she never backed them up here." She closed the computer.

Hannah let her head fall back against the cushion.

"I'll call Dana in the morning," Nikki said, evidently moving on to one of the next things she had been pondering. "I'm sure she can track down some information with her slippery lawyer ways."

Hannah gave her a weak smile. *How would I be getting through this without Nikki?* She couldn't imagine. "Thank you," she said softly, "for helping with all this."

Nikki hesitated. "Jordan's my best friend."

"I know." Of course, that was why she was here. She was worried about Jordan, too. "I just want you to know I appreciate it."

Nikki nodded, then shifted her gaze back to the laptop.

That odd unease stretched between them once again. Hannah had never felt it back when Nikki used to hang out with them. Had she? And what had happened with that? She would have to ask Nikki sometime. For now, she wanted to sleep, to escape all of this. Maybe when she woke, Jordan would be home. "Will you stay over again?" she asked.

Nikki looked resigned. "Yes," she said simply. "I'll stay as long as you need me to."

When Hannah crawled into bed, she could still hear Nikki in the bathroom. The sound soothed her, but the emptiness of the big bed caused an ache in her chest. She didn't want to be alone, didn't want Nikki as far away as the living room, but she couldn't very well ask her to share the bed with her. They were friends, but not that kind of friends, not the kind of girlfriends who would do a slumber party, or even sleep together for comfort. Still, the thought of being alone terrified her.

What if Jordan never comes home? What if the last time she would feel Jordan in bed with her had already taken place the previous morning, when she hadn't even noticed what Jordan was wearing? It wasn't the sex she was thinking of but the connection, that sense of belonging to, or with, someone. Had she and Jordan really had that, though? With all the things she hadn't known, how could she not question it?

Had she really never noticed what time Jordan left the house or who she hung out with besides Nikki? Had she never asked if Jordan had siblings? She knew she had asked about the rift with her parents and why they never spoke, but Jordan had refused to discuss that. Hannah had told herself she was respecting Jordan's boundaries. But was she? Or was it simply easier not to delve too deeply and let the relationship stay light and fun?

She couldn't bear the doubt. She had to stop thinking, stop wondering. On top of Jordan being missing, on top of the encroaching fear that something might have happened to her, Hannah couldn't face the shortcomings of their relationship, couldn't face her own part in it. She needed a distraction. She could call Kate. All she would have to do is ask about Kate's date the night before, and her mind would be blissfully inundated with irrelevant chatter.

She reached for the phone.

Jordan drifted through darkness, gradually becoming aware of the ache in her muscles, then the hard surface beneath her, unforgiving where it pressed against the bones of her shoulder, elbow, and hip. She lay on her side, stomach cramps forcing her into a fetal position and a sharp throb of a migraine pounding in her head. She started to turn onto her back but gasped and stiffened as shards of pain racked her torso. What the hell had she done? She felt like she'd just run a marathon and then gotten hit by a truck. She groaned.

She opened her eyes, then blinked rapidly against a light so bright it seemed to have no source. She tried to focus, to see through it, but quickly relented to the pain it caused. She clenched her lids shut and slung one arm across her face. *Where the hell am I?* She lay still, her breathing shallow.

With a start, she realized she was no longer restrained. Her hands were free. *My phone. Where's my phone?* Eyes still tightly closed, she reached for her pants pocket, but her fingers grazed skin. She felt around, her palm gliding down her bare thigh, then up to her abs. Also bare. *What the fuck?* Was she naked? She struggled to sit. She squinted and looked down at herself. *Yup. As naked as God's creation.* Where had *that* come from? Was it a saying? She'd heard it. Someone had said it...recently. She fought to clear her head. *Liz.* Liz had said it—but when, and to whom?

Nothing was making any sense. She remembered meeting Liz at the car garage, the cloth over her mouth, the restraints...the IV. In a panic, she felt her arm. The port was gone, but there was an itchy lump where it'd been...and the catheter Liz had told her about was gone, too. Then there was the bed, the movement, stopping for gas...a motor home. And Liz—always Liz. Who the hell was she? Someone Jordan had played racquetball with, who wanted... What? Had Jordan slept with her? This was all way too over the top for a disgruntled one-night stand. No, she'd never slept with Liz... She knew that from the bottom of her soul. So, what then?

She kept her eyes down to avoid looking directly into the brilliant light and surveyed some of her surroundings. She sat on a cement slab, about the size of a twin bed but with no mattress or covering of any kind. The floor was white linoleum with a drain in the center, the walls the same stark white, and a bare toilet stood in the corner. She tried to find a door, but the light sliced into her eyes and felt like it was cutting into her brain. She cried out and buried her face in her hands. Her head pounded.

Her fingertips grazed her forehead. Something was wrong. Something was *missing*. Her eyebrows! *Where are my eyebrows?* She touched the arched bones where they should have been, then moved higher until her hands ran over the smooth skin of her scalp. *Somebody shaved my head?* She looked down at her naked body again. Someone had shaved every inch of her! "What the fuck?" This time she said it out loud.

This is crazy! She pressed her fingers to her temples and squeezed her eyes shut. *Think. Think.* What could this possibly be? And why? And who? *And how do I get out of here, wherever here is?* There was too much. She didn't even know where to start.

The sound of a key sliding into a lock drew her attention, then the opening of a door. Footsteps.

"Do you want me to stay with you?" a man asked.

"No, thank you. I'll be fine." Liz's voice. "We'll be fine."

A door closed.

Jordan tried to look toward the voices. If she could only see something.

"How are you feeling, Jordan?" Liz asked. Her tone was sincere, like she really cared.

But she's the one who did this. "I feel like shit!" Jordan tried again to look up but had to shield her eyes.

"I'm sorry. You're experiencing some side effects of the sedative we used. They're not serious, though. They'll pass as the drug clears from your system."

"Will you turn off that dammed light?" Jordan's voice was a whisper. Her throat was dry.

"I can't do that." Liz moved closer and pressed her hand to Jordan's forehead. "Just close your eyes and lie back. Let yourself rest for a while. You'll start feeling better."

Jordan wrenched away from Liz's touch. Her aching muscles screamed. She winced. "I don't want to rest," she said, her voice rising. "I want to get the hell out of here. Who are you? And what do you want?"

Liz stepped back. "My name is Sister Katherine, and I want to help you find your way out of the darkness of sin and back into the light."

Jordan waited a beat to let Liz's answers match up with the questions. They didn't, at least not in a way that explained anything. "You're a nun?" She was lost.

"Not a nun. A servant of God in a different way, and I've answered a call to help save your soul."

Liz's voice was even. She sounded rational, as though she was explaining she was going to the store and would be back in a half an hour, as though she hadn't just kidnapped, drugged, and committed assault and battery against her racquetball partner by restraining, catheterizing, stripping, then *shaving* her entire body. Jordan wished she could look up into Liz's face to see if she was holding back laughter or about to break into a grin. Maybe Nikki would jump out from somewhere any minute, yelling, "Gotcha." But no. Her and Nikki's pranks were things like bribing a bartender to bring the other one a drink and tell her it was from a woman across the bar, then watching while she strolled over and made a fool of herself, or mixing a bunch of hot sauce into the other one's taco salad while she was refilling her drink. They weren't weird, never *anything* like *this*.

Jordan actually wished this were a prank. It would be a sick one, but she'd forgive everyone involved and join in on the laughter out of pure relief. But in her gut, she knew it wasn't. She knew she was in trouble. Her heartbeat quickened. "Liz, please."

"Sister Katherine," Liz said calmly.

"What?"

"My name is Sister Katherine."

Nausea rolled through Jordan's stomach. She felt weak, but an underlying rage began to work its way through her. "I don't give a shit what your name is. Give me my clothes, and let me the hell out of here."

"You've been chosen," Liz—or Sister Katherine—said, sounding, once again, as though the response should clear up everything. "You're being reborn into the light, stripped from all ties to who or what you've been and to your sinful ways." She pressed Jordan's shoulder. "Lie back, now, and put yourself in God's hands."

Jordan pushed past her and leapt to her feet, but her thigh muscles cramped, and she started to crumple to the floor.

Liz caught her and eased her onto the cement slab.

The throb in Jordan's head intensified. Her stomach roiled, and the side of her knee where she'd scraped it on the cement burned. She gasped for breath and clenched her eyes shut again.

"I'll leave you, now," Liz said. "Get some rest."

"No," Jordan said, grabbing for her hand. But she missed. She lay back on the hard surface, hoping that if she kept still enough, her head and stomach would settle. Her breath came fast. She heard a soft knock, then a key in the lock, and finally, the quiet click of the door closing. She was alone again.

She fought back overwhelming panic and tried to focus, but the pain finally led to darkness.

CHAPTER SIX

Hannah tensed as she listened to the front door close behind Nikki. She poured herself another cup of Kona blend and added cream. She thought of all the times she had heard the exact same soft rattle of the handle and quiet thump as Jordan had left for work or to catch up with buddies for some kind of sports game. How odd that there was no discernible distinction between the sound of her lover or her friend leaving the house. Shouldn't there be? She sipped her coffee.

She had never thought about it before—how, or if, things with her lover should be different than with anyone else. There was the obvious way, of course. By virtue of the very definition of the word, a lover was someone she had sex with, with whom she was sexually intimate, but was that all? It seemed it could be. After all, Nikki clearly knew Jordan far better than Hannah did, and *they* weren't lovers. How could that be?

This situation had brought up thoughts she hadn't had before, too many questions without answers. She hadn't been able to sleep the previous night, even after listening to Kate for an hour, then trying every relaxation technique she had ever learned. She had finally given up, wandering the condo until she eventually settled into the swing on the patio so she wouldn't disturb Nikki and listened to the night sounds. To keep her mind from heading straight into scenes from horror and thriller stories, she let herself consider what Officer Mullins had said about people who decided they wanted a fresh start and just walked away from their lives.

Who did that? Who would just walk away, leaving behind the people that loved them, that depended on them, without a word? Certainly, not Jordan. *Surely, it makes more sense to just break up with someone, right? To just break up with me?* What if it wasn't just Hannah she was escaping, though? Maybe in a couple of months, Dana would find Jordan had been embezzling funds. *Psh! Like Jordan needs to embezzle with the trust fund her grandparents left her.* There. *That* was something Hannah knew. Or maybe she was in trouble with the IRS. *No.* Hannah scoffed. But if Jordan hadn't just left her life behind, what was the alternative?

If she wasn't careful, Hannah would be back to those horrible scenes she had imagined, or worse, to the news stories about the real Ted Bundys and Jeffrey Dahmers of the world. She had to do something to keep busy, to keep her mind occupied. She couldn't just sit and wait for Jordan to come through the door after two days, for Nikki to come home from the doctor, for some nameless, faceless detective to call. She had to keep active, preferably with tasks that could lead to more information about Jordan. She thought of the laptop. There had to be something in there that might help. She and Nikki had only been in that iCloud thing.

She retrieved the computer from the office and settled onto the couch while it booted up beside her. They had checked the Phone Finder several more times throughout the previous afternoon and evening with the same result, and she made that her first stop now as well. When she read the same offline message, she exited the site and stared at the screen. *What am I looking for?* She set her mug on the end table and flicked a fingernail against the laptop's casing as she thought. Nikki had said she would ask Dana to try to track down Jordan's father, but maybe Jordan had some contact information for him, even if she didn't use it. *What about an email address?*

Hannah knew Jordan had a Gmail account, or, at least, she used to when they were dating. They didn't email each other now because they lived together, called, texted, even Facetimed occasionally. Maybe Jordan had an email address for her parents in her contacts, though. *Or that brother.* She frowned. The brother still irked her. *Three years together...how could I not know something like that?*

Hannah made her way back to the file Nikki had found and started down the list of IDs and passwords. It was, of course, alphabetized. Jordan was always organized. And there it was in the Gs, right where it belonged. Gmail: jnwsportsfan@gmail.com. Password: freethrow.

Within seconds, Hannah was staring at Jordan's Inbox. There weren't many messages—maybe twenty—and most of them, she could tell from the subject lines, were ads or promos. An unopened one was a reminder to reorder checks and a second, some sort of ticket confirmation. Curious about the latter, she glanced at the *From* field. *Impossible Dreams?* That didn't tell her anything. She started to open it, then caught herself. *You don't open other people's emails.* That was just wrong. What about what Mullins had said, though, about people leaving their lives behind? One might need some form of tickets to do that. Hannah's stomach knotted. Distractedly, she picked up her coffee. *But Jordan's in her car, wherever she is.* She wouldn't need tickets.

Oh, that's comforting. Wouldn't it be better to know that Jordan simply decided to leave? At least then Hannah wouldn't have to fight off images of her tied up in the trunk of a car or in some backwoods cabin being—Hannah drew in a sharp breath and tapped the screen to stop herself from following that line of thinking any further. The email opened to reveal a banner across the top that read, *Impossible Dreams! We get the Hard-to-Get!* Below was a purchase summary and confirmation number for two tickets to the sold out Pink concert the following month. Hannah had wanted to go so badly and had been disappointed to learn the tickets were no longer available.

And Jordan found some. Hannah's throat tightened with emotion. She took a swallow of coffee as she glanced at the total. *Nine hundred and fifty dollars?* She choked. The hot liquid shot out her nose. She dropped the cup, soaking her pants, and heard it hit the floor. *Damn it!* She tossed the computer onto the other end of the sofa as she doubled over in a coughing fit.

Nine hundred and fifty dollars. The words kept ringing in her head as she cleaned up the mess. What had Jordan been thinking? *An early birthday present?* It had to be *really* early. Her birthday was still five months away, and even then... *Nine hundred and fifty dollars?* Hannah *loved* Pink and had to admit she was touched by Jordan's thoughtfulness, but really? *Nine hundred and fifty dollars?* Jordan did things like that sometimes, though. Hannah ran her thumb over the face of the lady's Rolex on her wrist, Jordan's Valentine's Day present the year they had moved in together.

She returned to the couch and leaned her head back against the cushion. Her throat and nose burned from the heat of the coffee, her thighs still a little sticky beneath the clean jeans she had put on. She took a deep breath and positioned the computer on her lap. She would have to talk to Jordan—again—about such extravagant gifts. She enjoyed them—who wouldn't?—but she always felt a little uncomfortable because she couldn't do the same, at least not to *that* degree. Besides, she was just as touched by some of the other things Jordan did, like surprising her with a romantic picnic dinner on the beach, or taking off from work to care for her sometimes when she stayed home sick.

She didn't know how much money Jordan actually had in her trust fund, or even how much she made as a civil rights attorney, given that clients needing her services might not always have much. They had kept their finances separate other than a joint account they both contributed to for shared living expenses, and once when Hannah had broached the subject, Jordan's response had been a vague reference to silver spoons before distracting Hannah with her warm and oh-so-skilled mouth. Hannah hadn't minded the diversion in the slightest, and she hadn't bothered to follow up.

She sighed and closed the email. Would she have the chance to talk to Jordan about it? She blinked against the beginning of tears. *Where are you, Jory?* She looked through the rest of the messages but found nothing of any interest, never mind help, then remembered why she was actually there. She opened the contact list. It was relatively short, too. A number of names Hannah didn't recognize—Ashley Reynolds, Brian Davis, Gerald Simonson, Leslie with no last name. Nikki was there with an old AOL address, and Delia, along with a couple of other people with whom she knew Jordan played various sports. No other Webbers, though. *What about that Liz person?* She looked for a Liz or Elizabeth or even Beth but found nothing. Out of curiosity, she checked the Trash to find it empty. She frowned in frustration.

She returned to the list of IDs and passwords. *Maybe there's something else here.* There had to be. She scrolled down the page. At the very bottom, she found Work (backup): jwlegal@gmail.com with an accompanying password. Excited, she went back to the Gmail log-in page, then hesitated. Should she go into Jordan's work emails? Jordan dealt with a lot of confidential matters. *I won't read those, though. I'll just look through her contacts.* But even some of those could be confidential. *To hell with it.* She logged in. If Jordan didn't want people going through her things, she shouldn't just vanish off the face of the earth. And if her disappearance wasn't her own idea, she would be grateful for anything that could help find her.

In the Inbox, most of the messages showed as forwards from Jordan's actual work email address. Hannah assumed that, like her school district's server, the firm's system had a retention limit and dumped messages after a certain amount of time. Hannah had all of her emails sent to a backup address so she would have them on file for reference as long as she wanted. Intermingled with the forwards, however, was an occasional email that had come straight through to this address. *See You Next Time,* read the subject line of one from someone named Gen. *Re: Free Tuesday?* said another from Sylvia. *Thanks for Last Night ;)* from Marianna. And there were more from other women as Hannah scrolled down. She went numb. What was she looking at? Surely, this wasn't what it seemed. Jordan had just spent nine hundred and fifty dollars to take her to a Pink concert. How could she be seeing other women at the same time?

The screen blurred as her vision darkened and acid burned the back of her throat. *Maybe the tickets aren't for me. Maybe they're for Gen or Sylvia, or...* She felt queasy. A part of her wanted to turn away, to close the computer and pretend she had never seen any of this, but she had to know. She opened a message entitled *A Great Time.* It read:

If I'd known watching my sister play basketball could lead to so much fun, I would've started years ago. Thanks! Lydia xoxox

Okay, she *could* actually be talking about basketball. *You're a fool.* Hannah pursed her lips and returned to the top of the screen. She tapped on *See You Next Time.*

Thanks, hon, for the great time...as always. Be back in LA next month. Hope we can get together. You always do such a good job relaxing me. ;)

Hannah's stomach plummeted as though she was falling. There was no doubt about *that* meaning, even if she tried to make up something different. She knew very well Jordan's euphemism of *relaxing* a woman. She sat, dazed, staring unseeingly at the screen. *Jordan's cheating on me.* And not just with one woman, not a single fling or affair. *Anyone can slip, right?*

But no, there were many emails, many women, very few more than once. Hannah continued scrolling slowly and pulling up screens of older messages. Gen seemed to be the only one who showed up repeatedly—not necessarily frequently, but repeatedly. After a number of screen pages, Hannah stopped on one of Gen's emails and checked the date. Her eyes went wide and her lips parted with a small gasp. *Two years ago?* Jordan had been seeing this woman the whole time they had been living together. Hannah went numb. She moved to the next page. *Even when we were dating.* She couldn't look at anymore. *If that's what Jordan wanted, why was she even with me?* She slammed the computer shut.

She really didn't know Jordan at all. She had been with her for three years, and she'd had no idea Jordan was seeing other women, didn't know she had a brother, didn't know her friends. Was everything she thought they had shared a lie? The ground seemed to shift beneath her, and tears for the loss of something she apparently never even had burned her eyes. *How can I have been so blindly stupid?*

The telephone rang.

Hannah blinked, then stared at the cordless handset on the coffee table. Every time it had rung before since Saturday evening, she had snatched it up to see if it was Jordan. This morning, she still wondered if it could be and knew she should grab it, but what would she say, now that she knew about Gen and Marianna and Sylvia and Lydia and… She squeezed her eyes shut to try to quiet the drumming of each name in her head.

The phone kept ringing.

She had to answer it. She picked it up and checked the caller ID—Santa Monica Police Department. Had they found something? Had they found Jordan? She pressed the Talk button. "Hello?" Her voice trembled.

"May I speak with Ms. Hannah Lewis, please?" The woman's brisk manner almost left a crackle on the line.

Hannah took a deep breath. Could she take anything more right now—good, bad, or even neutral? She wished Nikki were here. "Speaking," was all she could manage.

"Ms. Lewis, this is Detective Morrison with Santa Monica PD, and I've been assigned to the missing person's case you filed on Jordan Webber." She paused, obviously wanting a response.

"Yes, hello, Detective." Hannah sat up straight, steeling herself.

"I just wanted to touch base with you this morning to see if Ms. Webber returned or if you've heard from her."

Hannah sighed, uncertain if in relief or disappointment that the police hadn't learned anything either. "No, we haven't heard anything," she said. "We called all of our friends yesterday and some of the places we've vacationed like the officer said, but no one's seen or heard from her." Should she mention the emails? The women? She couldn't. She couldn't say the words out loud—not yet, not to this stranger.

"What about her family?"

Shit. That's what she had been looking for in the email. She forgot all about contact information for Jordan's parents or brother. "We haven't been able to do that yet," Hannah said. "We'll keep trying, though."

"All right," Detective Morrison said, her tone softening just a bit. "I did speak with the manager of the gym first thing this morning, and she confirmed that Ms. Webber didn't keep her reservation for the court." The briefest pause. "And neither did Ms. Talbot."

"Ms. Talbot?"

"Liz Talbot. The other person on the reservation," the detective said.

Liz. Liz Talbot. The woman Nikki said had taken her place on the court. So, neither one had shown up? The implication lingered on the line like an obscene caller. Hannah rejected it. Maybe Jordan had to cancel for some reason. Or Liz. Or maybe Jordan had picked her up for the game and whatever happened to Jordan happened to her, too. "Have you talked to this Ms. Talbot to see if she heard from Jordan?"

"The address she listed with the gym is a hotel. I contacted them, and she checked out Saturday morning."

Hannah went cold. What did that mean? She didn't want to ask. She didn't want to hear what the detective thought it meant. It had been hard enough when Mullins had implied it with his questions about whether she and Jordan had a fight and if the relationship had any issues. Of course, they had issues. *Who doesn't?* But Jordan wouldn't just leave her. *Would she? What the hell do I know?* "What about a phone number?"

"I left a message on her voice mail." There was a note of finality in Detective Morrison's voice.

"That's not it, is it? You're not giving up?"

"Ms. Lewis, there isn't a lot we can do in a case like this. There's no sign of foul play, nothing to suggest any laws have been broken."

And here they were again. This was all the same stuff Officer Mullins had said.

"We've put an alert on the car, so if it turns up—"

"She was seeing other women," Hannah blurted. *God, how embarrassing.* "Maybe one of them—"

"Other women?" It was a question, but there was no surprise underlying it. Maybe this was one of those heard-it-all-before situations.

"Yes, I found emails when I was looking for contact information for her family." Hannah held her breath.

"Did you get in touch with any of them?"

Did I get in touch with any of them? How mortifying would that be? "No," Hannah said, keeping her voice steady. "I just found out this morning." *Two minutes before you called, actually.*

"Well, it would be good if you did," Detective Morrison said, clearly preparing to end the call. "Let me know if anything comes of it. I'll be in touch if we get a hit on Ms. Webber's car or if anything comes in with a match of her description. And be sure to follow up with her family, if possible."

After she hung up, Hannah stared into space. The reality of everything that had happened, everything she had discovered, since Saturday afternoon settled on her like a two-ton weight. And those emails, those women. *What am I supposed to do with that?*

If Jordan were here, she knew exactly what she would do. She would leave the computer on the table, signed in to Jordan's backup

Gmail account—maybe even with a message from *Gen* open on the screen—and she would wait in the bedroom and make Jordan come to her. That's what Hannah's mother used to do when she had caught Hannah or Kate at something. Her initial shock was wearing off and giving way to anger, but what was she supposed to do with the betrayal with Jordan missing? She couldn't be mad because what if something horrible really had happened to Jordan? And yet, she couldn't *not* be mad because, seriously, who *wouldn't* be mad and hurt and humiliated at finding out the person she lived with had *never* been faithful to her? Hannah's head felt like it was about to explode. The police clearly thought Jordan had just run away, and maybe she had—probably with one of those other women, probably with Liz.

The sound of a key unlocking the front door interrupted Hannah's escalating thoughts. *Jordan!* She leapt up, unsure if she planned to hurl herself into Jordan's arms or hurl the closest heavy object at her head. She waited, every muscle in her body taut, ready to spring.

Nikki stepped through the doorway. "Hey. I heard from Dana. She got us a number for Jordan's father's firm."

The disappointment was almost crushing. In that split second it had taken for the door to open, she had been so certain it was Jordan. It was a key in the door—not a knock, not the bell. She had been primed to take Jordan in her arms and cry in relief, to fly at her in a rage for not telling Hannah where she was, to hold her close, to throttle her—all at the same time. And now, here she stood, staring at Nikki. She began to shake and crumpled to the floor.

"Hannah!" Nikki rushed to her.

Hannah began to sob in frustration, in despair, in fury, in fear, in defeat. There were too many emotions. She couldn't sort them all out. "I thought you were Jory." She cried into the front of Nikki's shirt.

"I'm sorry." Nikki wrapped her arms around Hannah and pulled her close.

"I heard the key. I thought…" But how stupid. Nikki had a key, too. Hannah knew that. She'd had one since way before Hannah had even met Jordan.

"I'm sorry. I should have knocked. I just thought you might be resting. I heard you up last night and I didn't want to wake you if you were asleep." Nikki rocked her. "I'm so sorry."

Nikki's strong embrace felt so good, safe, reassuring. Hannah hadn't realized how alone she had felt in the short time Nikki had been gone. She burrowed into Nikki's chest and let her tears fall. Finally, her emotions ebbed, and she was able to ease away. "I'm sorry," she said, wiping her face on the sleeve of her blouse. "I didn't mean to fall apart."

"It's okay." Nikki kept her arms loosely draped around her. "Nobody's going to blame you for falling apart during this. Can you get up?"

Hannah nodded and pulled herself onto the sofa.

Nikki handed her a box of tissue from the coffee table and sat beside her.

Hannah blew her nose, then hiccupped.

"Can I get you anything?" Nikki asked.

Hannah shook her head. She cut a sideways glance at Nikki and took in the large wet spot on her chest. "I got your shirt all wet."

Nikki looked down and touched the tear-soaked fabric. "That's all right. It'll dry." She returned her gaze to Hannah's. "Are you sure you're okay?"

"I'm fine." It was a lie, of course. How could she be fine? She wasn't ready to tell Nikki about the emails, though, about the women and how far back they went, about what a fool she was. And she couldn't tell her about the call from Detective Morrison without bringing up the discovery that Liz Temporary-Racquetball-Partner Talbot disappeared, coincidentally, at the exact same time as Jordan, which then would lead to the revelation about the other women as well. She had a fleeting thought that with everything else Nikki knew, maybe she knew about Jordan's infidelities as well, but she immediately dismissed it. This was different from knowing about a brother that simply never came up, or having a coworker's phone number. Keeping this from Hannah would have been an actual deception, and Nikki wouldn't do that. She was Jordan's friend, but she was Hannah's friend, too. She would have told Hannah long ago. "Did you say Dana found a number for Jordan's father?" Hannah asked to stave off the inevitable.

"Oh, yeah," Nikki said, pulling her cell phone from her back pocket. "It's his office number. The one in New York. But if he's not there, they could probably give us the number for the one in California."

"Okay," Hannah said shakily.

"Are you ready for this, or do you need a little time?" Nikki watched her, concern showing in her eyes.

Hannah flinched. She realized she was becoming gun-shy, or in this case, conversation-shy. Every time she spoke with someone, she discovered some new disconcerting piece of information that revealed she had no idea who Jordan was. And now, she had to talk to the parents with whom Jordan didn't even exchange Christmas cards. God only knew what *they* might reveal. It was better than having to start writing emails to all those women, though—those women who had more than likely laughed at her while sleeping with her lover—*if* they knew about her at all. Hannah sighed. "I'll never be ready, but let's get it over with."

Nikki placed the call, then switched the phone to speaker.

"Good afternoon. Stevens, Webber, and Associates. How may I direct your call?"

Hannah straightened and composed herself. "May I speak with Mr. Webber, please?" She thought she sounded remarkably together.

"Which Mr. Webber are you trying to reach, ma'am?"

Shoot. There's more than one? Hannah had seen the name once in that interview Jordan had done. What was it? Something with a J? She looked at Nikki for help.

Nikki shrugged.

"Jonathan or David?" the receptionist asked before Hannah had to come up with an answer.

Wasn't David the brother? "Jonathan. Thank you."

"One moment, please." There was a soft click, then a classical piano piece began to play.

"That was easy," Hannah said, surprised. She would have thought it would be harder to get to a senior partner of a law firm.

"It's good to know David can be reached here, too," Nikki said. "I think if Jordan's talked to anyone in her family, it'd more likely be him than her parents."

Why? What had happened between Jordan and her parents? She regretted never pursuing the subject with Jordan.

The music clicked off, and a second woman said efficiently, "Jonathan Webber's office."

Ah, of course there would be another keeper of the gate. "May I please speak with Mr. Webber?" Hannah asked, hoping she had managed a patient tone.

"May I say who's calling?"

"Hannah Lewis," she said confidently.

"And what is this regarding, Ms. Lewis?"

Had there been the slightest pause before the question, or had Hannah imagined it? She wasn't sure what to say. She remembered her father's administrative assistant. Cheryl had taken great pride in being able to handle all of Hannah's father's affairs without ever having to speak with him. Hannah actually wanted to hear Jordan's father's voice, to be able to listen to *his* answers. "It's a personal matter," she said politely but firmly.

This time the pause was definite. "One moment, please."

More music.

"I'm sorry," the woman said when she came back on the line. "Mr. Webber is in a meeting. May I take a message?"

Hannah sighed with resignation. *Of course, a man with his own law firm wouldn't be easy to reach.* "Will you ask him to call me, please?"

"Of course, Ms. Lewis."

After leaving her number, Hannah started to hang up, then reconsidered. "Tell him it's about his daughter." The words rushed out.

"Yes, Ms. Lewis," the woman said. "Have a nice day."

The call ended.

"That was kind of weird," Hannah said under her breath. She couldn't quite put her finger on exactly why, though. *Had* there been a pause after she gave her name? And wouldn't the secretary have known already that her boss was in a meeting? Cheryl would have.

"Should we call back and see if we can get through to David?" Nikki asked.

Hanna tried to focus. "Sure," she said, tucking the wave of her hair behind her ear. "It's worth a try."

Nikki hit redial, and the same receptionist answered, but this time when she transferred the call, it went straight through.

"David Webber," a man answered, sounding a little frazzled.

"Oh," Hannah said in surprise. "Yes, hello, David. My name is Hannah Lewis? I'm your sister's—"

"Is Jordan okay?" Alarm rang in his voice.

Hannah could almost see him sit up straight behind a desk.

"Well..." Hannah faltered. How could she answer that? "I don't know. That's why I'm calling. Have you heard from Jordan recently?"

"No. Why?" David asked cautiously. "What's going on?"

Hannah steadied herself to say what needed to be said. "Jordan left for a racquetball game on Saturday morning and didn't come home. We're just calling everyone she knows, anyone she might have talked to recently who might know something."

The only sound was the long squeak of an office chair. "You're her partner," David said finally. "If you don't know where she is, how would I?"

Hannah thought she heard a hint of accusation in his tone, but what was she being accused of? "How do you know I'm her partner?"

"I saw a picture of the two of you in an interview a couple of years ago. Your name was mentioned."

"Oh," was all Hannah could think of to say.

"I haven't spoken with Jordan in years," David said resolutely. "Have you called the police?"

"Yes, they're the ones who told us to contact anyone she knows, including her family, even though you and she have been out of touch."

"I'm sorry I can't help you." David seemed to be softening. "I actually wish I *had* heard from her."

Hannah detected a sadness in his tone. "We put in a call to your father, but we haven't spoken with him yet. Do you think, maybe, your parents have heard from her?"

David barked out a humorless laugh. "Has hell frozen over?" He paused. "I'm sorry, but I'm sure Jordan hasn't been in touch with our parents. I would have heard *all* about *that*."

Hannah was curious about the comment but knew it would be inappropriate to ask. Besides, knowing what happened between Jordan and her parents would only be important now if Jordan came home, if she was okay, and if Hannah could stand to be in the same room with her knowing the rest of what she now knew. "May I leave my number with you, and if you do hear anything from her, would you let me know?"

"Sure." He wrote down the number as she gave it. "You know," he said slowly when he had finished, "this wouldn't be the first time Jordan just vanished from her life."

There it was again, the suggestion that Jordan had simply turned her back and walked away. "What do you mean?" Hannah asked.

"It's just... Well, like I said. I haven't spoken with her in years."

Hannah wanted to ask if he had tried—if he had looked for her or called her. He made it sound as though he had. "Thank you for talking with me," she said instead.

"Hannah," David said quickly.

"Yes?"

"Will you let me know when she shows up?" He paused. "Just so I know she's okay."

"Of course. And thank you again."

Hannah pressed her face into her hands as Nikki returned her phone to her pocket. "That was a bust," she said with a sigh.

"There's still the possibility her father might know something," Nikki said in an obvious attempt to bolster Hannah's sagging hope. "And at least we can tell the police we contacted Jordan's family when they call. If we can tell them no one who knows Jordan has seen her, maybe that'll prompt them into some kind of action."

It was time. As much as Hannah didn't want to have to say out loud everything she had learned, she had to tell Nikki. She walked to the front window and stared unseeingly into the street. "They already called."

"The police?"

"Yes. The detective who was assigned the case. She said Jordan didn't keep her court reservation. She didn't make it to the gym." Hannah squared her shoulders. "And neither did her friend, Liz." The words drifted in the air like a bird of prey circling menacingly on a high current.

"What does that mean?" Nikki asked finally.

Hannah turned, arms folded, hugging herself tightly. She shrugged. "The detective didn't come right out and say it, but the implication was the same as the officer's yesterday. That wherever Jordan is, she's there by choice. Liz *Talbot*," she emphasized the last name to indicate that they now knew what it was, "was staying in a hotel, and she checked out Saturday morning."

Nikki leaned back into the couch cushions and looked thoughtful. "Jordan said she was in town on a temporary job assignment."

"There's more," Hannah said before Nikki put any mental energy into that particular situation. A chill ran through her. She didn't want to have to tell Nikki her best friend was a liar and a cheater. Moreover, she didn't want to have to admit that about her own girlfriend. She struggled to find words. Finally, she walked to the coffee table and opened the laptop, then turned it toward Nikki.

It whirred awake, illuminating on the screen the last email—the one from Gen—Hannah had read.

Nikki went pale as she scanned the message. "Hannah—"

"There are more. A lot more." Hannah's voice broke. "From a lot of women." She sank down beside Nikki. "She's been seeing them the *whole time*." She began to cry.

Nikki wrapped her arms around her.

Hannah cried harder. All the emotions she hadn't been able to name, to acknowledge, as she had been scrolling through the emails inundated her. Hurt, anger, betrayal, rejection, her long-standing fear of not being wanted, all flooded her, and she was pulled under by their force.

Nikki held her close. "God, Hannah, I'm so sorry."

Hannah barely heard the words over the rush of the tide pouring over her, through her. But she felt Nikki's arms, her embrace, holding her, anchoring her. "I can't believe she'd do that," she said between sobs. "Why would she even be with me, if *that's* what she wanted?"

Nikki rocked her gently.

"I mean, she pursued me. I always knew I wasn't in her league, but then she…"

"No, Hannah," Nikki said against her hair. "This isn't your fault, in any way. You're amazing. This is Jordan. This is just what she does, what she needs. She's messed up."

Hannah gulped for air, trying to gain some control. "I just can't believe… And how could I not have known? She's been doing it the *whole* time we've been… I feel so stupid."

"No, Hannah." Nikki stroked Hannah's back. "You're not. How could you have known? Jordan's really good at covering her tracks."

"But I live with her. I should have seen..." Hannah stilled. What was Nikki saying? *This is what Jordan does? What she needs? She's really good?* Did Nikki already know? She eased back and stared at Nikki. A new deluge of emotion hit her, but this time, the clear frontrunner was anger. "You've known about this all along," she said flatly.

Nikki averted her gaze.

Even though Hannah already knew it was true, Nikki's lack of denial fanned the flame of Hannah's anger into a fury. Its heat dried her tears. She moved away and rose unsteadily. "How could you have known?" Her tone held a steely calm. "And not told me?" It sounded dangerous, even to herself.

Nikki stared at the floor.

"How could you come over here and have dinner with us? Sit up late with me, talking about books or movies when Jordan needed sleep for an early meeting? Comfort me through my grief when my father died? And all the while, you knew Jordan was sleeping with every woman she came across?" Hannah gasped with horrified realization. She pressed her hands to her heated face. "Oh, my God. I even talked to you about those things Jordan wanted me to do in bed, and you said I should be true to myself and only do what I'm comfortable with because you *knew*." She pointed an accusing finger at Nikki, and her voice rose. "You knew she could get any number of women to do those things with her."

Nikki jerked her head up. "No, Hannah. That isn't true. I did all those things as your friend. I care—"

"My friend?" Hannah shook with rage. "How can you sit there and say you're *my friend*—that you've *ever* been my friend? I know you were Jordan's friend first, but...Nikki..." Tears burned Hannah's eyes again. "You were supposed to be *my* friend, too."

Nikki stood and stepped toward her. "Hannah, I'm—"

"No." Hannah held up her hand to stop her. "You don't get to be that, now. Get out."

"What?" Nikki looked as stunned as if Hannah had slapped her. "Hannah, please. You can't go through this alone. You need—"

"I need what? A friend? You're right, Nikki, I *do* need a friend. I needed *you* to *be* a friend all this time so I could count on you now. But now, I have other friends. I have Marti. I have Kate. I have my therapist. And I have *real* friends calling me to find out how I am. *Any* of those people would be a better friend than *you* at this point."

Nikki squeezed her eyes shut. "Hannah, please…"

"Get out!" Hannah turned her back. She clenched her fists at her sides, her body rigid. "*Get out!*" she screamed. "*Get out! Get out!*"

In the resounding wake, the front door slammed.

Hannah dropped onto the sofa. Tears streamed down her face. She had never felt so alone in her entire life.

CHAPTER SEVEN

Nikki pounded her fist against the steering wheel. *Damn it!* She'd screwed this up big time. She'd always known that someday Hannah would find out about Jordan, but how could she have ever anticipated it unfolding like this? She should have said something when the cop had taken the report, or maybe even earlier. Maybe she should have told Hannah when Jordan hadn't come home that first night. At least, then, Hannah would have heard it from her. It still would have come out that she'd known all along and kept Jordan's secret, though, so would it have really been any different?

She sat in her car outside the condo for a long time, trying to come up with something—anything—she could say to make Hannah understand, make her forgive her. What could she say, though? What *was* there to say? She had known Jordan was cheating on Hannah— had known she'd never been with just one woman—and she'd never said anything. It was that simple. She *had* tried to point out to Jordan how great Hannah was and how lucky she was to have a woman like that love her, but Jordan had been unfazed. She hadn't even answered. *Maybe that's why Hannah knows so little about Jordan.* Maybe Hannah had asked all those things but Jordan had stonewalled her the way she did everyone else who tried to get close. As for Nikki trying to talk to Jordan about Hannah—Hannah didn't know that, and most likely never would. Nikki wouldn't blame her if she never spoke to her again. She was right—Nikki *wasn't* a friend. At least, not to Hannah.

And what had being a friend to Jordan gotten her? Jordan should be the one here taking the brunt of Hannah's pain and anger. Sure,

Nikki had known what Jordan did, but Jordan was the one who *did* it. And where was she now?

Nikki didn't believe for a second Jordan had just left her life behind and run off to lose herself in domestic bliss with some other woman—she was the closest she'd ever been to that right here with Hannah—or even by herself. She could, however, be holed up for the weekend, like she used to do, having mind-blowing sex with her latest conquest. She hadn't done that, though, not for days at a time, since she got together with Hannah, and even before that, when she did, she was always back for work on Monday morning.

Nikki leaned back against the headrest and blew out a breath. *Jordan. I don't want anything to have happened to you, but that doesn't mean I won't kick your ass when you get home.* She just wished she knew where she was. Then she'd know whether to be pissed or scared. *Somebody* had to know. But they'd talked to everyone they could think of, except Jordan's parents. She thought again of Jonathan Webber. There'd been something odd about that call, that slight hesitation at Hannah's name. Had the secretary known who Hannah was? She pulled out her cell phone and went into the Recently Dialed menu. Her fingers itched to put in a second call. But it wasn't her place—especially not now. Hannah would have to do it, if she didn't hear back from him.

Nikki forwarded Jonathan Webber's number along with a short note asking if Hannah could please let her know if she found out anything further about Jordan's disappearance, then sighed. She wasn't even sure Hannah would do that. She eased away from the shaded curb and headed for Aleyda's.

As she gained speed on the freeway onramp, she slid on her sunglasses against the bright spring morning and relaxed into the familiar mold of the driver's seat. She felt strange, as though a long-forgotten sense of lightness was trying to wriggle its way up through the long-standing guilt from somewhere deep inside. She couldn't quite smile, not with her best friend missing and the woman she'd always wished she'd met first so mad at her she'd thrown her out. There was a freedom, though, at no longer holding that secret she'd known for so long. The scene certainly hadn't played out the way she'd envisioned so many times, with Nikki being honest and noble and *doing the right thing*. There had been a time for that—one night—early in Jordan and Hannah's dating, when she could have given her a heads-up, then let her make her own choices. That night had come and gone long ago, though, and any opportunity since then would have brought up the same question Hannah had asked today. Nikki would just have to live with her decisions and hope Hannah would somehow be able to forgive her.

She pulled into Aleyda's driveway and climbed out of her car, gently putting weight on the foot that was freshly out of the cast she'd been stuck in for weeks. Her ankle was stiff, but the doctor had assured her its full range of motion would return as long as she did the physical therapy exercises he'd prescribed. She made her way up the brick walkway that split off to the house where her sister-in-law, two nephews, and niece lived. It led to the back of the property and Nikki's photography studio, with its side-yard landscaped for outdoor shoots. It'd been Aleyda's idea to build the studio on her property six years earlier when Nikki's business had taken off, in exchange for everything Nikki had done to help her with the kids since Ramon's death. It'd also allowed Aleyda to take a job as Nikki's assistant and still work from home so she could be more available for her children.

Nikki let herself in through the side entrance—only company used the front door—and kicked off her shoes on the service porch. "Anybody home?" she called as she strode into the kitchen. She retrieved her mail from her slot in the mail tray and started sifting through it.

"Aunt Nikki!" Cecelia raced into the room in boxer shorts, a tank top, and socks, sliding across the waxed floor and throwing her arms around Nikki's neck. At fifteen, she stood a couple of inches shorter than Nikki's five feet eight inches and was growing out of some of the gangliness of early teens.

"Hey, Cecil." Nikki still called her niece the nickname she'd given her as a two-year-old even though, or maybe because, it gave Cecelia a frowny face sometimes. "Why aren't you in school?" She gave her a one-armed hug.

Cecelia rolled her eyes. "School got out for the summer last Thursday."

"Oh, yeah," Nikki said distractedly as she finished her cursory inspection of her junk mail before dropping it into the recycle bin. She didn't know why she looked at the mail that came for her here. It was all business correspondence, and Aleyda handled most of that, only giving Nikki things that needed her specific attention. *Summer vacation. That's right.* She knew that. Not only had she known because of the kids, but that's why Hannah had been home today, too. "So, what do you have planned for your day?"

"I want to go to the DMV and get my learner's permit, but Mom says we can't. She has to talk to you to do some rescheduling stuff. Can't you do it some other time?" Cecelia finished with a whine.

"A learner's permit? You can't get a learner's permit," Nikki said, pushing Hannah from her mind.

Cecelia stepped back with an anxious expression. "Why not?"

"Because you're only four," Nikki said playfully. She grabbed Cecelia and started tickling her. "You can't drive at four."

Cecelia squealed. "I'm not four." She struggled to get away.

"Yes, you are. My niece is a little girl, not some teenager old enough to drive."

Cecelia doubled over, clutching at Nikki's fingers. "Stop," she cried through escalating laughter.

"Are you still my little girl?" Nikki couldn't help but let out some cackles of her own.

"Yes! Yes, always! I promise." Cecelia dropped to her knees.

"What are you two doing?" Aleyda asked, chuckling as she entered the kitchen.

"Cecil's trying to tell me she's all grown up and ready to drive," Nikki said as she straightened. "But I say she's still four and happy playing with her My Little Pony beauty shop."

Cecelia lay on the floor, giggling.

Aleyda smiled. "Oh, that we could go back to those days."

"No kidding." Nikki held out her hand to help Cecelia to her feet. "I can't believe it's time for her to get her learner's permit."

Cecelia let Nikki pull her up, laughter still dancing in her eyes. "Can we go today? Please, Mom?"

"Let me talk to Aunt Nikki and see what needs to be done this afternoon. Then, we'll see."

Cecelia made her way toward the door that led to the dining room, hands folded beneath her chin and giving Nikki pleading puppy dog eyes.

Nikki laughed. "We'll work it out. Don't worry."

Cecelia jumped up and down and dashed out of the room.

Aleyda smiled and shook her head.

"Where are the boys?" Nikki asked. Her oldest nephew, Tony, was a sophomore at UCLA, and though he still lived at home to save money, he was rarely there. His younger brother, Rob, had just graduated from high school and was busy getting ready to start classes in the fall at UC Davis.

"Oh, they're off doing their things," Aleyda said, evident affection deepening her voice. "They're all so grown up." She poured a cup of coffee and handed it to Nikki. "Jordan's home, I take it?"

Nikki smiled empathetically and went with the subject change. "No," she said, taking a seat in the breakfast nook.

Aleyda arched an eyebrow. "No? Any word from her?" She sat across from Nikki.

Nikki shook her head. "Nothing. Not a word. Not a clue. It's crazy. She just vanished."

"I'm sorry." Aleyda squeezed Nikki's hand. "Did you just stop by to check in, then? I thought you were staying with Hannah."

"Not anymore." Nikki sighed and sat back in her chair. She could still hear Hannah screaming for her to get out. She looked into her cup. She didn't want to tell Aleyda what'd happened. Aleyda had known about everything for years—about Jordan's flings and Hannah's ignorance, about Nikki's part in the deception, even about Nikki's growing feelings for Hannah being the reason she'd cut herself off from their friendship—and Aleyda had said all along that Nikki should tell Hannah the truth. "Hannah found out Jordan's been seeing other women and that I knew. She doesn't want me anywhere near her." She met Aleyda's gentle gaze. "You can say I told you so, if you want."

"No, *mija*," Aleyda said softly. "There's no joy in *I told you so*." She brushed her thumb over Nikki's knuckles. "Give her a little time. She's dealing with a lot right now."

"Thanks." Nikki turned her hand and laced her fingers with Aleyda's. "But I don't think time will help. She was really mad…and hurt." She closed her eyes. "I really blew it."

Aleyda just sat with Nikki in the quiet way she had.

"On top of hurting her, I screwed myself, too," Nikki said finally. She leaned forward, propping her elbows on the table, and pulled herself together. "Hannah's the contact person on everything we've done to try to find Jordan, so I don't have any way of knowing what's happening with that."

"You hadn't heard back from the police or the gym, yet?"

"Yeah, we got that information before it came out that I knew what Jordan's been doing." Nikki filled Aleyda in on what Hannah had shared from her conversation with the detective, then their calls to Jonathan and David Webber.

"It does sound like she might just be off with that woman from the gym," Aleyda said, her tone relaxed.

Nikki couldn't argue the point. Aleyda *did* know it was entirely possible. "Maybe." Nikki had to concede. "But I don't think so. Even when she used to spend whole weekends in bed with someone, she never stayed away this long. And she always at least checked in with me. At first, I was just pissed because I thought the same thing, but I'm starting to think… But from this point on, I won't know anything."

"Surely, Hannah will keep you in the loop. She knows you care about Jordan as much as she does. It would be cruel to cut you off completely."

"I hope you're right." Nikki took a drink of her coffee.

Aleyda smiled. "What did the doctor say about your foot?" she asked, her attempt to keep things from getting too dark obvious.

Nikki stretched it out in front of her and wiggled it. "He said it looks great. Just some exercises and it'll be good as new." She tried to grin but couldn't manage the emotion to back it up. She took a deep breath and shifted into work mode. "So, what do we need to reschedule from the last couple of days?"

"The most pressing is the shoot from yesterday for the prelude pictures for the Stillman and Blackmore wedding." Aleyda made the transition as seamlessly as she always did.

They'd always been in sync with one another, even before they'd started working together. Nikki had met Aleyda when Nikki's oldest brother, Ramon, brought her home to meet his family. Nikki had clicked with her instantly, and Aleyda had been the big sister she'd always wanted. For her part, Aleyda had doted on Nikki as though she'd helped take care of her from birth. The two things that bonded them the most strongly were their positions in their respective families as the only girls in a brood of brothers, and their love for Ramon.

"They were understanding, but they want to get it done as soon as possible," Aleyda said as she retrieved a file folder from the built-in desk at the end of the kitchen. "Then there's the meet with Mrs. Andrews to show her some sites you think might work for the family portraits she wants done, and the prelim meeting with a couple for engagement photos."

Nikki ran her hand through her hair. "Okay," she said, still distracted by the other matters.

"Are you sure you want to start scheduling again so soon?" Aleyda's tone held concern. "What if Hannah comes around and wants your help again?"

Nikki frowned. She supposed that could happen, though as mad as Hannah was, it didn't seem likely. "I can't just sit around and do nothing. All I'll do is worry about Jordan and dwell on how badly I screwed up with Hannah." She should be looking for Jordan. *But where could she be?* She could check the boat again, but other than that...

"How about if we take it a day or two at a time? I'll tell everyone you have a family emergency. They'll understand." Aleyda's attention was on the schedule in front of her. "Could you meet with Mrs. Andrews this afternoon, if she's available? And I'll see if the prelude shoot works for tomorrow morning. Then we'll go from there."

"What about Cecelia's learner's permit?" Nikki asked teasingly, knowing how Aleyda felt about her baby getting a driver's license.

Aleyda glared at her. "I'll take her to the DMV today."

Later, Nikki swiped the key card through the electronic lock and stepped through the gate at the marina. She'd headed over as soon as she'd dropped Mrs. Andrews back at her car at the studio. Since she couldn't go back to Hannah's, she'd decided to check out the boat again to keep from going stir crazy. Who knew? Maybe she'd find something useful. She turned off the paved path when she reached the dock and made her way to the slip that held Jordan's thirty-eight-foot cabin cruiser. It was Jordan's pride and joy, but no one knew about it except Nikki and the women Jordan entertained on it.

This was the first place Nikki had looked, following Hannah's initial call on Saturday night. She'd been sure she'd find Jordan here with some woman—maybe they'd fallen asleep or simply lost track of time—but everything had been dark and locked up tight. When Nikki had gone below, she'd found it clean, tidy, and unoccupied.

In the light of the late afternoon, it looked just as uninhabited from the outside, but maybe Jordan had been there. The thought struck Nikki as crazy even as it passed through her mind, but she was here. She might as well check. She hopped over the side onto the deck, then pulled her keys from her pocket and unlocked the door to the cabin below. Jordan had given her full access to the boat during the years they'd spent so much time together on it. That way, if Jordan were running late, Nikki could start getting it ready to take out on the water or to get things set up to entertain the women they had joining them.

As she stepped down to the top of the stairs, a sharp pain shot through her foot and ankle, and she realized she'd overdone it on her first day out of her cast. Tromping through sand all afternoon surveying possible beach sites with Mrs. Andrews probably wasn't conducive to the doctor's order to take it easy while she built up the strength again. She moved more gingerly, negotiating the rest of the steps. At the bottom, she glanced around her.

Everything looked completely in its place, the same as it had the night before last. The galley was spotless, the small dining table wiped clean and clear of any clutter, its surface gleaming in the sunlight that streamed through the elongated window above it. The door to the V-berth in the bow stood open, and Nikki could see the bed was made. She was more interested in the aft berth at the stern, the one Jordan used. She checked the head, just because, then opened the closed door to the back cabin. She studied the cozy room.

What was she looking for, now that it was clear Jordan wasn't there and hadn't been since Saturday? The blinds were closed over the high windows, and the room was bathed in soft, filtered light. She sat on the side of the bed and drew up her knee. As she massaged her tender ankle, she thought of the saying, *if these walls could talk*, and she wished they could. She'd ask them when the last time was that Jordan had been there, and if someone had been with her, who it was.

Jordan had always brought women there, even before there was a need to keep it secret, but she also liked spending time on her boat to get away. She liked taking it out on the water, either by herself or with Nikki, just to relax and escape the pressures of life. Before Hannah moved in with her, sometimes Jordan would spend entire weekends on the boat, either in its slip or taking short cruises out to Catalina, up the coast to Morro Bay, or down to San Diego.

Nikki had spent a lot of time there as well, kicking back with Jordan, joining her on the cruises, even bringing women back there. The V-berth had been hers. Once Jordan had gotten together with Hannah, though, she hadn't felt right about being Jordan's wingman and picking up women with her, and she certainly hadn't felt right about coming back there with them to party. She knew now what a big, juicy rationalization that had been. So what if she didn't actually go out with Jordan to pick up women anymore, when she still knew all along Jordan was doing it? Her stomach knotted, and she pushed aside the image of Hannah's devastated expression that flashed in her mind. Any realizations she had now about past decisions were way too late.

She pressed the release button for the top drawer to the built-in nightstand beside her. She was here to look for clues, for *something* that might tell her where the hell Jordan was. An array of sex toys greeted her—several vibrators, a harness, and a couple of different sized dildos, several silk scarves, a blindfold. Nothing that was any surprise. She opened the next drawer to find accoutrements for a little heavier play. She cringed at the memory of Hannah's accusation. She *hadn't* told Hannah to be true to herself because she knew Jordan was getting what she wanted someplace else. At least, she didn't think she had. Hannah really *did* need to be true to herself. *Would I have said something different if I hadn't known Jordan was getting this side of things taken care of?* How could she tell? She was so screwed up right now. *Damn it, Jordan!* She slammed the drawer.

The bottom drawer held an assortment of anthologies of erotic stories of varying kinds. She rummaged through the compartments beneath the bed, finding only clothing, then stretched across the mattress to check the contents of the other nightstand. She had no idea what she was looking for precisely, but she hoped it was like what they said about pornography—even if you don't know what it is, you'll recognize it when you see it.

There she found an iPod, charger, and a speaker port, along with several packages of earbuds and another stack of books—*Breakaway: Beyond the Goal*, a memoir by Alex Morgan; *Rita Will*, by Rita Mae Brown; and another that struck Nikki dumb. *The Final Freedom: Pioneering Sexual Addiction Recovery.* She stared in astonishment. Jordan was hardly the self-help type. Nikki read from the back blurb. *Sex addiction affects millions of people's lives today, and is on the rise with the Internet. This solution-focused book offers an intelligent understanding of sexual addiction as well as practical remedies.* This was *so* not Jordan. Intrigued, she dug deeper and came up with Stephen King's *11/22/63*. Okay. That was Jordan. The other one, though? No way.

Nikki had occasionally wondered if Jordan was a sex addict, but the thought of *Jordan* questioning it… That was almost enough to make Nikki laugh out loud. Jordan didn't question things about herself. And yet—Nikki stared at the book cover—here it was. She ran her hand through her hair. She'd thought she knew Jordan so well. Maybe none of us did.

The weight, or lack thereof, of the Stephen King novel drew her attention. She'd read that book. It'd been way heavier than this one, and three times thicker. The dust jacket slipped around loosely on this cover. She opened it. Page after page was filled with Jordan's handwriting. *A journal? Jordan keeps a journal?* This was getting way too bizarre.

Nikki's heart leapt at the realization of what information she might be holding in her hands. She flipped to the last entry and checked the date. Disappointment swallowed her excitement. *Mid May.* Two weeks earlier. So, there wouldn't be anything from last Saturday or even that last week Jordan was living her normal life. Still, though, there might be something that could offer some explanation for her disappearance. *Maybe.*

Nikki leafed through the journal, stopping occasionally to scan a page. There were recounts of time spent with particular women, always identified with only a single initial, and new sexual exploits she'd introduced them to right alongside paragraphs describing the peace and safety she felt being all alone on the water. There was a poem about deep emptiness and the darkness in her soul. Another about forgiveness. *What the hell?* Did Nikki really know Jordan at all? The journal entries began a little over a year earlier.

Nikki glanced back to the self-help book. The spine was cracked, but the book looked fairly new. Had Jordan read it? The corner of a piece of paper peeked out from the pages, and Nikki opened to its position at Chapter Three. The bookmark was a Barns and Noble receipt dated May seventh.

All of this was definitely more information, but none of it fit with anything Nikki already knew, except for the sex part. Even that, though, was out of context. Jordan didn't read about sex, or study it, or question it in any way, or, at least, she never had before.

And what was there to forgive? *Herself for all the lies she'd told?* Nikki thought for a minute. *Her parents, maybe?* Nikki remembered one night when they'd both gotten way too drunk and Jordan had broken down, telling her about being raised by nannies and feeling no connection with her mother or father. But the next day, everything was back to normal, as though nothing out of the ordinary had taken place. Was the emptiness she'd written about in the one poem getting too painful? Nikki knew from experience how much of a motivator pain could be.

There had to be something in all of this that explained what'd happened to Jordan, where she'd gone. And if there was, Nikki had to find it. She switched on the sconce above her head to ward off the encroaching dusk, settled back on the pillows, and opened the journal to the first page.

CHAPTER EIGHT

Jordan lay on the floor in a fetal position, hands covering her face, shielding her clenched eyes from the glaring light. The voice boomed in her head, that voice that now accompanied the light any time it was on, so loud it was slightly distorted.

"...the work of Satan...moves through history, beginning with Sodom and Gomorrah..."

Jordan moved her hands from her eyes to her ears. It'd been going on too long this time. She ached for the darkness and the silence she knew would come at some point, even knowing it, too, would eventually become too much. In its emptiness, her fear swelled within her, until it gripped her throat and threatened to strangle her, but for now, that deep well of quiet was all she wanted.

"Homosexuality...a tragic disorder of the fallen world...sin to be punished by death...Leviticus 20:13...to love the homosexual, homosexuality must be condemned...sinful and harmful to the homosexual..."

"Shut the fuck up!" Jordan screamed. Even she, though, could barely hear her voice. Her throat burned. How many times had she screamed? How many curses had she thrown out into the empty room? How many unanswered questions taunted her? What was this about? Who was Liz? What was Hannah doing? And Nikki? They had to be looking for her. They had to have called the police. Had they found her car? Were they close?

"...God's law...men belong with women and women belong with men..."

Jordan curled tighter.

Suddenly, the room went silent. The brilliance seeping through her eyelids went dark. She almost sobbed in relief at the velvet caress of total darkness, even as she knew it'd inevitably turn rough and scratchy and, eventually, crushing. She wouldn't break down, though, wouldn't give whoever might be watching, listening, whoever was outside this prison she was in, the satisfaction.

She lay still, panting. She never realized her physical state until the dark came once again. The harshness of the light and thundering of the voice were too overwhelming. She eased her hands from her ears and cracked open her eyes.

As blindingly bright as the light was when it was on, the darkness was equally deep and empty. She'd tried to see her hand only inches from her face and couldn't, regardless of how long she stared. She'd even widened her eyes and moved her gaze around the room she knew had to be there, but there wasn't a speck of light anywhere. The first time she'd awakened into the pitch-blackness, she'd panicked, truly thinking she was blind.

Now, however, she knew it would end, just as it had numerous times before. With the same lack of warning as they'd gone off, those lights would blaze back on, and with them would come that thundering voice, the combination sending piercing pain through her head. She'd lost track of how many times she'd gone back and forth, from one hell to the other. And she had absolutely no idea how many hours, or maybe even days, had passed since she'd been torn from her life and brought to this place.

She'd learned that when the lights were on, people might come in to bring her water and take away the previous bottle she'd emptied. The first time the pasty-faced guy from the motor home had come in, she'd hurled the full bottle at his back as he'd moved away and swore at him to let her go. He'd said nothing, simply tossed the water back into the room and closed the door behind him. At first, she'd refused to drink it, but after pounding on the door and screaming for help for what could have been twenty minutes just as easily as twelve hours, her throat was raw, and she'd taken a swallow. And when the room was plunged into blackness again, and she couldn't remember where she'd set the bottle, she spent that entire stretch of time until she could see again getting more and more thirsty. By the time she was able to drink again, she'd realized that water might be the only thing coming—not food—so, she'd taken a much stronger interest in keeping it close at hand and taking the new bottle—albeit begrudgingly—whenever one came.

She'd gone from furious, to terrified, to desperate, to despondent, then cycled back through the tempest of emotions countless times.

Now, she had to refocus, collect the shards of her consciousness shattered by the onslaught of anti-gay rhetoric and the sheer volume at which it was being projected. And she had to pee. She wouldn't do it in the light, though, wouldn't subject herself to the added degradation of someone walking in on her. It was humiliating enough being naked and shaved in front of anyone who wandered in. So she followed the wall in the dark, as she'd done several times before, to find the toilet.

Then she needed rest. Each time the lights went out, she tried—and a couple of times, succeeded—to escape into sleep in order to re-energize so, when the time came, she'd have the strength to make a break for her freedom. She was starting to suspect, though, that the periods of darkened silence were far shorter than those of the blazing light and thundering condemnations, because she was starting to feel exhausted.

As she wiped, she felt the soft scratch of stubble over her pubic area. That meant it'd been at least a couple of days that she'd been here. *Christ! How long does it take to go insane, to lose track of who you are?* She flushed the toilet and felt her way to the cement slab presumably meant to be a bed. As she bent forward to find the edge, her foot hit the partial bottle of water she hadn't finished, and she heard it skitter across the floor. Her stomach grumbled, and water was the only thing she had to fill it.

She dropped to her knees and crawled in the direction she thought the bottle had gone, feeling along the floor as she went. The farther she went, the more times her fingers met only tile, the higher her anxiety rose. She had to find it. Nothing else was in her control. *This* had to be. She groped, growing frantic. She knew it was irrational, but she couldn't get control of her escalating fear.

"Where the fuck are you?" Her words came out in a hiss.

Her hand brushed something, and she heard the bottle roll farther away. A cry escaped her. She clamped her mouth shut. She couldn't show weakness.

"It's okay."

Jordan stiffened. Was someone with her?

"Take your time. You'll find it." The voice was feminine, a whisper from somewhere deep within her.

She waited, but nothing more came. She moved more slowly, sweeping her hand across the floor more carefully. Finally, she found the water. With a shuddering sigh, she grasped it, sagging to her elbows, then to the floor. She clutched it to her chest and, curling around it, began to shake.

❖

Hannah sat in the swing on the patio and stared at the Encore azalea bush across the small yard, the purplish hue of its blossoms adding a rich contrast to the pinks, whites, and corals of the rest of the spring blooms. She loved azaleas, and when she had moved in, Jordan had planted that bush just for her. Well, she'd had the gardener plant it just for her. *Jordan doesn't do dirt.* Still, the gesture had touched Hannah. Jordan had said she had chosen the Encores because they were special, just like Hannah.

The memory almost made her gag. *Special. What a lie.* Hannah was no more special than any of those women in Jordan's emails she had been sleeping with. Hannah wanted to take a shovel to the roots and dig up the entire bush, but the flowers truly were too beautiful. Besides, Hannah was exhausted. She had gotten little enough sleep the first two nights following Jordan's disappearance when Nikki had been with her offering comfort and company. The last couple, however—since she had thrown Nikki out—had been nearly unbearable. Her mind had been shifting between images of Jordan with other women and her being tortured and killed, vacillating between thoughts of never seeing her again and what she would say to her when she walked in the door. So she had barely gotten three hours sleep combined. And *Nikki...*

Nikki had left her completely alone that first day Hannah had found out about her betrayal, but the next, she had called numerous times. Hannah hadn't answered once—though she had been tempted. God, she hated being alone. Nor had she listened to any of the voice mails. She couldn't think of a thing Nikki could say that would make her feel better, and *she* had nothing new to say to Nikki. She had made clear how she felt, and Nikki would just have to sit around knowing she was the one who made her feel that way.

"Yoo-hoo." Kate's voice drifted from the house through the screened patio door. She always managed to sound exactly like their mother when she called out that way. "Anybody home?"

"Out here." Hannah had held off from calling Kate for as long as she could. She loved her sister, but she took a lot of energy Hannah didn't have right now. Finally, she had reached a point she couldn't stand being alone any longer. She had thought of Marti, but Marti always had Ringo to deal with, and the rest of Hannah's friends were at work during the week. Plus, anyone else would need to be brought up to speed on everything, and Hannah couldn't bear the thought of that. She still had to tell Kate not only about Jordan's infidelities, but Nikki's betrayal as well. It was humiliating, but at least it was only Kate.

Kate stepped through the doorway from the kitchen and stopped short. "Christ, Hannah. You look like crap. When was the last time you slept? Or brushed your hair?" She crossed the patio and sat down beside her. "Or changed clothes?"

With dismay, Hannah realized she hadn't done any of those things, or showered or even brushed her teeth, since Nikki had left. Suddenly, she was grateful it had been Kate she had called and no one else. "Is it that bad?"

Kate sniffed and wrinkled her nose. "What's going on? When we talked yesterday, you said Jordan was still missing, but the cops were looking and you were waiting to hear. You said *we*, so I figured Nikki was still here." She looked around. "Where is she?"

Hannah sighed. "She left. We had a fight."

"A fight?" Kate's voice rose with an incredulous ring. "She was supposed to stay here with you until Jordan came home. She was supposed to *be* with you, not fight with you."

"It's all right, Kate. It wasn't her." Hannah's temper reignited at the memory of the moment she realized Nikki had known everything. "I mean, it *was*, but I made her leave. I kicked her out. She wanted to stay." *Why am I defending her?*

"What happened?"

Hannah sighed.

"No, wait," Kate said, settling back in the swing. "Start with Jordan. There's really still no word on her? They haven't found *anything*?"

Hannah began with a second phone call she had made to Jordan's father that proved just as fruitless as the first, then as much as she hated having to think about them again, covered the emails she had found and what Detective Morrison had said about them. By the time she had finished with, "I haven't talked to Nikki since she left," Kate had launched herself to her feet and was pacing the patio.

"That bitch! Those bitches! Both of them. I never liked either of them. Remember? I said—"

"Kate, please." Hannah massaged her forehead. One of Kate's rants about how she lived her life was the last thing she needed. "I'm already mad enough. Will you just give me a hug?"

Kate halted mid-sentence. "Oh, sweetie, yes. Of course." She sat beside Hannah and wrapped her arms around her. "You're right. This is about you. Not those bitches."

Hannah could tell Kate could barely contain the rest of her tirade. She cuddled close and sighed when they melded together as they had done all their lives.

"I have an idea," Kate said, still holding her.

"What is it?" Hannah felt the beginning of tears at the relief of not having to make the next decision.

"Never mind," Kate eased Hannah away from her. "You just let me handle things now."

Hannah wiped her eyes. She was reluctant—she and Kate *handled* things so much differently—but she was out of ideas at the moment and sick to death of sitting around doing nothing but crying.

"Come on. Let's go." Kate stood.

Dumbfounded, Hannah let Kate pull her to her feet. "Where are we going?"

"First of all, you need to get out of the house," Kate said firmly. "Then, I'm taking you to see Mrs. Romani."

Hannah stared at her, running the name through her mind. Recognition dawned. "Nooooo. Not that crazy woman who *sees* things."

"She's not crazy," Kate said with obviously forced patience. "And, yes, she is a seer. She can see things most of us can't."

"I don't want to see her," Hannah said. "I know you believe in that kind of thing, but I just can't right now."

Kate tilted her head. "What are you going to do sitting around here? Call the police again? They've already said they aren't going to do anything. Twice. You could call Jordan's father again, since he hasn't bothered to call you back. But then what? With everything you've found out, I'm surprised you still even *want* to look for Jordan."

Hannah sighed. "I just want to make sure she's okay. *Then* I can kill her."

Kate ran her hands over Hannah's shoulders, then began massaging them. "Sweetie, this is an unusual situation. I say, try something unusual."

Hannah relaxed into Kate's touch and stared at the ceiling. She considered Kate's words. This *was* an unusual situation, and nothing else was proving effective. But a psychic felt *too* unusual. "I think you're right. It would be good to get out of the house." She leveled her gaze on Kate. "But not *there*."

"Okay, where then? You name it. We'll go."

"Somewhere I can just get out of my head." Hannah thought. Shopping? *No.* She couldn't care less about buying anything at the moment. A movie? *How could I follow a plot line?* Someplace quiet, comforting. Someplace she could feel connected with life, *all* of life, not just the train wreck *her* life had become. "Zuma."

Kate grinned. "Zuma!"

When they climbed out of Kate's car in the parking lot at Zuma Beach, the oranges and golds of the setting sun were mingling with the cool blue of the ocean on the horizon. The salty air filled Hannah's lungs as she closed her eyes and breathed deeply, and the rhythmic rush of the breaking waves washed away all stress and tension. It wasn't simply the beach that affected Hannah this way. Since she had moved in with Jordan, she lived only blocks from a beach. It was *this* beach, where her parents had brought them for picnics and afternoons of swimming so many times in her childhood. The beach where she could still feel the solace of her parents' presence, where she could see herself and Kate as little girls running hand-in-hand into the surf. The beach where, later in their teens, they would come in the evening—like now—and walk along the water's edge or lie on a blanket and plan the future.

Hannah clutched the old quilt she had grabbed to her chest, while Kate retrieved the bag of deli sandwiches and fruit juice they had picked up. Wordlessly, they made their way to the water and walked along the wet sand until the stars were visible in the sky. Finally, they stopped and spread out the blanket.

This was one of the few places Hannah had ever found where Kate seemed capable of not talking. Tonight, she was eerily quiet. Of course, she knew that was what Hannah needed most. Hannah was thankful for the peace.

She ate, then stretched out beside Kate and gazed up into the night sky. She couldn't help but wonder if Jordan could see it from wherever she was, if she were somewhere she could hear the ocean. *Is she with someone? Or all alone, in pain or trouble?*

Images drifted through her mind, first of Jordan with other women, then of Jordan crumpled and broken, but soon of Jordan smiling, bringing her coffee and bagels in bed. She remembered Jordan's hot breath in her ear as she pushed Hannah on a sled, then jumped on behind her as they sailed down the snow-covered mountainside in Shasta. She heard Jordan's soft laugh following Hannah's thank you kiss the day Jordan had shown up at career day at the high school with flowers for Hannah and a killer talk on civil liberties law. How could *that* person be the same one who had never been faithful in their relationship? And where does infidelity fall on the scale with injury, death, maybe even murder?

Hannah jerked awake, her heart pounding, her shoulders tight again.

"Bad dream?" Kate whispered. She brushed the hair from Hannah's eyes.

Hannah rolled onto her back. "I didn't realize I was asleep."

"You've been out for a long time. I didn't want to wake you, since I don't think you've slept much lately." Kate unplugged her earbuds from her phone and tucked them into her pocket.

Hannah sat up and rubbed her face. "What time is it?"

"Late. Getting close to dawn."

Hannah lifted her gaze to the horizon, and her breath caught. A huge full moon sat in almost the precise spot the sun had been when they had arrived, casting a pathway of white light across the water. It looked like a shimmering bridge. It reminded her of something, but she couldn't place what. She stared in wonder. "Wow!"

"Yeah," was all Kate said.

They took another walk along the beach, until the sun rose and their stomachs grumbled, then headed back to the car.

On the way home, Hannah deleted two more voice mails from Nikki on her cell phone and, at the condo, found a missed call from her on the house phone. Still nothing from Jordan's father.

"Why don't you lie down and try to get some more rest?" Kate asked, while she straightened up the kitchen. "I'll run out and get us something to eat."

When Kate had gone, Hannah snuggled under a throw blanket on the couch. She was cold, even though it was June. She felt scattered. She thought of Kate, wanting so badly to help, but never quite sure of what to do. She thought of Nikki and all her calls and messages. Maybe Hannah should have listened to at least one. What if Nikki had found something? If that was the case, though, why didn't she just come over when Hannah didn't call her back? *Would I go to her house if she had thrown me out the way I did her?* She thought of that gorgeously brilliant moon and its reflection on the water. What had it reminded her of?

Suddenly, it struck her. It had looked like a bridge of light into the beyond. That's what people said, wasn't it? People who died and came back talked about going into the light? In her mind, she saw Jordan walking along that pathway into the light of the full moon. Of course that thought had occurred to her before, but now she couldn't shake the idea that Jordan could be dead.

She wanted to talk to Nikki, wanted to feel her presence, to be with her. She was still mad at her, still hurt, but she couldn't deal with this alone...or with Kate. Kate would want to drag her off to Mrs. Romani's again. No, if Jordan was dead...

Jordan wasn't dead. She couldn't be. Hannah wouldn't let herself go there. She thought of everything she had found out, though, all the lies, all the women. Liz Talbot. Even if Jordan wasn't physically dead, wasn't the Jordan she'd thought she had known, thought she loved, thought loved her—wasn't *that* Jordan dead to her? Even if she walked through the door right this second, she would be a stranger.

Hannah's Jordan *was* dead.

The realization ripped through her. She needed somebody with her, somebody strong, somebody who also knew and loved Jordan. She needed Nikki.

She picked up the phone and dialed.

Chapter Nine

Nikki's phone rang. "Eye of the Tiger." *Jordan's ring.* When she glanced at the screen and saw it was Jordan's home number, she realized it was most likely Hannah and was almost as relieved as if it *were* Jordan. She answered quickly. "Hannah, thank you for calling me back."

"Nikki, I need you to come back." Hannah's voice broke. "I'm still mad at you, and think you were a horrible friend, and I hate that you're the only person I want here, but I can't do this without you."

Nikki didn't know what to say. She'd expected to hear that Hannah was as intrigued to learn about Jordan's journal as Nikki had been to find it and that she was at least a little interested in what it might say. She certainly didn't expect no mention of it at all, especially with the number of messages Nikki had left for her. Had Hannah learned something from the police? Nikki's heartbeat quickened. "Is everything okay? Did they find Jordan?"

"No. Nobody's found anything. I just…" Hannah inhaled shakily. "I just need you here. Please, come back."

"I'll be right there." Nikki ended the call and took the last swig of her coffee as she got to her feet.

"Jordan?" Aleyda asked, looking up at her.

"No, nothing yet. But Hannah doesn't sound good." Nikki rinsed out her cup at the sink. "At least she called, though. Maybe she's letting me back in. Can you handle things here?"

Aleyda smiled. "I can handle everything that doesn't require the photographer, herself."

Nikki knew how true that was. Over the years, Aleyda had learned almost every aspect of the business, including processing, categorizing, and filing all the pictures so Nikki could find them easily. "Thanks, Aleyda." Nikki kissed her cheek. "What would I do without you?"

Aleyda squeezed Nikki's hand. "I could ask the same thing about you, *mija*. Keep me posted, okay?"

"You got it."

Nikki pulled up behind the same black Camaro she'd parked behind five days earlier, the evening of the day Jordan had gone missing, and assumed it was Kate's. She cringed slightly at the thought of facing a double dose of unhappy Hannah—especially since Kate had left Hannah in her hands—but she steeled herself for it. She'd face anything in order to be allowed back in. Not knowing anything for the past couple of days had driven her crazy, not to mention wanting to talk to Hannah about the journal. She'd read through the whole thing, and there were things in it that would hurt Hannah, but Nikki knew it had to be Hannah's decision whether she wanted to read it. Nikki hadn't found anything in it that seemed like it would be helpful to the police in any way—nothing that indicated the *sign of foul play* they said they needed in order to do anything—but that would be Hannah's call as well.

When Nikki knocked, the front door opened almost immediately, and there stood Hannah—or Kate, Nikki couldn't tell which—one fist planted on a hip and a hard expression on her face. "How could you do that to her? You were supposed to be *her* friend, too, weren't you?"

Ah, Kate. "I know. I'm sorry. And I told her I'm sorry, too."

"You should have told her everything first thing," Kate whispered. "Not let her find those emails."

"What about you?" Nikki could feel herself getting sucked in. "You obviously had your suspicions about Jordan. Did you ever say anything?"

"I only had suspicions. You *knew*."

"What are you two whispering about?" Hannah asked as she strode into the living room.

"I was just telling her what a schmuck she is," Kate said.

Hannah frowned. "I've already covered that." She looked at Nikki sheepishly. "Thank you for coming back."

Nikki relaxed a little. "Thank you for calling. Hannah, I'm so sorry—"

Hannah held up her hand. "I don't want to talk about that. I'm still so mad...and hurt...but, like I said, I really need you here. If we could just get through this and find Jordan, maybe we can talk about...you know...later."

"Whatever you need," Nikki said. "I'm here."

"I'll go finish up breakfast," Kate said. "Nikki, you want some coffee?"

"I'm good. Thanks." Nikki crossed to the sofa, meeting Hannah in front of the coffee table. She tentatively stroked her arm.

"Hey," Hannah said, glancing down at Nikki's foot. "You got your cast off."

"Yeah." Nikki was tempted to add that it'd been off on Monday but decided against it. "Have you heard anything else?"

Hannah shook her head as she sat on the couch. "I tried calling Jordan's father again, but his assistant only took another message. And then last night, Kate and I went to the beach, just to get out of the house. It really helped at first. But then I saw the moon, and it was reflecting across the water..." Tears filled her eyes. "And it made me think of the people who die and come back and talk about seeing a bright light."

"Oh, Hannah." Nikki slid an arm around Hannah's shoulders. "Don't go there. We don't know that Jordan's dead. We can't jump to that."

"I know." Hannah began to sniffle. "But it made me realize that with everything I've found out about her, everything I never knew, even if she comes back, she won't be the Jordan I thought I knew, the Jordan I thought I was in love with. So, she might as well be dead."

Nikki understood what Hannah was saying, and it was true. Hannah really never *had* known Jordan, and there were entries in the journal that would bring that forward even more strongly. Suddenly, Nikki had doubts about showing it to her. *Jeez, have I learned nothing in the past five days about trying to keep secrets?*

"Nikki?" Hannah was staring at her. "What's the matter?"

"Uh, nothing." She had to tell her. "Did you get my messages about the journal?"

Hannah blushed and looked away. "I deleted all your messages without listening to them. I'm sorry."

All of them? Wow, she really was pissed. "That's okay."

"What journal?" Hannah asked.

"I'll get it." As Nikki retrieved the book from her car, she was actually grateful Hannah had known nothing about it. This gave her the opportunity to start over, to start fresh with everything up front. When she returned to the living room, she held it out to Hannah. "It's Jordan's."

Hannah looked at it. She raised her hand tentatively, then stopped before touching the cover. "Jordan kept a journal?"

"Yeah. I didn't know either."

"Did you read it?"

Nikki nodded.

A wary expression settled on Hannah's face. "Is there anything in it that might lead to what happened to her or where she is?"

"Not that I found," Nikki said, setting the book on the table. "There's a lot, though, about what Jordan thinks and feels about herself that explains some things, helps us to understand her."

Hannah pursed her lips but said nothing for a long moment. "I don't think I care about understanding her right now," she said finally. "Where did you find it?"

The change in subject took Nikki by surprise. *Christ, she doesn't know about the boat either.* Maneuvering through Jordan's life was like making one's way through a laser maze. "Where did I find it?"

Hannah looked up sharply. "If I even think you're keeping anything else from me, Nikki, I swear to God, I'll—"

"On her boat," Nikki blurted. "Jordan has a boat."

Hannah went still. "A boat?" She blinked in evident disbelief. "How long…? How can…? Did she ever go out on it?"

"She used to, quite a bit. Before she got together with you, we'd take it out a lot on the weekends and go up or down the coast. Sometimes she'd go by herself."

"Why wouldn't she have told me about it, or taken me along?" Hannah's brow creased.

"Well, because…" Nikki couldn't hold Hannah's gaze.

"Because that's where she took all those women," Hannah said with sad resignation. She bowed her head and massaged her temples. "Of course, she needed some place to take them."

"I'm sorry, Hannah."

Hannah waved a hand in obvious dismissal.

"Breakfast's ready," Kate said as she swooped into the room and deposited three plates holding scrambled eggs, cut fruit, and toast onto the coffee table. "I'll be right back with juice."

"Thanks, Kate," Hannah said, discreetly slipping the journal beneath the sofa cushion behind her as Kate retrieved the drinks. She gave Nikki a slight shake of her head.

"So," Nikki said as Kate joined them again, "nothing more from the police?"

"No," Hannah said with a sigh. "I don't think they're going to do anything. And I still haven't been able to make myself start emailing those women. All I've been able to do is hope Jordan's father will call, but him having any answers is wishful thinking. I really don't know what else to do." She took a drink of her orange juice but didn't touch her food.

"Have you thought about a private investigator?" Nikki asked.

Hannah and Kate both looked at her. "Do you think that would help?" Hannah asked.

Nikki shrugged. "It couldn't hurt. At least we'd know someone was actually *doing* something to find her. He could start by contacting the women in the emails so you wouldn't have to, and maybe there's another way of tracking cell phones that we don't know about. Really, any PI would know more than we do."

"Do you know any?" Hannah asked.

"No, but I'll bet Dana does. Lawyers use them sometimes. And she might even be able to give him some information about Jordan that we don't have." Nikki saw a flash of hope in Hannah's eyes. "You want me to call her?"

"Would you?" Hannah asked. "Thank you." A note of what sounded like relief tinged her voice.

Dana had checked in with Nikki a few times over the past several days to see where the investigation stood, so it didn't take long to bring her up to speed. Within minutes, Nikki had the name and contact information for a PI Dana recommended highly, and five minutes after that, she was making an appointment to meet with an investigator named Lantz Jansen the following morning at ten o'clock. For the first time since the disappointment of hearing that the police couldn't do anything unless there were signs of foul play, Nikki felt some genuine optimism. Bolstered somewhat, she considered the calls to Jonathan Webber. "When you called Jordan's father the second time, did you leave any more information than the first time?" she asked Hannah.

"I said no one's heard from her. Why?"

"I don't know. I'd just really like to know why he hasn't called back." Nikki tried to remember exactly what Jordan had told her about their relationship. "I mean, I know he's busy and all, and they don't get along, but she's still his daughter. You'd think he'd be curious."

"It might explain *why* Jordan doesn't talk to him." Hannah picked at her toast.

"Why don't you call the brother again?" Kate scooped up a forkful of eggs and held it to Hannah's lips. "Eat."

Looking abashed, Hannah obeyed.

"Maybe he could talk to her dad for us," Kate said, finishing her thought.

"That's not a bad idea," Nikki said, impressed with both the suggestion and Kate's demeanor with Hannah. "Are you up to it?" she asked Hannah.

"Sure, I can do that. That *is* a good idea." Hannah grabbed her phone.

"And afterward, you need to eat your whole breakfast," Kate said, sounding like the older sibling. It made Nikki wonder which one had actually been born first and by how many minutes. "You need to take care of yourself."

"David Webber," Jordan's brother said, following the third ring.

"Hello, David. This is Hannah Lewis. I spoke with you a couple of days ago about Jordan?"

"Yes. I remember," David said. "Did she show up?"

"No. We still haven't heard anything," Hannah said. "We've hit a bit of a dead-end, which is why I'm calling you again."

"What can I do?"

"I've put in a couple of calls to your father, and he hasn't returned them."

"Oh," David said flatly. "Yes, Jordan isn't among his favorite topics."

"I was wondering if you might be able to talk to him, either to see if he's had any contact with her or to get him to call me."

David hesitated a long moment. Nikki realized both she and Hannah were holding their breath. Just when it was about to become uncomfortable, David said, "I can do that."

Hannah and Nikki exhaled. "Thank you," Hannah said. "I really appreciate it."

"No problem," David said. "One of us will get back to you. Give me a day or two. And if you hear from Jordan in the meantime, be sure to let me know."

When they'd finished the call, Hannah genuinely smiled. Was it weird that such a small thing could give them so much hope? Was it desperate? Were they grasping at straws? After all, it wasn't likely Jonathan Webber would be the one to have any helpful information.

"That went well," Kate said brightly.

Nikki smiled in an attempt to add to the encouragement.

Kate picked up Hannah's fork and handed it to her. "Now, eat."

Hannah took a bite.

"And now, if Nikki promises to behave and you think you can get along without me for a while," Kate said to Hannah, shooting a quick glare at Nikki, "I have an appointment with Francois at Le Boutique to cut my hair. I've been waiting for months."

Nikki blinked. Keeping up with Kate was like trying to catch a mosquito with chopsticks.

"Oh," Hannah said. "Of course. I'll be fine. Thank you for coming over." She rose and hugged her sister.

Within seconds, Nikki and Hannah were alone.

"What the heck was that about?" Nikki asked as Hannah sat down beside her again.

Hannah took a bite of melon. "It's just how Kate is," she said. She gulped her orange juice. "I'm glad she had somewhere to go. I didn't want her to come with us."

"Come with us? Where are we going?" Nikki asked, trying to catch up.

"I want to see that boat," Hannah said resolutely.

❖

Nikki paused at the gate to the marina. "Are you sure you want to do this?" She tried to catch a glimpse of Hannah's emotional landscape in her eyes but was met with only her own reflection in Hannah's mirrored sunglasses.

"I'm sure." The tremor in Hannah's voice belied the certainty of the words.

Reluctantly, Nikki swiped the electronic key card, then held open the gate. As she guided Hannah onto the dock that ran alongside the slip that held Jordan's boat, Hannah slowed and stared. Her lips parted.

Nikki waited. "Are you okay?"

"Yes," Hannah said after a brief hesitation. "I just didn't expect it to be so big. I guess I pictured a small sailboat or something."

Nikki reached over the side and unlatched the gate so Hannah could step onto the deck. She watched as Hannah took in the glassed-in cockpit on top and the molded lounge chairs positioned around the stern.

Finally, Hannah moved closer and took Nikki's offered hand as she stepped onto the boat.

Nikki followed as she fished her keys from her pocket and found the one that unlocked the door to the cabin below.

Hannah stayed close, but continued to take in her surroundings.

Nikki wished she knew what Hannah was thinking. She was pretty damn sure this wasn't a good idea. When the door was open, she moved down several stairs, then reached back for Hannah. "Watch your step here."

Hannah made her way slowly, and as they reached the floor to the lower cabin, she stopped and slid her sunglasses to the top of her head. Without a word, she took in the galley, the small refrigerator, the dinette.

Nikki remembered the dinners or midnight snacks she and Jordan had made for dates they'd brought back here or taken out on the water for an overnight cruise, and she imagined Hannah standing here seeing it all. A pang of guilt twisted in Nikki's stomach. But no, Nikki hadn't done that once Jordan had gotten involved with Hannah. That had to mean something. Didn't it? She started to turn away, but followed Hannah's gaze to the open door of the V-berth.

"Is that where she..." Hannah's tone held something Nikki didn't recognize.

"No," Nikki said. She knew her answer meant having to show Hannah where Jordan *did* sleep with other women, but the time for keeping things to herself was over. "Back here." She moved past Hannah and pushed open the door to the aft berth.

Hannah stepped into the doorway. She stood still and silent for a long time, her eyes seeming unfocused while, at the same time, absorbing every detail. Her pallor was ashen.

The low rumble of a boat motoring past outside in the marina broke the incessant silence. Nikki shifted uncomfortably. "Hannah, you don't have to—"

"I need to start facing the truth," Hannah said desolately. "To be blind to it for so long makes me pathetic enough, but to pretend it doesn't exist now that it's in my face... Well, that would just make me pitiful."

"You're not pathetic or pitiful, Hannah," Nikki said. "This is all just Jordan. It's just the way she is. It isn't you." She lifted her hand to Hannah's shoulder.

"Don't touch me," Hannah whispered sharply.

Nikki froze.

"I don't want to be touched. Not here." Hannah's attention lingered on the bed a moment longer, then she turned in the doorway and let her gaze roam once again over the rest of the cabin. She stopped again on the galley, then the dinette, then the V-berth. "Is that your room? Is that why you have a key?"

Nikki's throat closed. She didn't want to have to admit it out loud. "It used to be. I haven't been here in a long time." She knew it was a weak defense. "And yes. That's why Jordan gave me a key."

Hannah's expression gave nothing away. "Thank you for telling me the truth." She looked as though she was going to say something else, but moved toward the steps instead. "I'm done here." She didn't wait for Nikki to lock up or to help her back onto the dock. She was standing beside the car when Nikki reached the parking lot.

The ride home was quiet. While Nikki drove, Hannah found a station on the radio, then stared out the window.

Her silence grated on Nikki's nerves, and she flexed her grip on the steering wheel. She wished Hannah would say what she was thinking. Anything would be better than not knowing.

The phone was ringing as they walked into the condo, and Hannah grabbed the handset off its base. She glanced at the caller ID. Her eyes went wide. "It's the Webber law firm," she said, pressing the speaker button. "Hello?" she said into the receiver.

"Ms. Lewis, please?" the now familiar administrative assistant's voice said.

"This is Hannah Lewis." She shot a look of anticipation at Nikki.

"Please hold for Jonathan Webber." There was a click.

The wait was only seconds.

"Ms. Lewis," a man said, his tone brusque, its temperature chilly.

"Yes, Mr. Webber," Hannah said. "Thank you for returning my call."

"I'm not returning your call, Ms Lewis. My son has informed me that you are harassing him, and I've called to tell you to leave my family alone, unless you'd like to find yourself facing stalking charges."

"What? No, Mr. Webber. I just wanted—"

"I know what you want, Ms. Lewis. My secretary is very efficient, and my son was thorough in his report. Whatever trouble Jordan has gotten herself into is none of our concern. She made her choice to leave our family years ago."

Hannah looked at Nikki, her mouth agape. "I'm sorry, Mr. Webber. The police thought that maybe—"

"Good-bye, Ms. Lewis. I expect no further contact from you with me or any member of my family."

The line went dead.

Hannah's cheeks flamed. She glared at the phone. "What a jerk. Can you believe that?"

Nikki remembered a few entries in Jordan's journal in which she wrote about her father's complete detachment from her any time she did anything other than exactly what he wanted her to do. She had hoped it was more of a child's perception hanging on into adulthood rather than the truth. *Apparently not.* "There's some stuff in that journal—"

"I don't want to hear about that right now." Hannah tossed the phone onto the couch. "I don't think I can take one more thing today. Can we just not talk for a while?"

"Sure." Nikki shifted off her weak ankle. It was starting to ache. Hannah glanced down. "Is your foot okay?"

"It's fine," Nikki said. She appreciated the inquiry, but there were more important things to focus on. "I'm going to get a beer. Is there anything I can get you?"

"A glass of wine would be nice," Hannah said, turning away. "I'll be outside." She crossed to the sliding door and disappeared onto the patio.

Nikki exhaled deeply, unsure if it was because of frustration or relief at the brief reprieve from being in Hannah's immediate presence. She rubbed the back of her neck. Even in Hannah's absence, though, she couldn't shake the look on Hannah's face as she'd stood in the doorway of the aft berth and stared at Jordan's bed. Had she been imagining Jordan there with someone else? Would she have tortured herself with images like that? Nikki couldn't believe Hannah had even wanted to see the boat. That took strength. And what Hannah had said about needing to face the truth? How many women in her circumstances right now would be able to do that?

Nikki went to the kitchen and grabbed a beer from the fridge. She twisted off the top and took a long pull. She wanted to give Hannah a little time to herself. She found some crackers in the cupboard and spread cream cheese on them, then poured Hannah a glass of white zin. When she stepped outside, she found Hannah in the swing, her head tilted back and her eyes closed.

Her cheeks were wet.

Nikki hooked the leg of a small glass-topped table with her foot and scooted it in front of Hannah. She set the plate of crackers and the wine on it before sitting in a chair across from her.

Hannah straightened and wiped the moisture from her face.

"I thought you might want some food, too," Nikki said. She wanted to sound as firm as Kate had, but who was she to tell Hannah what to do? She was partly responsible for how Hannah was feeling—hell, for Hannah even *being* in this situation, if you looked at things a certain way. If Nikki had been honest with Hannah in the beginning, had actually been her friend, Hannah might never have moved in with Jordan, wouldn't now have a girlfriend who'd simply vanished, and wouldn't be finding out she'd never even known her. *Okay, maybe the vanishing thing isn't my fault, but still...* What was that saying? *Oh, what a tangled web we weave, when first we practice to deceive?* Something like that. No, Nikki had no business telling her what to do.

"Thank you," Hannah said, taking a bite of a cracker. She still didn't look at Nikki.

Nikki hated the formality in her manner. Sure, she had called her and asked her to come back, said she needed Nikki there, but ever since she'd first seen the boat, it felt like a door had been closed. Did she still want Nikki there, now? "Hannah," Nikki said hesitantly. "Do you want me to leave?"

Hannah looked up. "No," she said, alarm in her eyes.

"Okay." Nikki held up her hands. "Okay. I just asked because I know you're not happy with me. And I don't want to make things worse."

Hannah's expression tightened. "I'm *not* happy with you. I told you that. But I need you here. You have to see me through this. You owe me that, at least."

Nikki nodded. "You're right. And this is where I want to be. I just wanted to check and make sure it's still what you wanted."

Hannah seemed to relax again and took a sip of her wine. She was quiet for a long time, staring past Nikki at some flowers. "You know, when we were on that boat, I thought about canceling the appointment with that private investigator tomorrow. Just let Jordan be wherever she is." There was a bite in her tone.

"Is that what you want to do?" Nikki wasn't sure *she* could do that, but if Hannah didn't want a part in it...

"No." Hannah pushed her toe against the cement and started the swing moving. It somehow softened her demeanor. "Regardless of anything else, I have to do whatever I can to find her if she needs help. Even though I know we'll never be together again—were never together in the first place—I need to know I did everything I could."

"That's admirable," Nikki said softly.

Hannah cut her a sharp glance. "The rest of what I'm thinking isn't admirable. I think I actually hate her for all the things I've found out. But then, how can I hate her when she might be hurt or dead? And then, I want to hate her for that, too. For the fact that she couldn't just *do* all those things, and I couldn't find out about them, and break up with her and hate her for that. Like normal people. No, she has to disappear so that I don't know where she is or what's happening to her or if she's even still alive, and *then* find out all the ways she lied to me and cheated on me…" Tears spilled down her cheeks again.

Nikki moved to sit next to her on the swing.

Hannah held up her hand. "No. Stay over there. I can't… Not yet."

Nikki swallowed the lump of regret in her throat and settled back down. "I'm sorry, Hannah," she said. "I'm so sorry."

"Just sit here with me," Hannah whispered. "I just want to sit here and not think about anything for the rest of the day."

Resigned, Nikki nodded. She could do that. *It's not like I have any new ideas anyway.*

CHAPTER TEN

This time, when the voice fell silent, following a discourse punctuated by the words "abominations," "America's tolerance," "terrorism," and "all evil," something different happened. Rather than the blinding light vanishing completely, leaving Jordan yet again in utter blackness, a dim illumination remained, enabling her to make out the toilet and cement slab of a bed she'd only been able to catch glimpses of before.

She didn't know whether to be grateful or apprehensive. On one hand, she was thankful for a break from the two versions of hell she'd been volleying between for... She had no idea for how long. At the same time, however, now she didn't have a clue what to expect. Would someone come in? Liz? She hadn't seen her since Liz had reintroduced herself as Sister somebody and told her some bullshit about saving her soul. Would she be taken somewhere else? She huddled in a corner. *What the fuck do they want?*

She sat, waiting and wondering, tense with apprehension, but nothing happened. As her vision adjusted, she could see more clearly. The room was as bare as she remembered, everything—the linoleum floor, the walls, the porcelain—all stark white. She tried to find the door, but it blended in too seamlessly. She ran her hand over the prickly stubble on her head. She recalled Liz's words. *You're being reborn into the light.* She had to get out of there. These people were insane. She just had to wait. There'd be an opportunity. In the meantime, she had to preserve her strength, what little she had left with no food in her stomach. She sighed and leaned back against the wall.

Time passed—she was sure—but she could no longer distinguish between minutes and hours, maybe even days. The only sound in the room was her own breathing, the chafe of the skin of one leg against the other, or of her butt against the floor as she changed positions, trying to get comfortable. Her head fell forward each time she nodded off. She jerked up and forced her eyes open wide. She had to stay awake. She had to be ready.

The sound of a key in the door made her jump. It was deafening in the dead silence.

She tried to scramble to her feet to meet her captors on equal footing, but she was weak. She lost her balance and grabbed for the wall. Leaning against it for support, she made her way to the cement slab and sat on the edge.

The door opened.

The pasty-faced man stepped into the room.

Jordan flinched. She'd grown accustomed to her nakedness to some degree, given that she'd been alone for the most part, and when anyone had come in, she'd been preoccupied, curled up in a ball, fending off the assault of light and sound. Now, however, she wanted to try to cover herself, fold her arms over her breasts, or turn away. She also wanted to stand—or at least sit—tall and defiant. She opted for the latter.

Pasty-face looked at the floor.

Liz came in, followed by another woman carrying an assembled TV tray with something on it. They wore identical below-the-knee-length, drab, tan dresses. A savory aroma wafted in the air, making Jordan's mouth water and her stomach growl loudly.

"How are you feeling?" Liz asked, as though she didn't know what Jordan had been going through.

Pasty-face lingered behind, blocking the doorway.

"How do you think I feel?" Jordan's throat was raw, her voice hoarse.

"We brought you some broth," Liz said. "It will help you start adjusting to food again. If you behave ungraciously, we'll assume you don't want it. Do you understand?"

Jordan glared at her. "If I throw it in your face, I won't get any more."

Liz pursed her lips and gave a single nod. "And if you misbehave in *any* way, you'll have to begin again."

Jordan didn't know what that meant, but at the moment, it was difficult to think about anything but the cavernous ache in her stomach.

Liz turned to the other woman and motioned her forward.

She looked younger than Liz and Jordan, with shoulder-length, wavy brown hair and large, dark eyes. She positioned the tray over Jordan's lap, never meeting her gaze or saying a word. She stepped back.

Jordan breathed in the steam from the chicken broth and could actually taste it. She moaned. She dipped the spoon into the liquid and started to bring it to her lips. Her hand shook. The broth spilled back into the bowl. She hadn't realized she was trembling.

"Here, let me help you." The brunette moved forward and sat beside her. She filled the spoon again and brought it to Jordan's mouth.

Jordan opened and took it in. The flavor exploded on her tongue. After so long with only water, it was almost too much. She squeezed her eyes shut and swallowed slowly.

"More?" the brunette asked.

When Jordan opened her eyes, another spoonful awaited her. She looked at the brunette.

The other woman's eyes widened slightly at the attention. She tensed, then shifted her gaze to the spoon. Her frightened demeanor made her seem vulnerable.

There was something familiar about her. The eyes, maybe? Jordan couldn't pinpoint what, but something made her want to comfort her. "Thank you," she whispered.

The gesture seemed to increase the brunette's anxiety rather than ease it. She glanced nervously at Liz, then slipped the spoon back into Jordan's mouth. They settled into a steady pace, each swallow soothing the pangs of Jordan's hunger. When the bowl was empty, the brunette looked at Liz again.

Liz smiled and nodded.

The brunette picked up the tray and scurried from the room.

What the hell was that about? Before Jordan could wonder too much, a cramp gripped her stomach. She doubled over and lay on her side.

Another man stepped through the doorway.

"Please, come with us," pasty-face said.

Come with us? Where? Jordan was grateful for the distraction of her discomfort. "I can't," she said with a wince. "I can't get up." It was a lie, but it might buy her a few minutes.

The two men looked to Liz. She was clearly the one in charge. "Give her ten minutes for her stomach to settle." She started toward the door.

"Liz," Jordan said, a bit frantic. She had to know where they were taking her, what was going to happen.

Liz turned back to her. "Sister Katherine," she said firmly. "My name is Sister Katherine."

Liz? Sister Katherine? Crazy bitch? Who cares. "I forgot. I'm sorry." She had to keep on Liz's good side. From what Jordan could see so far—which, granted, wasn't much—she might be Jordan's only hope. They'd had a connection, hadn't they, albeit a superficial one? Or had that just been a ruse to lure Jordan to that isolated street? The thought turned to fear and chilled her like a winter wind. What if she were completely alone here? She hadn't realized she'd been holding on to a thread of hope tied to Liz. She suddenly got it. There *was* no Liz. *Only Sister Katherine. Only crazy bitch.* She blanched. "I'm sorry," she said again, this time meaning it, in her own way. "Sister Katherine. Will you tell me what's going on? Why I'm here?" She fought to keep her anger from rising again.

Sister Katherine's manner softened. "God rested on the seventh day, so we're resting today. Brother Noah and Brother Isaac will come back for you in a little while." She left the room, the men close at her heels.

Jordan was stunned. *The seventh day?* Had she been there *seven days?* Was that possible? Or had Liz…or Sister Katherine… Had crazy bitch meant Sunday, the Christian Sabbath, the traditional seventh day when God needed a break? She sat up and shook her head to clear it. She had to count. It'd been a Saturday she'd gone to meet crazy bitch. So, if today was Sunday a week later, she'd been there… *Nine days?* Holy fuck! Why hadn't anybody found her?

Her heart began to palpitate. Her breathing quickened. *Nine days?* She had to get out of there. There had to be a way. She forced herself to breathe deeply, to calm down. She couldn't do anything, she couldn't even think, if she let herself panic. The guys were coming back for her, to take her someplace. That meant leaving this room. It meant a chance. She sat up and bent over, hanging her head between her knees. She inhaled, deeply, slowly. When she straightened, she was able to focus. She'd stay calm. She'd observe. She'd take whatever chance presented itself.

A few minutes later, the two men returned. "Are you feeling better?" pasty-face asked.

"Yes," Jordan said. "A little."

He smiled. "That's good. Please come with us?"

"Where?" Jordan eyed the other man, but she stood. The first step to getting out of there, wherever there was, was to get out of that room. "Can I have a robe or something?"

"Please come along."

They moved to either side of her and each took a gentle hold on one of her arms.

She started to balk, but stopped herself. She had to go along with it. *Breathe.*

They led her out the door and into a long hallway. As they turned to the left, she glanced in the opposite direction. The corridor, like the room, was all white. Doors, all closed, were spaced at seemingly random intervals along both sides. When Jordan looked forward, she found the exact same sight. There were no distinguishing numbers or signs anywhere.

When they came to another hallway that teed off to the left, Jordan saw crazy bitch coming out of a side door and heading toward another one at the far end. Through a small window, Jordan could see stairs leading up. When crazy bitch drew near, the door opened automatically.

Without a thought, Jordan broke free and raced down the hall. Her legs were shaky, but she pumped hard, her whole focus on the open door.

Just as Jordan reached it, crazy bitch spun around and pushed it closed from the other side. She stared at Jordan through the small window.

Jordan yanked on the handle. Locked. It was only then she heard the footsteps behind her. Someone grabbed her and held her firmly. She felt a needle stab in her arm. Within seconds, she was falling.

❖

Hannah reached groggily for the phone on the nightstand. She had no idea how many times it had rung. She squinted at the small caller ID screen, but her eyes wouldn't focus. "Hello," she said, her voice husky with sleep.

"May I speak with Jordan Webber?" a woman asked.

Hannah blinked awake. "Who's calling, please?" It was a woman. Did Hannah really want to know who she was?

"My name is Stephanie Wood. I'm her accountant."

Accountant. Hannah relaxed as the word registered. When she had first moved in and asked about her share of the expenses, Jordan had told her she had an accountant who handled all the monthly bills and some of her investments. At Hannah's insistence, they had set up their joint account from which to pay for groceries and entertainment, and Hannah deposited the amount of her previous rent and utilities into it each month as well. She didn't know anything else about the bills or Jordan's money. "I'm sorry. She isn't here."

"I've been trying to reach her on her cell for the past several days, but I haven't been able to get through. May I leave a message for her to call me?"

A message? What would I do with a message? Hannah tried to quell the tide of emotion that constantly ebbed and flowed within her these days. She was going to have to give this woman some sort of explanation. "I'm sorry Ms. Wood. I don't know when Jordan will be back." She filled her in on the pertinent details, then waited in the silence that followed. She couldn't blame her for not knowing what to say.

"I see…Well," Ms. Wood said finally. "And to whom am I speaking?"

"My name's Hannah Lewis." She sighed. She wouldn't say *I'm her girlfriend* anymore.

"And you're living on the property?" Ms. Wood seemed to have regained her stride.

"Yes. For the time being." Hannah hadn't thought about it before now, but of course, she would need to move out. So, in addition to the question of whether Jordan was okay, Hannah would have to start thinking about *that*, too. She couldn't bear the idea. She was so tired most days she had difficulty getting out of bed. How would she be able to look for a new place to live, shop for everything she would need, and actually manage a move? She realized she didn't have any legal right to be there. "Is that okay?"

"I don't know anything about your and Ms. Webber's arrangement," Ms. Wood said. "So, I really can't say. I haven't heard anything different from her, so my job is to continue to do what I've been doing, and save my questions for when she returns. I'll contact the police to see if they have any questions I can answer without violating any confidentiality, but other than that, I'm sure she'll be in touch with me, unless..." She cleared her throat. "If you do find out anything new, would you please let me know?"

"I will," Hannah said. *So, that's it? The bills will just magically continue to be paid for a while?* Everything was getting more surreal by the day. Of course, Hannah would also keep contributing her share. And she would start looking for a new place to live as soon as she could pull it all together.

When she had taken down the accountant's contact information and hung up, Hannah rolled onto her back in her and Jordan's big bed—or rather, in Jordan's big bed. She looked around the sunlit room. Jordan's bed. Jordan's dresser. Jordan's matching nightstands. Jordan's lamps. Everything visible in the room belonged to Jordan, except the teddy bear Hannah was hugging, which Jordan had won for her at the fair, and her robe draped over the back of Jordan's chair in the corner. Hannah sighed.

It had made sense at the time she had moved in. All of Jordan's things were nicer than hers, and they went with the style of the condo. It *fit*, and Hannah had liked that. It all worked together to present the up-and-coming, successful couple image Hannah enjoyed, being Jordan's girlfriend. She had kept her own furniture in storage for the first year after she had moved in with Jordan, but when it seemed things were working out between them—actually, everything had seemed perfect—she had sold it all on Craigslist. She had still been living with mismatched remnants from her college years, with a few new pieces purchased here and there in a gradual upgrade of her apartment. Most of her disposable income, however, had been spent on some amazing summer vacations with Kate and some ski trips in the winter.

The smell of coffee drifted in through the open bedroom door, and as much as she would have loved to pull the covers over her head and hide from everything, Hannah took it as a sign she might as well get up. Another day of waiting. She slipped her robe over her pajama shorts and camisole, but didn't tie it, and walked out into the living room.

Nikki lay on the sofa, one bronze leg on top of the rumpled sheet and an arm dangling off the side of the cushion, her fingers trailing on the hardwood floor. She didn't stir at the sound of Hannah's footsteps, but Hannah didn't think she could possibly still be asleep. How could she be? Neither of them had been sleeping more than a few hours a night.

"You awake?" Hannah asked quietly.

"Yeah." The muffled answer came from under the pillow.

"I'll get the coffee." *Thank God for the timer on the coffeemaker.* Hannah filled two mugs, added cream to her own, then trudged back into the living room. Her limbs were leaden.

Nikki sat up and took the cup Hannah handed her. "Thanks."

Hannah dropped into the chair across from her and drew up one knee. She took a large swallow. The hot liquid and creamy texture soothed the ragged edges of her nerves.

Nikki turned away and took a drink of her coffee.

Had she been staring at Hannah? *Do I look that bad?* Hannah finger-combed her hair and glanced down at her jammies. *What was she looking at?*

"Who was on the phone?" Nikki asked in a mumble.

"Jordan's accountant," Hannah said. "I'll tell you about it later. I need coffee." Nikki rubbed her eyes, then ran her hand down her face. "I'm so exhausted, but I can't sleep."

Hannah yawned. "It's the waiting," she said without thinking. The memory of the last time she had been this down-to-the-bone tired crept into her. "I remember feeling like this when my mother was dying. When my dad and Kate and I were camped beside her hospital bed at the end." She heard her voice as though from a distance. "The macrobiotic diet hadn't worked. The colloidal silver didn't work. The chemo and radiation… We'd said our good-byes, so… It was so draining…just waiting."

"Was she in pain?" Nikki asked softly.

Hannah met her gentle gaze. "Not by then. She was in a coma. She actually seemed peaceful. And when she released her last breath, I felt her move past me and kiss my cheek." The last sentence came out in a whisper.

A tender smile lifted the corners of Nikki's mouth. "That had to be amazing."

They looked at each other as though a spell had been cast over the moment.

Hannah cleared her throat and glanced down. "What's amazing is that I told you that." She gave a little laugh. "I've never told anyone. Not even Kate."

Nikki tilted her head. "I'm honored." She hesitated. "I've never told anyone my brother Ramon comes to visit me sometimes."

"Does he?"

Nikki nodded. "He doesn't say anything, but I can feel him. I miss him."

"Me, too. My mom." Hannah smiled. "I could talk to her about anything. When Ramon died, was there waiting? I know he died in a car accident, but… Was there waiting?"

"No." Nikki looked away. "He was killed on impact. I can't imagine going through what you did."

Hannah frowned. "Even that, I think, was easier than *this*." She waved her hand, indicating the all-things-Jordan that surrounded them. "At least then, we knew there was an end and what it was. Now, there's nothing but the waiting. Waiting to hear something. Waiting for Jordan to come back. Now, I understand what people mean when they say it's the not knowing that makes you crazy. I'm going *crazy*,

Nikki. I can't take another day of just waiting. Can we do something today?"

"Like what?" Nikki asked. "We've already done everything the police said to do. We've looked through all Jordan's stuff. And now we've hired Lantz and given everything to him."

The initial meeting with the private investigator three days earlier had felt anticlimactic. Hannah didn't know what she had expected—a dark office with an air of moral ambiguity, or film noir elements like a man in a black hat seated behind the desk and an old-fashioned telephone with a large black receiver. There had been nothing like that. They could have been sitting in an accountant's office. Lantz Jansen had seemed competent, though, and they had given him all the information they had.

"I meant something…I don't know… Normal?" A wave of guilt washed over Hannah. How could she be thinking of doing something *normal* when her girlfriend was missing? Then again, the angry voice in her spoke up, how could her girlfriend have done the things *she* did?

"Sure," Nikki said gently. "You want to see a movie?"

Gratitude swelled in Hannah for Nikki's easy acceptance of what she needed. She considered the idea. "I don't think I could concentrate on a movie. Maybe something outside?"

"How about the zoo?" Nikki asked as though it were an everyday occurrence.

Hannah couldn't remember the last time she had been to the zoo. "The zoo?"

"Yeah. It's a fun day," Nikki stretched and propped her feet on the coffee table. "We could see if Marti and Delia and Ringo want to go, if you'd like." She wiggled her eyebrows. "You could pet a goat."

Hannah laughed. "Oh, well…if I can pet a goat…" The sound of her own laughter startled her. It seemed as though it had been forever since she had last laughed. She looked at Nikki, taking in the warmth in her lush brown eyes, her toned arms and shoulders, the snug fit of her tank top, her loose navy boxers, the strong lines of her legs. Hannah's long-standing appreciation of Nikki's appearance swept through her like a hot summer breeze. Was *that* what Nikki had been doing earlier—appreciating *her*? When she returned her gaze to Nikki's face, she was met with a broad grin.

Jordan would never in a million years have suggested going to the zoo, never mind inviting a couple with a baby to join them, and Hannah had always assumed—because they were best friends—that Nikki was exactly like Jordan. *Why should she be?* But then, if she thought about it, she should have known better. She had met Nikki's family a couple of times, seen how close she was to them, watched her play with her nieces and nephews. Aleyda had told her how much Nikki helped with the kids.

"Do you go to the zoo a lot?" Hannah asked, genuinely curious.

Nikki shrugged. "Sometimes."

"When was the last time?"

A light blush bloomed beneath the natural tan of Nikki's cheeks. "Two weeks ago. Ringo and I went."

"Just the two of you?"

"Delia and Marti needed a date," Nikki said. She turned her coffee mug in her hands, as though it was suddenly a necessary task. "So, Ringo and I went on one, too, along with Cecelia, who came to help, since I still had the cast on." She wiggled her bare foot.

Hannah smiled. "That was nice of you."

"Well, you know…Ringo likes the monkeys."

They called Marti and Delia, and two hours later, they were all standing at the entrance to the Los Angeles Zoo. As they made their way from one animal exhibit to the next, Hannah relished the heat of the sunshine on her face, and the caress of the breeze on her skin. She was acutely aware of all the people around her, all the normal people enjoying perfectly normal days. She wondered at what point in her own mind she had become Hannah, the poor, distraught woman with the missing, cheating girlfriend instead of Hannah, the happy high school counselor who laughed easily and loved to dance and sing karaoke—after a few drinks, of course. She walked arm in arm with Marti, laughed as Delia and Nikki mimicked the orangutans so Ringo wouldn't cry when they left the Red Ape Rain Forest, and ate a ridiculous amount of caramel corn, until she was almost able to forget the surreal-ness of her actual life.

She shouldn't have let down her guard, though. Standing in the shade of a large tree enjoying the sight of Marti and her family oohing and aahing over the beauty of a peacock opening its tail into full display, Hannah felt her earlier realization sniffing around the edges of her consciousness: Jordan *was* dead to her regardless of whether she was still physically alive. Instantly, the gorgeous colors of the peacock's plumage and the joy in her friends' expressions blurred, as Hannah's eyes burned with unshed tears.

Nikki's first touch, a light press of fingertips to Hannah's shoulder blade, was tentative, questioning.

How had she been so aware of the shift in Hannah's emotions?

Hannah hadn't let Nikki touch her, or even sit very close to her, since she had found out about Nikki's knowledge of Jordan's affairs. Even with the moment they had shared that morning, Hannah wasn't sure she was ready to trust Nikki's friendship again. As angry as she had been, though, it galled her to admit that Nikki was the only one she really wanted with her throughout this ordeal, and since Hannah had allowed Nikki to come back, she had shown her commitment to her. She had been honest with her about the journal and that damned boat—even taken her to see it—and had been at Hannah's side every second, except for the previous afternoon and evening when she'd had a wedding to shoot. Even then, she had invited Hannah to come along, but Hannah couldn't imagine watching two people in love begin their life together amidst the wreckage of her own shattered dreams.

Hannah stiffened at Nikki's hand on her back, but the touch was so tender, ultimately, she couldn't resist its solace. She leaned into Nikki, then hesitantly, looked into her eyes.

"I'm sorry," Nikki whispered. Of course, she knew the ambivalence Hannah was feeling. And, of course, she *was* sorry.

Hannah pressed a finger to Nikki's lips. She didn't want to hear any excuses, any explanations of Nikki's betrayal. She couldn't. Not yet. Deep down, she knew Nikki had reasons for what she had done, and they would make sense, once Hannah was able to hear them. For now, she just needed Nikki's comfort. She leaned in and allowed herself to be held. For the rest of the afternoon, Nikki never left her side, ready with the squeeze of a hand or the strength of her arm around Hannah's shoulders.

"So," Nikki said as the day seemed to be coming to a close, "you ready to pet that goat?"

Hannah laughed. "I think I can manage without it."

"What? You can't spend the day here without going to the petting zoo." Nikki was clearly incredulous. "Besides, Ringo likes it."

"Ringo's not even a year old yet," Delia said. "*She's* the one who has the relationship with the goats." She grinned and shot Nikki a teasing look. "You going to dance with them again?"

"I wasn't dancing," Nikki said.

"Be nice," Marti said to Delia, but she was laughing.

"You danced with a goat?" Hannah asked Nikki.

"I wasn't dancing," Nikki said again, this time more obstinately.

"Looked like dancing to me." Amusement sparked in Delia's eyes as they all walked through the inner gate to the petting zoo. "Look, I think that was your partner over there." She pointed to a black goat eating from a little girl's hand in the far corner.

"Come on, Ringo." Nikki lifted the baby from Marti's arms. "Let's go pet some animals." A small smile played on her lips.

"You should've seen it, Hannah. It was beautiful," Delia called after Nikki as Nikki walked away. "It was grace personified. Nikki stepped one way, and the goat moved right with her. Nikki twirled the other way, and he followed flawlessly." Delia reenacted the steps.

Nikki squatted so Ringo could touch the thick wool on a sheep's back. She shook her head, a wide grin on her face.

Hannah smiled at Delia's antics.

"Then she leapt into the air," Delia said and performed the jump with a dramatic flair, "tripped over the goat, and landed wrong on her ankle when she came down. She ended up in a heap in the dirt." She doubled over, laughing.

Nikki chuckled. "It wasn't pretty," she said to Hannah.

Hannah laughed.

"It was valiant," Marti said with obvious admiration. She turned to Hannah. "There was a little boy across the yard getting squished between two sheep and the fence, and he was crying. Nikki was trying to get to him, and the goat kept moving in the same direction. She lost her balance, and when she tried to jump over him, she fell. That's how she broke her foot."

Hannah covered her mouth with her hands. "Oh my, that must have been a bad fall."

"It's all over," Nikki said with a shrug. "And my foot's as good as new."

They finished petting the goats and sheep—the only animals in the petting zoo—and said their good-byes to Marti and Delia. Nikki kissed the baby, and Hannah gave him a squeeze, then they headed for Nikki's car.

When they got home, Nikki grilled some turkey patties outside while Hannah threw together a green salad and sliced onions, tomatoes, and cheese for the burgers. They settled on the couch to watch *Sliding Doors*, one of Hannah's favorite movies, while they ate.

"Have you seen this?" Hannah asked a bit hesitantly.

"No." Nikki took a bite of salad.

"It's kind of different. Are you sure you're okay with it?"

Nikki chuckled. "I'm sure. I know what kind of movies you and Jordan like." The mention of Jordan's name brought her into the room.

Hannah pursed her lips and set down the remote without pressing the play button. "I'm sorry," Nikki said quietly.

"It's okay." Hannah pinched off a piece of her hamburger bun and nibbled on it. "It's not like she isn't still with me most of the time anyway, or at least my worry or anger or questions about where she is or the things she did. But, you know, there were times today when I forgot it all, when I was just enjoying being outside with friends, having a normal day. I felt so free. Does that make me an awful person?"

"No." Nikki took her hand gently. "It makes you a person who's going through a lot, who just needed to escape it all for a little while." She stroked Hannah's knuckles with her thumb.

Hannah wondered if that were true. "I think I've already let her go." She looked at Nikki. "Because of all the women and all the lies."

Nikki's expression softened into one of understanding.

"I hope nothing bad has happened to her, but I know I'll never watch another movie with her. Or have drinks at Fontaine's with her. Or make love—*if* that's what we ever really did."

Nikki just squeezed her fingers, and Hannah was glad there weren't any platitudes or excuses.

They ate while they watched the beginning of the movie, then Hannah paused it while Nikki took their dishes into the kitchen. When she returned, she kicked off her shoes and stretched out her leg, flexing and pointing her recovering ankle.

Hannah started the movie again, but her attention remained on Nikki. She had watched her carry out the exercises the physical therapist had prescribed for the past five days, so she knew the routine. Next would come the full rotation of the ankle for fifteen minutes, then the application of pressure, both pushing and pulling back, to build up the strength again. Tonight, however, Nikki stopped after only a few minutes and began rubbing the top and side of her foot. "What's the matter?" Hannah asked.

"Oh," Nikki said her attention still on the television screen. "Just kind of sore from all the walking." She shifted, drawing up her knee and changing the angle. She seemed to be having trouble getting to the right spot.

Hannah continued to watch. She realized that if Nikki extended her leg and put her foot in Hannah's lap, Hannah would have full and easy access to the spot Nikki seemed to be struggling to rub. She remembered all the times throughout the day Nikki had been there for her with a comforting touch, getting her something to eat or drink, even tonight, clearing away the dishes. She could pretty much guarantee Nikki had put them in the dishwasher while she had been in the kitchen. She thought of all the meals Nikki had cooked over the past several days, the lead she had taken with Lantz Jansen, all the other ways she had helped Hannah since Jordan's disappearance, and here she sat, offering nothing.

What the hell is wrong with me? Was she that self-absorbed? "Here." She shifted on the sofa and sat cross-legged. "Let me do that."

Nikki looked at her in evident surprise. Her completely shocked expression told Hannah that yes, indeed, she had been *that* self-absorbed.

"You don't have to. I've got it."

Hannah felt horrible. "Please, let me."

Slowly, Nikki changed positions and stretched out along the length of the couch, settling her foot in Hannah's lap.

Hannah began a gentle massage.

Relief replaced the astonishment on Nikki's face, and she leaned her head back and closed her eyes. "That's perfect. Right there." She released a deep sigh.

Hannah warmed at being able to give something back. She let her fingers widen their circle and began to rub the length of Nikki's sole. She was surprised at its softness. In that moment, she realized she had never touched Nikki before, not like this. She had hugged her hello or good-bye when Nikki used to hang out with her and Jordan, and she had let Nikki touch her in that affectionate, comforting way Nikki did—even let Nikki hold her when her father died, and now with everything going on with Jordan—but *she* had never touched Nikki. Had she ever offered her anything, done anything for her?

Back when Nikki had been around a lot, Hannah had been too wrapped up in everything she had thought it meant to be Jordan's girlfriend to notice anything else. *Yeah, and now I know exactly what it means to be Jordan's girlfriend.*

And Nikki had been there then, too. Even when the three of them would get together for the evening, Nikki had been in the kitchen helping Hannah make dinner or clean up, while Jordan watched a game or took a work call.

That's when Nikki had known everything, though, had known Hannah's girlfriend was cheating on her. She had only been pretending to be her friend. *No. Jordan and I weren't actually together then, not exclusively. I was still dating other people, too.* Hannah thought back. It had been when she and Jordan had *become* exclusive—or, at least, Hannah had—that Nikki had vanished. Hannah suddenly knew that was when Nikki would have had to *start* lying to her if they had remained friends. *That's why she had to leave.* A sadness at the loss overcame Hannah, along with disgust at herself for not even noticing the loss before now. Her hands stilled as she stared at Nikki.

After a moment, Nikki's eyelids fluttered open. "Thanks," she said and started to sit up.

"No." Hannah tightened her grasp. "Let me finish."

Nikki hesitated, giving her an uncertain look.

"Just relax," Hannah said.

Slowly, Nikki lay back, but a question lingered in her eyes.

Hannah answered it with a smile of newfound appreciation and began a gentle rotation of her ankle. It was time for *her* to start being a friend.

CHAPTER ELEVEN

Nikki and Hannah unloaded the camera equipment from the back of the car and headed up the walk to the studio. Aleyda had planned to assist on the shoot for the Andrews's family pictures, but when Hannah had learned the photos were being shot on the beach and asked if she could help, Aleyda had decided to stay home and work on the proof package for the wedding they'd shot a couple of weeks earlier. Hannah had done great as an assistant. Nikki had to tell her what she needed more often than she did with Aleyda, but that was to be expected. After all, she and Aleyda had worked together for years and were as close as sisters even before that. Mostly, Nikki was thrilled just to have Hannah there with her.

Hannah flashed a bright smile from beneath Nikki's baseball cap, which she'd commandeered halfway through the afternoon when her cheeks and nose had begun to burn. A lot of things had been different between them since the day at the zoo two weeks earlier. Hannah had been different. She seemed to be more aware of Nikki, more interested in knowing about her—her family, her work, her life apart from her friendship with Jordan. She seemed more attentive in their conversations. Hannah had always been somewhat self-absorbed. *This* was unusual.

She also touched Nikki a lot more these days. That'd started the day of the zoo, too. When Hannah had taken Nikki's sore foot into her lap and rubbed it, then worked it through the physical therapy exercises, Nikki had been speechless—not only because it'd been so odd, but because Hannah's gentle caress on her skin had ignited every response and emotion she'd ever had for her. And since then,

Hannah's touches had become much more frequent. Nikki knew it was friendly affection and nothing more—the way Hannah was with Marti—but Nikki's body and heart still responded. When Nikki touched Hannah in comfort and affection, she knew it was coming and could brace herself for it, but when Hannah touched her, there was no way to be ready.

And the intimacy growing between them from all but living together was playing havoc with her as well. Seeing Hannah in her pajamas, or loungewear, or a towel, or sharing a drink, or a dessert from the same fork, reminded Nikki of how much she'd wanted that when she'd first met Hannah. And now, here they were, but under such different circumstances than anything Nikki could ever have imagined. Regardless of it all, though, even with Jordan gone, Hannah was still Nikki's best friend's girlfriend, so she'd keep it all under control and to herself. Besides, Hannah didn't think of *her* that way at all.

"How'd it go?" Aleyda asked from behind the computer at the worktable.

"It was so much fun," Hannah said, hefting her camera bag off her shoulder and into a chair. "And the beach was beautiful."

Aleyda smiled and looked at Nikki.

"We got some great shots. I think Mrs. Andrews will be very happy," Nikki said, answering the real question Aleyda had asked. "And Hannah was a great assistant. She even got a genuine smile out of a sullen teenager." She gave a light tug on the short ponytail sticking out the back of Hannah's hat.

"That's my superpower. It's why I have the job I do," Hannah said. "I keep teenagers from going completely over to the dark side so their parents don't kill them before they hit twenty."

Aleyda laughed. "A noble profession."

"How's your day?" Nikki asked, stepping up behind Aleyda. She scanned the pictures on the computer screen.

"Productive, but I was just about to knock off." Aleyda stretched her shoulders. "I need to get dinner started. You two want to stay?"

"We'd love to. But maybe another time?" Nikki said, half of her attention still on the wedding shots. "I'm kind of beat." Her foot was killing her. She felt Hannah move up beside her. She glanced at her.

Hannah stared at the pictures on the screen, a tight expression pinching her face. Her gaze moved from one photo of the happy couple to the next, a faraway look in her eyes. It was the look she got when she was thinking about Jordan and all that now entailed.

Nikki regretted drawing focus to the pictures. "In fact, we should probably take off," she said quickly. "Hannah, you ready to go?"

At the sound of her name, Hannah snapped back to the moment. "Yes," she said, then cleared her throat. "We should go."

In the car, Nikki sighed. "I'm sorry about that."

"It's all right." Hannah stared out the windshield. "Do you think about her a lot?" she asked.

"Yeah," Nikki said quietly.

"What do you think?"

Nikki looked straight ahead and let her mind wander. "I wonder where she is, what she's doing, if she's okay." She didn't want to say *if she's alive,* but the words still hung in the air between them. "I think about her at the times we'd be at the gym, now that my ankle's getting stronger." She turned and looked at Hannah. "I miss her when I want to just call somebody to talk. Weirdly, she's the one I would've called to talk to about all this."

Hannah remained still except for pressing her lips together in a firm line. "Do you know Jordan and I didn't talk like that?" she asked after a long silence.

"Like what?"

"When something was bothering one of us, or we'd had a bad day, we didn't talk to one another about it. I talked to Kate, or one of my friends. And she…" Hannah paused as though thinking. "I guess she talked to you."

"Not really. I don't think Jordan talked…" With a start, Nikki realized they were speaking of her in the past tense. "I don't think she *talks* much to anyone."

Hannah looked at her. "It's so hard not knowing, isn't it?"

Nikki's phone rang. She checked the screen. "It's Dana." She answered the call. "Hey, how's it going?"

"Pretty good." Dana sounded hurried. "I came into the office this afternoon to catch up on some work, and there's something that came in the mail for Jordan last week while I was gone. I don't think it's work related. Do you or Hannah want to come pick it up?"

"What is it?" Nikki felt Hannah's eyes on her and knew she could hear Dana in the confines of the car.

"I don't know. I didn't open it," Dana said. "It's from some place called Impossible Dreams?"

Hannah stiffened. "I don't want it."

"You know what it is?" Nikki asked in surprise.

"They're tickets, and I don't want them. Tell Dana she can have them. Or you can. Or she can give them to whoever she wants." Hannah's voice trembled.

"Tickets to what?"

"The Pink concert next weekend." Hannah turned away and stared out the side window.

"Nikki? You there?" Dana asked.

"Yeah, hold on a sec." Nikki touched Hannah's hand. "Are you sure?"

"Positive." Hannah's voice was hard.

"Dana? Hannah says it's tickets to the Pink concert, and she doesn't want them." Nikki relayed the message while still watching Hannah. "She said you can have them or give them to someone else."

"I can understand her not wanting to use them without Jordan," Dana said. "That's a nice gift. I heard that concert's been sold out for months."

Hannah's reaction seemed more furious than sad, but Nikki didn't say anything. "I heard that, too." She rubbed the back of Hannah's hand. When she got no response, she pulled away. "Give them to someone who'll enjoy it. Okay?"

"Sure, I'll talk to you soon." Dana hung up.

"I found an email invoice for those when I found the others." Hannah answered the question before Nikki had even settled on what to ask. "They probably weren't even for me. She probably would have told me she was going to work, and then gone with someone else."

Nikki wanted to argue to try to make Hannah feel better. She wanted to point out that Hannah loved Pink, and Jordan did surprise her with those kinds of things periodically, but what was the point? Hannah was right. The tickets could have been for anyone. "I get mad when I think about her sometimes," Nikki said, returning to the previous conversation. She punched the button to start the car. "And I think she's an idiot for risking what she had with you. I always have."

Hannah leaned back against the headrest and closed her eyes. "Thank you," she said softly.

Nikki backed out of the driveway. *And I'm an idiot for risking what I had with you for* her.

❖

Hannah stood in the shower and let the cool water cascade over her skin as she rinsed the shampoo from her hair. It felt good on her sunburned face and neck. The day had been wonderful—the sunshine, the peace that being near the ocean always gave her, the fun of being a part of the large and playful Andrews family, the reward of that first glimpse of a smile from Josh Andrews. *And Nikki.*

Nikki was so easy to be with, so relaxed and unflappable. Hannah had watched her smooth Mrs. Andrews's ruffled feathers when her eldest son and his family still hadn't shown up a half hour after the shoot was to begin. Then she'd turned right around and corralled the three-year-old who thought they were all there just to find sand dollars all afternoon and coaxed her into sitting on great-grandma's lap for a series of shots of the elderly woman and all the children. Nikki was always so gentle, so attentive. Throughout everything with Jordan's disappearance, whatever Hannah had asked her to do, whatever she needed, even when Hannah had been angry and impossible to deal with, Nikki had been there for her. And today, being at Nikki's side, seeing and being in Nikki's life rather than being so wrapped up in hers, had been such an escape.

Of course, she hadn't fully forgotten everything. It was all always right there, Jordan and all the questions, but today they had seemed willing to fall to the back of her mind and allow her some respite. Today had been like the day they had spent at the zoo. Until those damned tickets had shown up. Even before that, though, looking at those wedding pictures had reminded her of everything she once thought she might have someday with Jordan.

She stood under the stream of water for another few minutes, trying to move back into a peaceful place in her mind. She had known since the morning after she and Kate had gone to Zuma Beach that the future she thought she would have with Jordan was gone, and she had known since she had discovered Jordan's infidelity that what she believed they'd had for the past three years never was. So why did it come as such a jolt to her each time she came face-to-face with those truths? She sighed. She knew why.

"Hey." Nikki's voice through the bathroom door startled her. "How does pizza sound for dinner?"

Hannah turned off the water and pulled her towel from the bar. "It sounds like a lot less work than cooking," she said, trying to push the other thoughts aside again. She wanted to go back to how she felt on the beach with Nikki, wanted to forget everything else—maybe forever. There wasn't anything else she could do anyway. Those other thoughts were back, though, along with all the unanswered questions. She began drying herself. When she stepped out of her bedroom in a comfortable pair of athletic shorts and a loose-fitting T-shirt, she found Nikki on the couch flipping through the TV channels and drinking a beer.

Nikki gave her a quick glance—very quick—then returned her attention to the television screen. "The pizza will be here in about forty-five minutes."

Hannah stepped over Nikki's outstretched legs resting on the coffee table, then settled onto the sofa beside her. "Okay," she said, still trying to find a way to gain more control of her thoughts. Maybe it was being back in the condo. The times she had felt the most free were when she had been out in the world. *Not here.*

"Are you all right?" Nikki asked.

Hannah sighed. "Yes," she said wistfully. She wanted it to be true. "No."

"You want to talk about it?" Nikki asked.

Hannah slipped the beer bottle from Nikki's grasp and took a swallow, while she tried to decide. None of it was anything new. "I was thinking in the shower about why seeing those wedding pictures was all it took to ruin such a nice day on the beach. I mean, I know things are over with Jordan and me. I've known it since I found those emails."

"It's only been a few weeks," Nikki said, her tone filled with compassion. "Your head might know all that, but it might take a little while for your heart to catch up."

Hannah took another drink. "I don't think it's that."

"What then?" Nikki retrieved the bottle and took a long pull, then handed it back to Hannah.

Hannah was reluctant to say. She hardly ever spoke about these feelings. It was silly, though, to hold back from Nikki. Nikki already knew from one of those late night conversations they had shared years ago. "It's all that stuff about my birth mother." She picked at the label on the bottle. "I've struggled for so long, trying to come to terms with my own mother not wanting me. Even after all the therapy, I can't help feeling like I must not be worth someone sticking around for. And now, if Jordan simply left her life with me behind like the police suggested, I can't help but feel like maybe I've been right all along."

"Hannah." Nikki covered Hannah's hand with her own, stilling Hannah's fidgeting fingers. "Everything Jordan's done just proves what an idiot *she* is. Anyone with any intelligence would cherish what she had with you."

Nikki's voice was low and gentle and soothed like a lover's tender caress in the afterglow. Hannah looked into her eyes, and in that moment, she believed it. She smiled and held Nikki's hand tightly.

Nikki encircled Hannah's shoulders and pulled her close.

Hannah burrowed into her. "I just wish all of this were over. One way or another." She took another swallow. "I wish Jordan would come home, perfectly fine, and we could just go through separating our lives and move on. I feel so stuck. I mean, I can't change anything that's happened, and because of the circumstances, I can't even act on what I now know. But I don't feel like I can go forward with anything either, not without knowing where Jordan is or if she's ever coming home."

Nikki slowly stroked Hannah's upper arm.

"If she had been here when I found those emails—and I know, if she were, I never would have found them, but still. If she had been, I'd be gone by now. I wouldn't still be living here. I'd have some emotional healing to do, but my life choices would be free of Jordan." Hannah felt herself getting stronger with each word. Or was it angrier? "I'd be done with her, and I wouldn't have to think about where she was or if she's okay..." To her utter shock and humiliation, a rush of tears hit her so fast she didn't have a chance in hell of stopping them.

"Damn it! I'm so mad at her." She pounded her fist into the couch cushion.

Nikki bolted upright and grabbed the beer, setting it on the table, then slipped her arms around Hannah.

Hannah fell against her. "I'm so damned tired of crying over her," she said through short hiccups of breath. "I'm sick to death of not knowing if she left me, or…" She clutched Nikki's shoulders and sobbed.

Nikki held her tightly and rocked her. She let her cry.

Finally, Hannah calmed. "I'm sorry." She sniffed. The blended scents of the sea and sunshine and Nikki's salty sweat—the aroma of their day—soothed her further. "I didn't know that was coming. If I had, I would have done it in the shower."

Nikki smoothed her hair. "You don't need to be sorry," she said softly. "And you don't need to do it by yourself in the shower. That's why I'm here."

Hannah squeezed her eyes shut. *And thank God you are.* She sat up and wiped her eyes on the sleeve of her T-shirt.

The doorbell rang.

"I'll get it." Nikki rose and fished some bills from her front pocket on the way to the door.

Hannah finished off the beer and started toward the kitchen to get a couple more.

"Good afternoon, I'm Detective Morrison with the Santa Monica PD," a woman said from outside. "Are you Hannah Lewis?"

Hannah's heart began to pound.

"No," Nikki said, her tone as shaky as Hannah's knees. "But she's here. Please, come in. I'm Nikki Medina, a friend of hers."

A tall, slender woman in gray slacks and a black blouse stepped through the doorway.

Hannah quickly swiped the rest of the moisture from her cheeks.

Detective Morrison's sharp eyes found her immediately.

"I'm Hannah." She held out her hand and shook the detectives.

Morrison flashed her badge. "Detective Morrison. We spoke on the phone a few weeks ago?"

"Yes, of course," Hannah said. "Please, sit down." She motioned to the recliner with a trembling hand. What had she said not thirty minutes earlier? *I want this over. One way or another.* Could she take it back? What if the detective was there to tell her Jordan was dead?

"We got a hit on Ms. Webber's vehicle over the weekend." She waited for Nikki and Hannah to sit, then went on. "I just finished checking it out and was on my way past here, so I thought I'd stop by and fill you in. I know it's been a while with no news."

"Where's her car?" The words spilled from Hannah's lips without warning.

"I got a call from security at LAX. Ms. Webber's car was in one of the long-term parking lots, and there was a break-in. When they ran the plates, it came back as being connected with our missing persons case, so they called me."

"You didn't find Jordan?" Hannah's emotions vacillated between relief that they hadn't found her dead and disappointment that they hadn't found her alive. Mainly, though, she ached at the knowledge that they still didn't know a thing about Jordan herself. Just her car.

"Well, we did and we didn't, ma'am."

"What does that mean?" Nikki asked, taking Hannah's hand.

"Two tickets to Philadelphia were purchased and used on the day of Ms. Webber's disappearance. They were in her and Ms. Talbot's names."

Ms. Talbot. Liz Talbot. So, there it was. The police had been right all along. Jordan *had* left her for Liz Talbot. *But to Philadelphia?* "What's in Philadelphia?" Hannah asked stupidly, as though the detective would know.

Morrison's manner softened. "I don't know, ma'am," she said kindly.

"Wait a minute," Nikki said. "How do you know Jordan is the one who actually used the ticket? Were there security cameras?"

Morrison's expression remained patient. "We have no reason to pull any security footage. It would take a pretty elaborate scheme to obtain false IDs in advance for someone to pose as a passenger under her name, and there's nothing in this case that points to anything illegal or even suspicious. Not even in Ms. Webber's caseload, according to her supervisor."

Hannah's mind was spinning. She couldn't grasp what was being said. "So, you're saying Jordan woke up that morning, had sex with me, then just got on a plane and flew away with someone else to Philadelphia?"

The detective shook her head, looking uncomfortable. "I don't know about the first part, Ms. Lewis, but everything indicates the second." She paused, then added quietly. "I'm sorry, but we're closing the case."

Nikki jumped up. "How can you close a missing person's case when the person's still missing?" She looked panicked.

"It isn't a crime to be missing, Ms. Medina." Detective Morrison stood. "People walk away from their lives all the time. There's no reason to believe Ms. Webber didn't do exactly that."

"What about their jobs?" Nikki sounded desperate. "Their careers? Jordan wouldn't just walk away from *that*. Isn't *that* worth keeping the case open for?"

"I'm sorry," the detective said again. "I know it sounds strange, but it really does happen all the time."

Nikki turned away and shoved a hand through her hair.

Still stunned, Hannah walked Morrison to the door. "Thank you, Detective, for coming by." She closed it and pressed her forehead to the jamb. *So, that's that.* She had said she wanted it to be over, one way or another, and now it was. *Now what?*

She heard a soft sob and turned to find Nikki standing in the middle of the room, head down, arms folded across her middle, her shoulders shaking. A sudden realization hit her. Nikki had been so strong for her throughout all this, so concerned for Hannah, it had been easy for Hannah to think of her as being there only for her. But Nikki loved Jordan, too. She had her own grief to deal with in learning Jordan had just walked away without a word. Jordan had left Nikki just as cruelly as she had left Hannah. *God, I'm such an ass.*

Hannah moved up behind her and cupped her shoulders, then pressed her cheek to Nikki's nape. She gently turned her until they were face to face and took Nikki in her arms.

Nikki grabbed on to her, pulling Hannah against her, but this time she was the one needing comfort. She was the one who needed to know she wasn't alone and that everything would be all right. She cried into Hannah's neck.

Hannah combed her fingers through Nikki's hair, then rubbed her back. "It's okay," she whispered. "It will all be okay." And somehow, she knew it would be—eventually.

❖

Jordan swallowed a spoonful of chicken broth gratefully and opened her mouth for more. She was so hungry, she wanted to pick up the bowl and drain its contents, but she was trembling too badly. This was her second. The brunette had brought her the first a while earlier, shortly after the bright lights and sermons had ended, just like twice before.

She still didn't know where she was or why she was there, didn't know the brunette's name. Didn't know a lot of things. What she did now know, however, was what the crazy bitch had meant when she'd said if Jordan misbehaved, she'd have to begin again. After she'd run and tried to reach the door and been sedated, she'd awakened once more alone, on the cement slab, the stubble of hair that'd begun growing back shaved smooth again, and the preacher's voice booming.

And *then*, she'd done it again. The next time, she'd run in the opposite direction, but the result had been the same. She had to get smarter.

She'd figured out that each time the room went dim and quiet, each time she was given some broth and led into the hall, another six days had passed, and it was the seventh day of rest.

This time, when the brothers—she didn't remember their names—came for her, she went quietly. In reality, she couldn't have run if she'd wanted to. She was too weak, too emaciated, and too tired. She'd decided it was time for a different tactic. She needed to watch, to observe, to see who and what was behind some of the other doors. She needed more information in order to know what she was dealing with.

She'd wondered several times, while trying to keep her mind occupied with *anything* other than the religious rants, about Hannah and Nikki—what they were doing, if they'd somehow learned anything about what'd happened and where she was. Surely they'd notified the police. Were they any closer to finding her? Every time she thought of them, however, it led her to questions about whether Hannah had found her backup email account, if Nikki had revealed all she knew, if Hannah knew about the boat and Jordan's use of it. *What would Hannah do with all that?* Jordan didn't want to think about it. All she knew right now was that it seemed as though no help was coming and she needed to figure out her own escape.

Now she walked between the men down the long corridor, past the T, to the double doors at the far end. As they entered the room beyond, the lights flickered on automatically, revealing a shower and bathtub along one wall, a sink and counter along the other, and a bench stretching between them that held a neatly folded stack of clothing and towels. A toiletry kit sat beside it.

Someone came in behind them. "Since you're unsteady, I think a bath would be best," crazy bitch said. She moved past them and began filling the tub.

The two men helped Jordan to the bench, then stepped back and looked away.

Jordan breathed in the soft flowery fragrance of the salts being added to the steaming water and closed her eyes. It reminded her of times she'd caught the first scent of a woman in front of her in a line, or leaning in to say something on a first meeting. Mostly, though, the heat rising from the water warmed her exposed skin.

When the bathtub was full, crazy bitch nodded to the men, and they helped Jordan into it.

She couldn't have done it without their assistance. Her once beautiful and toned athletic body had been reduced to slack, blotchy skin that hung loosely on her frame and weakened muscles that could barely hold her weight standing, never mind as she lowered herself into the tub. As the water enveloped her like a lover's embrace, she moaned and reclined into it. It burned the abrasions where her skin had repeatedly scraped against the cement slab, but even that sensation comforted her. She let out a deep sigh.

"You can relax for a while, and when you're ready, you can clean yourself with these." Crazy bitch set a washcloth and a bar of soap on the edge of the tub, then sat on the bench.

"You're going to watch?" Jordan asked, only half sarcastically.

"I'm going to pray." She closed her eyes.

"So, all of you are religious—" She almost said nuts, but caught herself. "People?"

"Yes, we are. We're servants of our Lord."

"Then why are those guys allowed to hang around when I'm naked? Isn't that some kind of sin?" Jordan wanted to get the woman talking, wanted to find out as much as she could about what flavor Kool-Aid these fruitcakes were drinking.

Crazy bitch opened her eyes and gave Jordan a searching look, as though trying to determine if her question was sincere. "You're naked as a baby is naked. You've been reborn into the light and are now being washed clean. There's no temptation for them in seeing a baby naked. Also, rebirthing is arduous and exhausting. You needed their support."

"What about you? You could support me." Jordan made sure there was a challenge in her voice. *Liz* would rise to it. She needed to see if any part of Liz was still around. "You can kick my ass at racquetball. Surely, you can help me down a hallway." The Liz Jordan she knew wouldn't be able to resist that one.

There was no reaction, not even the hint of a shift in expression. "You're in Satan's grasp, in the clutches of homosexuality. For you to be too close to or touched by another woman would release Satan's power over you. You'll be cleansed and exorcised of it, but at this point, it's too strong for you to fight."

Is she serious? "Believe me, honey," Jordan said derisively. "In your case, there's nothing to fight." At least her question had been answered. There really was no Liz.

Crazy bitch folded her hands and closed her eyes again. Her lips began to move ever so slightly.

Jordan lay back in the water. She was in deep shit. She wondered again who was in charge, who was directing this horror movie. Whoever it was had to be a *complete* lunatic. Of course she knew about the ex-gay ministries and groups that claimed to "cure homosexuality," and "save the souls of the sinners." Was that what this was, some kind of conversion program? But that didn't make sense. Conversion therapy was now illegal in California. Hell, even Exodus, the largest ex-gay ministry in the world, had disbanded and offered a public apology for their claims that homosexuality could be cured. And even then, most of those programs targeted teenagers whose parents signed legal consent forms, and adults who entered the program voluntarily. They didn't kidnap full-grown adults and hold them captive. She was an attorney, for God's sake. If she ever got out of there—no, *when* she got out of there—she'd bring whoever was behind this down so hard, there'd be brain matter on the pavement. They were all certifiably insane. She shot crazy bitch a glare.

Except for the brunette. Jordan thought about her. There was still something so familiar about her. What was it? Whatever it was, *she*, at least, was still holding on to enough sanity to be scared in this loony bin. And Jordan was, too.

She dunked her head beneath the water and scrubbed her hands over her face and the prickly cap of her scalp. It was time to see what was next. She washed herself with the soap she'd been given, only then realizing how badly she'd needed it. If her calculations were correct, she'd been locked in that room for a little over three weeks. When she'd finished, she managed to get to her feet in the tub. "Can I have that towel?" she asked flatly. "I'd come get it, but I wouldn't want to lose control and endanger your immortal soul."

Crazy bitch remained still except for the movement of her lips a few seconds longer, then opened her eyes. She did as Jordan asked, then walked to the door. "You can dress in those clothes." She indicated the folded pile on the bench. "We'll be waiting in the hall."

Jordan dried herself and picked up a pair of white cotton underwear, staring at them in amazement. *Granny panties?* She pulled them on. The bra was just as nondescript and fit awkwardly, but after being completely exposed for so long, it felt good to be covered. Finally, she donned the shapeless, tan, cotton dress, then slid her feet into a pair of white canvas slip-on Keds, completing the outfit identical to the ones worn by crazy bitch and the brunette. She found a toothbrush, toothpaste, and dental floss in the toiletry kit. When she finished, she stepped into the corridor and found the two men waiting for her.

They both smiled and each moved to take one of Jordan's arms as they had before.

"I'm fine," she said, pulling away. "I can make it on my own." As one knee threatened to buckle, she hoped she was right.

They led her directly to the door she'd seen crazy bitch coming out of the first time she'd attempted an escape—at least, she thought it was the same one. They all looked alike. One of the men opened it with a key, while the other stood behind her. The first entered and stepped aside.

Jordan froze.

A long table dominated the center of the white room, at the end of which sat the Reverend Thomas A. Palmer, the minister of the church Jordan's parents had insisted the family attend during her childhood and adolescent years. He was older and heavier, but definitely Reverend Palmer. Jordan had grown up listening to him rail against fraternizing with the devil in all manner of ways, not the least of which was homosexuality. Then, when she was fourteen, he'd started an ex-gay ministry for teens at the urging of several concerned parents. That'd been the very thing that'd prompted Jordan to keep her blossoming sexuality to herself—that *and* a private conversation with the *Mrs.* Reverend Palmer, in which she'd promised Jordan a more interesting way of *fighting off her demons* than sitting around in a circle, confessing her temptations and memorizing Bible verses. Jordan had sometimes wondered if Loraine Palmer had managed to break free of her lie of a life and let herself love a woman.

To Reverend Palmer's right sat Jordan's mother, and behind her stood the formidable Jonathan Webber.

Stunned, Jordan stumbled backward, almost collapsing. She was caught and gently helped to a chair at the end of the table opposite the others. Her mouth was dry, and she began to shake again.

Reverend Palmer smiled.

Jordan remembered that smile. She'd hated it. It'd always felt creepy, as though it was the prelude to something horrible like, "I'm sorry, but your puppy is dead," or, as it'd been back then, "God loves you, but you could still burn in hell for eternity if you trip up in the slightest." Or, as it was now, "I'm insane, and your fate is entirely in my hands."

"Hello, Jordan," he said, lacing his fingers together on the table in front of him. "It's been a long time."

Her parents didn't smile. Nor did they speak.

"Can Brother Isaac get you anything?" Palmer asked.

Jordan steeled herself. Anger spread through her in a slow burn at the realization that these three were behind all this. She wanted to leap across the table and tear into them for everything they'd put her through in the past several weeks, but the last thing she could take was to *begin again*. "What the hell is this?" she asked, holding her voice steady. Still, it came out weaker than she would have liked. "Why am I here? And why the hell are *you* here?" She swept her gaze over all three of them.

"You're here to be cured of homosexuality and liberated from Satan's clutches," Palmer said, his demeanor composed. "*We're* here as God's servants to assist in your redemption."

It was almost exactly what crazy bitch had said. They were *all* crazy. Jordan looked at her father. He'd never believed anything about God, not even back when he and her mother insisted on going to church. It'd all been for show as he was working his way up the rungs of the corporate ladder with his sights set on becoming a partner.

Jordan's father met her eyes, cool superiority in his own. He still said nothing.

"What do you want?" she asked him.

"He wants the salvation of your soul," Palmer answered for him.

A harsh laugh tore from Jordan's throat. "All right, let's go with that for a second." Her gaze never wavered from her father. "Why now? You haven't given a shit about my soul, or any other part of me, in…Well, I'd say *ever*."

"Your parents love you, Jordan. They want their daughter back in the loving arms of God and the bosom of her family. It's never too late for that." Palmer rose and walked around the end of the table. "So much so that your father has become the sole investor in our mission to save as many souls as possible from the degradation and damnation of homosexuality. As soon as we have you to hold up as a shining example of what we can do even with adult homosexuals who've been steeped in a life of sin for years, there will be no end to the number of families who will seek us out."

Jordan glared at him. That might be why *he* thought she was there, but she didn't buy for a nanosecond that was her father's motivation. She could tell she wouldn't get another answer now, though. "Uh-huh. Rich families, no doubt?"

There was that smile again. "It isn't about money. It's about doing God's work."

"And are you going to kidnap all of them like you did me?"

"If need be."

Jordan wanted to be able to laugh at the sheer absurdity of it all, but Palmer's serious tone and her father's cold expression terrified her. *They fucking mean it.* And what was her mother thinking? She glanced at her. She'd never been able to see past the mask Marion Webber kept so firmly in place, and now was no exception. She turned her attention to her father. She knew this was all him. She didn't know why, but it had to be him. "Conversion therapy's illegal in California—you know that—never mind kidnapping and assault. You're all insane."

"You're no longer in California." Again, Palmer answered instead of Jordan's father.

She turned on him. "All the better. That turns the kidnapping into a federal offense, which brings the FBI to the party. You're breaking so many laws, you'll never see the light of day again. When I get out of here, I'll make sure of it."

"We adhere only to God's law. No other," Palmer said resolutely. "And you won't be getting out of here until God cures you."

The declaration sent a chill up Jordan's spine. *Holy fuck!* From what she'd seen of this place, they might very well be able to make good on that threat. *No. I can find a way out. I will find a way out.* She had to think…and watch.

"Brother Isaac and Brother Noah will escort you," Palmer was still talking, "where Sister Katherine is waiting for you. She will explain some of the details of your redemption program."

Panic clutched at Jordan's gut. She took a deep breath. She had to stay calm. She had to be able to think. There had to be some way out of here. She just had to find it. And Hannah… Hannah and Nikki had to be working with the police. *They have to be looking for me. Don't they?*

Chapter Twelve

Nikki let herself into the condo and made her way toward the kitchen to put away the groceries she'd bought for dinner.

"What's all that?" Kate asked from her sprawled position on the couch, her fingers moving swiftly over her phone screen. Her appointment with Francois had made it impossible for anyone to mistake her for Hannah any longer, since her blond hair was now short, spiked, and had pink tips.

"I promised Hannah spaghetti tonight." Nikki glanced at the PI report on the credenza, as she did every time she passed it. She still intended to read through it, but they already knew all the basics.

It'd been three weeks since the police found Jordan's car and closed the case—a little over six since her actual disappearance—and during that time, there'd been no activity on her credit cards, no usage on her phone, and no contact from her of any kind. It was strange, but then not. On the one hand, Jordan would need access to money, wherever she was. On the other, she had tons of it, certainly far more than was reflected on the statement that came to the house for her and Hannah's shared account and probably even more than her accountant handled. She'd once mentioned having investments all over the place. And the phone? Well, if someone was truly leaving her life behind, she'd have no use for existing contacts and a number at which she could be reached. Hannah had considered having Lantz check into any possible connections Jordan might have in Philadelphia, but decided if that's where Jordan wanted to be, that's where she should be. She'd thanked him for the work he'd done and taken the report.

It *was* weird, though. Nikki kept remembering what Detective Morrison had said about people walking out of their lives all the time, and all the people they left behind probably thought it was weird, too. Having to admit to herself that Jordan hadn't given any more thought to her than to anyone else had been a blow. Jordan had always said being best friends meant something, but apparently, it didn't. Every time she thought about it, she got angry. Aleyda reminded her that was a good thing, though, that anger was part of the grief process.

"Is there enough for me," Kate asked, following Nikki into the kitchen.

Nikki smiled. "Always." She and Hannah had continued spending a lot of time together even though Nikki went home most nights, unless they'd stayed up too late watching movies, and in the process, she'd grown more accustomed to Kate. She'd taken some getting used to, but Nikki was actually starting to enjoy her. "I thought you had a date, though."

"I do." Kate slouched against the counter. "But I don't feel like going out."

"Hey, you," Hannah said in evident surprise as she came in the back door with a basketful of cut roses. She ran a hand over the small of Nikki's back.

Nikki's body responded as it always did, but that was something else she'd gotten used to—holding herself in check. "Hi," she said. "How was your day?"

Hannah bumped Kate aside and retrieved a vase from the cupboard above her. "It's been nice. Kate and I went shopping for a while, then saw a movie."

"Ah, the life of teachers during summer break."

"We only have two weeks of vacation left," Kate said. "We have to start doing *something*."

"What did you see?" Nikki filled the vase with water for Hannah and set it on the counter.

Hannah shrugged. "What was the name of it, Kate?"

Kate gave her a smirk. "Did you even watch it?"

"I looked at the pictures." Hannah began trimming the stems and arranging the flowers in the vase.

Ever since the news about the plane tickets and the official closing of Jordan's case, Hannah had been different. She'd seemed calmer and more at peace, no longer worried that Jordan might be dead in a ditch somewhere. She told Nikki she'd rather know Jordan was someplace happy, even if it was with someone else, than to have learned something horrible had happened to her. However, there was a distracted and far-away, concerned look in her eyes much of the time. Nikki often wondered what she was thinking, but when she'd asked, Hannah simply smiled and offered some vague reassurance.

"Since you're here early, can we eat early?" Hannah asked Nikki. "I'm starving."

"That's because you picked at your lunch," Kate said, holding up a pink rose and sniffing it. "What's bugging you?"

"Nothing's bugging me." It wasn't convincing.

"Oh, come on. That was pathetic. I know you *way* too well to buy that," Kate said. "But I'll bet even Nikki wasn't fooled by that denial."

Nikki smiled at Hannah as she started dinner. She liked this. She'd have to remember to sick Kate on Hannah when she wanted to know something.

"I've just been thinking." Hannah finished the flower arrangement and set it on the table.

"About what?" Kate sounded impatient.

Hannah gave her a cautious look. "That thing we always argue about."

Kate's eyes widened. "You're thinking about not being gay anymore?"

Hannah rolled her eyes. "The *other* thing."

Kate furrowed her brow, obviously in deep thought. Then she gasped. "Nooooo. We've settled that."

"I need to, Kate," Hannah said in a rush. "This whole thing with Jordan has—"

"Whoa, whoa. Hello?" Nikki waved a hand in the air. "You two can't do that twin telepathy thing. I want to know what's going on, too."

Kate glared at Hannah. "She wants to find our birth mother."

"Really?" Nikki looked to Hannah, then back to Kate.

"Why now?" Kate asked, her tone hard. "What does Jordan's disappearing act have to do with finding the woman who never wanted us?"

"Jordan leaving and cheating on me with all those other women has brought up all my feelings of abandonment again." Hannah looked at Nikki. "I thought I'd dealt with them in therapy, but Jordan leaving me for someone else, without the slightest hint, without a word..." Tears welled in her eyes. "It's the same feeling I have about my mother, like no one will ever stay."

Instinctively, Nikki slipped an arm around her shoulders.

"*I've* stayed," Kate said, her voice rising. "And I always will. Doesn't *that* count? And Mom and Dad never let us down. Doesn't that count too?"

"Oh, Katie, of course it does." Hannah took Kate's hand. "You know I love you, and you know how important you are to me. It's just... If I could know what her circumstances were... Maybe she *couldn't* keep us, or she didn't feel like she had a choice. That would make a difference. Wouldn't that matter to you?"

Kate softened slightly. "I don't know, Hannah." She lifted a shoulder, shook her head, and grimaced all at once in that conflicted way people do. "I just don't need to. I still think she had her chance to know how amazing we are, and she threw it away. It's *her* loss."

"But I think I do, Kate," Hannah said softly. "And I don't want to sneak around behind your back to do it or lie to you. I want you with me."

Kate studied her. "Will you give me some time to think about it? To get used to the idea? Because I *really* don't want to do it."

Hannah's face brightened. "You *will* think about it, though?"

Kate frowned. "I will." She turned to Nikki. "Now, what about dinner? What can we do to speed this up?"

When they'd eaten, Nikki picked up Lantz's report, while Hannah and Kate squabbled over what movie to watch. After listening to what Hannah had said about needing to find her birth mother so she could know the circumstances, Nikki had begun to wonder if there could still be something more to know about Jordan's disappearance. Granted, there might very well be nothing new, but she needed to make sure she hadn't overlooked anything.

She'd been surprised at some of the things she'd read in Jordan's journal—the depth to which Jordan felt unworthy to be loved, the reason she slept with so many women being that those moments were the only times she felt loved, and as soon as it was over, how she felt lonelier than she had even as a child—but they had helped her understand Jordan better, helped her understand the things she did. Maybe there was something, some small thing, in the report that would shed some light in some way. It wouldn't be anything personal, but there might be something.

"What are you doing?" Hannah asked.

"I'm going to read through this." Nikki held up the file.

Hannah arched an eyebrow, but only tapped the sofa cushion beside her. "Can you sit with us while you do it? Kate wants to watch a scary movie, and I don't want to be on the end."

Nikki laughed. She ignored the spark of arousal at the thought of being so close to Hannah all evening. "Sure."

They settled in, Hannah in the middle, and Kate pressed play as Nikki started reading.

The report was dry and highlighted all the things they already knew, either from their own inquiries, from the police, or from their conversations with Lantz. Nikki read every word carefully, though. She'd initially only skimmed the list of names he'd compiled from Jordan's email and a log of the responses he'd gotten when he'd contacted the women, but when she'd finished the rest of the report, she returned to it and read through it slowly. It was arranged by date, earliest to most recent. When her gaze landed on the last one, she tensed. It'd come in three days after Jordan went missing. It read: *Hey, what happened to you on Saturday? I waited for you all day. Left a bunch of voice mails. Call me.* It was from Kristin West, one of Nikki's exes.

"What's the matter?" Hannah asked.

"Hm?" was all Nikki could manage.

"You went all stiff," Hannah said. "Did you find something?"

Nikki only half heard. *Jordan was supposed to see Kristin the day she went missing? Why?* There was really only one reason Jordan spent time with women who didn't play sports.

"Nikki?" Hannah's hand was warm on Nikki's thigh through her jeans.

Nikki swallowed. "Just…something…" She retreated from all the questions suddenly inundating her. "Do you remember Kristin?"

Hannah looked at her blankly. "Kristin who?"

"Kristin West," Nikki said. "I went out with her for about a year. You met her at my birthday party the first year you and Jordan were dating."

Hannah shook her head. "Sorry."

"Anyway, apparently, she and Jordan were supposed to meet the day Jordan disappeared. Kristin sent her an email a few days later asking why she didn't show up."

Hannah looked at her expectantly.

"I don't know. I just think it's weird." Why did she think that, though? She and Kristin had broken up two years earlier and hadn't even crossed paths since. She and Jordan had never talked about exes being off limits. It'd never come up. *Was that because Jordan just hit on friends' exes without saying anything?*

"Are you okay?" Hannah asked.

"I'll be fine," Nikki said, trying to shrug the whole thing off. But she couldn't. It niggled at her, demanding attention, even after she closed the file and set it aside. *Why do I care about someone I broke up with two years ago?* She was surprised at the anger behind the question. It wasn't at Kristin, though. It was at Jordan. Weren't there enough women in the world for her to sleep with without dipping into Nikki's relatively small pool of exes?

"You're fidgeting," Hannah whispered. "Do you want to talk about it?"

Yes. Nikki did want to talk about it, but not with Hannah. She wanted to talk to Kristin. "I think I'm going to go," she said as she rose.

"Where?" Hannah asked.

"I want to talk to Kristin. See if she knows anything."

"Lantz didn't contact her?" Hannah was up now, too.

"She didn't respond."

Kate paused the movie. "What's going on?" she asked.

Hannah quickly filled her in, then returned her attention to Nikki. "Can we call her?"

We? Nikki glanced at her. "I thought you didn't want contact with any of the women Jordan was sleeping with."

Hannah hesitated. "I don't want you to do it alone. You seem upset."

Nikki was touched by her concern, and a little surprised. This was the new Hannah, though. "I don't have her number anymore, and she was never listed. But I know where she lives." She pulled her keys from her pocket. "If she still lives there. I'm okay, though. Really."

"I'm going with you," Hannah said firmly.

Kate jumped up. "I want to go, too."

"Why?" Nikki and Hannah said simultaneously.

"Are you kidding? I love drama. I'm not going to miss this," Kate said with a scoff. "I just wish we could stop on the way and get popcorn."

Thirty minutes later, Nikki stood staring at the numbers 319 on the apartment door in front of her and remembered all the times she'd stood there in the past, all the times she'd kissed Kristin up against it—either on the inside or out—all the times she'd left in the early hours of the morning. She wondered how many times Jordan had done the same. She shook off the thought. *Why does it matter?* She knocked.

"Who is it?" someone called from within. It wasn't Kristin.

"Robin?" Robin had been Kristin's roommate the whole time Kristin and Nikki had dated. They'd been friends since high school. She was nice, but she'd always kept somewhat of a distance. Nikki leaned closer. "Hey. It's Nikki. Nikki Medina." She added the latter to cover the passage of time.

"Nikki?" There was surprise—and maybe a little excitement— in Robin's response. The deadbolt clicked, and the door opened. "Oh my gosh, it's great to see you."

Nikki smiled. "Thanks. You, too. How are you?" Nikki shot a glance past her into the living room.

"I'm great," Robin said, smiling at Hannah and Kate, in turn. She lingered on Kate, maybe noting the mirror resemblance to Hannah, maybe the pink-tipped spikes. "Come on in."

Inside, an awkward moment passed. Nikki wasn't sure how to start. "Is Kristin here?" she asked finally.

"No, she's not." A question flashed in Robin's eyes before it quickly turned to unease. "You're not dating her again, are you?"

"No," Nikki said, a bit too quickly. Then she wondered about Robin's response. "Why?"

Robin's cheeks pinkened. "No reason." She waved a hand. "Kristin's out of town for the week. She'll be back on Sunday."

"Oh." Nikki heard her own disappointment in the single word. Then she realized Robin had to know about Kristin and Jordan. "Well, maybe you can help. Do you remember my friend, Jordan?"

Robin's lips curved in a faltering smile. "Yes."

Nikki thought she saw a hint of wariness pass through Robin's eyes, but she continued. "She went missing about a month and a half ago, and we found an email from Kristin…"

Robin looked down at the floor.

"You already know all this, don't you?" Nikki asked.

"Yes," Robin said softly, returning her focus to Nikki.

At least that cut down on the amount of needed explanation. "Do you know how long they'd been seeing each other?" Nikki asked, cutting to the chase.

Robin looked uneasily at Hannah and Kate.

"I'm sorry," Nikki said. "This is Hannah and Kate Lewis. Hannah is Jordan's girlfriend—"

"*Was* Jordan's girlfriend," Hannah said, extending her hand. "Until I found out about many more like Kristin. So don't worry. You're not telling me anything I don't already know."

Robin seemed to relax some. She shook hands with Hannah and Kate.

"So, did you know Kristin was supposed to get together with Jordan the day Jordan disappeared?"

Robin nodded. "Kristin went to the marina to meet her. They were going out on the boat, but Jordan never showed. Kristin hasn't heard from her since."

"How long had they been seeing each other?" Nikki asked.

Robin waited a beat, a shadow of regret darkening her eyes. "A long time, Nikki."

And suddenly, Nikki knew why she was there. She needed to know. She needed to hear the words actually spoken that made it impossible for her to deny the truth she knew in her heart. "How long?" She sank her teeth into her lower lip to keep it from trembling.

"They started sleeping together about six months into your and Kristin's relationship."

There it was. She'd survived it, but it hurt like a bitch. How could Jordan do that to *her*? Nikki couldn't speak.

Robin gently touched her arm. "I'm sorry, Nikki."

"Why didn't you tell me?" Nikki asked finally, but she heard the words in Hannah's voice.

And Robin's answer came in her own. "She's my best friend. It's just what she does."

The ride home was silent. When Nikki pulled the car up to the curb in front of the condo, both Hannah and Kate opened their doors to get out. Nikki sat stone still, staring out into the twilight.

Hannah paused and turned around. "Aren't you coming in?" she asked. She covered Nikki's hand on the steering wheel with her own.

"No," Nikki said, her voice gravelly. "I need to be alone."

"Nikki," Hannah said gently, "I know what you're feeling. Obviously. Please, come in. I'll send Kate home. Let me be here for you tonight."

Nikki snorted. "Like *I've* been there for you?" She shook her head. "Hannah, I am *so* sorry."

"For what?" Hannah asked with a note of incredulity. "You've been by my side through this whole thing."

"I'm sorry I never told you. I should've in the very beginning. If I had, you wouldn't be going through any of this now, because *you're* smart enough to have dumped her sorry ass right then. I'm sorry for telling you she's my best friend and that's just how she is and thinking it would make up for anything or ease the amount of pain you're feeling. I'm sorry for choosing her over you, and for being a crappy friend…"

"You're not a crappy friend." Hannah pressed her hands to Nikki's cheeks and turned her to face her. "You're a wonderful friend. I couldn't have gotten through this without you. Please, come inside. The last thing you need right now is to be alone."

"If I were a good friend, I'd have a good best friend. I wouldn't have a best friend who sleeps with *my* girlfriends at the same time she's cheating on hers." Nikki's voice broke. "I'm sorry, Hannah. For everything."

"Nikki, please, come inside with me."

"Just go. I'll be fine."

"Nikki—"

"Hannah, go." Nikki's voice rose in the quiet of the car.

Reluctantly, Hannah climbed out and closed the door.

Nikki sped away. She wanted as much distance as she could get between her and anything to do with Jordan Webber.

❖

Nikki flopped onto her couch. She'd tried to escape her pain and regret, first with a grueling run on the beach, then a hammering game of one-on-one at Delia's, during which Delia was not allowed to ask any questions, and finally, a boxing match with the wall of her parking structure until her fist bled. Her earlier anger had spiked into rage at several points, but now she was just exhausted. She draped her arm over her face and closed her eyes, but sleep didn't come.

She had no idea how long she'd been lying there when a sharp rap sounded at her door. She ignored it. It was the middle of the night, for God's sake.

Another knock, this time louder.

"Nikki?" It was Hannah.

Nikki groaned. She couldn't see her yet. She had to pull herself together before that happened. She turned over and burrowed into the back of the sofa.

"Nikki?" Hannah yelled. Then she started pounding. "I know you're in there. I saw your car."

"Hey, shut up, will you?" Bernie from next door hollered. "It's two in the morning."

Grudgingly, Nikki rolled over and off the couch, landing on the floor on all fours. She pushed to her feet and staggered to the door. "Come in," she said as she swung it open and turned back toward the couch. "And thank you for accepting my invitation to come over."

"Okay, I deserve that," Hannah said, closing the door behind her. "I've been mean to you once or twice when I've been upset."

Nikki groaned and dropped back down to where she'd been lying. Her muscles had stiffened in the time she'd been trying to sleep. The past three months with little exercise—six weeks in the cast and another almost seven dealing with Jordan's ordeal—had left her sorely out of shape. "What are you doing here? I told you I wanted to be alone."

"Yes, you did." Hannah set her purse on the coffee table. "But when Delia called, frantic, wanting to know what the hell had happened that made you go over there and run her into the ground under the pretense of a basketball game, then leave skid marks pulling away, I knew leaving you alone wasn't working." She perched on the edge of the sofa cushion and gazed down at her. "You smell horrible. What have you been doing?"

"Running. And basketball." Nikki looked at Hannah, suddenly glad she was there.

Hannah wrinkled her nose. "Let's get you into the shower. You'll feel better in the morning if you go to bed fresh."

"I don't think I can," Nikki said. "I hurt."

"I'll help you."

The mere thought of Hannah helping her into the shower brought Nikki's body screaming to life. "That's okay," she said quickly. She clasped Hannah's hand as it closed over the button of her jeans. "I can do it." The last thing she needed tonight was to add raging arousal to her ragged emotions and aching limbs.

Hannah looked at her as innocently as Bambi blinking his long lashes in the sunshine.

"Really, I got it," Nikki said, patting Hannah's hand.

Hannah looked down to where their fingers touched. "Oh, my God." She gasped. "You're bleeding."

"It's no big deal," Nikki said, struggling to sit up.

"It's always at least a little bit of a big deal when your blood is on the outside." Hannah examined Nikki's skinned knuckles. "Wash it out really well in the shower, and I'll see if I can find something to wrap it in."

The hot water worked out some of Nikki's aches, and while the soap stung the abrasions on her hand, she felt a lot better when she stepped out of the shower. She did find herself wishing she weren't alone, though. She briefly wondered about a world in which she could shower with Hannah.

"Here," Hannah said at the same instant the door opened.

Nikki jumped and grabbed a towel. *This* wasn't that world.

Hannah stuck her arm through the opening, offering some clothes. "I got you these to sleep in."

Relaxing some, Nikki took the T-shirt and underwear. Had Hannah gone through her dresser? As quickly as she'd asked the question in her mind, an answer came. It seemed only fair. Nikki knew where everything was in Hannah's house, had put away her laundry, and even folded her panties. *That was a tough day.*

"I found some gauze and tape to wrap your hand when you're finished," Hannah said without interruption.

"Great. Thanks." Nikki calmed more. She was kind of liking this. It was helping her let go of everything else she'd been feeling all night.

She found Hannah waiting for her, seated sideways on the edge of the bed and the blankets pulled back. She stood in the doorway, wanting so much for the circumstances of finding Hannah waiting for her in her bedroom to be different. She thought of what Hannah had said earlier about her birth mother's circumstances possibly making a difference and realized just how important circumstances could truly be.

"Come here." Hannah patted the sheet in front of her.

Nikki complied, although she wasn't sure it was a good idea if she ever wanted to be able to sleep in her bed again.

Hannah took her hand and examined the scrapes and bruises. "Wow, you really went at it, didn't you?"

"I was mad," Nikki said.

Hannah lifted her gaze to Nikki's. "I know," she said softly.

And Nikki understood that what Hannah knew was how much her heart hurt.

Hannah rested Nikki's hand in her lap and opened a tube of antibiotic cream. She gently rubbed some into the abrasion. Her touch was tender and light. Her fingers moved slowly.

She was so close, Nikki could smell her shampoo and had to tamp down the urge to breathe her in completely.

Hannah pulled a gauze strip from a box and began wrapping Nikki's hand. When she was finished, she taped it securely, then pressed her lips to the bandage. She kept them there for a long moment. When she looked up, her green eyes were darker than Nikki had ever seen them.

It would take only the slightest movement to close the distance between them, to feel Hannah's lips pressed to hers as she'd always wanted. *Am I dreaming? Did I go to sleep?* Nikki swallowed. "Hannah—"

Hannah touched a fingertip to Nikki's lips. "Shh. It's okay. We can do this," she whispered.

For a split second, Nikki wanted to do it for the sole purpose of taking something of Jordan's, but the fire of her long-denied desire flamed in an instant and burned away everything else. She shoved her fingers into Hannah's hair and crushed her lips to hers. Her center flooded with wet heat. She parted her lips, and Hannah's tongue swept into her mouth, dancing against hers. She felt Hannah's hand beneath her shirt, her nails dragging across her stomach. She moaned at the hard throb between her legs.

Without warning, Jordan was there in Nikki's mind—Jordan with Hannah, Jordan with Kristin. Jordan with every woman Nikki had ever wanted. Her anger flared again. She thrust her hands under Hannah's shirt and kneaded her way up the smooth skin of her back, around to her breasts. She wanted to take, to take what was Jordan's. To take what she'd wanted for so long, but stayed away from out of *respect* for Jordan. She squeezed Hannah's breasts, catching the nipples between her fingers through the thin bra.

Hannah arched and cried out. "Nikki!" She pushed Nikki backward onto the pillows and crawled up over her body. Her thigh pressed between Nikki's as one of Nikki's came up between hers. She ground against it. Her mouth came to Nikki's again, firmly, but this time softer.

Nikki tasted her, smelled her, felt her body against her. Not Jordan's girlfriend, but Hannah. *No.* She heard the word as a scream in her mind. *No. Not like this.* She wanted Hannah, but not out of anger or hurt—or revenge. *What am I doing?* And what was Hannah doing? If she ever got to be with Hannah, she wanted it to be out of desire, maybe even love, and she wanted to know that Hannah wanted her the same way. She never wanted to be a mistake Hannah would regret. She had to stop.

Just as Nikki started to push Hannah away from her, Hannah pulled back.

"Wait," Hannah said, breathing hard. "I don't... I'm sorry." She dropped onto the mattress beside Nikki.

Nikki struggled to catch her breath. She stared at the ceiling. What had she almost done?

"I'm sorry," Hannah said again into the quiet.

"*I'm* sorry," Nikki whispered.

"I started it," Hannah said. She pulled the hem of her shirt down. "I think I just... I wanted to get even with Jordan, for both of us. But I shouldn't have..."

Nikki turned her head and considered her. "I had the same thought. I don't think it would have worked, though."

"I don't ever want to be like her." Hannah rolled onto her side and touched Nikki's arm. "And I don't ever want to hurt you."

"And *I* don't ever want to hurt *you*...again." Nikki looked into Hannah's eyes. They were still a couple of shades darker than normal.

Hannah gave her a tender smile and laced her fingers with Nikki's. "Apology accepted."

And with those two words, Nikki felt Jordan's secret, one she'd hated carrying for so long, fall away. But what about the shadows in her own life?

CHAPTER THIRTEEN

Hannah opened her eyes and blinked, trying to remember where she was. With her next breath, she caught the scent of Nikki's lotus petal body wash where she had lain against the pillows, fresh from the shower, the night before, and the full memory rushed in. Her lips had been so soft, even as the kiss had been demanding, her body so firm beneath Hannah's, her hands... Oh God, her hands had felt so good. Now, Hannah was alone—Nikki had insisted she stay for what little remained of the night and take the bed—but she still felt Nikki there with her.

She had grown used to Nikki's presence over the past seven weeks and to knowing that even if she wasn't physically there, Hannah still wasn't alone. All it would take was a phone call. This was different, though. This morning, Hannah actually *felt* her. She touched a finger to her lips, reliving that first kiss, remembering the dark, hungry look in Nikki's deep brown eyes right before she had claimed Hannah's mouth with her own. Had it been hunger or anger driving her?

It didn't matter. Hannah was the one who had started it all. She grimaced. *What was I thinking?*

She hadn't been thinking. That was the problem. After the conversation with Kristin's roommate, Hannah had gotten even madder at Jordan than she had been before. It was bad enough Jordan would betray *her*, but her *and* her own best friend? Hannah now fully understood she had never had any idea who Jordan was. And once she had gotten to Nikki's and seen Nikki was okay, the anger that had been simmering all evening ignited, and she just wanted to get even. This morning, in the light of day, she saw how ridiculous that was, but last night, in that moment when she was holding Nikki's hand, when Nikki had been so close, it made perfect sense. Thank God she had caught herself.

Not that sex with Nikki would be any kind of hardship or sacrifice. She remembered thinking, when they had first met, that if she hadn't already accepted a date with Jordan, she would definitely have been interested. Nikki was sweet and intelligent and attentive. She had interesting things to say about almost any topic, *and* she had been sexy as hell in her tight black jeans and tank top.

Jordan had already asked Hannah out, though, and Jordan… Well, Jordan seemed to be all those things, and then some. She *seemed* to be everything Hannah had dreamed of and thought important at the time. She was an up-and-coming attorney with success written all over her. She had a ton of charm and knew exactly how to use it. And she had a charisma that demanded attention. When Hannah was with her, all eyes were on them. Now, Hannah understood that those were all the same things that drew other women to Jordan as well. She also understood what a fool she had been for falling for any of it.

She wondered what things would be like had she met Nikki first. She would have gone out with her. She knew that. Would she have considered anything serious with her, though? Whereas Jordan was clearly on her way to success, Nikki had struck Hannah as the creative artist, struggling to earn a living through her passion. She recalled the first time she had seen Nikki's apartment when she and Jordan had stopped by to lure her to a surprise birthday party her family was throwing for her. She had thought the tiny, one-bedroom place with its worn carpeting and view of the parking lot was romantic in that *follow my dream* kind of way. But here it was, three years later, and she was surprised Nikki still lived in the same place, especially now that she had gotten a glimpse of her photography business and how in demand she was.

Hannah took in Nikki's bedroom—the walnut dresser, one mahogany nightstand and the other birch. The head and footboards of the bed were marred, giving the impression they had been handed down from some family member who had redecorated. It should seem shabby by applied reason, particularly in contrast to the perfectly matched, modern style bedroom Hannah had awakened in at Jordan's for the past two years. Instead, it felt comfortable and cozy. It made Hannah want to snuggle back into the sheets and enjoy another hour of sleep, but she wondered what Nikki was doing.

As though conjured by the thought, a soft knock sounded on the bedroom door, and Nikki eased it open. "You awake?" she asked softly.

"Yes," Hannah said, instantly aware of her embarrassment about the previous night. "Come in."

Nikki held out a cup of coffee.

Hannah was certain it would have the perfect amount of cream in it. Nikki knew exactly how she liked it. She smiled. "Thank you."

Nikki lifted a shoulder. "You know what the Greeks say about unexpected visitors."

Hannah tilted her head in question.

"That they could be a god or goddess in disguise, so you better treat them with the utmost hospitality." Nikki's eyes sparked with humor, but she didn't hold Hannah's gaze, as if she were uncomfortable.

Hannah laughed. "The utmost?"

"Yes," Nikki said, "which is why I came in to see if you want breakfast before I head over to Aleyda's."

Hannah thought it odd that Nikki always referred to her studio as Aleyda's. Granted, it was on Aleyda's lot, but Aleyda had told Hannah that Nikki was the one to have it built and how much it upped the property value. Maybe it was part of that unassuming nature Nikki had. "I'd love it," Hannah said, noticing that Nikki was still wearing the T-shirt Hannah had found for her the night before, its length not quite covering the boy briefs beneath.

"Okay. Well, you enjoy your coffee, and I'll get it started." Nikki edged toward the dresser. "I'm just going to grab these." She pulled a pair of shorts from a drawer, her face reddening, and stepped into them as she hopped out of the room.

Hannah almost giggled. She couldn't remember the last time she had seen Nikki blush. Not like this. This was almost a bashfulness. It wasn't as though Hannah hadn't seen her in her underwear before. There had been a lot of mornings in the past weeks when she had been in only a tee or a tank and a pair of boxers. It had to be because of what had happened between them the night before. *Maybe we should clear the air.*

After dressing and with coffee in hand, Hannah slipped onto the lone stool at the bar that acted as a divider between the kitchen and living area in the small apartment.

Nikki stood at the opposite counter, her back to Hannah, beating the eggs for what looked to be a veggie omelet. Mushrooms, onions, and broccoli sizzled in a pan on the stove.

"It smells great," Hannah said.

"Good, because the last thing I want is the wrath of the gods raining down on me." Nikki stirred the vegetables, then opened the refrigerator and retrieved some cheese.

Seemingly of its own volition, Hannah's gaze dropped to Nikki's bare legs. They were so toned, so strong. Her calf muscles tightened and flexed as she moved. A flash of heat caught Hannah off guard as she remembered the firmness of Nikki's thigh between hers, pressing against her center. She barely contained a soft moan.

"Here you go," Nikki said, setting a plate in front of her. She placed a bottle of hot sauce beside it. "I'm sorry. I don't have any sour cream."

Hannah snapped her gaze up to Nikki's face. "That's okay," Hannah said quickly. "It looks great."

"Are you okay?" Nikki asked.

"Mm-hm." Hannah wished Nikki would turn away long enough for her to get a grip on herself. "I'm fine." This was ridiculous.

"You're flushed."

"Nope, I'm fine. Really. Go ahead and make your omelet." Hannah waved her fork toward the stove.

Nikki turned and cracked two more eggs into a bowl.

Hannah blew out a quiet breath and composed herself. Once they talked about it, this would pass.

"I'm sorry about last night," they both said simultaneously. Nikki glanced over her shoulder, and they burst out laughing.

"So, you feel as weird about it as I do?" Hannah asked.

"I'm mortified," Nikki said. "I'm so sorry, Hannah. I crossed a line."

"It wasn't just you. I shouldn't have…" Hannah watched as Nikki slid her omelet onto a plate. *What shouldn't I have done? Thought what I thought? Felt what I felt? Responded the way I responded?* Definitely the last. Nikki was her friend. "I think we were both just mad and upset." It didn't feel exactly right, but she didn't know what else to say. She was confused.

"I just don't want it to make things awkward between us," Nikki said.

"I don't either. So, we won't let it." Hannah heard the determination in her own voice and hoped it would be enough. "I've been furious at Jordan all these weeks, and when I saw how hurt you were last night, I got mad for you, too. And when I got here and saw you, I thought, what better way to get even with her than for the two of us to sleep together. It was stupid."

"It might be stupid, but I had similar thoughts." Nikki set her plate on the bar across from Hannah and took a drink of her own coffee. "I wanted to take something of hers. To hurt her the way I was hurting." She met Hannah's eyes. "But not at your expense."

The sincerity in Nikki's tone and expression pulled a tide of emotion from within Hannah. She blinked back tears. She remembered at the precise moment she had broken the kiss, she had felt Nikki gently push against her, moving her away. She trusted that if she hadn't been able to do it, Nikki would have. "Me either, at yours." She squeezed Nikki's hand.

They shared a smile, then started eating.

After a couple of bites, Hannah glared at Nikki. "Just for the record…" she said defiantly. "I'm *not* Jordan's."

"You're right. I'm sorry." Then she cocked her head and grinned. "In that case, we're safe. There's *really* no reason to sleep with you."

Hannah knew it was a joke, one she might have found funny even yesterday, but it stung just a little. Why was that?

A cell phone chimed.

Both of them looked around the room.

"It was mine," Hannah said. "A text." She retrieved her phone from her purse on the coffee table and opened the message:

From: Kate

OK. Search 4 Momzilla is on. But U O me. And B warned, I might make you give up women. Hope it's worth it.

Hannah laughed. "It's from Kate," she said to Nikki as she typed back *Smiley. Thanks Big Sis.* "She's agreed to look for our birth mother."

"Huh," Nikki said as she finished her omelet. "That surprises me. She seemed so against it."

"She probably still is." Hannah returned her phone to her purse. "She says she's going to make me give up women in exchange."

Nikki laughed but looked at Hannah thoughtfully. "Can I ask you something?"

"Of course." Hannah shot her a smirk. What a silly question with everything they'd been through together recently.

"Does she really have a problem with you being a lesbian?"

"No. She just doesn't like anything that makes us different." Hannah returned to the bar stool to finish her breakfast. "She gets a lot of comfort out of being a twin and knowing I'm so much like her that I understand her without her having to explain herself. I guess I do, too, with her. The lesbian thing sets us apart, and she doesn't like it."

Nikki nodded.

"Now, I get to ask a question," Hannah said.

"All right."

"*Why* do you still live in this tiny apartment with all the same furniture you've probably had since you moved in, when clearly your business is doing well and you're in high demand?" Hannah tried to keep it light, but she really wanted to know.

Nikki shrugged. "There's never been a reason to move." Her manner was casual, but the slight blush that crept up her neck and into her face spoke to something more.

"The *reason* is that you can," Hannah said teasingly.

Nikki grinned. "Well, for now, I have to change clothes and *get* to my successful business. I have a set of two-year-old triplets to coax into smiling all at the same time." She rinsed her plate and put it in the dishwasher, then headed toward the bedroom.

"Don't think I don't recognize deflection when I see it," Hannah called after her.

❖

"No!" the brunette screamed. She jerked free of Jordan's grasp.

The tray crashed to the floor, sending the dishes from Jordan's meal clattering loudly across the linoleum. The sound echoed off the bare walls.

"No! No! No!" She dashed toward the door but stopped short when she realized it was closed. She ducked her head and yanked at her hair. "No! No! No!"

Jordan stared in horror. Her heart pounded. "I'm sorry," she yelled over the shrieks. She'd learned the woman was called Sister Sarah, though Jordan just thought of her as Sarah. She seemed so different from the others. Without thinking, she stepped toward her.

"*No!*" Sarah scurried to the corner and huddled behind the toilet. She buried her face in her hands and began to murmur.

Jordan had no idea what to do to try to calm her. She knew a couple of the brothers—there were four now—or Sister Katherine— she'd decided it was worth calling her that because she'd learned that not doing so held repercussions—would be there in another heartbeat. They were never far away. Jordan had discovered a while ago two camera lenses set into the diagonal corners of her room and flush with the stark white walls so as to be almost undetectable. She knew the whole scene had been witnessed.

Right on cue, the door burst open. Sister Katherine rushed in, Brothers Simon and Nathaniel close behind. She paid no attention to Jordan; she simply looked at Sarah. Was that sadness in her eyes? She crossed to the far corner and knelt near her, keeping the toilet between them. She spoke gently.

Jordan couldn't hear what she was saying, but it seemed to have little effect.

Sarah's shoulders shook as she cried into her hands.

Sister Katherine motioned the two men over, and they knelt with the women. They began to sing.

What the hell? Jordan listened, dumbstruck by the whole scene. She remembered the song. It was a hymn. Something about walking in a garden.

It took several verses, but Sarah began to quiet.

Sister Katherine rose. "Take her to her room," she said softly to the men.

Sarah's head snapped up. She shook it vehemently, staring at Sister Katherine, eyes wide. "No, please. I'm sorry."

"It's not your fault." Sister Katherine stepped back as the men got to their feet. "Go with your brothers," she said to Sarah.

Sarah's lips quivered. A fresh batch of tears rolled down her already wet cheeks as she started to cry again, this time silently. She rose and moved toward the door.

The men fell in behind her. They stayed close, at the same time maintaining some space between themselves and Sarah.

Jordan realized she'd never seen anyone touch Sarah in any way, not even to assist her out of a chair as was offered at times to Sister Katherine, or even to get her attention. "What's wrong with her?"

Sister Katherine didn't respond for a long moment, as though deciding whether or not she would. "Satan was strong with her," she said finally.

"Satan? What the hell does—" Jordan caught herself, but not in time. She'd pay for that.

Following the first meeting with Palmer and her parents, Jordan had been taken back to her room, where Sister Katherine had explained how her "redemption program" was to work. First, from that day forward, she would begin a strict regimen of prayer, Bible study, and work as a means of *remembering God's word* and *showing her devotion to her Lord*. The result of her cooperation and sincere efforts would be the acquisition of comforts, privileges, and when true milestones were reached, an actual reward. Any defiance or disrespect toward God or any of *His workers* would bring the loss of the same, or in severe cases, actual punishment. Violation of any of the Ten Commandments, profanity, escape attempts, and unclean behavior would not be tolerated and would result in punishment to fit the severity of the infraction. She would be addressed as and expected to answer to Sister Jordan, and she would address those caring for her by their designation as Sister or Brother. Everyone referred to Palmer as Father. The first time Jordan actually spoke that one, she almost gagged on it.

Sister Katherine pursed her lips.

"I'm sorry," Jordan said. "I ask for forgiveness." She was getting better at playing the game.

"Forgiveness isn't mine to give," Sister Katherine said as she always did. The request was mandatory. "You will be cleansed by the strap."

The punishment for the word hell, as Jordan already knew, wasn't too bad. Five lashes with a well-worn strip of leather. She'd taken that easily in the past as warm-up for play scenes with particularly adventurous women. The first time they'd taken the strap to her, she'd endured it by thinking about a woman she'd been with who'd been adept at combining it with pleasure, and it had worked well. She wasn't an extreme player, though. So the whipping that'd finally claimed her attention was the twenty-five lashes that'd left the skin of her back split and seeping when she'd lost her temper after Sister Katherine had left her alone again and she'd pounded her fists against the door, screaming, "God damn it, you're a bunch of fucking psychos." She'd learned a lot in the three weeks since then.

"What does that mean, Satan was strong with her?" Jordan asked, returning to her earlier question about Sarah. Then it hit her. "She went through this." It *wasn't* a question. "She went through a redemption program."

Sister Katherine's expression remained impassive. "Yes."

Jordan's stomach turned at the thought of that seemingly fragile woman going through what *she* was going through. She glanced out into the hallway, as though Sarah might still be there. She'd recently earned the privilege of having her door open as long as one of God's workers was with her. "And it left her like that?" she asked incredulously. "Freaking out at the slightest touch?"

Sister Katherine knelt and began picking up the scattered dishes. "As I said, Satan was strong in Sister Sarah. She was the first to undergo the program as an adult. She graduated from the teen program, but later, they discovered she'd been sneaking a sinful lifestyle for several years, and Satan had a deep hold on her. Father had to use stringent methods."

"You mean he went too far. He destroyed her."

Sister Katherine placed the last of the dinnerware on the tray. "Sister Sarah is cured. She no longer has impure desires for women."

Jordan scoffed. "That's *cured*? She can't stand being touched by *anyone*. That's why the men didn't help her up and support her like they did me, isn't it?"

"You shouldn't have touched her." Sister Katherine searched Jordan's face. "Why did you?"

In truth, Jordan liked Sarah's quiet company, and she hadn't wanted her to leave when Jordan was finished eating. She'd grabbed her hand to keep her from getting up. She wanted to ask her to stay and read scriptures with her. That was all they were allowed to do together. Jordan never got the words out, though, before Sarah lost it. She wasn't going to tell Sister Katherine that. "I took her hand to say thank you for staying with me while I ate."

Following that first whipping, Brother Isaac had tended to Jordan's back, then called for Sarah who brought in some fruit, rather than the broth she'd had before. Due to her weakness from being starved—they'd called it fasting, of course—and the pain she was in, Sarah had stayed to help her eat. Halfway through the meal, Jordan had tried to talk to her. Even that early, she'd known Sarah was different from the others. "Can you help me?" she'd asked under her breath. "This is illegal. They're all going to prison. If you help me, I'll make sure you don't."

Sarah had paled, and her eyes grew wide. She glanced over her shoulder at Brother Isaac, then back to Jordan. She gave the slightest shake of her head, but it didn't seem like she was saying no. It was more of a warning.

"Please," Jordan mouthed.

Sarah fed her a bite of watermelon. The fork trembled in her hand. Her lips moved slightly. "Play along. They're watching."

That was what Jordan had needed, a reminder to be smart, to stop acting so rashly. This group was organized. Palmer and her father had a definite plan, and had obviously put a lot of time, money, and energy into it. She'd be wise to find out more about it before trying anything else. She'd given Sarah a grateful look, then settled back to take more fruit. Clearly, that little bit of reality hadn't meant she could touch the woman. *Stupid mistake.*

Sister Katherine looked skeptical. "Father has instructed that your actual Redemption Program is to start tomorrow."

It's to start? What had she been doing there all this time if it hadn't even started yet? "I thought that's what we've been doing." Dread seeped into the pit of her stomach.

"This has been the beginning of your religious training. That will continue. Your Redemption Program is different. You'll understand more as we go." Sister Katherine picked up the tray and turned to leave.

"What about you?" Jordan asked. She'd been dying to know, but this was the first time crazy bitch had seemed open to telling her anything.

"Me?" She looked genuinely confused.

"Yeah. Did you go through a program? Did you used to...you know?" A few lewd descriptions floated through Jordan's mind, but she didn't want to add to whatever punishment she knew was already coming. "Did you used to desire women?"

"I was cured when I was seventeen in Father's ex-gay ministry for teens."

So, he'd continued that after Jordan had graduated and left for college. Sister Katherine must have come to the church after Jordan was gone, so she was evidently younger than Jordan had realized. Jordan thought of Sarah again, and something tugged at her memory, but whatever it was eluded her.

"Father saved me," Sister Katherine said, clearly grateful to Palmer. "He saved all of us here now doing the Lord's work. That's how we can have compassion and empathy for you."

"The brothers, too?"

Sister Katherine nodded. "And I'm now married to Brother Isaac."

Jordan arched an eyebrow. *Crazy bitch and pasty face?* She couldn't see it, especially with the vibe she'd gotten from Liz. She and Jordan hadn't slept together, but Jordan never slept with any of the women she played sports with. It was easier to find a willing bed partner than someone who could give her a challenge on the courts. Liz had definitely set off Jordan's gaydar, though. She wondered how *Sister Katherine* had liked her short-lived freedom and if she'd been tempted to disappear into the big, anonymous world.

"Someone will be back to take you for your punishment." Sister Katherine left without waiting for acknowledgement.

It wasn't as though Jordan had a choice. She sat on the edge of her bed, thankful for the thin mattress she had earned to soften the cement slab a little and picked up the Bible from the small table beside her. After her rocky start of having to *begin* three times and that first severe punishment, her intelligence had kicked in, with some help from Sarah.

Jordan opened the Bible and rested it on her lap. She lowered her eyes to the page. This was something else she'd learned—as long as she was pretending to read scriptures or pray, all seemed well. She needed to remember to turn the page occasionally and to actually read a passage now and then so if questioned, she had something to say, but other than that, it was ideal. No one interrupted her. She earned privileges. And she had time to think.

She thought about Sarah and what might be happening to her. Would they punish her, too? Sister Katherine had said it wasn't her fault. No, it was Jordan's. Guilt and anger twisted together into a tight knot in her chest. And...remorse? She needed Sarah's help, but she couldn't stand it if Sarah suffered any more than she clearly already had because of her.

What *had* she suffered? There were the whippings, but those wouldn't cause a reaction like the one Jordan had seen. She'd heard about some of the more extreme methods used particularly in the early days of conversion therapy. Was *that* what they'd done to her? *And Christ! What's in store for me?*

CHAPTER FOURTEEN

Nikki sat at her worktable, staring at her computer screen as she'd been doing for hours. There were images of the Jamison wedding party looking back at her, but all she saw was Hannah the way she'd looked three nights earlier in Nikki's bedroom, in Nikki's bed. Nikki had never seen her aroused before—her skin so flushed, the green of her eyes so dark, her lips so swollen—and now that she had, she couldn't see anything else. No matter where she was or what she was doing, she couldn't get Hannah out of her mind.

She finally knew what it felt like to hold her, to touch her, to kiss her, not as the friend she'd been, but as a lover. She'd finally tasted her mouth, cupped her breasts, felt the heat of her desire, albeit ever so briefly. She had experienced Hannah in ways she'd ached for at times over the past three years, and even the knowledge that Hannah had been motivated by nothing more than a desire for vengeance didn't diminish the exquisite memory.

Nikki now knew what it could feel like to love Hannah fully, what it might feel like to have Hannah love her in return. How could she go back to the way things were? And yet, she had to.

She'd spent the last two evenings at Hannah's, as she normally would have, and had played her part as the loyal and committed friend. They'd promised they wouldn't let what happened make things awkward between them, and Nikki intended to hold up her end. It had been excruciating, though. Every brush past one another making dinner, every whiff of Hannah's scent when she stood close, every touch of her mouth to a shared soda or beer shot Nikki back to that night in her bedroom. She had to find a way to ensure they each had their own drinks without making it obvious. And when Hannah had leaned over to snip a rose from the bush and the hem of her tee had ridden up to reveal a glimpse of bare skin, Nikki had to turn away and focus on the chicken on the grill to block out the memory of just how soft that skin was.

Nikki let her thoughts return to the moment her palms stroked that softness. She knew she shouldn't. It drove her nuts. But she did. She let herself relive the sensation of Hannah's swollen nipples between her fingers, the thrill of hearing Hannah cry out her name in response.

"Nikki?" A hand touched Nikki's arm.

Nikki jumped, her heart pounding.

"I'm sorry," Aleyda said, a smile in her voice. "I didn't mean to startle you."

"Jesus Christ!" Nikki clutched at her chest. "Are you trying to kill me?"

Aleyda laughed. "I would never." She rubbed Nikki's shoulder.

"What are you doing sneaking up on me like that?" Nikki straightened, then leaned back in her chair.

"I called your name three times," Aleyda said defensively. "Twice from the doorway and once from right here. You were *gone* gone. And I don't think you were engrossed in your work because you're staring at the same pictures you were looking at when I stuck my head in to check on you an hour ago."

Nikki searched for what to say, but came up with nothing.

"I brought you something to eat, since you skipped lunch." Aleyda retrieved a tray from the desk behind them and set it beside the computer. She pulled up her own chair.

Nikki plucked a strawberry from the bowl, dipped it into sour cream, then coated it with brown sugar. The snack was a part of their repertoire of standard comfort foods when one of them had something to work through. "Is something bothering you?" she asked. She took a bite of the berry and moaned with pleasure.

Aleyda gave her a knowing look. "I've been waiting for three days for you to start talking. I bought these yesterday, and I couldn't stand it any longer." She popped her own berry into her mouth.

"You think you're pretty smart, don't you."

"I *think* I've known you since you were twelve and know when something's wrong." Aleyda bumped her with her shoulder. "Let's have it."

Nikki sighed and stared down at her keyboard. "Hannah and I..." She paused. What *did* they do?

"Hannah and you...?" Aleyda arched an eyebrow.

"We..." Nikki met Aleyda's gaze and pursed her lips. How could she tell Aleyda what'd happened? Maybe she needed to back up. "I finally read Lantz's report the other night, and I found an email... from Kristin." By the time she got to the point in the story where Hannah was looking into her eyes on the bed, she was stuck again.

Aleyda drew in a breath. "You slept together."

"No," Nikki said. They hadn't slept together. *Why is this so hard?*

"You kissed?" Aleyda tried again.

Nikki looked away. "More than that."

When Nikki turned back, Aleyda was smiling. "Nikki, that's wonderful."

"No," Nikki said emphatically. "It's not wonderful."

"Why not?" Aleyda's expression displayed genuine confusion. "You've had feelings for Hannah ever since you met her."

"Because we're friends," Nikki said with frustration. "Because she's always been with Jordan. Because she doesn't see me in that way." She smashed another berry into the sugar.

Aleyda studied her speculatively. "A lot of couples start out as friends. There's nothing wrong with that. Your brother and I were friends for over a year before we actually started dating."

"But Ramon wasn't your best friend's lover for three years."

"No, but he did date one of my roommates for a while."

Nikki cut her an it's-not-the-same-thing glance. "And we don't know if Jordan's coming back."

Aleyda slipped her hand over Nikki's. "*Mija,* even if she does come back, do you really think Hannah is going to want anything to do with her after everything she's learned?" She caressed Nikki's knuckle with her thumb. "Would you, now that you know about Kristin?"

The hurt and anger Nikki had locked away in the deep recesses of her heart started rattling the lid. She thought of the years they'd known each other…all the time they'd spent together and the laughter they'd shared, then the betrayal. She winced. "I don't know. Probably not."

"Oh, *mija*." Aleyda leaned close and took Nikki into a tender embrace. She stroked the back of her head.

Tears burned Nikki's eyes, and she put her arms around Aleyda. "I thought we were best friends." Her voice broke, and she began to cry.

"I know, *mija*," Aleyda said softly.

Nikki let herself be comforted until her eyes dried, then gave Aleyda one last squeeze and sat back in her chair. "Thanks," she said, grabbing a tissue from the box on the table. "I needed that." Aleyda was the one person she'd always been completely comfortable with seeing her cry.

Aleyda smoothed Nikki's hair, then tucked a few errant strands behind Nikki's ear. "I think you're wrong about the last thing."

"What last thing?" Nikki asked.

"That Hannah doesn't see you that way," Aleyda said, reaching for another strawberry. "I've seen the two of you together quite a bit lately. I've seen how she is with you."

"What do you mean, how she is? How is she?"

"She looks to you for emotional support."

"That's just because of the thing with Jordan," Nikki said. "She turned to me as Jordan's friend."

"The way she smiles at you sometimes is more than just friendly."

"No, it isn't." Nikki felt herself blush lightly.

Aleyda smiled. "She watches you when you're not looking."

Nikki stilled before taking the prepared berry Aleyda held out to her. "She does?"

"Mm-hm. And she watches you the way a woman who's interested would watch you. *Not* like a friend."

Nikki's heart did a little flip at the thought. That wasn't true, though. Hannah had never given any indication she had any interest in Nikki.

"And she touches you…a lot," Aleyda said, continuing without prompting.

Nikki couldn't deny that one, but that was recent. "She just started doing that," she said. "I think it's only because she's mad at Jordan, and that's what the other night was, too. She said so."

"She did?"

"Yeah. She said she was sorry she started it. She was just mad and wanted to get even with Jordan for hurting both of us." Nikki licked some sour cream and sugar off her fingers. "It wasn't because she likes me *that* way."

"Well, isn't that what you told her, too?"

Nikki shot her a quick glare.

"It wasn't true when you said it. Maybe it wasn't when she did either."

"It was partially true when I said it." Nikki sounded like a sulky kid.

Aleyda eyed her. "Have you fallen in love with her, *mija*?"

"What?" Nikki fidgeted. "Why would you think that?"

"When she and Jordan started getting serious—"

Nikki smirked.

Aleyda lifted a shoulder dismissively. "Okay, when you stopped spending time with them…" She changed her approach. "You said you needed distance from Hannah because you thought you might be falling in love with her. Now that you've been with her so much, have you? Fallen in love?"

And there it was—the question Nikki had been avoiding asking herself. She looked into Aleyda's kind eyes. She knew the answer, and Aleyda did, too. She turned to the computer screen. Two happy brides smiled back at her. "I know. I'm a fucking idiot."

Aleyda let out a quiet chuckle. "That wasn't where *I* was going with it."

Curious, Nikki looked at her expectantly.

"I think Hannah might be falling for you, too."

Nikki couldn't help but laugh. "That's a leap."

"Really?" Aleyda folded her arms. "Okay. How did she end up wearing your hat the day of the Andrews shoot?"

Nikki blinked. "What?"

"When you two got back, she was wearing your baseball cap. How'd she get it?"

Nikki held up her hands in bewilderment. "She took it."

"She just took it off your head?"

"Yeah." Nikki recalled the moment. "We were waiting for Mrs. Andrews to round up her sons, and I mentioned to Hannah that her face was getting red. And she said, 'Give me your hat, then,' and she grabbed it off my head. But I don't get—"

"Uh-huh. And was she laughing?"

Nikki remembered the sound and the light in Hannah's face. "Yeah." She couldn't figure out what this had to do with anything, though.

"And then did she run off with it and look back at you like she wanted you to chase her?" Aleyda cocked her head.

Nikki remembered that exact moment, the smile on Hannah's face, the teasing glint in her eyes—the swell of happiness in Nikki's chest. How did Aleyda know all this? "Yes."

"Doesn't that sound like a scene right out of a romantic movie?" Aleyda seemed pleased with herself.

"So, what? This is life, not a romantic movie," Nikki said, but she felt hope rising in her at Aleyda's implication.

"It's still what women do to try to get the attention of someone they like." Aleyda wasn't giving up.

"I'm a woman, and I don't do that."

Aleyda shook her head. "I'm sure you've done the butchie version of it, whatever that is."

"I have not," Nikki said, but even as the words left her lips, she knew they weren't true. She'd done her version of it that very same day with Hannah. She *had* chased her. She'd let Hannah dodge her once or twice even though she could have easily caught her. Then, she'd let her keep the hat so the next time she wore it, she could feel close to Hannah. "And it's butch, not *butchie*." Could Aleyda be right? Could Hannah be attracted to *her*, too?

Aleyda was watching her in that way she did when she was waiting for something to sink in.

"It wouldn't change anything anyway." Nikki couldn't let herself go there. "We're friends, and I don't want to mess that up. And things are still too up in the air about Jordan. No matter what Jordan's done, she was still my friend. She was still with Hannah for three years. She's still between us."

Aleyda sighed. "All right. I'm just going to say this. There's something we've needed to talk about for a long time. Today's the day. Ramon would kill me if he knew I'd waited this long."

"Now what are you talking about?"

"Why won't you let yourself be happy?"

Nikki blinked. "What?"

"You've never let yourself be happy with any of the women you've been with. And there have been some really nice ones," Aleyda said. "In fact, it seems like the nicer they are, the faster you get rid of them."

"That isn't true." Nikki picked at the few remaining strawberries. "And I am happy."

"You know what I mean, *mija*. You've never allowed yourself to be with anyone." Aleyda softened her voice. "And the only one you've even let yourself have real feelings for is Hannah. Someone who's been completely unavailable. She wasn't only in a relationship. She was with your best friend."

Nikki felt the same pang of envy and disappointment that'd eaten at her for three years at the thought, sight, and knowledge of Hannah being with Jordan. She'd never been able to escape it. She didn't need it in her face now. "What's your point?"

"Do you remember after the accident, after Ramon died, you told me you were sorry for ruining my happiness? You said it was your fault I didn't have the husband I loved anymore and the kids didn't have a father. That since you destroyed our happiness, you didn't deserve to ever be happy."

"I remember." Nikki stared into the bowl. She remembered that day perfectly. Second only to the actual day of the accident, it'd been the worst day of her life, the day that all of her emotions around her brother's death broke loose.

Aleyda was studying her.

"I remember," Nikki said again.

"Is that why you won't let yourself be with someone who makes you happy?"

"Course not." Nikki shifted in her seat. "I went to therapy. I worked all that out."

"I know you went to therapy," Aleyda said. "But the evidence in your life says there might still be something there."

"There isn't. I just haven't met the right person," Nikki said flatly.

"Until now," Aleyda said firmly. "The woman you've had feelings for for over three years is no longer with your best friend. And even if Jordan does come back, she can hardly expect anything to be the same. And I guarantee you Hannah's feelings for you are changing. I've seen it. So all I'm saying is give yourself a chance. *I* want you to be happy, and Ramon would, too."

"Look, I appreciate your concern," Nikki said, weary of the entire conversation, of all the emotions that'd been churning away inside her since the night with Hannah. "I just think you're off on this one." Aleyda was rarely *off* on anything. But this? *Hannah* wanting *her*? If Nikki opened her heart to it and it wasn't true, there'd be no way she could still be around Hannah. She wasn't willing to risk it. *And I am happy.*

A gentle frown touched Aleyda's lips. "Okay. I won't push." She started collecting the dishes. "Just…think about it. Okay?"

Nikki answered with a shrug. She tossed some berry stems into a bowl.

"Mama and *Papi* called last night," Aleyda said with a wide smile. "They're coming up for Robbie's going away party next month."

Nikki's mood brightened and she grinned. She hadn't seen her parents in almost a year. When they'd moved back to Mexico four years earlier to look after her grandmother, she'd tried to go down for a visit every six months, but she'd postponed her last trip due to a heavy work schedule at the time, and then when everything with Jordan had happened, it'd dropped by the wayside. "That's great. I can't wait to see them. Rob's going to be thrilled."

A twinkle flashed in Aleyda's eyes. "Maybe you could bring Hannah. Introduce her to them as your new girlfriend."

Nikki groaned. "I thought that subject was closed."

Aleyda laughed. "You know what Ramon used to say about me? No subject is fully closed until it's crystal clear I'm right." She picked up the tray and started out of the room. "Don't forget you have the Gilmores coming in a half hour."

Nikki smiled after her as the door clicked shut. Their conversation lingered in her mind. Could Aleyda be right about Hannah?

❖

Hannah threw open the front door. "Where have you been?"

"I got here as soon as I could," Nikki said, a tiny smile playing at the corners of her mouth. "I had to finish up a shoot. You're not excited or anything, are you?"

"Come on." Hannah grabbed the thick manila envelope off the table beside the entrance and stepped onto the stoop, pulling the door closed behind her.

"What? I don't even get to sit and relax for a minute? I've had a long day."

"No." Hannah grabbed her hand and pulled her down the sidewalk toward her car. "You can relax later. I'll take you out for dinner."

Nikki laughed. "You know, if it was this hard to wait, you could have gone without me?"

"I didn't want to do this alone. This is big." Hannah could barely contain her enthusiasm. She had waited twenty-two years for this day.

"You could have taken Kate." Nikki opened Hannah's door and waited while she slipped into the passenger's seat.

"Kate doesn't want to go. You know how she feels about this." In truth, Hannah hadn't asked her. She wanted Nikki with her for this. She had been thinking about Nikki a lot since the night at her apartment, and she had come to realize she wanted Nikki with her for most things. What she was working on now was why. But in this moment, all she wanted was to get to Lantz's office.

"Where is she tonight?" Nikki asked as she slid in behind the wheel.

"I don't know. A date, I think." Hannah watched Nikki start the engine. "Thank you for going with me."

Nikki chuckled. "Of course. I know how important this is to you. I'm sorry the shoot ran over."

The meeting with Lantz was a formality, really. She had already told him over the phone that she wanted to hire him to find her birth mother and the little bit she knew about the adoption. He had explained the kinds of things he needed that would help him get started and the challenges that he might run into in the process. Once they'd handed over the paperwork and had a bit of chitchat, they thanked him and left him to it.

"Well, it's started," Nikki said as they headed back toward the car. "How does it feel?"

"I don't know. It's a little bit of a letdown," Hannah said. "I mean, I knew nothing would actually happen tonight. It's not like I expected my birth mother would be waiting there in Lantz's office to be found as soon as he had the adoption papers, but it still feels like nothing is different."

Nikki was quiet for a minute. "How about this," she said finally. "Picture your birth mom the way you've always thought she'd look, sitting at a table in a kitchen somewhere. And as soon as you handed Lantz that packet, a soft bell rings in her subconscious, and she sits up straighter to listen."

Hannah smiled at the image.

"She doesn't know what it is," Nikki said, continuing the narration as they walked, "but she knows it's something really important, something she needs to listen to."

Hannah warmed, not just at the thought, but at Nikki's obvious attempt to lift her spirits.

"Then she gets up and moves to the window and looks outside, knowing something super important is on its way. So, she's waiting."

Hannah slipped her hand into Nikki's and leaned into her. "Thank you."

Nikki's fingers gently closed around Hannah's. Her grasp was so tender, so protective, but there was something more tonight. There had been something *more* since the night they had kissed.

Or… Maybe the difference wasn't in Nikki's touch, but in Hannah's reaction. Nikki's touch lit something in Hannah—arousal, excitement—like Jordan's touch, like other lovers' touches, but not. It was more than the flame of desire. It was—Hannah didn't know— something she hadn't felt before. Something that made her happy and uncertain at once.

"Hey," Nikki said, "you owe me dinner."

Hannah startled. *What was* that *road I'd been going down?* "Oh. Okay. Where do you want to eat?"

"How about here?" Nikki gestured to an open doorway beside them. "Fat Jack's," she said, looking at the Chinese symbols on the window.

Hannah giggled.

"Oh, wait. Great Wall Chinese Cuisine," Nikki read from the small lettering beneath.

"Have you eaten here?" Hannah peered inside and inhaled the delicious aroma.

"Nope. Never heard of the place," Nikki said. "Shall we?"

When the waiter brought the menus, Nikki waved them away. "Just bring us your three favorite main dishes and your favorite soup," she said with a smile.

He grinned. "Very good."

Hannah stared at her in astonishment. She had been eating out with Jordan for so long, she had forgotten there was any other way of ordering other than long deliberation of every menu item, then meticulous choosing based on past experience or recommendation from someone she knew. Jordan would never turn the order over to the waiter. She would never walk into a restaurant she'd never heard of to begin with. Unbidden, the question of where Jordan might be eating that night drifted into Hannah's mind. *Is she with Liz Talbot?* She let it drop away. Jordan never would have made up that silly little scenario to make Hannah feel better. She would have just told her to be patient and let Lantz do his job—*if* she had come with Hannah to the meeting at all. *How could I have ever thought Nikki was exactly like her?*

"What's the matter?" Nikki asked, sounding concerned. "Did I do something wrong?"

Hannah shook her head. *Just the opposite.* Nikki had done— did—everything right, except for that one thing. Except for not telling Hannah the truth about Jordan. That was over and done, though. When Hannah had seen the pain in Nikki's eyes after finding out about Jordan and Kristin and learning that Robin had known all along, suddenly she didn't want to hold on to her anger at Nikki any longer. Maybe because she knew Nikki now truly understood what she had done. Maybe because Hannah didn't want anyone to hurt the way she had. She didn't really know. She just knew something had changed in that moment.

And now, she was curious. "Will you tell me something?" she asked as the waiter set soup bowls, spoons, and a tea pot on the table.

"Sure." Nikki filled a cup for each of them. She sounded a bit wary.

"I understand that you didn't tell me Jordan was cheating on me because you were being loyal to your best friend, but what is it about Jordan that made you so loyal to her?"

Nikki went still. Her eyes went unfocused, as though she were looking at another time and place. "Jordan helped me when we first met," she said finally. "A lot."

Hannah could see that. Jordan had quite a bit of money. Maybe she had given some to Nikki for her business or to pay off some debt. "With what?"

"With my confidence. My belief that I could have something good in my life, like success."

The waiter brought their soup and dished it up. "Hot and sour," he said.

"Thank you." Nikki smiled at him.

Hannah looked at her expectantly.

She took the cue. "When I first met Jordan, I was struggling with my business, barely staying afloat. I got to the point I was about to give up and shut it down. Jordan sat me down and told me, point-blank, the reason it was failing was that I was sabotaging myself every time things started going well. I'd screw up a big shoot I'd finally landed or turn down a high-visibility project with some excuse about it not feeling right."

Hannah could hear Jordan saying those things. She was very matter-of-fact when it came to business dealings and put work as a high priority.

"She started calling me on it every time she saw it, then following up with reassurance that I could do it and reminding me of all the projects I'd done that'd gotten recognition and even some awards. Little by little, that voice in my head that said I couldn't or didn't deserve to be successful was replaced by hers." Nikki met Hannah's gaze. "I always felt I owed her for that."

Hannah couldn't imagine Nikki sabotaging her success. She seemed so comfortable with it now. "Why did you think you didn't deserve to be successful?"

Nikki gave her a measured look, then glanced down, and absently folded and unfolded the corner of her placemat. "Aleyda says I don't allow myself to be happy because of guilt about my brother."

"Guilt about what?"

Nikki didn't answer right away. She continued fidgeting with the placemat, then she met Hannah's gaze. "I was driving the car when Ramon was killed. We were coming home from a camping trip. It was late. I fell asleep and crashed into a tree."

Hannah heard her own small gasp. "Oh, Nikki," she whispered. She slipped her hand over Nikki's, stilling her fingers. "I'm so sorry."

Nikki looked at their hands, then turned hers to clasp Hannah's. "I was twenty. It took me five months to even cry," Nikki said.

Her voice was so low Hannah had to strain to hear.

"I remember I was standing in my mother's kitchen, and I burned a piece of toast. And suddenly, that was the last thing I could take. I didn't cry when I woke up in the hospital and found out he was gone. I didn't cry at his funeral. I didn't even cry any of the times he wasn't someplace he should've been." Nikki's eyes shimmered. "On Saturday mornings when he'd barge into my room and literally drag me out of bed to go to the swap meet for Aunt Rosita's *menudo*. When he didn't walk in my parents' door with Aleyda and the kids for the monthly family dinners. When he didn't call to find out how a date, or a test, or just my day, had gone. Then, all of a sudden, that day, I lost it over that damned piece of burned toast. I cried for hours and begged Aleyda and my mother to forgive me."

"I'm sure they don't blame you," Hannah said softly. "But have you forgiven yourself?"

"That's what Jordan helped me do for my business," Nikki said. "She didn't know that's what she was doing, but the more she pointed out that I could do it and that I deserved success, the more I could believe it and let go of the guilt."

Nikki paused, but Hannah could tell there was more.

"Then there was one night when we were really drunk that she started telling me about her childhood. How empty it was. She said the people she was closest to were paid to be there with her, and they came and went like all employees. She started crying when she talked about how her parents only had kids to complete a public picture and doled out what she thought *might* be love as a reward for being what she was supposed to be."

Hannah stared at Nikki in disbelief. *Jordan had cried?* Hannah had never seen her the slightest bit vulnerable.

"I could feel the pain she was in when she talked about how lonely she'd felt and how unworthy she must be of being loved, if her own parents didn't even love her." Nikki absently stroked Hannah's palm. "That's when I knew I had to be there for her, no matter what. She isn't a bad person. She just has a crap-ton of baggage." She looked at Hannah, a request for understanding in her eyes.

Hannah nodded. She did understand, now. She understood the depth to which Nikki felt things, the strength with which she loved.

"You know," Nikki said, clearly present in the moment again, "there's a lot in her journal that might help you know her better."

Hannah pursed her lips and shook her head. "The time for me to know Jordan has passed," she said quietly. "I didn't ask that to know her better. I asked it to know you better."

Surprise flashed in Nikki's expression. "Oh," was all she said.

Then the waiter was there with a broccoli dish and two others Hannah had no idea how to identify. Suddenly, everything seemed so new—a new restaurant, new food, a new beginning to knowing who she was and where she came from, a new life without Jordan. She looked across the table.

And maybe a new way of seeing Nikki.

CHAPTER FIFTEEN

Nausea rolled through Jordan's stomach. She clenched her eyes shut, blocking out the images on the screen, but there was no escaping the sounds—the soft moans of pleasure and arousal of two women making love. Bile rose in her throat.

She knew what these psychos were doing to her. She'd read about it. Aversion therapy. She was being conditioned to have adverse reactions to any stimulus involving women. An IV kept a steady flow of meds that induced nausea as long as the stimulus involved women engaged with one another in sexual situations. Then, as those drugs were flushed from her system and her stomach began to settle, the pictures or movie before her changed to the images and sounds of straight couples in bed.

On the first day of her *actual* redemption program, as Sister Katherine had called it, Brother Simon had come for her. A first. Sarah had been removing her breakfast tray and had slipped her that look Jordan now recognized as a reminder not to fight. She'd been taken to a room she'd never been to before and strapped into a chair. She hadn't known what to expect. She'd started to resist at the restraints but decided against it at the threat of a punishment.

The second day, she fought. The thought of them messing with her head any more than they already had, infuriated and terrified her. She took a swing at Brother Simon and landed a solid punch on his left cheekbone.

He fell backward against the wall.

Jordan froze. She hadn't thought. She'd just reacted. Now, there wasn't anything to do but keep punching until more Brothers arrived to restrain her, or she could make a break into the hallway. But then what? She already knew the futility of that. Rage at her impotence flooded her. She went after Brother Simon again.

He didn't fight back. In fact, he simply doubled over and covered his face for protection and waited.

Jordan got in a few more solid hits before she was pulled off of him and wrestled to the floor.

Two men held her while Sister Katherine gave her an injection.

The fucking drugs! How could she fight those fucking drugs? Jordan drifted into blackness.

When she awoke, she was strapped into the chair, Brother Simon with a swollen eye beside her, and the screen in front of her. Within minutes, the scene of a beautiful brunette and a boyish blonde in the throes of passion played before her while saliva filled her mouth. A wave of hopelessness broke over her.

When she returned to her room, the thin mattress on her bed was gone, and she was left in total darkness, the passage of time marked only by deepening hunger. Her momentary rebellion had felt good, had given her a surge of power, but it'd been stupid. What had she thought she could do? Where did she think there was to go? As she lay on the hard cement in the dark, she felt that same fear from her initial days creep back in, and realized the conditioning had begun the very first day. She had to figure out how to play along without actually losing control of who she was. However, by the time the lights came back on and she was allowed to eat again she was a trembling mess. She barely felt the whipping.

In the days that followed, she tried to counteract the effects of the sessions by thinking of sex between women while she was alone or staring at the pages of the Bible, times when her system was drug free and no nausea accompanied her thoughts and responses. Sometimes, she thought of Hannah. Sex with Hannah had always been good, and remembering it gave her something solid to focus on, especially if she went back to their early days, prior to any talk of monogamy, before she had to admit to herself she wasn't good enough for Hannah. These fantasies, whether of Hannah or nameless strangers, were the only way Jordan could think of to fight back.

Sometimes during the sessions, it even helped to think of Nikki, not in a sexual way, but just remembering that easy connection they'd always had, the laughter and fun they shared doing almost anything together. She'd revealed more of herself to Nikki than to anyone else in her life, and she valued what they had. The intensity of the sessions was increasing, though, and Jordan struggled to keep from vomiting.

"Just a little longer," Brother Simon said.

His patient demeanor irritated the hell out of her. She thought it odd that he ran this procedure when Sister Katherine seemed to be the one overseeing everything else. But maybe Sister Katherine couldn't. Maybe the images made her sick, too. *And videos of men made Simon ill?* Jordan didn't know if this type of tactic had been used in the teen program. It seemed extreme for that. Hell, it seemed extreme for anything. She turned away from Simon.

He switched the IV bag to one filled with saline and restarted the drip as a new couple—a woman with a man—appeared on screen and began kissing. "There you go."

The man on the screen began fondling the woman's breast and moaning.

As Jordan's belly began to settle, she took in deep breaths, feeling her stomach muscles unclench. She turned away from the images and tried to block out the sounds. She called Nikki to her mind and let herself relive their high-five-victory-dance after the final game of the racquetball tournament they'd won just before Nikki broke her foot. The happiness from that moment warred with her remorse in this one. *Will we ever have another moment like that?*

Simon released one of her hands and gave her a cup of water.

She drank slowly.

The door opened, and Sister Katherine hurried in, glowing like a sunbeam. "Father has a surprise for you." Her eyes sparkled.

How could everyone seem so normal? How could they act like nothing out of the ordinary was going on, like they didn't have someone strapped into a chair, forcing them to watch soft porn, and punishing them if they did anything to avoid it? In the name of God, no less. Jordan was exhausted from trying to figure it out. *I don't care about any dammed surprise.*

"As soon as you're finished here, I'll take you to him." Sister Katherine busied herself, disposing of the used IV bag and straightening some items on the counter.

When Jordan stepped through the doorway of the room where she'd met with Palmer and her parents several weeks earlier, she stiffened.

"Sister Jordan," Palmer said. He flashed that smile she hated. "You have a visitor."

Jordan's father sat at the table, dressed impeccably in a navy Ralph Lauren polo and gray slacks, his usual air of superiority and arrogance hovering around him like an entourage.

Jordan flushed with embarrassment. It was abject humiliation to stand in front of him—the man responsible for her kidnapping, for everything she'd gone through—beaten down in her frumpy attire with her hair growing out in uneven tufts, so utterly under his control.

"Please, come in and sit down, Sister Jordan." Palmer motioned to several empty chairs at the table.

Jordan's face burned. No, *this* was abject humiliation, what came next. She had to address Palmer as Father and do as he said, when what she really wanted to do was tell them both to fuck off and hurl a chair across the room. If she didn't acquiesce, though... She didn't want to think about what would happen if she didn't, especially in front of her father. She instinctively knew *that* was a bad idea. The thought of submitting to anything in this situation in front of Jonathan Webber, though, ate at her soul. She winced at the rip and tear of every bite. She looked at the floor and murmured the required response. "Thank you, Father." From the corner of her eye, she saw her real father smirk. She seethed.

"Since you've been having some trouble with the next phase of your program, I thought it might be good for you to have a visit with a family member," Palmer said, placing a hand on her father's shoulder. "Someone who loves you and deeply cares about your salvation."

Does he really believe that? Jordan glanced at him as she took a seat.

"Now, I'll leave the two of you alone to visit." Palmer patted her on the back as he moved toward the other door.

"So, are you having fun?" Jordan's father asked when they were alone. His eyes held a mocking glint.

Jordan glared at him. "What do you want?"

"I'm getting what I want." He had always been cold—not as downright frigid as her mother, but fairly icy when he wanted to be—but today he felt glacial. "I want you back under control."

"Really?" Jordan let out a sharp laugh. She knew it was dangerous to taunt the beast under the circumstances, but she heard the words come out of her mouth anyway. "You think you've ever had control of me?"

Her father steepled his fingers in front of him. "Fair enough. I *have* learned you weren't who you pretended to be, but now, all that's over. Thomas has assured me he can cure your sick perversions and get rid of your rebellious streak, so you can return to your loving family." He finished in a tone of mocking sentimentality.

Jordan ignored it. "Why are you doing this? You haven't given a crap where I was for almost a decade. I'm thirty-seven. Why would you even care what I do now?"

"No, I haven't cared, that's true. I admit it was a bit of a blow when you walked out after going to an Ivy League college and law school on my dime, but having my deviant daughter work for me and eventually become a senior partner wasn't anything I was interested in, so I let you go."

"Then, why do you care anything about me, now?" Jordan was genuinely curious.

Her father leveled his cool gray eyes on her. "You have no one but yourself to blame for that. If you'd just kept your distance."

Confused, Jordan studied him. Then his meaning dawned. "You mean that case against your firm a few years ago."

He remained silent, evidently waiting for more.

"And the interview." She nearly laughed.

"You always were smart. It's too bad you didn't apply your intelligence back then and turn down those bitches when they first came to you." He folded his hands on the table, a mannerism she knew meant he was about to make a point. "Surely, you didn't think I could let you get away with that."

She remembered her words in the interview. She'd felt invincible when her clients were awarded a million each. Five women who'd been fired from her father's firm had come to her with accusations of sexual harassment and wrongful employment terminations. Two were lesbians, who'd been told all they needed was a real man to satisfy them. All of them had been told the only way up the corporate ladder for them was through a bedroom, and at some point, after refusing to comply, had been fired for various fabricated reasons. Jordan's quote had been, "*Stevens, Webber, and Associates has a longstanding history of misogyny and homophobia, and it's time they were held accountable for wrongs, both past and present.*"

"*That's* what this is about?" Jordan asked incredulously. "Your hurt pride because I kicked your corporate ass in the courtroom? It's about your fucking ego?"

"Oh, no. It's about a lot more than that," her father said, his tone still even but his expression hardening. "I lost three of my biggest clients as a result of your antics, and have had to agree to numerous additional settlements. You've cost me quite a bit of money, and created a tarnish on my reputation that's going to take me years to rebuild. I've spent the last several years rectifying the mess you made. You're paying for it now."

"And how is *this* going to help that?" Jordan asked, unable to hold back her sarcasm.

"Well, first, you have quite the past to expose, that will easily discredit anything you said." He rose as though preparing for a closing argument. "You call me misogynistic, but isn't that hypocritical? What about you?"

"What about me?" Jordan had no idea where this was going.

"You parade that pretty blond girlfriend of yours for the cameras and the interview, then move her in with you in domestic bliss, but all the while you're screwing other women—or whatever you dykes do—on that boat of yours. Which of those women were you not treating *misogynisticly*? Your little girlfriend? Or the ones you used for your playthings?"

Jordan was stunned. She didn't know what shocked her more—his knowledge of all that, or that he had nailed her on her behavior and called it what it was. Guilt flooded her, the same guilt she felt every time she left a woman to go home to Hannah, the same guilt she tried to escape by buying her expensive presents. She'd tried to stop seeing other women when Hannah moved in with her, tried to be different, but she'd failed at every turn. Finally, she'd resigned herself to meeting Hannah's needs and giving her the things she seemed to want and hoped that would be enough. "How do you know about that?" she asked, deciding any defense of herself was ludicrous.

Her father laughed. "Do you think we just threw this together at the last minute? We had you watched for over a year. It took a lot of planning to extract you from your life without leaving a trace. And to plant other things intentionally."

"What do you mean?"

"Your little girlfriend thinks you ran off with Liz Talbot, thanks to plane tickets purchased in both your names. But there is no Liz Talbot, is there?" He smiled. "There's only Sister whatever her name is, so there isn't even anyone to look for. The police closed your case weeks ago. Everybody's done with you."

Jordan went cold, as though icy tentacles were wrapping around her. *That's why no one came.* Of course, they'd worked out every detail to ensure that. That's what her father did.

"Oh, and you might be interested to know that your little girlfriend and your best friend have gotten very cozy since you've been gone." He strolled around the table and leaned close to her ear. "They even visited your boat together."

Jordan fought not to react. She couldn't, not in front of her father. She doubted very much they'd *done* anything together on the boat. Nikki wouldn't have taken Hannah there for that. No, their presence there meant Hannah knew everything. Had Nikki told her, or had she found Jordan's private email? And if they'd found her email, did that mean Nikki knew… *Christ.* Why had she done that to Nikki, of all people? To the one person who stood by her, no matter what, who was always there for her, who somehow, by some unimaginable miracle, understood her. *Why am I such an asshole?*

She closed her eyes and drew in a long breath. She couldn't do this here...now. She had to keep it together. She collected her fragmented thoughts, reeled in the tendrils of emotions that'd begun to unravel. She steeled herself. "So, what's the rest of your plan? You could have discredited me with all this information without bringing me here," she asked her father, desperate to hear *anything* else. "I'm sure you have every detail already worked out."

He straightened and returned to his seat. "When you come back into the fold of our loving family," he said with a satisfied smile, as though he'd been waiting for this moment forever—and maybe he had. "It will be with deep contrition and a public apology and statement that you regret taking the case, and you're sorry for any pain and suffering it caused your mother and me. You'll publicly thank Thomas for helping you heal your sinful homosexual tendencies, and we'll announce your engagement to a suitable young man to whom you'll profess your gratitude and love for being able to forgive your sinful past."

Jordan couldn't hold in a humorless laugh at the absurdity of what she was hearing. "Who would that be?"

Her father narrowed his eyes. "Whoever I pick for you. Then you'll come to work at Stevens, Webber, and Associates, side-by-side with me and your brother, and you'll be the daughter *I* say you're going to be, or you'll end up right back here, undergoing a second *redemption program*. Our family will no longer be a laughing stock. I worked far too hard to get where I am, to let my dyke daughter cost me my clients and reputation. And based on your past record, you're bound to keep causing me problems. But having you killed would be messy. Besides, *this* will be much more fun. This way, I get to see you suffer. It's a win-win."

The depth of his hatred and the simplicity of his plan made Jordan feel so weak the room began to sway.

"You see, I've paid for most of this facility, so you can be kept here as long as needed. You'll bend, or you'll break. I don't really care which."

The door opened and Palmer strode in, followed by Sarah carrying a tray. "How is your visit going?" he asked, gesturing for Sarah to put the tray on the table.

Jordan looked down, trying to compose herself.

"Very well, I think," Jordan's father said. "Sister Jordan seems to understand more about what she needs to do to find her way back to God." He smiled. "And to our family. You're doing good work with her, Thomas. Her mother and I thank you."

Palmer beamed. "It is not I who doeth the work. It is the work of our Lord."

Sarah set out a plate of cookies, a carafe, and two cups. "And Sister Jordan, of course, is making more of an effort as well."

Jordan knew what was expected following any praise or compliment from Palmer. She gritted her teeth. "Thank you, Father," she said barely loud enough to avoid repercussions. She glanced up.

"Thank you, Lena," Jordan's father said, touching a lock of Sarah's hair that'd pulled loose from its bun. "I'm sorry, I mean Sister Sarah."

She stiffened. "You're welcome, Brother Jonathan."

Lena? Jordan snapped her gaze to Sarah in astonishment. That was it! That was why Sarah seemed so familiar. She stared. There it was. Those eyes, those sad brown eyes that'd looked up at Jordan through black, plastic framed glasses. She'd certainly grown into an adult. Her teeth had been straightened. She'd matured into her mismatched features, but it *was* Lena—poor, lonely, mercilessly teased, little Lena. "Jesus Christ." Jordan turned on Palmer. "You did this to your own daughter?"

Palmer's pleasant manner morphed into the demeanor he carried when administering punishment. "That's fifteen, Sister Jordan, for taking our Savior's name in vain."

Jordan didn't care. Lena had been a gentle, fragile little girl with no friends and parents who treated her like her birth was their punishment for past sins. Her two older brothers had been the golden children. She was six or eight years younger than Jordan, so she'd still been a child when Jordan had left, but Jordan had stood up for her a number of times, shielding her from the harsh ridicule the other younger kids heaped on her. Jordan leapt from her chair. "You son of a bitch. You're a fucking monster."

"Jordan, no!" Lena said, her voice stronger than Jordan had ever heard it.

Jordan looked at her in surprise, just in time to see her mask drop back into place.

"Sister Jordan, you mustn't swear," Lena said, lowering her gaze. "It displeases our Lord and leaves the way open for Satan."

"Listen to your sister," Palmer said. "Surrender your anger to God. His will for Sister Sarah isn't your concern."

Jordan glanced at Lena, who was keeping her eyes lowered. She knew she should take Lena's cue. It was the smart thing to do. Rage still consumed her, though, at the memory of that little girl in relation now to this woman, who shrieked and cried at the slightest human touch. But she had to shut it down. Nothing good would come from a further attack on Palmer. She was already looking at fifteen lashes with the strap, and she didn't want to get Lena into trouble. *I can do this. I can do it.* "I'm sorry, Father," she said, looking to the floor. "Please, forgive me."

"You'll be cleansed by the strap," Palmer said. "Then there will be nothing to forgive."

Jordan heard her father chuckle.

"Yes," he said, "I think your program is working quite nicely."

Jordan lay on the hard cement slab in her room. Her back burned and throbbed from the lashing, even with the ointment and dressing Brother Isaac had administered. She could tell she'd really pissed off Palmer this time. *This* time it'd been personal.

The darkness enveloped her. For now, it soothed her, but she knew it was only a matter of time before the fear crept in and claimed her every thought. She considered Lena while she still could. *What happened to her?*

When Jordan had left for college, Lena had been eight, maybe ten, at the most. *She must be gay to have ended up in the teen ex-gay ministry.* What had Sister Katherine said? She was the first to go through the program as an adult, but she'd graduated from the teen program earlier. Then she'd been caught *sneaking a sinful life. Jesus, what must that have been like? To have gotten away, then been dragged back into this insanity?*

Satan was strong in Sister Sarah, Sister Katherine had said. *Why'd they change her name?* They'd turned her into an emotional invalid. But no. Lena wasn't as debilitated as she pretended to be. She'd been trying to help Jordan since the very first day Jordan had seen her. It was all an act. *Not all.* That day she'd completely lost it when Jordan had touched her…That hadn't been an act. Nor was the terror in her eyes when she'd been taken away.

Jordan had to find a way to talk to her, to find out how she really was, what she really knew. She had a room there. Sister Katherine had told the men to take her back to her room. Did that mean *she* was being held captive here, too? Even if she were, she seemed to have free rein of the place, and that might be enough to make her Jordan's only hope. She now knew Hannah and Nikki hadn't gotten anywhere with the police.

And what about Hannah and Nikki? Was what her father dangled in front of her true? Were they getting closer to each other? Were they together? Or had her father simply been trying to get a rise out of her, trying to torment her?

The truth was, she'd betrayed them both, individually *and* together. She'd known from the very beginning there was a connection between them. For a moment, she'd even thought she should step back and let them discover it, but Hannah had been so enthralled with her. It'd felt so good. Hannah wasn't the kind of woman she usually spent time with. She was something special. She had an air of class about her. Even at that, Jordan had never loved her—Jordan didn't know how to love—and she knew Nikki would, if given half a chance. She knew Nikki *did* love Hannah, and that was the reason she'd stopped hanging out with them. She'd never needed to say it out loud.

And yet, Jordan had stayed with Hannah, continued dating her, even let her move in when it'd come up, all the while, still fucking other women. She hadn't been able to give that up either. She'd gotten that book about sex addicts to see if that's what she might be, but she'd read only a few chapters, because the bottom line was she didn't know how to change. Or maybe she just didn't want to.

She was an asshole—she knew it—and Hannah deserved better. Hannah deserved Nikki. Nikki was a good person, a good friend, a good girlfriend, when she let herself get involved. None of her relationships had ever lasted very long, though. Perhaps one with Hannah would.

If that was the only good thing that came from all this, then it was something. It meant she was really alone, now, though, but hadn't she always been?

The welts on her back throbbed harder. She clenched her teeth against the pain, but she felt a strange sense of release. Even freedom, maybe. She was no longer cheating on Hannah, no longer lying to Nikki. They knew *exactly* who she was. *No more hiding.*

Now, if she could just figure out how to get out of this insane asylum. Maybe, once she was out, she could start fresh, and find the person she actually wanted to be.

CHAPTER SIXTEEN

Nikki stepped into the living room of the condo, carrying the large pan of enchiladas she'd made for Rob's going away party, and kicked the door closed behind her.

Hannah looked up with a start from where she sat on the couch. "Oh my God, is it that late?" She shifted and began to rise.

"No, no. I'm early. Relax," Nikki said on her way to the kitchen. "I'm just going to put these in your fridge until it's time to go." She made room on the top shelf and slid the pan in before returning to say a proper hello.

Hannah sat cross-legged on the sofa with the coffee table pulled close and her computer open in front of her. She was obviously showered, with her hair already dry and pulled up in a style that swept seductively across her forehead, and her makeup was applied expertly to highlight the deep green of her eyes and her supple lips. She wore only her short terry robe, the cut of which showed off her long, shapely legs and the delicate hollow of her throat.

"Where'd you get that shirt?" Hannah asked, clearly conducting a perusal of her own.

Nikki glanced down at her black button-up shirt with an intricately embroidered design of what almost, but not quite, looked like numerous open bird wings fluttering across a night sky. The red, orange, and bright blue and green threadwork covered the yoke and shoulders. "My grandma made it." She ran her hand over the soft fabric enveloping her torso, knowing that her *abuelita* spent many hours washing and working with it before ever cutting the pattern to ensure its comfort and that the wearer felt her love. "She always brings something for each of us."

Everyone had been so excited when Nikki's parents had shown up a week earlier with her eighty-four-year-old grandmother as a surprise. Nikki had spent the better part of the past six days at Aleyda's, visiting and helping to ready the house and yard for the party tonight. She'd spoken with Hannah on the phone and texted, but she hadn't seen her much. The separation had been simultaneously good for her and difficult. She'd come over early tonight to catch up with her as well as to meet with Lantz.

"It's beautiful." Hannah's gaze loitered on the design, then dipped lower and traversed Nikki's black jeans and polished boots before moving back to her face.

It felt like fingertips exploring her body. Nikki heated. Would she ever be able to be in the same room with Hannah without that feeling? *This is wrong. We're friends.*

Hannah smiled. "You look great."

"Thanks." *So do you.* She almost said the words out loud but caught herself. "What are you doing?" she asked instead.

Hannah's expression shifted to one of uncertainty, and she frowned. "I'm seeing what apartment rents run these days."

Nikki crooked an eyebrow and sat across from her in the recliner. "You're ready to move?"

Hannah nodded. "It's time. I've regained some of my energy, and I certainly don't want to still be living here if Jordan comes back." She looked around the room. "Besides, it doesn't feel right being here with Jordan's money still paying for most of it. I'm sure she has a new place by now, but she might want to do something with this one. I talked to her accountant and told her I'd let her know when I'm out so she can tell Jordan if she hears from her."

Nikki glanced at the laptop. "Finding anything?"

Hannah looked at the screen. "There's a place in Silverlake, but it's a little farther from school than I'd prefer, and I'd need to check the neighborhood. I just feel like I have to get out of here, so I might take something temporarily until I can find a place I really like."

"What about Kate's? Could you stay with her?" Nikki could almost physically see the elephant in the room, plodding around, looking as uncomfortable as she felt. Of course, she didn't have the space for Hannah in her little one-bedroom, but she felt like she should at least offer. She couldn't, though. Hannah had already asked her why she still lived there, already suggested she move. What if she brought it up again and wanted them to be roommates? There was no way in hell Nikki could live with Hannah, not now that she knew what it felt like to kiss her, to hold her—not without her head exploding in the first week.

"She offered, and I might take her up on it, at least while I'm looking." Hannah furrowed her brow. "I don't think she's there much right now anyway."

"Where is she?"

"I don't know," Hannah said, sounding conspiratorial. "She's been acting strange lately."

Nikki laughed. "Stranger than usual?"

"I know." Hannah giggled, a light and happy sound that went with the love in her voice.

Nikki couldn't help but smile.

"She'll tell me what's going on eventually. She always does. I can count on Kate." Hannah closed the laptop. "Like you," she said, meeting Nikki's eyes.

Nikki wanted so badly to tell Hannah how much she could count on her, how much Nikki wanted to be there for her all the time, and not simply as a friend. She'd thought a lot about Aleyda's question a few weeks earlier, and she'd had to admit, at least to herself, that yes, she had fallen in love with Hannah this time. Fully and completely. And she'd thought about what Aleyda had said about Hannah not being with Jordan any longer, and that she never would be again. For some reason, though, Nikki couldn't let herself go there, couldn't allow herself to consider the actual possibility of really *being with* Hannah. She'd continued telling herself that Hannah wasn't interested, didn't see her as anything but a friend, but with moments like this one, when Hannah had run her gaze over Nikki like she wanted to explore every inch of her, that denial was getting more difficult to hold on to. "I'm glad you know you can count on me," Nikki said quietly, unable to say anything else.

Hannah waited an awkward moment, then cleared her throat. She rose and straightened her robe. "I should get dressed. Lantz will be here soon."

Nikki was more than ready for Hannah to get some clothes on.

"I wish he'd given me some indication on the phone of what he found," Hannah said. "Do you think he found my birth mom?"

"We'll know soon." Nikki's cell chimed an incoming text. She pulled it from her pocket and read it.

From Cyndi

Just checking to see if you decided about tomorrow night. Would love to see you.

Nikki had been putting off an answer for a week, but maybe it was time. Hannah was doing well. She was back at work with plenty to occupy her mind and time. Maybe the thing to do was to go back to dating a little, to get everything back into perspective.

"Who's that?" Hannah asked.

Nikki looked up, startled that Hannah was still there. She hesitated, then remembered her promise never to lie to Hannah again. "A woman I met a few months ago. In fact, she's the one I was out with the night you called looking for Jordan."

"Oh," Hannah said, in evident surprise. "Are you dating her?"

"I haven't been." Nikki slipped her phone back into her pocket. "But she wants to get together now that things have settled down." A shard of her attention was still on Cyndi's text and whether it would be best to see if that might lead to something. Most of it, though, was on Hannah's legs. "Go get dressed. If Lantz gets here and sees you like that, he's going to forget anything at all he found out about your birth mom."

Hannah smiled, but a shadow dimmed her expression. "I'll be right back," she said as she turned to leave.

Alone, Nikki took a slow survey of the living room she'd spent so much time in over the past nine years. There were the past few months with Hannah, but more than that, all the evenings and weekends she'd spent here with Jordan, watching games, barbecuing, just hanging out. She wondered what Jordan was doing right then. It was a Saturday, heading into the evening. Was she relaxing on a different couch? Getting ready to go out with Liz Talbot? Or maybe not home at all, but on a basketball court somewhere in Philadelphia, shooting hoops? She'd probably never know. But she'd miss this place when Hannah moved. Hannah stepped back into the room. "Okay, I'm dressed."

All Nikki could do was stare. If she'd thought her body had heated with desire at Hannah in her robe, now it burned. The deep vee of the red and orange swirled halter dress she wore revealed just enough cleavage to make Nikki want to beg for more, and Hannah's bare neck and shoulders called for Nikki's mouth, her lips, her teeth. Strappy heeled sandals showcased Hannah's long, smooth legs, making Nikki ache to feel them draped over her shoulders. She and Hannah had spent so much time hanging out around the house together in shorts and T-shirts over the past few months, Nikki had almost forgotten how mouthwatering Hannah looked when she went out. Nikki's pulse throbbed between her thighs. "Wow," she said, trying to collect her thoughts. "You look amazing."

Hannah smiled. "Thank you. It feels good to be dressed up and going to a party."

Great. She feels good. It's going to kill me.

The doorbell rang.

Hannah's eyes widened, and she inhaled sharply. "It's Lantz."

"I'll get it," Nikki said, thankful for the distraction. "You relax."

Once they'd all settled, Lantz handed Hannah a folder. "Everything I'm going to tell you is in here, but if you have any questions, or if any come up for you afterward, don't hesitate to ask."

"Okay," Hannah said. She looked excitedly at Nikki.

"I won't draw this out because I know you've had your hopes up. I want to let you know right up front that your birth mother passed away in 1992."

"Oh," Hannah said, all of her enthusiasm extinguished. Her shoulders slumped and her eyes watered.

Nikki took her hand.

"I'm very sorry," Lantz said. "I did find out who she was and where she was living, and I can go over that with you, if you'd like. There was no information on who your father was, though. No one I spoke with knew anything about him."

Hannah looked up. "You talked to people who actually knew her?"

"Yes. The last seven years of her life, she lived in a little place called Tehachapi. It's in the desert foothills of the southern Sierra Nevada mountain range. She went by Ellen Graham, although it doesn't appear that was her real name. I wasn't able to find any record of her prior to the year you and your sister were born."

"Why would she change her name?" Hannah asked.

Lantz shrugged. "We'll never know. It could have been anything. It might have been she was hiding from your father for some reason. Or maybe he was someone famous and married and she was protecting him. People change their names for all kinds of reasons. Maybe she just wanted a fresh start."

Just like Jordan? Nikki encircled Hannah's shoulders. This whole conversation was reminiscent of the ones they'd had with the police.

Hannah sighed. "Thank you, Lantz," she said sadly. "I'll read the rest in the report and call you if I have any questions."

"I'm sorry, Hannah," he said.

Nikki walked him to the door and was just about to close it behind him when Hannah spoke again. "What did she die from?"

"Congestive heart failure," he said.

She only nodded.

When she and Hannah were alone again, Nikki sat beside her, uncertain what to say.

"That's that, then," Hannah said, before Nikki had to decide. "I guess I'll never know anything more about my birth mother *or* Jordan."

"Do you want to go talk to some of the people that knew your mother?" Nikki picked up the folder and leafed through the pages, finding some names. "Here's a woman she worked for. Maybe she could at least tell you what she was like."

"I don't even know where that place is."

Nikki pulled out her phone again and Googled it. "It's only a couple of hours from here. We could do a day trip. Or maybe a weekend." She clicked on a link to some images. "It looks pretty."

Hannah rested her elbows on her knees and cradled her chin in her hand. She looked at Nikki thoughtfully. *My mother's gone. I'll never actually know her.* Would talking to people who *had* make any difference? "Let's just go to your nephew's party and have a good time," she said finally. She couldn't think about yet another disappointment right now.

❖

Hannah stood on the back steps off Aleyda's kitchen and watched Nikki across the yard, dancing with her niece. She couldn't take her eyes off her. Nikki looked so incredibly hot all in black, the colorful embroidery on her shirt adding a flourish of celebration to the outfit. The fabric looked so soft, Hannah had wanted to run her hands over it all evening, but she was afraid if she touched Nikki in any way, she wouldn't want to stop. Nikki's brothers and nephews wore similar shirts, only with different embroidered designs, and Aleyda, the other sisters-in-law, and the nieces wore tunic style tops with colorful stitching down the front, around the open neckline.

She watched all of Nikki's family members and their friends dancing, in conversation clusters at tables around the large yard, playing Frisbee under the white twinkling lights strung along the trellises and draped over the shrubbery. Music filled the air. Hannah felt so much a part of this big family, even though she'd met most of them only once before, some never. It alleviated some of the remaining disappointment from her conversation with Lantz, at least for the evening. They'd all been so welcoming. Nikki's father was a flirt, her mother an angel. Her brothers had teased Nikki mercilessly about keeping Hannah a secret, as though she were Nikki's date. Hannah had been grateful Nikki hadn't corrected them and reminded them she'd been to a couple of Nikki's birthday parties as Jordan's girlfriend. She wasn't Jordan's girlfriend anymore, and it was time for a fresh start of her own.

It was Nikki's grandmother, though—Nikki had told Hannah to call her *Abuelita* or just *Lita* like everyone else—that had captured Hannah's heart. She was a tiny woman, no more than five feet tall, in her eighties, who didn't speak a word of English. She had just stared and smiled at Hannah, then taken Hannah's face in her hands and kissed her tenderly on the cheek. She then said something to Nikki in Spanish that made Nikki redden. Nikki had said she had simply told her it was nice to meet Hannah, but Hannah didn't believe her. She smiled thinking about it.

"She's a sweetheart, isn't she?" Aleyda said, stepping up beside her.

"I'm sorry?"

"Nikki." Aleyda nodded in the direction Hannah had been staring. "She's a sweetheart."

Hannah blushed at being caught. "Yes, she definitely is." She looked across the yard again just in time to see Nikki drop into a chair at a table with two of her aunts and one of her brothers.

Nikki scanned the party until her gaze fell on Hannah, then she arched an eyebrow in obvious question.

Hannah smiled and gave her a little wave, letting her know she was fine. "I don't know what I would have done without her these past few months," she said to Aleyda.

"You two have been through a lot together." Aleyda rested her hands on the railing. "It seems to have made you closer."

"It has," Hannah said, thinking back to some of the moments they had shared. "Even with everything else going on, I've really enjoyed getting to know her better. And now that life seems to be moving on, I want to pay back some of what she's done for me."

"That's nice," Aleyda said. "I'm sure that will mean a lot to her."

"At the very least, I'd like to get her into a better apartment."

Hannah had meant it as a joke, but when she turned to Aleyda for a conspiratorial chuckle, Aleyda's expression was serious. It softened as she returned her attention to Nikki. "She's never told you why she lives there?"

"She just said there's no reason to move." Hannah waited, curious.

Aleyda smiled. "Of course, she'd say something like that."

"What's the real reason?"

Aleyda studied Hannah, as though weighing whether to answer. Finally, she spoke. "After my husband died, Nikki moved in with me and the kids to help me manage everything. She babysat while I was at work and arranged her work schedule around when I could be home. She helped take care of the house and its maintenance. She contributed financially. But when the boys reached an age when they wanted their own rooms, Nikki got that apartment. She found the cheapest place she could—without getting mugged every night when she got home—so she'd still be able to help with everything the kids needed." Aleyda turned to Hannah. "And she stays there, now, because in addition to paying my salary from the business, she's also covering part of the boys' college expenses and putting money into a family college fund for Cecelia. The kids do their part with scholarships and grants, but Nikki puts in quite a bit of what she makes."

"I had no idea." Hannah felt a little embarrassed.

"I used to think she did it out of guilt, but all I have to do is see her with the kids to know it's pure love." Aleyda was watching Nikki again, her eyes shining with a veneer of tears in the soft lighting.

A gentle stroke on Hannah's back drew her attention, and Nikki's grandmother slipped between Hannah and Aleyda.

"Ah, *Lita*," Aleyda said, squeezing the small woman's shoulders.

Abuelita pressed a folded garment into Hannah's hands and said something in Spanish.

Hannah smiled but shook her head. "I'm sorry, I don't—" She looked helplessly to Aleyda.

"She made that for you," Aleyda said. "As a welcome to the family." A smile lit her face.

"What?" Hannah ran her fingers over the finely stitched embroidery in awe. "It's beautiful." She shook out the tunic and admired it. "But how did she…"

"She told me she had a dream about you, that you'd be coming into the family," Aleyda said, affectionately rubbing the older woman's arms. She said something to her, and *Abuelita* answered. "She says you're everything she dreamed and more. She knows you'll be good to Nikki."

"I… I don't understand."

Nikki's grandmother took Hannah into a long hug and began to rock her.

Hannah melted. She felt like a child being loved so deeply nothing could ever frighten or disappoint her again. She wrapped her arms around *Abuelita* and closed her eyes.

Finally, the older woman released her, gave her a brilliant, sparkling-eyed smile, and disappeared into the house.

"I'm so touched," Hannah said, trying to collect herself. "But I don't want her to misunderstand. Nikki and I are just friends."

"Are you?" Aleyda asked. "Are you sure?"

All of the thoughts Hannah had been having about Nikki lately, the closeness, the feel of her touch that night in her bed, rushed in on her. Arousal licked at her senses. She looked away. She found Nikki, back on the dance floor, with a voluptuous redhead pressed so tightly against her they could have been conjoined twins. She went rigid. "Who's *that*?" She heard Aleyda chuckle.

"That's Kayla," Aleyda said. "She used to live next door to the family. She and Nikki and the boys all grew up together. You don't need to worry about her."

"I'm not worried," Hannah said, too quickly to be convincing.

"Friends don't react the way you just did when their *friends* dance with someone else," Aleyda said, making her point clear.

Hannah pursed her lips. Was she ready to admit it, even to herself? "I don't think Nikki feels—"

Aleyda cut her off with a deep sigh. "I shouldn't say this, but I'm going to. She does."

Hannah searched her eyes for confirmation.

"Don't let her push you away." Aleyda patted Hannah's hand and moved down the steps to join the party.

Hannah was speechless and watched as Nikki finished her dance with Kayla. She twirled her off the dance floor and into the arms of a tall guy in a cowboy hat.

Nikki smiled and waved at the couple as they walked away, then headed across the yard toward a gate that led behind her photography studio. Her stride was strong and easy, just like her presence in Hannah's life had been since Jordan's disappearance. But that was how friends were supposed to be in times of trouble, right? Wasn't that just what friends did?

Nikki had been more, though. Aleyda was right. Hannah remembered moments, the flash of something in Nikki's eyes, the warmth of a touch, the heat of Nikki's kiss that night in her bedroom. It *hadn't* been anger, not completely. Emotion stirred in Hannah's depths, conjuring that swell that she had written off as something else so many times before. She felt something for Nikki, something strong, but she wasn't sure what it was. It wasn't love, was it? She had loved Jordan, and this felt so very different. It felt unlike anything she had felt for any woman in the past. She was sure she could figure it out in time, but now there was that woman who had sent the text asking for a date.... *Damn her.*

Hannah moved down the steps and followed Nikki through the gate. It was darker at this distance from the party lights, more difficult to see. She could make out Nikki in shadow and heard the soft clang of bottles jostling against one another as Nikki fumbled with a trash bag. Hannah moved closer. "Nikki? Can I talk to you?"

"Yeah," Nikki said, sounding surprised. "Hannah? Is that you?"

"Yes." Anxiety fluttered in Hannah's stomach. What was she going to say?

As if from nowhere, soft light illuminated the area.

Nikki closed the door of a control panel mounted on the wall.

"What is this?" Hannah asked, taking in the scene.

"It's an outdoor shoot area for smaller parties, where we don't need to go off site." Nikki turned and gestured across the lawn to the outer fence line. "There are six different stations."

Hannah crossed to an alcove that held a mountain backdrop with a partial cabin porch angled into one corner, replete with rocking chairs, and a small cluster of trees reminiscent of a forest in the other. The next area ensconced a cropping of rocks on a sand floor that could have been nestled into a beach cove waiting for picnickers or someone wanting to sit and watch the sunset.

Nikki walked along side her as Hannah took in each one. They stopped in front of a park scene with lush grass and a wooden bench, worn smooth from use and surrounded by an array of multi-colored flowers in sculpted beds.

"They're beautiful," Hannah said.

"Thanks." Nikki's voice was quiet and close to Hannah's ear.

Hannah shivered with the desire for actual contact. She pulled her attention from the scene and looked into Nikki's face.

Nikki met her gaze, an expectant look in her rich brown eyes. "What do you want to talk about?" Her breath feathered across Hannah's cheek.

Only inches separated them. Hannah warmed. "What?"

"You asked if you could talk to me?" The hint of a smile lifted the corner of Nikki's mouth.

The subtle shift of Nikki's lips drew Hannah's attention. Did she want to talk? Or, did she just want to kiss her? *I can't do that.* "Oh. Yes." But what had she wanted to talk about? She was having a hard time thinking. *The text. The woman. That was it.* How could she, though? It wasn't her place.

Nikki touched Hannah's forearm, then ran her hand down and interlaced their fingers.

Hannah quelled a sigh and the urge to tighten her grip.

"Are you okay?" Nikki asked. "Do you want to leave?"

No! She didn't want to leave, not this spot, not this moment. She wanted to stay close to Nikki. She needed to feel what she was feeling so she could figure out what it was, but mostly, she simply wanted to be right here with her. So close and so wanting. Her hand tingled where Nikki grasped it. She shook her head. "I..." She had to get this out, to force herself, if necessary. "I want to ask you..." She faltered, then tried again. "I know I don't have any right..."

"What is it?" Nikki asked with evident concern.

"I don't want you to see her." Hannah pushed the words from her throat.

Nikki blinked. "What? Who?"

The heat of a blush flooded Hannah's cheeks and neck. "The woman. The text. The one you were with before." *There!* She'd said it. She looked at the ground.

A long silence stretched between them.

Finally, Nikki crooked a finger beneath Hannah's chin and lifted her face to hers. "Why not?" she whispered.

Suddenly, Hannah knew. She knew what she wanted. She still wasn't sure why, couldn't put an actual name to it, but she knew what it was she wanted. She pressed her hands to Nikki's chest, curled her fingers into the softness of her shirt. She traced the embroidery, then brushed two fingertips over the hollow of Nikki's throat. She lingered on the hard pulse in Nikki's neck, desire surging at the knowledge that Nikki's heart was pounding as fast as her own. Then, she looked at Nikki's mouth again. She lost all other thought. The only thing she could think about was the way Nikki had kissed her that night—and she wanted it again. She ran her thumb across Nikki's lower lip.

Nikki sucked in a breath and opened for her. She slipped her fingers around the nape of Hannah's neck and dispensed with the mere inches between them. She tentatively covered Hannah's mouth with her own.

For a moment, that was all there was—just the pressing together of lips, the confirmation that something had changed. Then, Hannah trailed the tip of her tongue along the slight opening of Nikki's mouth.

Nikki groaned and pulled Hannah against her. Their bodies melded.

Hannah felt the heat of Nikki's entire length. She arched into her, encircling her shoulders, at the touch of her hands on Hannah's bare back.

Nikki ran her palms slowly up the length of Hannah's spine, finding that spot right in the center that made Hannah's knees weak.

Hannah's nipples stiffened against Nikki's breasts, and she moaned softly into her mouth.

Nikki kissed her, thoroughly, deeply, excruciatingly slowly. She caressed Hannah's back with her fingertips, from the nape of her neck to the hollow just above the fabric of her halter dress.

Arousal burned between Hannah's legs, and she pressed her hips into Nikki's. She swept her tongue over and around Nikki's, returning the kiss with equal fervor.

"Hannah." Nikki gasped for air and started to pull away.

Hannah slipped her fingers into Nikki's hair and held her to her. "Not yet," she murmured against Nikki's lips. "Let me feel you a little longer."

Nikki relaxed into her. "God, yes," she whispered. She kissed Hannah again.

Hannah took in the taste of Nikki's mouth, the softness of her lips, the scent of her skin mingled with that of lotus. She felt the imprint of her taut, toned body on her own, the silkiness of her hair between her fingers. She wanted to memorize it all, to be able to recall it, to relive it, in case she could never have it again.

The thought jarred her, made her cling more tightly, suck Nikki's tongue in more deeply. *People leave. They walk away and give you up.*

Nikki wouldn't do that, though. But she had thought Jordan wouldn't either. *And what mother does that?* She didn't want to, but she slowed the kiss, then eased out of it. She needed to think. She knew this was what she wanted, no lingering doubt, but she wanted more than just an urgent orgasm in the shadows. She needed to know it was more.

Nikki watched her, her eyes hooded and dark with need. There was something else in them, too, though—tenderness, concern.

Of course there is. This is Nikki.

They both panted as they looked at one another, but neither spoke.

Finally, Nikki touched her hand to the back of Hannah's head and guided it down to her shoulder.

Hannah relaxed against her and let Nikki hold her.

Nikki began to sway, and Hannah became aware of the music drifting on the night air. A gentle breeze cooled her skin. A woman sang seductively in Spanish.

"What's she saying?" Hannah asked after a while.

"She's saying she never wants this moment to end..." Nikki waited, seemingly for the next line. "She never wants time to begin again...to have to return to a world where her love isn't hers."

Hannah turned her face into Nikki's neck and smiled. "Is that really what she's saying?"

"I have no idea. I'm not listening." Nikki held Hannah close and moved them in a gentle circle.

Hannah laughed and lifted her head. She searched Nikki's face. "Is this okay?"

"This is *so* okay." Nikki's eyes still smoldered, but a question lay in their depths.

"I feel something for you," Hannah said, answering it. "Something more than friendship. I'm not sure what it is, but I'd like to explore it, if that's something you think you'd like, too."

"How long have you felt it?" Nikki asked.

Hannah shook her head. "I don't know. The last few weeks, at least. Maybe longer. It's hard to say with everything that's gone on."

Nikki kissed her tenderly on the lips but said nothing.

"So, is it?" Hannah asked.

"Is it what?"

"Something you think you'd like, too."

Something passed through Nikki's eyes, leaving behind a sheen of moisture. "Yes," she said, her voice breaking a little.

Hannah lowered her head to Nikki's shoulder again and snuggled against her. Her body still craved more, her arousal right on the verge of reigniting, but under control. It felt so right to be in Nikki's arms, so right to have Nikki in hers. How could that be after all this time? Part of her didn't care. Part of her wanted just to be right here, in this moment, looking only forward, not behind. And what did forward hold? She remembered the text. "So, you won't get together with that woman?" She needed to hear Nikki say it.

Nikki laughed so softly Hannah only felt it. "No," she whispered and squeezed Hannah tightly. "I won't."

Hannah smiled and relaxed into Nikki's embrace. That was all she needed for now.

CHAPTER SEVENTEEN

Jordan knelt in front of the toilet and threw up. She was losing the battle. The only defense she'd had was no longer working.

During the first week when they'd given her the drugs that induced nausea, she'd countered the effects by fantasizing about sex with women at other times of the day in hopes of keeping the conditioning from taking hold. As the intensity and frequency of the sessions had increased, she'd begun feeling sick even with the meds out of her system. She'd still kept trying, though. She'd fought the nausea, focusing the thoughts more strongly on the images and memories she pulled up—mind over matter, and all—but instead of warding off the churning in her stomach, now she simply reached the point that she vomited.

How are they doing this? She wiped the sweat from her forehead, then swiped her mouth. *I should be able to fight it.* She thought of Lena and the number of times she'd warned Jordan not to. Had Lena fought? Is that how she'd ended up the way she was? What was the alternative, though—just to concede and end up unable to ever be with a woman again, married to some asshole her father chose, and working for the man who'd done this to her? *I have to fight.*

She hadn't had the opportunity to talk to Lena yet. There had to be a way to do that. Maybe if she kept pretending to go along with everything, behaved herself... Maybe spending some *Bible study* time with Lena could be a privilege she earned again.

Jordan pushed herself to her feet, flushed the toilet, and curled onto her side on her bed. Her biggest battle, and probably the most important one, was the one against despondency. In some moments, the hopelessness of her situation all but consumed her. She couldn't give up, though. She had to keep control of her mind. She closed her eyes and went to a place where no one could touch her.

It was a place from her childhood she'd remembered after one of the sessions a while back. It was a meadow filled with long, swaying green grass and wild flowers. A cabin sat on the edge of a wooded area nearby, and she'd always been able to hear the ocean, though she could never see it. And she'd heard a voice, one from inside her, that'd given her the strength she'd needed.

When she was young, she'd escaped there when the emptiness and the knowledge that she'd never be good enough for her parents got to be too much. There, the truth always resonated within her. That inner voice reminded her that who she really was wasn't determined by her parents. Once she'd grown up and turned her back on her childhood world, she'd forgotten about it. She'd no longer needed it. Or maybe she'd just replaced it with the arms of nameless women.

She'd remembered it here, though, had heard that voice in the early days of constant darkness. She'd gone there for solace and to ward off the encroaching fear and hunger. For a while, she'd found Hannah waiting for her there, and they had only sat in silence. Recently, however, it was only her, warmed by the sunshine, soothed by the rhythmic rush of the unseen waves, comforted by that inner voice. It'd been hard to hear at first, as though it had a great distance to cross, digging its way out of the past Jordan had so deeply buried. But little by little, it strengthened, and she could hear it clearly once again.

Crazy! But that place, and that voice, had gotten her through her empty childhood. And now they were back, right when Jordan needed help. And she was grateful, crazy or not.

She lay in the tall grass, the sunshine on her face, listening.

Relax. Let your stomach settle.

Jordan inhaled deeply and felt the nausea subside. She knew what to do.

Breathe. Slowly.

In, then out. In, then out. She began to calm, not just physically, but her fears, her doubts. But she was still here. As soon as she opened her eyes, she'd be in hell again. Tears threatened, and she held back a sob. She couldn't take anymore.

Yes, you can. Be strong. You can beat them. You can't give up. There will come a time for you to act, but until then, know you're never alone.

Jordan calmed. She wanted to believe it. She had to, otherwise, she had nothing.

"Sister Jordan." Another voice broke the spell of that quiet place, and Jordan was back. She groaned with disappointment—only a dream. Then, anxiety gripped her. *Another session?*

"Sister Jordan?" It was Sister Katherine. "Father wants to see you."

Jordan blinked awake, the words from her dream still in her mind. Could she trust them, or was it part of the insanity? She had to trust. She sat up, feeling dangerously docile.

"Please, come with me," Sister Katherine said, moving to the door.

Without a word, Jordan followed. When Sister Katherine led her into the room where she'd met with her father both times, Jordan filled with dread. Nothing good ever happened in that room.

Palmer sat at the other end of the table, a woman on the corner to his right, their heads bent together as they looked over some papers.

Sister Katherine remained at Jordan's side.

Palmer looked up. "Ah, Sister Jordan. I hope you're feeling better," he said with a hint of sympathy.

Jordan didn't buy it. "Thank you, Father," she said robotically.

The woman beside him lifted her gaze and smiled. "Hello, Sister Jordan."

Jordan stared in disbelief.

"You remember my wife, I trust," Palmer said.

Loraine Palmer, the first woman Jordan had ever touched, the first to have touched her, looked back at her with the cool expression she gave to the world. Jordan, however, had seen, heard, felt, what lay beneath. All of that was missing, along with even the slightest trace of surprise. "You're in on this?" Jordan asked stupidly. *Of course she is. Why else would she be here?*

"Mrs. Palmer is overseeing your program. She oversees all of them," Palmer said, as though Jordan hadn't spoken. "And she takes part in some of the more difficult ones. She feels Satan has a tight grip on you in this phase, which is why you've been sick. She feels stronger methods might be warranted."

Jordan couldn't take her eyes off Loraine's once golden blond hair, now a shimmering silver, her smooth skin only touched by faint brackets around her mouth. Jordan couldn't believe she was here, still married to her fanatic husband, an active part in his lunacy. Jordan had always pictured her far away somewhere, living happily with her female lover. Even if that weren't true, though, for her to be *here* and actually taking part in Jordan's kidnapping and torture… They'd shared a lot all those years ago, spent many hours, some whole nights, together, exploring and pleasuring one another. Jordan knew it hadn't been love—she hadn't been that naïve even in her teens—but hadn't it been *something*? "Loraine?"

"You'll address her as Mother," Palmer said with mild reproach. "And you'll treat her with the same respect you show me or face similar consequences."

Mother? There was no way. She'd tasted this woman, been inside her, made her come. There was no fucking way she could— or would—call her Mother. A sudden fury blew through her. Every muscle in her body clenched. "So, *Loraine* feels stronger methods are warranted?" Jordan asked Palmer, her glare never wavering from Loraine. "Has *Loraine* told you she was the first woman I ever *fucked*? Has she told you she *taught me* how to fuck a woman? How to eat pussy?"

An expression of distaste settled on Palmer's face. "These aren't your words, Sister Jordan. We know that. Some of the girls in our teen program have cast the same lies." He shook his head. "We know it's Satan within you. That's what Mrs. Palmer suspected."

"Oh, really?" Jordan scoffed. "Other girls have said the same thing? Imagine that." She cut Sister Katherine an accusatory glance. "How about you?"

Sister Katherine averted her eyes.

"Yeah, that's what I thought." Jordan leaned closer. "She's a great fuck, isn't she?"

"That's enough," Palmer said, his tone hard.

"Is it?" Jordan's voice rose. She knew better, but she couldn't stop. "I don't think it is."

Palmer pressed a button beside the door behind him.

Jordan picked up a chair and hurled it across the table at the couple.

They dodged it.

She grabbed another. "It's not *nearly* enough," she screamed as she threw it so hard, it bounced off the wall, then clattered across the floor. She could see Lena, giving her that pleading look that said *play along*. She could hear that voice inside, saying, *be strong*. But without fighting back, she couldn't be strong. *No more! No fucking more!*

The door behind her burst open, and two of the brothers grabbed her. In an instant, like clockwork, Sister Katherine sank a needle into her arm.

That Goddamned needle.

❖

When Jordan came around, she was restrained on a table, and she was pretty sure she was naked beneath the sheet that covered her. She was alone in a room she'd never seen before.

How could I have been so stupid? She remembered Loraine Palmer's expression the whole time she was losing it. It was that unreadable mask she'd worn at the church years ago, the countenance that allowed no one to see past it. Jordan had seen what, or who, lay behind it, but never in public, only in their private moments.

Jordan knew now that Loraine Palmer was a predator, who should have been brought up on charges for having sex with underage girls, but it hadn't felt that way back then, at least not at first. Jordan had felt so unworthy of being loved, so invisible in her house, Loraine's attention made her feel special, like someone saw her, valued her. How fucked up was that? As time passed, though, it started feeling sordid and sleazy. Jordan began to realize she should be exploring her sexuality with girls her own age, but when she and Jenny Winters, one of the other forwards on her varsity basketball team, discovered a mutual attraction and Jordan had tried to end things with Loraine, Loraine had threatened to tell both of the girls' parents. Then, she'd made it perfectly clear that Jordan belonged to her. Jordan now wondered how many other girls over the years had belonged to Loraine.

The door opened and in she walked.

Brother Simon followed and began preparing something at the counter behind Jordan.

"How are you feeling?" Loraine asked, her expression conveying sincerity. "Better, I hope."

How could they all walk around here like all this wasn't a nightmare? Jordan got the impression the little minions truly believed in what they were doing, which didn't make it right, but it was something. Her father, however, just wanted revenge and was using Palmer and his craziness to get it, and Loraine... Christ, Loraine was the worst. She was a *lesbian*. Jordan knew that, because despite her predilection for teenage girls, Loraine had been with other women, had even lived with one in college. She'd shown Jordan pictures of the two of them, their house, their life. They'd even had cats, for God's sake. So, how the hell could she be a part of this? Not just a part, like Sister Katherine or one of the brothers, but a key player?

Jordan refused to answer. She was afraid if she did, all that would come out was a long string of pejoratives. She knew she was already in enough trouble, and now, apparently once again, in Loraine Palmer's hands. She turned her head away.

"You *will* need to talk to me, Sister Jordan," Loraine said. "We have things to discuss about your program."

Jordan kept her expression hard. She couldn't make her talk. She could feel Loraine's eyes on her.

"Brother Simon," Loraine said after a moment. "Would you please leave us? I'll call you when we're ready."

"Of course, Mother."

Jordan cringed at the title. She heard the door click closed, then the clack of Loraine's heels on the tile floor. She glanced over just in time to see her flick the lock on the knob. As Loraine returned, Jordan met her veiled gaze with a glare.

"Perhaps we need a little time to ourselves." Loraine actually smiled. "Maybe to alleviate the tension between us? Get reacquainted? Once you left for college, you never came home."

Jordan remained silent.

"You grew into a beautiful woman, Jory."

Jordan clenched her teeth at the pet name Loraine had always called her in private, the one she'd hated every time Hannah had used it. She'd never brought it up because she didn't want to explain.

"You were very cute as a teen, but when I saw the first pictures of you as a woman, before you came here..." Loraine gave a slight shake of her head. "You took my breath away," she whispered.

Jordan snapped. "Before I *came* here?" Her tone was sharp. "I didn't *come* here. I was *kidnapped* and brought here against my will."

"It was unfortunate that it had to happen that way." The words were empathetic, but no emotion showed in Loraine's eyes. "You know what they say. God does work in mysterious ways."

Jordan squeezed her eyes shut and tightened her jaw. She was so sick of hearing about their insane God. "If there *is* a God, *she* doesn't give a shit who someone fucks. *She* made gays just the way we are."

Loraine tsked. "Jory, you have to get your mouth under control." She brushed a fingertip across Jordan's lips. "There's no reason for you to be undergoing so much punishment."

Jordan jerked her head to the side. "Fuck you."

"And your temper," Loraine said, continuing her caress.

The building waves of rage constantly rolling through her finally crested. She lurched, trying to sink her teeth into Loraine's skin.

Loraine pulled her hand back and laughed. "I guess I shouldn't tease the animal." Her expression softened. "But I do remember that mouth. I taught you well."

Jordan's stomach turned. She didn't know if it was the thought of pleasuring a woman with her mouth that brought up the effects of the conditioning, or if it was the thought of ever having touched or tasted Loraine in particular.

"You should thank me. I understand you've gotten quite a bit of enjoyment over the years, sharing what you learned from me." Loraine paused long enough to draw Jordan's gaze back to her, then smiled. "But all of that's over. By the time you leave here, you won't be able to take pleasure in a woman ever again."

Jordan felt her face pale.

Satisfaction flashed in Loraine's eyes. Then something else. Sadness. "It's too bad." She moved around the table and behind Jordan. "I'd love to leave just enough desire in you so that you and I could have some fun once in a while."

Jordan heard a cabinet door open.

"But that would be wrong. Jonathan's paying a small fortune to support our mission to save as many souls as we can from the damnation of homosexuality in exchange for getting you back, so I can't disappoint."

The more Loraine spoke, the more strongly terror clawed at Jordan's throat. It seemed that each new character who came into this horror movie was a little bit crazier than the one before. "What about you?" she had to ask. Maybe if she could punch a hole in the twisted thought process... *Maybe, what?* "Obviously *you* haven't *been saved* from damnation..."

Something clinked against the counter, and paper tore.

"I've sacrificed myself," Loraine said as conversationally as if she'd merely declared her preference for pie over cake. "I need to be able to feel my temptation, and sometimes give in to it, in order to be able to be compassionate and understanding with the girls, and women, I work with."

Jordan couldn't restrain a loud snort. "Yeah, right."

Loraine returned to Jordan's side. "All that being said, it's time to see how much, if any, effect your resistance has had."

Jordan tensed. What did that mean?

"Yes, I know what you've been doing. Your increase in meditation and prayer time along with more Bible study was a bit transparent. It *was* smart of you, however. I would have expected nothing less." Loraine checked Jordan's restraints. "I actually instructed a girl to do the same thing a while back, just to see if the tactic worked." She moved closer. "It didn't. But let's see." She slowly pulled the sheet that covered Jordan down to her waist. She stared at Jordan's bare breasts, and sucked a breath between her teeth. "Mmm, beautiful."

Jordan flushed with anxiety, fear, helplessness. Suddenly, she fully understood how vulnerable she was.

Loraine touched a fingertip to one of Jordan's nipples. "I seem to remember these were *very* sensitive. Are they still?" She pressed down and worked it slowly.

Jordan tried to twist away, but her restraints restricted her movement. She remembered a time when a similar touch would have felt so good, but not here...not like this...not by *her*. Even the memory turned her stomach.

"I think so," Loraine said quietly. She rolled the nipple between her thumb and fingers as she began fondling the other one with her free hand.

The feminine lilt of Loraine's voice brought back scenes from the movies Jordan had been subjected to. She didn't feel an actual sexual response. She was too terrified. She was back under the control of the woman she'd had to move to a different city in order to get away from, and this was sexual assault, possibly heading toward rape. But the soft voice, the words themselves, so like what Jordan had experienced in the conditioning sessions, brought back the nausea.

"Doesn't that feel good?" Loraine whispered close to Jordan's ear. Her breath was a warm caress.

Jordan's stomach roiled. She struggled against it, trying to think of anything but what was happening.

"That's it, Jory." Loraine almost crooned the words. "Let's bring that devil out." She squeezed Jordan's nipples and tugged gently. "Remember how much you liked it when I sucked these?"

Saliva filled Jordan's mouth. She swallowed hard.

"Would you like that now, Jory? Would you like me to suck them?"

The mere thought of Loraine's lips and tongue on her made Jordan sick. Her throat tightened. "No!" She gasped with revulsion. She had to stop her. "No, please." Let her think what she wanted.

"Oooh." Loraine let out a low chuckle. "A please. I like that." She straightened and released Jordan's nipples.

Jordan slumped back to the table, aware for the first time she'd been straining against her bonds. She gulped for air, desperate to settle her stomach.

Loraine pulled the sheet up to Jordan's shoulders, and watched as Jordan inhaled deeply. "You see, Jory. No IV. No drugs. And yet, you still feel the effects. This will help you with any kind of temptation, because by the time we're finished, you won't be able to even think about sex with a woman without becoming violently ill."

Jordan steeled herself. She had to get control. "Is this what you did to Lena? Did you play with your own daughter?"

"Don't be disgusting." Loraine's air of authority never wavered. "We did learn from our mistakes with Lena, however. We'll continue more slowly with you. And while you'll remain far more functional in the world, the desired result will be the same."

A chill crawled up Jordan's spine. Cold sweat broke out on the back of her neck.

Satisfaction crept across Loraine's face. Her eyes narrowed slightly. "You'll *never* again be able to stand a woman's caress." She rested her hand on Jordan's thigh. "Never again be able to have a woman's mouth between your legs or yours on her. Whoever that last woman was, I hope she tasted good."

Jordan remembered Hannah, the way she'd come that last morning they'd been together. She concentrated on her beautiful smile.

"You'll never be able to have a woman's fingers inside you again, Jory. Never have a woman fuck you again. I remember how much you like that." Loraine teased Jordan's inner thigh with her nails. "Would you like it one last time, Jory?"

"No!" Jordan thrashed against her restraints. She swallowed rapidly.

"You might still be able to come—one last time," Loraine whispered.

Jordan lurched. Her stomach heaved. Vomit pumped up her throat and out her mouth. She turned her head, trying to spit it out.

Loraine stepped back, and her heels tapped as she moved across the room.

Jordan lay panting, her abdomen quivering from stomach cramps.

A beep.

"Brother Simon?" Loraine said, her tone casual again.

"Yes, Mother?"

"Please come in here. Sister Jordan needs some cleaning up before we begin."

Jordan lolled her head to the side and met Loraine's smug expression.

"Do you understand now, Jory, who's in control?" she asked flatly. "*No one* will listen to a word you say about me. *I* will be in charge of your sessions from this point on. And you will be returned to your father as the daughter he wants you to be. Or, you'll stay here with me."

Jordan's breathing began to slow, and her nausea ebbed.

Loraine unlocked the door, and Brother Simon came in. "Please get Sister Jordan cleaned up and give her a few minutes to collect herself," Loraine said, deftly conveying concern. "Then get her ready for her session. I finished prepping the electrodes. They're on the counter. I'll be back shortly."

"Yes, Mother," Brother Simon said.

"Oh, and we won't be using anesthesia." Loraine glanced back at Jordan. "I'm afraid Satan is very strong in her." She met Jordan's gaze. "It won't be easy to get her back."

Jordan's mouth went dry. Her heart pounded. She thought of Lena, and terror seized her again. *I can't end up like that.*

CHAPTER EIGHTEEN

Nikki knocked on Kate's apartment door. She knew Hannah wasn't home yet. She'd gotten a text from her earlier saying she and Marti were going shopping when Hannah got off work but that she'd be home for dinner, and it was Nikki's plan to have it waiting for her.

The past two weeks since the party had been surreal. They'd been everything Nikki had dreamed of since she'd met Hannah. Well, not *everything*. They'd agreed to hold off sleeping together until Hannah was completely moved out of Jordan's condo so they could have a brand new beginning, totally separate from both of their pasts with Jordan and everything that'd happened. It'd been difficult at times, since they *had* gone out on a few dates, *had* spent some evenings curled on the couch together in front of the TV, *had* kissed and held each other with the exquisite anticipation of more. Nikki knew she could wait, though. She'd waited three years for Hannah. She could handle it a little longer.

Hannah had decided to move in with Kate for a while, since she hadn't found an apartment currently available that met all of her needs. Once she'd made up her mind to leave the condo, however, she hadn't wanted to linger. The move was simple. She'd brought her clothes and personal items with her immediately, and there were some boxes of books, a couple of shelving units, and her grandfather's desk that still needed to be put in storage. That was it. Anything she and Jordan had bought together, she was leaving behind. When she'd let Jordan's accountant know she was vacating the property, she'd given her David's number in case she needed to contact the family. It all seemed so coldly final, but they didn't know what else to do. Jordan was living somewhere else now. It was time for them to move on, too.

Still, Nikki had some moments of guilt. Sometimes, it all felt so unfinished. Sure, Jordan was gone and hadn't left a trace of a trail to be followed, but there were so many unanswered questions. They didn't change Nikki's feelings for Hannah, or Hannah's for her. Nor did they justify anything Jordan had done. They just nagged at Nikki. Maybe the guilt she felt was simply habit.

Kate opened the door. "We need to get you a key if you're going to be a permanent fixture around here." She stepped back, looped a bracelet around her wrist, and tried to fasten it with one hand. It slipped from her grasp. "Damn it."

Nikki chuckled and scooped it up. She opened the clasp and held the gold chain out for Kate's arm.

Kate gave her a coy smile. "Aren't you chivalrous?" She let Nikki hook the bracelet around her wrist. "No wonder Hannah fell for you."

"You look nice," Nikki said, enjoying the acknowledgement of Hannah's feelings for her. "Another date?"

"Yep, and I'm running late."

Nikki watched as Kate rounded the end of the bar that separated the kitchen and dining area, retrieved some cash from a drawer, and tucked it into her wallet. "So, are all these dates ever with the same guy, or different ones?" Nikki knew it was none of her business, but she'd grown to really care about Kate.

"Awww," Kate said, sending her a tender glance. "Are you worried about me?"

Nikki shrugged. "Not worried. You stay safe, though, right?"

Kate smiled. "Always." She returned her wallet to her purse, then patted Nikki's cheek. "You're so sweet. You'll be happy to know I've been seeing the same person for over a month now."

Nikki raised an eyebrow. "Really? Why haven't you told Hannah?"

"I didn't want to jinx it. And I probably shouldn't have told you." Kate gave herself a last cursory inspection in the mirror by the front door. "So, if it all falls apart now, I'm blaming you."

"All right." Nikki laughed. "I'll take full responsibility."

"Tell Hannah not to wait up," Kate said over her shoulder as she closed the door behind her.

Nikki plugged her phone into the iPod port on the bookshelf, keyed up the playlist of soft instrumentals she liked to relax to, and started dinner. An hour and a half later, when she heard a key in the lock, she struck a match and touched the flame to the wick of one of the tapered candles on the small dining room table. The lights were already dimmed.

Hannah slowed as she came through the door. "Oh my. What's all this?"

"Just dinner," Nikki said, lighting the second candle.

A smile lit Hannah's face. "I'll be right back." She carried her shopping bags into her bedroom, then reemerged, seconds later, still in her floral print skirt and teal silk blouse she'd worn to work but with bare feet and her silky blond hair freed from its clip. It was an enticing combination of dressy and intimately casual.

Nikki drew in a breath to steady herself. *Maybe I* can't *wait much longer.*

Hannah came to her and threaded her arms around Nikki's neck. She kissed her lightly on the lips. "How was your day?" she whispered. She pressed her body to Nikki's.

Nikki groaned and claimed Hannah's mouth.

Hannah molded against her, her fingers tangling in Nikki's hair. She parted her lips for Nikki's tongue and teased it with soft flicks of her own.

Nikki wanted to sink more deeply into the kiss, to take Hannah's lower lip between her teeth, to suck it between her own, but she held back. Her pulse was already racing, arousal pooling in her center, and she could feel the intensity of Hannah's desire in the tension of her body. She eased away. "What day?"

Hannah released a throaty laugh and caught her breath. She ran her hand through her hair, then glanced at the table. "What's the occasion?"

"I just wanted to surprise you." Nikki let her hands slip to Hannah's hips, then kissed her forehead.

"Is that your spaghetti I smell?" Hannah rested her forearms on Nikki's shoulders and trailed her fingers across her nape.

Nikki closed her eyes. "I took the refrigerator being filled with all the ingredients as a hint that you'd like me to make it soon."

Hannah giggled. "I love your spaghetti." She moved closer again and nuzzled Nikki's neck, then grazed the pulse point with her teeth.

Nikki jerked. "If you don't stop that, you're not going to get any dinner at all."

"Mmmm, you're right," Hannah murmured. "And I *am* hungry."

Nikki gathered her strength and released her. "Have a seat on the couch. I'll put the water on to boil for the pasta and bring you some wine."

Hannah sighed. "I won't argue with that."

Nikki returned and handed Hannah a glass, then sat beside her.

Hannah took a sip of the merlot. "I have a surprise for you, too," she said, shifting sideways and leaning back into the cushions.

"Oh yeah?" Nikki brightened. "Did you buy me something?"

Hannah smiled playfully. "I did."

"What is it?" Nikki stretched her legs and propped her feet on the coffee table. "Can I have it now?"

"No, you have to wait until after we eat." Hannah took a deep swallow.

Nikki watched as the tip of Hannah's tongue darted between her lips to swipe a drop of wine. "Why?" she asked, managing only a whisper. She cleared her throat. "Why can't I have it now?"

"Because it'll ruin your appetite."

"Oh, so it's edible," Nikki said thoughtfully. "Is it chocolate?"

"No," Hannah said.

"Is it cheese?"

"No."

"Is it those pickled pigs' feet?" Nikki feigned an excited grin.

Hannah drew her brows together and wrinkled her nose. "Eww. No. You don't really eat those things, do you?"

Nikki stared at her with innocence. "Why? Is that a deal breaker?"

"It might be." Hannah eyed her as though trying to decide. "Or, at least, we might need to have a one-hour rule before you can kiss me after eating them."

"Forget it, then," Nikki said seriously. "I'd never do anything that would keep me from being able to kiss you. I've waited too long."

She leaned over and pressed her lips to Hannah's. As their kiss turned from playful to heated, she shifted and set her glass on the table, then took Hannah's. She explored Hannah's mouth as she slipped an arm around her waist and pulled her close.

Hannah drew her thigh up between Nikki's, then caressed Nikki's calf with her bare foot.

Nikki squeezed her legs together, but resisted the urge to move against her.

The timer in the kitchen dinged.

Nikki groaned and broke the kiss. "I have to put the pasta in."

Hannah nodded.

When the noodles were in the boiling water, Nikki took the salad from the refrigerator and dressed it.

"Can I help?" Hannah asked, coming around the end of the bar.

Nikki needed to keep her distance. "You can put this on the table and refill our wine glasses."

Hannah took the salad bowl from her and did as directed.

"And now you can put the garlic bread in and keep an eye on it," Nikki said when Hannah returned.

Hannah slid the broiler pan into the oven.

Nikki retrieved the colander from the cabinet and set it in the sink.

Before she could turn around again, Hannah pressed up against her backside and snaked her arms around her.

Nikki turned in her embrace.

Hannah looked into Nikki's face, her eyes dark with desire. She kissed her lips, then the hollow of her throat.

Nikki moaned and arched her neck, giving Hannah more access. "This isn't helping," she whispered.

"It isn't?" Hannah opened the collar of Nikki's shirt and brushed her lips across the bare skin, then trailed her tongue along the slant of her collarbone.

"No." Nikki's breathing quickened. "Definitely not helping."

Hannah opened another button and dropped a tender kiss on Nikki's chest. She pulled the hem free from the waistband of her jeans and slipped her hands beneath it.

Nikki groaned at Hannah's touch to her heated flesh. *You're killing me.* She drove her fingers into Hannah's hair and tipped her mouth to hers. "Oh, God, Hannah," she said against her lips.

Hannah leaned her hips into Nikki's.

Nikki kissed her hard. "Oh, God, Hannah." Her voice was almost a growl.

Hannah's teeth closed on Nikki's lower lip, then she sucked it greedily.

"Oh, God, Hannah." Smoke touched her nostrils. Her eyes fluttered open. "Oh God, Hannah!" She tried to break free. "Fire! Hannah, the bread's on fire!"

Hannah jerked back, and Nikki grabbed an oven mitt. She yanked open the door, pulled out the broiler pan, and threw it into the sink. She turned on the faucet and doused the flames.

They stared at one another, wide-eyed.

Nikki began to calm and grinned. "Okay, now look what you've done. No bread for you."

Hannah started laughing. "You're right. That wasn't helpful."

Nikki looked at her with mock reproof. "Go sit down," she said, pointing to the table. "And stay over there while I finish."

The meal was uneventful, comparatively. They sat on opposite sides of the table, managed to actually have a conversation about their days, and set nothing on fire. Hannah's eyes kept dipping to Nikki's open shirt collar, to the flesh her lips and tongue had been teasing, but Nikki couldn't blame her for that. Nikki's own gaze drifted numerous times to Hannah's mouth, her lips still swollen from their hungry kisses. As they cleaned up the kitchen, Hannah was quiet and kept her distance, but each time she caught Nikki's eye, desire sparked in her own.

"Would you like your surprise now?" Hannah asked when they'd moved to the living room.

"Sure." Nikki stretched her arms over her head. "Is it something we can share?"

"Mm-hm. Wait here." Hannah disappeared into the hall.

Nikki leaned her head back and closed her eyes as she listened to the soft piano notes of "Clair de Lune," the rustling of bags from Hannah's room, the closing of the bathroom door. Over the months, she'd gotten used to the sound of Hannah's movements around her, the predictability of her routines, the feel of her presence even when she wasn't in sight. Being with Hannah, no matter where they were or what they were doing, felt so right. As the minutes passed, she grew antsy. She wanted Hannah nearer. "Everything okay?" she called. "You need some help?"

"Everything's perfect," Hannah said quietly.

Nikki opened her eyes. Her throat went dry. Her earlier arousal reignited and swept through her like a brush fire.

Hannah stood in front of her in a black lace teddy, her breasts barely covered by the plunging front as it veed to just below her navel. The sculpted lace trim of the thong bottom highlighted her bare hips, ensconcing them in a deliciously high cut.

"Fuck," Nikki whispered. Her nipples went rigid. Her clitoris throbbed.

Hannah straddled her and nestled into her lap. "Yes," she said, her voice husky with lust. "Please." She wound her arms around Nikki's neck, her tantalizing cleavage level with Nikki's mouth.

Nikki ran her hands up Hannah's firm thighs, then brought them to Hannah's sides. "I thought we were going to…" She faltered as her fingertips tangled in thin, crisscross straps at the small of Hannah's back, smooth skin caressing her pads.

Hannah gasped and arched, offering the inside curve of her breasts to Nikki's lips. "I finished moving my stuff to storage last night." She lowered her head and kissed the corner of Nikki's mouth. "That's your surprise."

Nikki groaned. She raked her gaze over the sexy lingerie and ran her hands up Hannah's sides to caress the outer swell of her breasts. "I thought *this* was my surprise."

Hannah moved against her. "All of it."

Nikki slipped her thumbs beneath the lace and grazed Hannah's nipples.

Hannah threw her head back and cried out. She thrust her hips.

Nikki watched in wonder, in love, in need. Hannah looked just as she had the night in Nikki's bed, the night they'd stopped because too much still stood between them. This time, though, *nothing* stood between them. She cupped Hannah's breasts beneath the thin fabric, then squeezed her swollen nipples.

"Oh, yes, Nikki." Hannah tightened her thighs.

Nikki buried her face in Hannah's cleavage. She kissed and nibbled the inner sides of her breasts while still teasing her nipples.

Hannah gasped for air. She ground her center against Nikki's jeans.

Nikki's desire heightened with the pressure against her clitoris, and her desperately needed orgasm grew close. She didn't want their first time to be over so quickly. "Hannah, wait." She grasped Hannah's hips. "Not so fast."

Hannah slowed, but dropped her head to Nikki's shoulder with a whimper. "I can't, Nikki. Please. We have all night to go slow. I need you right now."

And with those words, the desperation in Hannah's voice, Nikki's arousal inflamed. She knew she couldn't deny her, even if she'd wanted to. She gripped Hannah's bare ass and lifted her as Hannah's mouth came down hard on hers again. She found Hannah's hot, wet sex and plunged inside her.

She keened into Nikki's mouth and clamped down around Nikki's fingers.

Nikki set a steady rhythm, taking Hannah more deeply with each thrust.

Hannah broke the kiss and arched upward. She pumped her hips. "Ooooh, God. Yes. Yes."

Nikki sucked one of Hannah's stiff nipples into her hungry mouth through the lace of the teddy and bit gently.

Hannah came instantly, crushing Nikki's hand with each wave of pleasure. She tightened her arms around Nikki's neck and writhed against her.

Nikki remained deep inside her until Hannah began to calm and relaxed her hold.

"Oh, my God," Hannah murmured in Nikki's ear. "Oh, my God." Her voice broke slightly.

Moisture trickled down Nikki's neck. She tried to ease Hannah away to see her face. "Hannah?"

"No," Hannah said. She sucked Nikki's earlobe between her lips and flicked her tongue beneath it. "I want you, Nikki." She began working the buttons of Nikki's shirt. "I want you now."

Nikki's clitoris ached. She moaned and leaned her head back, letting Hannah have her.

Hannah made her way down Nikki's neck. She pushed her shirt off her shoulders and kissed the bare flesh. She trailed the tip of her tongue along the edge of Nikki's sports bra, teasing her nipples through the material with her fingernails. She wasn't slow. She wasn't gentle. She was greedy and determined. She yanked up the bra and clamped her mouth around one of Nikki's nipples, sucking it hard.

Nikki groaned and twined her fingers in Hannah's hair. She held her firmly against her breast.

Hannah fumbled with Nikki's belt buckle, finally yanking it loose and unbuttoning Nikki's jeans. She feasted on Nikki's nipples a little longer, finishing with a quick nip that brought Nikki up off the back of the sofa. Then she dropped to her knees between Nikki's legs. She tugged on Nikki's pants, making her desire clear.

Nikki lifted her hips, and Hannah pulled down her jeans and briefs just enough to get to what she wanted. She brushed her lips over the triangle of hair as she raked her nails across the skin.

Nikki trembled. Her hands still in Hannah's hair, she brought Hannah's mouth to her throbbing clitoris.

Hannah licked it, then sucked it between her hot lips.

Nikki bit back a scream and came hard and fast.

Hannah gentled, keeping a soft swirl of her tongue moving through Nikki's drenched folds and around her clitoris.

Nikki jerked with each pass, eventually loosening her hold in Hannah's hair. She struggled to catch her breath.

Hannah climbed up Nikki's body and settled again astride Nikki's lap. She touched a fingertip to Nikki's lips, then kissed her tenderly.

Nikki opened her eyes.

"Now, take me to bed and make slow, sweet love to me," Hannah whispered.

In the bedroom, the sheets were already pulled down, the nightstand lamp already lit. Nikki quirked an eyebrow. "Pretty sure of yourself, weren't you?"

Hannah smiled as she slipped Nikki's shirt the rest of the way off her shoulders and down her arms. "Some things are inevitable."

Nikki stripped her bra, then kicked off her shoes and shoved her jeans down her legs. When Hannah started to slip the teddy off, Nikki grasped her wrist. "Leave it on a while. I want to take it off of you later." She already felt her arousal building again, as though an all-consuming orgasm hadn't just ripped through her.

Hannah stepped closer and spread her hands over Nikki's breasts, palming her still stiff nipples. "I'm glad you like it."

Nikki moaned as she took in the contrast between the black lace and Hannah's fair skin and the way the seductively thin fabric revealed everything that lay beneath while still covering it. "I love it," she murmured. She caressed the exposed skin of Hannah's hips, coaxing her against her. The texture of the lace softly scratched her sensitized nipples. She kissed Hannah as she eased her onto the mattress.

Hannah stretched beneath Nikki and pulled her down on top of her. She ran her hands up and down Nikki's back.

Nikki made small circles with her fingertips along Hannah's sides, lingering to toy with each indention between her ribs. Finally, she left Hannah's mouth and made her way down her throat, to trail her tongue down Hannah's chest as she shifted lower, letting her hip slip between Hannah's thighs.

Hannah gasped and pressed up against her.

Nikki cupped the sides of Hannah's breasts, pushing them inward so that each nipple barely peeked from beneath the edge of the black lace. She licked one, then the other. Then the first again.

With each flick of Nikki's tongue, Hannah moaned.

Nikki quickened her pace until her tongue moved rapidly between the two and Hannah arched up to meet her mouth. With one final slow swipe of the flat of her tongue, Nikki began to suck one swollen, engorged nipple. She squeezed the other between her thumb and fingers and gently rolled it.

Hannah cried out and reached above her head to grip the spindles of the headboard.

Hannah's sighs, her moans, her cries, the sound of her calling out Nikki's name all drove Nikki wild with her own need. Her pounding pulse throbbed between her thighs.

Hannah pushed up into her, rubbing her wet center against Nikki's hip.

Nikki knew Hannah's orgasm was close, and hers grew more imminent each time she met Hannah's thrusts and her aching clitoris brushed against Hannah's thigh. But she had to taste her. She had to know the feeling, the flavor, of Hannah coming in her mouth. She'd imagined it, dreamed of it, waited so long for it. With a groan of anticipation, she moved farther down Hannah's body.

"No," Hannah said, obviously desperate with need.

Nikki slipped the straps of the teddy off Hannah's shoulders and opened the bodice before spreading Hannah's thighs and settling between them. She breathed her in, closing her eyes to revel in her scent. She pushed the thong aside, then parted Hannah's soaked labia and gazed hungrily at what awaited her.

"Hurry, Nikki," Hannah whispered hoarsely. She squirmed, rotating her hips.

Nikki kissed her, full on.

Hannah screamed and bucked.

Nikki ran her tongue through Hannah's wetness, savoring every drop. She dipped inside her, then circled the opening. She pressed her lips to Hanna's hard clitoris and sucked gently.

Hannah pumped against Nikki's mouth.

Nikki reached up and caressed Hannah's nipples while she explored every millimeter of Hannah's sex with her lips and tongue.

Hannah twisted her hands into Nikki's hair and pulled her hard against her center.

Nikki circled her clitoris, then flicked her tongue across its tip.

"Inside me." Hannah groaned. She moved against Nikki's mouth. "Inside me," she said more emphatically.

Nikki slipped a finger into Hannah's slippery opening, then two. Then three.

Hannah lurched upward and bucked. "Yes. More." She held Nikki's mouth to her clitoris.

Nikki sucked and pumped into her.

Finally, Hannah cried out unintelligibly, her torso lifted off the bed, and her muscles clutched at Nikki's fingers. When she dropped back to the mattress, she thrashed through the last spasms before eventually quieting. "Holy shit."

Nikki crawled up over her, dropping kisses here and there onto bare flesh as she made her way, then eased down beside her.

Hannah cuddled against her. "That was amazing," she whispered. "I hope nobody's home next door."

Nikki chuckled and tucked an errant lock of hair behind Hannah's ear. "That is a drawback to apartment life."

Hannah exhaled sharply, still trying to steady her breathing. "Well, being with you, I'm definitely going to have to keep that in mind when I'm looking for a place."

Nikki wondered at the comment. Surely Hannah had been no louder with her than when she was with Jordan, but she didn't want to ask. She didn't want to bring Jordan into this conversation, this moment, at all. "I could just give you quickies," she said teasingly.

"Not now that I know what you can do." She brushed her lips over Nikki's, then raised up on an elbow and kissed her properly.

When they parted, Nikki was panting.

"Your turn." Hannah toyed with one of Nikki's nipples, then lowered to it and pressed her lips around it.

Nikki moaned. Hannah's mouth was warm and soft, her hand that traced languid circles on Nikki's stomach deliberate.

With each curve, Hannah dipped a little lower, until her fingertips combed through the hair that concealed Nikki's clitoris. She gently worked the tip with two fingers. "You're so hard," she murmured, rubbing her lips across Nikki's breast, then returning her mouth to Nikki's aching nipple.

Nikki lifted into Hannah's hand and opened for her. Her orgasm was so close. She wanted it so badly, and yet, she wanted this to last. What if this was the only time? What if Hannah woke the next morning and decided this was a mistake? She shook the thought. She couldn't ruin this moment. She cupped the back of Hannah's head as Hannah continued pleasuring her nipples.

Hannah draped her leg over Nikki's thighs and moved over her.

Nikki moaned in protest at the loss of Hannah's hand between her legs, only to groan with need at the pressure of Hannah's center against her mound and swollen clitoris. She gripped Hannah's thighs and clenched her teeth to keep from coming.

Hannah sat up, changing the angle of their joining, dragging a guttural sound from Nikki's throat. "Look at me," she whispered.

Nikki hadn't realized she'd clenched her eyes shut. She opened them and almost came at the sight of Hannah straddling her, that taunting teddy, now back in place, covering just enough to drive Nikki mad.

Hannah's wetness, her heat, mingled with Nikki's as she gently rotated her hips.

Pleasure tore through Nikki's sex. She jerked and moaned Hannah's name.

Hannah took Nikki's hands and guided them to her breasts. She held them there until Nikki started fondling them through the lace, kneading them, tenderly pinching the nipples.

Hannah sighed and began rubbing herself against Nikki's mound, teasing and tormenting her aching clit.

She looked so beautiful, felt so good. Nikki could barely believe all this was really happening. And yet, she couldn't deny the reality of how it felt, the intensity of the connection, the pure hedonistic pleasure coursing through her body. This was definitely real.

"I'm going to come with you." Hannah's voice was gravelly with need and lust. She quickened the thrusts of her hips.

Nikki thumbed Hannah's nipples as her own pleasure overtook her. "I can't wait."

"Oh, honey, you won't have to." Hannah's pitch rose and she pressed herself harder against Nikki.

Nikki's orgasm racked her entire body. She knew how close she'd been, but it was that one word, that simple little endearment that'd tipped her over the edge. *She* was Hannah's honey. She gripped Hannah's hips and held her firmly as she ground up into her.

Hannah dropped forward, bracing herself with her hands, and met Nikki's desperate movements with a force of her own. "Oh God, Nikki! Don't stop."

Nikki was nowhere close to stopping.

They worked against one another, eking out every last wave of pleasure, every last spasm, until, finally, Hannah fell across Nikki, panting.

They lay together, not speaking, not moving, not doing anything that might shatter that moment of pure happiness in Nikki's heart, for a long time. Hannah seemed just as content to remain right where she'd dropped, draped across Nikki, only the fingers of one hand curling and uncurling in an absent caress of the hollow of Nikki's shoulder. Soft music drifted in from the living room. If Nikki hadn't been able to feel the flutter of Hannah's eyelashes on her skin each time Hannah blinked, she would have thought Hannah had drifted to sleep.

"Nikki?" Hannah said, finally breaking the silence.

"Hmm?" was all Nikki could manage.

"I think I want to go to that town where my birth mother lived and talk to the people who knew her," Hannah said, her tone quiet but certain. "Will you go with me?"

Nikki blinked. "Sure," she said, trying to find a connection. "What we just did made you think of your mother?"

Hannah laughed softly. She drew a design on Nikki's skin with her fingertip. "What we just did was so incredibly amazing," she said slowly, "it made me feel so connected to you. And that made me think of all the times I've felt alone. Even having Kate. Even after making love with someone. Even in a roomful of people. And then that made me feel pathetic, like it always does when it happens, like no matter what I do or where I am, or who I'm with, I'm always going to be alone because no one really wants me."

Nikki tightened her arms around Hannah. She wanted to argue the point, reassure Hannah, but she knew it was more important for her to be able to say what she needed to say.

"And then that made me think of Jordan and how I could have been with her for so long, lived with her and slept with her, and never known anything about her." Hannah raised her head and looked into Nikki's eyes as though searching for answers there. Then, her expression held a trace of sadness. "And *that* made me wonder how *you* could have been so close, so right in front of me, all this time and I didn't see you. I might not have felt *this*." She squeezed Nikki's torso, then dipped her head and kissed Nikki's shoulder.

"And then that made me think about what else I could be blind to, what else I might miss because…I don't know. Just because. And I thought of wanting to know about my birth mother all those years, wanting to understand why she gave me away, and now, just because finding her didn't match my little fantasy I've always had about our reunion, I was going to walk away from *anything* I could know about her. And then that made me think how stupid that is, and that made me want to go see where she lived and hear what people who knew her have to say. And," she said with a note of finality, "I want you to be with me."

"Wow. How long have we been lying here?" Nikki kissed the tip of Hannah's nose.

Hannah chuckled.

"Of course, I'll go with you." Emotion swelled in Nikki's chest. "I'll go anywhere with you. I'll do anything you want me to do. I'll be with you through anything."

Hannah's eyes shimmered with a sheen of tears. Her gaze settled on Nikki's lips, and she touched them. "I think I believe you," she whispered.

Nikki kissed her fingertip. "Good. And if you still have doubts about being wanted, I intend to show you every day how much *I* want you."

Hannah smiled and pressed her mouth to Nikki's. "You can start now."

Nikki's desire, still hot and ready, leapt into flame. "What do you want?" Her tone was low and husky.

"Get me out of this teddy," Hannah murmured against Nikki's lips. "I want to feel you, skin on skin."

CHAPTER NINETEEN

Jordan sat on the bench in the garden, Lena beside her, their Bibles open on their laps. She didn't remember coming outside. That was becoming more common, not being able to remember anything immediately before or after the electric shock treatments. Mercifully, the amnesia sometimes included the sessions themselves. She was losing other memories too, though, or, at least, she thought she was. It was hard to know for sure. Sometimes there seemed to be a hole in her thinking, as though she knew something should be there, but nothing was.

She couldn't remember when she'd first been allowed to sit outside or walk in the garden with Lena. She loved the fresh air in her lungs, the breeze on her face, the birds singing in the trees, and sitting next to Lena, listening to her voice. Lena was always reading something about hell and homosexuality, God's wrath and vengeance, always praying for forgiveness, but Jordan escaped into the sanctuary of the cadence, blocking out the words themselves. Then she'd hear it, a slight shift in tone, and Lena would be talking to her, quietly, softly, under her breath so only Jordan could hear.

"Jordan?" Lena asked as though not for the first time. "Are you with me?"

"Yes," Jordan said, keeping her voice low as well.

"How are you?" Lena turned the page, signaling Jordan to do the same. "How are you feeling?"

"Headache," Jordan whispered. "But it helps being outside."

Jordan finally understood and had accepted the importance of not fighting, glad for the stability that even the smallest reward or comfort brought her. It gave her a twisted sense of control in a situation in which she was otherwise completely powerless. She'd learned from watching Lena that it was the only way to hold on to any remnant of sanity. And then, there was Lena herself offered up as a reward. Jordan's time with her brought her peace. She couldn't risk losing it.

"You're trembling," Lena said, her eyes downcast to her Bible. "Take some deep breaths."

Jordan complied. She hadn't realized she was shaking, but that wasn't unusual. Jordan couldn't imagine how Lena had gotten through on her own. "Tell me some more about you," she said, grateful for any distraction.

Lena had already shared the series of events that'd taken place in Palmer's ex-gay teen ministry. She'd explained how it'd initially grown, but then lost congregational support when conversion therapy and its detrimental effects had been brought to the attention of the media, and groups like Exodus had begun backpedaling on the idea and practice. Now, though, Jordan wanted to know about Lena herself.

"What do you want to know?" Lena asked.

Jordan struggled to think. Her mind was always so foggy now. "Sister Katherine said you graduated from the teen program and went to college, but that you were caught...you know." Jordan had to be careful around the subject of women together in fear of triggering a bout of nausea or pain or seizure associated with the electric shock sessions. "How did that happen?"

Lena toyed with the corner of the page in front of her. She was quiet for a long time. "Sister Katherine and I met in the teen program," she said finally. "And we became...close. She really didn't want to be gay, though, so after a while, she broke things off. But during the time we spent together, I'd told her I was only going through the motions of my father's program until I could get away, so when she became one of his *workers*, she told him that. He sent her to visit me at the college I was attending to see how I was living. And she saw."

"And she told him?" Jordan asked, astonished.

Lena only nodded.

"So it's her fault you've gone through all this and that you're still being held here?" If Jordan ever wanted to tear into the woman for her part in Jordan being here, she wanted to rip her into tiny pieces for doing that to Lena.

Lena shrugged stiffly. "That's all in the past. I was devastated by it, furious. I hated her. But none of that changes anything. And she *has* done what she can for me here."

Jordan seethed. "Bitch."

"Don't, Jordan," Lena said gently. "Don't get angry and lose your privileges again." She glanced at Jordan from the corner of her eye. "I need to be able to sit here with you. It's made all the difference in the world to me to spend time with you and know you're here for me again."

Jordan understood Lena's reference to when they were young and Jordan had stood up for her. She flinched inwardly at the sting of her own helplessness now. "I can't protect you here."

"I know," Lena whispered. "I don't need you to. I've learned how to survive this. And I'd do anything for you not to have to be here with me, but given that you are, I just want to be able to sit beside you and not be alone anymore. And maybe help you the way you helped me."

Jordan calmed herself for Lena's sake, but she knew if she ever got the chance, she'd make sure that bitch paid. "Okay," she said to Lena. "I'll behave." She heard what might have been the tiniest of laughs slip from Lena.

"Thank you," Lena said.

They sat in silence, enjoying the warmth of the afternoon sun—as much as they could enjoy anything—and pretended to read. "I need to tell you something," Lena said softly, sounding almost like the child she used to be. "So you can prepare yourself."

Jordan closed her eyes. *That's never a good phrase.* "What?"

"I overheard Father and Mother talking about you earning a family visit. It's supposed to take place tomorrow morning."

"Family visit? You mean with my father again?" Jordan *would* have to gear up for *that.*

"I don't know who's coming, but I think they said *they.*"

The door on the side of the building opened, and Palmer stepped outside.

Lena lapsed into the Lord's Prayer, and Jordan lowered her head.

Palmer approached and waited. "Amen," he said in unison with Lena and Jordan at the end. "It's a lovely day, isn't it, ladies?"

"Yes, Father," they said together.

He drew in a deep breath and looked to the sky. "Praise God our Lord," he said, raising his hands.

Not very long ago, Jordan would have wanted to roll her eyes, but not now. She understood now that what she once thought was ridiculous, was actually truly dangerous.

"Sister Sarah," he said, turning to them. "You're needed in the kitchen to help start preparing our evening meal."

Lena had told Jordan that Palmer had changed her name when they'd started her in the adult program because he felt Satan had too strong of a hold on her as Lena, like changing her name would trick the devil.

"And, Sister Jordan," Palmer said without a pause. "It's time you begin serving in some way. Sister Sarah, will you please take Sister Jordan to the janitorial room? Sister Katherine is waiting for her there to show her the housekeeping protocols."

"Yes, Father," Lena said, closing her Bible.

After dinner, Jordan spent the evening in her room doing what she could to bolster herself to face her father, and maybe her mother, again. She had difficulty focusing, though. Instead, she spent most of the time before bed remembering what Lena had said about needing their time together. If for no other reason than not to jeopardize that, Jordan would be the perfect ex-gay candidate during her parents' visit. If she couldn't do anything to help herself, she could at least help Lena in that way. She slept fitfully, waking from nightmares of electrodes and Loraine and dark hallways that led nowhere, and woke in the morning exhausted and achy. She followed a Brother up some stairs to a new visitation room, one that looked like a living room.

She quieted her thoughts just as the door at the other end of the room opened and Palmer and Loraine strode in, followed by Jordan's parents—and David. *David?* What the hell was her brother doing here? Jordan felt like she'd been sucker-punched. *Christ! Is there anyone who isn't in on this?* She glanced back to the doorway, half expecting Hannah and Nikki to appear.

Palmer grinned. "You've been doing so well, we wanted to surprise you," he said to Jordan. "From the look on your face, I see we succeeded. We're all very proud of you."

The crushing weight of utter despair and betrayal threatened to buckle her knees. "Thank you, Father," she heard herself say. She'd never once considered that her brother might know what was going on. They weren't close, but still…

"Please, everyone sit down." Palmer waved a hand, indicating the sofa and several accent chairs.

Jordan dropped into the seat beside her, maybe a little too quickly, but she couldn't support herself in that moment. "This *is* a surprise," she said as cordially as she could manage.

"It's good to see you, Jordan," her mother said. "Your hair is growing out."

Had Jordan heard right? *She's commenting on my hair?* She wanted to laugh, not that anything was funny, but that nervous, hysterical laughter that came instead of words in ludicrous situations. What was she supposed to say to that? "Thank you, Mother," was all she came up with.

"Thomas and Loraine tell us you're finally starting to behave properly with this new phase of your program," Jordan's father said as he ushered her mother to a seat on the couch and sat beside her.

Pain popped in Jordan's head and her stomach soured at the mention of *her program*. She swallowed. "I'm doing my best, sir."

"We're happy to hear that." Her mother smoothed the skirt of the casual suit she wore, then adjusted the cuff of the jacket. "It will be nice to have you home where you belong and all of this nonsense behind us."

Jordan wondered what her mother was referring to as *nonsense*. Was it her being in this place, enduring the torture of electric shock and psychological conditioning? Was it her being forcibly taken from her life and held prisoner until she agreed to live a lie? Or was it the life Jordan had chosen, itself? She wanted so badly to ask, she could barely keep the words in her throat. But she'd promised Lena she'd behave, so she would. She wouldn't do anything to jeopardize the time they had together. Both of their sanity could very well depend on it. "Yes, Mother, I'll be happy to be home, too." From the corner of her eye, she saw David staring at her. She glanced at him.

As soon as their gazes met, he looked away.

Jordan was amazed at how much he'd changed. He still had the dark hair and gray eyes he shared with her and their father, but he was now a man, his chest and shoulders filled out, his carriage and posture controlled and deliberate. Tiny lines creased the corners of his eyes. The last time Jordan had seen him, he'd been twenty-four and still a little gangly and undisciplined. Now, he looked spookily like Jonathan Webber. Was he?

"Aren't you going to say hello to your sister, David?" their father asked.

David returned his attention to her. "Hello, Jordan." His tone held no emotion, no surprise.

Her heart sank at the confirmation that he had known about this and was a part of it. That didn't make sense, though. He wasn't crazy like Palmer, or cold and vindictive like their mother, or even controlling and vengeful like their father. At least, he hadn't been any of those things years ago when she'd known him. She'd left him alone, though, with them. When she'd walked away, she'd walked away from *him*, too, and hadn't looked back. She cringed inwardly. Another casualty in her wake. *Hannah. Nikki. David. And how many others I probably don't even remember?*

"David," she said in acknowledgement, but her voice was weak with regret for the life she'd lived.

When I get out of here, I'll do better. I'll be better. I just need a second chance.

Chapter Twenty

Hannah, Nikki, and Kate all climbed out of Nikki's car on a side street in the little town of Tehachapi. It'd taken a month for Nikki to clear a weekend in order to be able to come with Hannah, and that had only happened because the Burnside/Bennett wedding had been cancelled due to an unscheduled elopement, but they were finally here.

They had spent the past hour driving around, looking at everything, Hannah trying to imagine her mother—a woman she had never seen before—moving along the streets, shopping in the stores, simply living a life. They had seen a grocery store, the post office, a movie theater—places that anyone might frequent in their daily dealings, and Hannah wondered if Ellen Graham had walked through those very doors. Granted she'd lived there twenty-five years earlier, and the town could have changed drastically since then, but Hannah liked the thought. She had tried to pull Kate in, but Kate had promptly reminded her that she was only there for a weekend in the mountains. She'd spent most of the trip so far texting in the backseat.

"This is so beautiful," Hannah said as she closed the car door. She took in the vibrant, multicolors of the fall leaves, some still clinging to the branches of mature trees, others covering the yards and sidewalks that lined the street. As they had neared the freeway off-ramp that brought them into town, they had seen a sign that read: *Welcome to Tehachapi. The land of four seasons.* It had been years since Hannah had seen such a gorgeous display of autumn.

She glanced at the paper in her hand and checked the scribbled address against the numbers on the six bungalow style houses that occupied the short block. She walked to the gate of the one that matched and stared at the cement porch with the half-wall enclosure and the front door beyond. "This is it," she said, almost to herself. "This is where she lived."

Nikki stepped up beside her and encircled her waist. "You okay?"

Hannah pictured a woman sitting in the swing on the porch reading a book or doing some kind of needlework. She wished they had been able to schedule their meeting with Mrs. Peters, the owner of the local drugstore where Hannah's mother had worked, when they had first gotten to town. Instead, the visit was still an hour away. "Yes," she said to Nikki. "More than okay. I'm excited to be here. It feels…" She searched for the right word.

"It feels like we're stalkers," Kate said.

Hannah laughed. "Maybe, a little."

"Can I help you?" a man asked from down the sidewalk. He ambled toward them. A cowboy hat was pushed back on his head, and a shopping bag dangled from one hand.

"Oh! No, we're sorry," Hannah said. "We were just…" How could she explain it without truly sounding like a stalker?

He stopped in front of them and waited.

"Their mother lived here years ago," Nikki said easily. "They wanted to see it."

"How long ago?" he asked, seeming genuinely interested.

"A long time," Hannah said. She waved her hand dismissively. "Over twenty-five years."

The man studied Hannah, then shifted his gaze to Nikki, then Kate. "I'm Blake," he said, tipping his hat. "Would you like to see inside?"

Hannah gasped with enthusiasm. "Could we?" she asked at the same time Kate said, "That's not necessary."

Blake looked between them again and laughed. He settled on Hannah. "Give me a second to pick up a little bit." He opened the gate and gestured them through. "You can make yourselves comfortable on the porch, if you like."

When he'd gone inside, Hannah grabbed Nikki's hand and squeezed it tightly as she let out a quiet squeal. She did a little dance.

Nikki smiled and kissed her.

Kate smirked and shook her head.

After a few minutes, the door opened and Blake invited them inside. "You'll have to excuse the fact that I'm a bachelor. I'm sure your mother kept it much neater."

Hannah stepped directly into a brightly lit living room with a dining area connected to the other end. Brown leather furniture with heavy oak tables dominated the space, but Hannah easily replaced it all in her mind with a more feminine décor.

"The kitchen's back there." Blake pointed to a doorway across the dining area. "And there's two bedrooms through there." He indicated a short hallway. "Feel free to look around."

Hannah moved through rooms, caught somewhere between the present and the past. She could almost see a woman who looked like her sitting on the couch, chopping vegetables at the kitchen counter, asleep in the bed. She thought she could feel her. A sudden wash of emotion flooded her. She had never been able to *feel* her before, and maybe she was losing it in this moment, but right now, she really believed she could. Tears welled in her eyes and spilled onto her cheeks.

Nikki was at her side. "Baby?"

"I'm okay," Hannah said, resting her head on Nikki's shoulder. She sniffed. "I'm really okay."

They thanked Blake.

"No problem," he said. "I understand how places can make you feel closer to someone."

Outside again, Hannah snapped a few pictures of the house before they walked down the street, enjoying the small town atmosphere and cool afternoon. Again, Hannah thought she could feel her mother's presence. By the time they got back to the car and drove the few blocks to Mrs. Peters's house, she wondered briefly about her mental stability, but at the same time, was beginning to get comfortable with this new feeling. It felt right.

"Oh, my word," Mrs. Peters said, her hand fluttering to her mouth. She looked from Hannah to Kate as they stood at her front door, Nikki behind them. "You two are the spitting image of Ellen. I can't believe it! Come in, come in. I made some lemonade and cookies. Please, sit down."

"Thank you so much for seeing us," Hannah said as Mrs. Peters filled their glasses.

"It's my pleasure." Mrs. Peters looked in her late sixties, with gray streaks through her dark auburn hair. She emanated an air of class in black slacks and a soft green, cowl neck cashmere sweater on a Saturday afternoon. "Ellen was such a special person. I'm thrilled to meet her daughters."

Her daughters. Hannah let the words sink in. What would it have been like to be Ellen Graham's daughter?

When Lantz had contacted Mrs. Peters, he hadn't shared the details of the case, but when Hannah had called to ask if she would see her and Kate, she had explained the basics of the situation. "So, you knew her well?" Hannah asked.

"As well as anyone, I suppose." Mrs. Peters looked thoughtful. "She kept to herself for the most part. Didn't socialize a lot. But she and I spent quite a bit of time together at the store. After you and I spoke, I dug these out. I thought you might like them." She handed Hannah and Kate a picture each. "I don't need to tell you which one is Ellen."

Hannah stared at the photo of four women in white pharmacy jackets. On one end, clearly a younger Mrs. Peters, on the other, a blonde who could easily have been either Hannah or Kate in their twenties. Hannah's vision blurred with tears, and she drew in a steadying breath. *My mother.* She touched a finger to the woman's small smile.

"They're not the best pictures," Mrs. Peters said. "Just a couple of the annual photos we used to take for the store. You can keep them, if you'd like."

"Thank you," Hannah said, wiping the moisture from her cheeks. "That's so nice of you." She glanced at Kate in time to catch her swiping at a tear of her own. "She never mentioned having had two babies?" she asked Mrs. Peters.

"No, dear, I'm sorry. She didn't talk at all about her life before she came here." Mrs. Peters sat back in her chair. "She didn't even mention she was sick until it became obvious and she had to start making changes."

"What kind of changes?" Hannah didn't know exactly what she wanted or needed to hear, but she hoped she would recognize it when she did.

"Well, as she started getting winded more easily, we had to turn some of the restocking she'd normally handle on her shift over to someone else. And eventually, she had to cut back on her hours." A sadness flickered in Mrs. Peters' eyes.

She must have been so scared to be so alone. Because she had always had Kate, and their adoptive parents because of Ellen Graham's decision, and now she had Nikki, Hannah could only imagine. Was that a gift her mother had given her? "Did she know she was sick before she moved here?"

"She never said, but I think she must have." Mrs. Peters' expression softened. "What are you looking for, dear?"

The directness of the question startled Hannah, but she considered it seriously. "I'm not sure. Maybe just something that would tell me..." *Tell her what? That my mother loved me? That she didn't want to give me away? That I mattered?* She couldn't say those things. It would leave her too vulnerable, too exposed.

"I can tell you this," Mrs. Peters said. "Ellen was a warm and kind-hearted woman. She'd do anything for anyone, always helped in any way she could." A gentle smile touched her lips as she spoke. "Tehachapi's a small town, and was even smaller back then. Our lives cross on a daily basis, and even though she didn't share details of her life with us, she always had a smile and a kind word to give. Even toward the end. When we held her funeral service, that sanctuary was packed."

So, her mother was kind and warm and obviously generous and giving, so why had she given up her babies and started a whole new life? And how had she left her old one? Had she simply gotten up one morning and walked away, like Jordan? Was she another one of those people who simply vanished? And if so, who else had she left behind besides Hannah and Kate? Hannah sighed. There were too many questions that would never be answered. She thought of the little house they had seen. "Who went through her belongings afterward?" she asked Mrs. Peters.

"I did." Mrs. Peters took a bite of a cookie. "Well, I followed her instructions as far as what to do. She didn't have anything to go through, really. She gave her clothing to Good Will, and there weren't any other personal possessions, which I admit, I thought was strange. She told me a couple of specific things she wanted on her headstone, so I took care of that."

"What were they?" Hannah asked.

"The writing on it. There was something odd about the dates." Mrs. Peters tapped her chin as she thought. "I can't remember now, though. It was so long ago. But you can go see it for yourself. She was laid to rest in the cemetery across the tracks. I can give you directions."

Hannah looked at Kate for any indication as to whether she would like that, but she was still staring at the picture she held. "Okay." Hannah said, making the decision on her own. "That would be nice. Thank you." Maybe actually seeing her mother's grave would give her some closure.

"She sounds like a nice person," Kate said when they were in the car again. It was the first opinion she had offered about anything to do with this trip since they had left home.

Nikki looked at her in the rearview mirror, surprise evident in her expression.

Hannah turned in her seat and studied Kate. "I wasn't sure you were listening."

Kate shrugged. "I was. Her life sounds kind of sad. Lonely. Don't you think?"

"It does," Hannah said.

"It sounds like she came here to wait to die," Kate said softly, her customary rigidity on the topic gone.

Hannah looked out the window at the beauty of the small town. She considered what Mrs. Peters had said about it being a place where everyone's paths crossed every day, and reflected on Blake's friendliness and openness in letting three complete strangers into his house. *I guess if you go somewhere to die, this is a nice enough place to do it.* She wished she had been able to be here with Ellen Graham, to give her comfort if she had needed it. "I want to take her some flowers," Hannah said to Nikki. "Can we stop and get some?"

Nikki smiled and brushed her thumb across Hannah's cheek. "Of course."

The cemetery was relatively small, and they spread out to look for the grave. Hannah came across it first. "Over here," she called and waved. She read the name several times and wondered whose name it really was. Lantz had said he hadn't been able to find anything on her prior to her pregnancy. Hannah's gaze dropped to the date. May 3, 1962, the date their mother had been born. When she read the next date, she balked in confusion.

"Hey, that's our birthday," Kate said, stepping up beside Hannah.

And it was. The day and year their mother had died was the day they were born. But no. That wasn't right. She had lived here in Tehachapi for another seven years.

"She died on your birthday?" Nikki asked, moving up to Hannah's other side and slipping her hand into Hannah's. "How can that be?"

Hannah shook her head. "That must be what Mrs. Peters meant when she said there was something strange about the dates."

"What do you think it means?" Kate asked.

A warmth passed through Hannah, and suddenly she knew. She would never know who Ellen Graham really was, anything about her life before this quaint little town, or the circumstances of her pregnancy. She would never know who their father was, or any other secrets Ellen kept. But she now knew what she had always wanted, needed, to know. She had been loved, and the mother who loved her had given her away because she knew she couldn't stay to take care of her. "I think it means she felt like she died on the day she had to give us up."

Kate inhaled sharply and swiped at her eyes. Then she began to cry.

Hannah took her in her arms and rocked her. "You *do* care," she whispered.

"I blame you for this," Kate said in an obvious attempt to reclaim the upper hand. "I blame you for a lot of things right now."

"What does that mean?" Hannah laughed through her own tears. "Like what?"

"Never mind. You'll find out soon enough." Kate squeezed Hannah tightly and let herself cry.

❖

When they had checked into the lodge where they were staying for the night, Hannah stood at the railing of the large deck outside the dining room and watched the shift of shadows among the trees below as dusk began to creep over them. She let herself ruminate on everything that had happened in the past five months. It seemed like her life had changed so much, it left her feeling like a completely new person, one who saw things more clearly, understood things more deeply, felt things more fully. And with today's revelation, maybe she would be able to love more easily.

Nothing externally had changed. Her mother had still given her away at birth. All of her relationships had still been shallow due to her fear of rejection and abandonment, and, if she were honest with herself, her own selfishness. The one relationship she'd thought was her most significant had turned out to be a farce. Her girlfriend was never really her girlfriend and had walked away without a word. But none of those things had been finalities in her life. They had all led to other things, better things.

"What are you thinking about?" Nikki's voice was soft in Hannah's ear. She handed her a glass of wine she'd brought her from the bar.

Hannah sighed at the comfort of Nikki's presence. "The vicissitudes of life."

Nikki arched an eyebrow. "Sounds deep. Care to share?"

Hannah smiled and turned back to the view and the setting sun. She took a sip of her wine. "I've spent a huge part of my life believing my mother gave me away because there was something wrong with me," Hannah said, continuing her thought process. "And that belief has affected every relationship I've had. But now that I can let go of that and see things more clearly, I can see how it all fits together. My mother knew she was dying, so she gave me a new life—even though I think it hurt her. She gave me one that wouldn't involve knowing and loving her, only to lose her at a young age and have to learn to love strangers. Or worse, end up in the system, where I could have lost Kate." That thought had never occurred to her before. She shivered.

Nikki laced her fingers between Hannah's and ran her thumb over Hannah's knuckles in a soothing caress.

Hannah calmed. "And I had an amazing childhood with parents who cherished me, who gave me so much of themselves and their hearts, and so many opportunities I wouldn't have had in other situations. And there are a lot of other, smaller things, that I've judged as losses or failures that I now can see led me to something even better." Hannah turned to face Nikki. "And then, there's you."

"What about me?"

Hannah looked into Nikki's rich brown eyes that revealed so much depth, so much emotion, so much of who Nikki was. Hannah hadn't realized she was going to go there, hadn't realized *she* was there, but in that instant, she suddenly knew everything she hadn't understood about the two of them before. She set her glass on the railing. "I've been so confused about you, about what I feel for you, ever since I started seeing you differently. And I don't even know when that happened. It just sneaked up on me. But ever since I realized I was feeling something stronger than friendship, I haven't been able to put it into words. I knew it couldn't be love, because I thought I'd loved before. I thought I loved Jordan. And this doesn't feel anything like that." She touched Nikki's cheek. "This is so tender, so sweet. But at the same time, it's so hot." Her voice went husky. "Sometimes, I want to rip your clothes off, no matter where we are, and make you mine. Other times, I could be happy forever, sitting with you in the quiet, listening to you breathe."

"Hannah." Nikki's eyes had grown darker, her fingers tightening on Hannah's hand.

"No," Hannah said. She pressed a fingertip to Nikki's lips. "Let me say this. It's important." She caressed the softness of Nikki's mouth. "That first time we kissed, I was so confused. My feelings were so jumbled and twisted with anger at Jordan, but there was something else there, too. Something for you that I couldn't shake the next morning or the days following. I've never been able to shake it." She ran the pad of her thumb over Nikki's lips, along the slight opening where they met.

Nikki moaned softly.

Hannah's own body heated with desire, but there was more. Her heart swelled with emotion, with an ache for expression. "Nikki, I didn't think what I feel for you could be love because it doesn't feel anything like what I thought was love. But now, I understand. What I've felt *before* wasn't love. It was…I don't know, infatuation, maybe, lust, satisfaction at being with someone who looked good on the surface. And I feel all those things with you, too, but…oh, my God, there's so much more." She felt tears sting her eyes. "I love you so much, Nikki."

Nikki took Hannah in her arms. She exhaled and closed her eyes. Moisture seeped from beneath her lids. "Oh, Hannah. *I* love *you*." She found Hannah's mouth with her own and claimed it in a long, passionate kiss.

Hannah threaded her arms around Nikki's waist and molded against her. She tilted her head, changing the angle, and took Nikki in deeper. When Nikki groaned, Hannah remembered they weren't in the privacy of their room. She eased away, but kept Nikki in her embrace.

Nikki swallowed hard. "I love you, Hannah," she said again. "I *love* you." She grinned. "I've waited so long to say that."

Hannah hugged her tightly. "Why did you wait?"

"Because you were with Jordan." Nikki nestled her against her.

Hannah leaned back and searched Nikki's face, curious. "You've wanted to say it since then?"

Nikki looked away. "I wanted to say it three weeks after I met you."

Hannah was surprised. "Why haven't you said it in the past couple of months then?"

Nikki lowered her gaze. She released Hannah and turned to the railing, resting her elbows on the cross beam. "Do you remember what I told you about me sabotaging my business, that I didn't believe I deserved to be successful because I was driving when Ramon died?"

"Of course."

"Aleyda helped me see I've been doing that with relationships, too. Especially with you." Nikki stared out into the night sky.

"What do you mean?" Hannah moved beside her and drank from her wine as she listened.

"When Ramon died, I felt like I took Aleyda's husband from her, like I stole her happiness. So, I didn't feel I deserved to be happy with anyone. With most women I dated, it didn't really matter because I wouldn't have wanted to stay with them anyway. And I didn't." Nikki took a deep breath. "But when I met you, I knew in the first minute, I wanted to be with you. But I didn't think I deserved anybody like you. Besides, you were already dating my best friend."

"Well," Hannah said quietly. She trailed her fingernail along Nikki's forearm. "I'm not dating your best friend anymore."

"No, you're not." Nikki smiled. "And I'm ready to leave the past behind and let myself be happy...with you." She cupped Hannah's cheek.

Hannah pressed into her palm. "That's what Aleyda meant when she told me not to let you push me away."

Nikki laughed softly. "I don't seem to be very good at that with you anyway. Not that I've tried lately. Even back when I did try, though, even when I stayed completely away from you, I still dreamt about you, still thought of you when I saw something I knew you'd like. Even when I went months without seeing you, the first time I stepped into the same room with you again, I wanted to tell you how I felt."

Hannah gripped the front of Nikki's shirt playfully. "You'd better not ever try again."

"Oooh, I kind of like it when you're bossy." Nikki kissed the tip of Hannah's nose.

They moved into each other's arms again.

"Good." Hannah smiled and looped her arms around Nikki's neck. "That will work out well for me." She slipped her fingers beneath the hair at Nikki's nape. "Tell me again, now, how you feel about me."

Nikki leaned into Hannah's caress. "I love you, Hannah. And I'm going to spend the rest of my life making you happy."

"And letting me make you happy?" Hannah whispered.

"Absolutely." Nikki brushed her lips across Hannah's.

"Jeez, you two. Get a room." Kate emerged from a door off the lobby of the dining room. "Oh, wait. You have one. Why aren't you in it?"

"Because I need food," Hannah said, glad to see a spark in Kate again.

"That's why God created the miracle of room service," Kate said with a flash of a smile.

"Where have you been?" Nikki asked.

"Just hanging out." Kate glanced at her watch.

"Are you joining us for dinner?" Hannah asked.

"I don't think so," Kate said, drawing out the words. She smiled, her attention on something over Nikki's shoulder. "Give me one minute."

"Is that her on-the-prowl look?" Nikki asked with a chuckle.

"I have no idea. I've never been on the prowl with her. We don't prowl for the same thing."

"Well, you won't be prowling for anything but me from now on." Nikki leaned in for another kiss.

Hannah pulled her attention from Kate, then did a double take as Kate stepped into the arms of a woman coming out onto the deck. And then... She blinked rapidly.

"What's the matter?" Nikki asked.

"Kate's kissing a woman," Hannah said in utter astonishment.

"What?" Nikki turned and stared. "Kate's kissing Robin," she said.

"Who?"

"Robin. You remember, my ex's roommate?"

Kate eased away, then slipped her arm through Robin's and led her over to Hannah and Nikki. A bright smile lit her entire being.

Hannah and Nikki both merely watched in stunned silence.

"*This* is the person I was telling you about," Kate said to Nikki.

Robin gave Nikki a little wave and blushed slightly.

Hannah opened her mouth to speak, but she found no words. Finally, she managed, "What...how..." But that was all.

"That night we went to Robin's apartment, I felt something," Kate said, looking at Robin adoringly, then back at Hannah. "And I couldn't stop thinking about her. So, I went back."

Hannah couldn't hide her shock. She glanced at Robin.

"She did," Robin said, answering the unasked question. "And I had felt something that night, too, but I didn't have any way of reaching her, and didn't know if she was straight, and didn't know if she was attracted... You know, all those things."

"Anyway, we went out for coffee, and then lunch. Then dinner. And one thing led to another..." Kate studied Hannah. "Are you ever going to say anything?"

Nikki laughed. "It might take her a week or so."

Hannah shook her head. "I don't under—You've never—"

"I said those things, too," Kate said excitedly. "But then I remembered something Mrs. Romani said once about me finding love where I'd least expect it. And...voila. Besides, you were never going to go back to men, and I really do hate not being identical," Kate said playfully.

"Well," Hannah said, finally getting out a full word. "As long as you're happy."

Kate grinned. "Very." She took Robin's hand. "And now, since this beautiful woman drove all this way simply because I discovered I couldn't go a whole weekend without seeing her, I'm going to take her to my room, and we're going to enjoy God's miracle of room service—among other things." She winked. "I suggest the two of you do the same."

Hannah stared after them until they disappeared around a corner on the other side of the large windows of the lodge. "Wow!" she said, still looking a little shocked. "I never saw that coming. I think I'd better pick up the pace on finding somewhere to live." She moved back into Nikki's arms. "Speaking of which..."

Nikki drew her in close.

"Aleyda also told me why you live where you live."

Nikki frowned. "I can see I'm going to have to keep you two apart. Who knows what she'll tell you. She might reveal my secret identity."

Hannah frowned. "It's too soon to joke about that."

Nikki chuckled. "I guess you're right."

"What *I* was thinking is that it would be a whole lot easier for me to focus on making you happy if we lived together." She trailed her fingertip along Nikki's jaw. "And if we find a place where half the rent is what you're paying now, it will be big enough for two, *and* you can still contribute what you do to your nephews and niece's college fund." She pressed her lips to Nikki's.

Nikki kissed her. "You have this all figured out, don't you?" she murmured against Hannah's mouth.

"I do." Hannah nipped Nikki's lower lip.

Nikki moaned quietly. "You know you'll always get what you want from me."

"I do," Hannah said again.

Nikki laughed. "All right, then. A new place it is."

Hannah hugged her tightly.

"For tonight," Nikki whispered in her ear. "How do you feel about following Kate's suggestion and taking advantage of God's miracle instead of eating in the dining room?"

Hannah giggled. "I'm *always* open to a miracle."

CHAPTER TWENTY-ONE

Jordan stared at her reflection in the mirror—well, in the sheet of shiny metal mounted on the bathroom wall. Externally, she looked well enough. Her pallor from the months of being locked inside was beginning to bloom with some color, the result of the privilege of being allowed time in the garden, and her hair now skimmed the tops of her ears. Sister Katherine had trimmed it into a short style to even it out. Jordan absently wondered how long it took hair to grow a few inches.

Her eyes were dull, though. And her brain... Her brain wasn't hers anymore. It was foggy and sluggish. Sometimes it took full minutes for her to even remember what she was doing. Sometimes, she never did.

She finished brushing her teeth, then pulled a clean, tan dress over her head. She'd finished her chores of cleaning the bathrooms and mopping the floor of the main corridor, she remembered that. Then her shower. Now, what? She studied her reflection again. There was something.

The door opened behind her.

"Your visitor is here," Sister Katherine said. "Are you almost ready?"

That was it. *A visitor.* Her father. He was always her visitor. Anger coiled tightly in her stomach like a snake ready to strike. Jordan had given up the fight, though. There was nowhere for her anger to go that didn't land it right back on herself somehow. There was no help here for anything other than how to simply survive the days. There was no way out. The only escape she'd found was her retreat into her childhood place, and her only solace, her quiet time with Lena. "I'm ready," she said through only slightly clenched teeth.

Sister Katherine accompanied her down the long hall to the door leading out to the garden. She carried her Bible. The lock released as they approached.

"You've been doing so well." Sister Katherine smiled. "You've earned a reward."

Jordan kept her eyes down. She couldn't look at Sister Katherine anymore, not without the temptation to throttle her, to pay her back for what she'd done to Lena. How could she have done that to someone she'd cared about, and how could she now look at Lena every day, at what she'd been turned into, without being consumed by guilt? Jordan's own guilt for what she'd done to the people *she'd* supposedly cared about reared its ugly head at the summons. She choked it back down. "Thank you, Sister Katherine," she said, although time with her father hardly seemed like a reward.

They stepped out into the sunshine, the warmth instantly quieting Jordan's jumbled emotions.

"Here she is," Sister Katherine said pleasantly.

The man standing on the path that wended through the garden, his back to them, turned around.

Jordan blinked. He looked like her father, but wasn't. She'd seen him…sometime…maybe. A while ago? She couldn't remember exactly. She tried to clear her head, call up the mottled memory. It was getting harder to do. Then, it came to her…*he* came to her. "David," she said.

He smiled. "It's good to see you." He looked at Sister Katherine. "This is lovely." He spread his arms, indicating the surroundings.

"Father thought you might enjoy your visit out here on such a nice day."

"Tell him thank you," David said with a nod.

"I hope you don't mind if I do some reading in the gazebo," Sister Katherine pointed toward the far wall. "I promise, I won't disturb you."

"Not at all," David said. He glanced at Jordan.

"Of course not," Jordan said with practiced politeness.

"Can we take a walk?" David asked Jordan and gestured down the path.

"How are you?" Jordan asked as they moved under the shade of a large tree. She remembered clearly now. She saw David, sitting with their parents and Palmer and Loraine. *That's right. He's in on this.*

"I'm well," he said, slipping his hands into the pockets of his slacks. "I've been working with Dad in the New York office, waiting for my Bar results."

Dad. The word tumbled around in Jordan's mind. When was the last time she'd thought of him as *Dad.* Had she ever? *Bar.* That's right. David was going to be a lawyer. Like their father. Like her. *I'm a lawyer.* She remembered. "I'm sure you did great," she said. And she was. David knew how to get what he wanted. He was smart. He was like her. So, how did he fit into all this?

He chuckled. "You always believed in me. You were always there for me." He reached above him and pulled a leaf off a branch they were passing beneath. "You know, until you weren't."

A pang of guilt rippled through her. "I'm sorry." She said the words because she'd learned to say what she thought was expected, but this time she felt it. She meant it. "I shouldn't have left you. I should have stayed in touch."

"That's okay." David twirled the leaf between his fingers as they walked. "Dad says you're coming home, that you'll be working with us. When you're done here." He cut her a questioning glance. "Is that true?"

Jordan tensed. Was this some kind of trick? A test? David was one of them. She couldn't trust him. "Yes, it's true."

"I'm glad. I've missed you." He glanced over his shoulder in the direction of the gazebo, then looked at her for a long time.

An uneasiness stretched between them.

"Jordan," he said finally. He lowered his voice. "I need to know if you're the one actually doing this. If you're here voluntarily like Dad says."

Jordan felt herself pale. She turned her head, pretending to look at some flowers. Was this it? Was this her chance? Or was it a setup to see if all of her good behavior and correct words were a pretense. Were they testing her to see what she might say once she was out in the world? That would be something they would do. She swallowed. "What do you mean?" she asked, stalling for a little more time to think.

The air between them seemed weighted with uncertainty, thick with apprehension.

David began to walk again. "I don't know. When you came out, it just seemed like you were sure of who you were. What you wanted. And now, you've checked yourself in here without so much as talking to your girlfriend."

Girlfriend? If he wasn't in on it, how did he know about Hannah? She had to be careful. "You talked to Hannah?"

"She called, looking for you. She said you disappeared and the police told her to check with family."

Jordan looked straight ahead, trying not to display any reaction, but she could feel David's eyes on her. *They did look for me. They cared enough to call the police—and David.*

"I asked Dad about it, and, at the time, he said he didn't know anything." David's tone was casual, but it seemed to hold the slightest bit of an edge. "Later, he told me Reverend Palmer had contacted him and that you asked Palmer to help you change."

Just the thought of that lie, with the way her father had taunted her with his overall plan and how they'd watched her and figured out how to take her, made Jordan livid. She couldn't react, though. David was *with* them. He was in on this.

But what if he's not? Jordan's head began to hurt. What if he was telling the truth? What if he was here to help her? What had her inner voice said? To be strong and not give up? That a time would come to act and to be ready? Was *this* that time? Her heartbeat quickened.

She had to say something. What had they been talking about? *Hannah.* They were talking about Hannah. What could she say? "I couldn't face Hannah," she said, not knowing where the words had come from.

"So, it's true? You're here voluntarily?"

No! I'm not! Jordan screamed in her head. She had to tell him. She had to take the chance. But what if he was lying and she told him everything, begged him for help? The punishment for such an infraction would break her. She knew that. Loraine, the craziest of the bunch, would break her. She had control of the electric shock machine. And the placement of the electrodes. And the duration of the sessions. And the pain. She knew Loraine would break her, and she'd end up like Lena. Or, worse. Her palms began to sweat. Her breathing became shallow.

"Jordan, talk to me," David said, his voice low. "Do you need help? I'm taking a big chance here, but I need to know."

Jordan fought to keep from trembling. It was now, or maybe never. Her father and Palmer and Loraine seemed so sure that she'd be cooperative when she got out of here, when she was *back in the fold of her family*. Maybe by then, she wouldn't be *able* to talk about this at all. Maybe the bits of memory loss she was experiencing now were only the beginning. She had to take a chance, in this moment, with David. She sucked in a deep breath. She closed her eyes. "Please help me." Her voice broke.

David's gait caught, but he continued walking. "Okay, keep moving. Slowly, like we've been doing." He looked up at the sky, then behind him, as though he was merely enjoying the beauty of the day. "I don't know where that Sister Katherine is."

Terror threatened Jordan's composure. Was he looking for the woman to alert her or avoid being overheard? She surrendered to the moment.

"Is Dad in on this?" David asked, falling, once again, into step beside her.

She nodded, relief peeking around her constant companion, fear.

"Is he behind it?"

Another nod.

"Shit. I was afraid of that. He was furious over that case you won against the firm. And then, that interview… He went ballistic. Went on about it for months. He made some threats, but I never thought…" David was quiet for a moment. "Okay…well, let's go."

"What?" Jordan looked directly at him for the first time.

"Let's go," he said.

"David, they're not going to let you just walk out of here with me." She almost laughed at the idea.

"What are they going to do?" he asked boldly. "They can't stop me."

Jordan's fear ratcheted up a notch. "Yes, they can. Believe me. If we try that, neither one of us will ever see the other side of these walls again." She angled to a bench along the path and sat. "David, these people are absolutely crazy. Every single one of them. *Dangerously* crazy."

"They can't keep us here against our will."

Jordan stared at him. *Is he serious?* She didn't blame him, though. All of this was so far out of the realm of possibility. How could she make him understand? "When did Hannah call you?" she asked, trying to be patient.

He shook his head. "Last summer sometime. Maybe June."

That's right. It'd been the beginning of June. "And what's today's date?"

"January twenty-first."

Jordan blanched. "Seven months?" *What must Hannah think by now? That I'm dead? Or just living somewhere else, happy as can be?*

An expression of comprehension dawned on his face. "Oh my God."

"That's how long they've kept *me* here against my will," Jordan said, trying to recover from her shock. "*So far.*" She drove her point home. "You don't think in all that time I've tried to get out of here?"

David ran his hand over the back of his neck and dropped onto the bench beside her. He chewed his lower lip. "I have to think," he said finally.

The fact that he didn't seem to have any ideas past marching out the front door made Jordan queasy, but then, she'd run out of ideas long ago. The fact that someone was even thinking about a possible solution was hope in and of itself. "You have to get us out of here, David. Please."

He blinked, returning from his thoughts. "Us? Who else is here?"

"You remember Lena?"

He looked at her blankly, then his eyes widened. "Lena Palmer?"

Jordan nodded. "I don't even know how long they've had *her* locked away. A lot longer than me. There may be others, too. I don't know."

"Jesus," David whispered.

Jordan wondered if he regretted coming today, but she was too afraid to ask.

"Sister Jordan?" Sister Katherine's voice drifted through the quiet of the garden. "It's time for our afternoon prayer circle."

Panic gripped Jordan. She riveted her gaze on David. "David, please." The words were almost a hiss. "Please, don't leave here and change your mind."

"I won't," David said, covering her hand with his.

"Get us out of here."

"I will. I promise." He pressed his lips together. "I don't know how or when, but I promise, I will."

"There you are," Sister Katherine said, rounding the curve in the path. "We need to go in for prayer," she said with a smile at David.

"Of course," David stood. "Do I leave the way I came in?"

"Yes, Brother Isaac is waiting for you. Did you have a nice visit?" She looked from David to Jordan.

"Yes. We did," David said. "I look forward to the next one."

When Jordan stepped back into the confines of the corridor and the door locked behind her, the walls closed in. Her heart pounded. What had she done? What if she'd been wrong to trust David? Was he, right now, telling Palmer and Loraine—and their father—everything she'd said? Would they come for her? Of course they would—*if* she'd been wrong.

She'd had no choice, though. She'd played the only hand she had. Now, all she could do was wait and see.

As she sat waiting for prayer circle to begin, each time the door opened and someone came in, her heart leapt into her throat. She forced herself to glance over, to see who it was, to check their expression. Were they simply coming to prayer circle? Or were they coming for her? But no. All of them simply entered and found a seat. Then Palmer stepped through the doorway.

Jordan froze. She held her breath.

He surveyed the room, his gaze landing on each face in turn. His expression gave nothing away.

Cold sweat ran down Jordan's spine. She kept her head down, but watched him peripherally.

Finally, he smiled and moved to his seat.

Jordan fought to keep from trembling as her clenched muscles released.

At dinner, she started when someone dropped a cup, tensed every time the door to the dining room opened, stiffened and waited when anyone walked her way. By bedtime, her vigilance, her anxiety, and her fear, had exhausted her, and sleep gave her no reprieve. In the small patches she managed, Loraine loomed over her with electrodes, and endless darkness swallowed her into its pit, never to see light again. In between, she lay awake, reliving the conversation with David over and over in her mind. *Did it really happen? Was it a delusion? Am I starting to hallucinate? Was it a trick, and now they're fucking with me?* She lay in the dim light of her room, waiting, listening. When she finally heard a key in the lock, she almost lost control of her bowels. But it was only her door being unlocked for the morning ritual.

Each day, it was more of the same. Morning prayer. Breakfast. Chores. All the while, Jordan jumped, jerked, started at every opening or closing door, tensed any time Sister Katherine or any of the brothers approached. By the time Brother Simon came to take her for her session with Loraine, her head pounded and her stomach roiled. When he tightened the restraints, she knew this was it. If David had been a plant, if he'd gone to Palmer and her father after they'd talked, she'd know in a few minutes. Loraine would make sure she knew.

But the torture was the same as it always was, and Jordan took small comfort in the fact that she hadn't been betrayed. Yet.

The days passed, long and slow. Jordan constantly wondered what David was doing, if he'd come up with a plan, how he could possibly circumvent such an elaborate scheme. As the days turned to weeks, she began to doubt.

Maybe he couldn't come up with anything. Maybe he gave up. No, he'd promised. He'd said he didn't know how *or when*, but he'd get them out.

Jordan wanted to tell Lena, to try to prepare her, but how could Jordan prepare her for something even she didn't know anything about? Even if she did, though, she knew it'd be better if Lena knew nothing. That way, if the plan failed, maybe she wouldn't be punished along with Jordan.

Jordan stepped from the shower and began to dry herself. The lights in the whole facility had been dimmed, as they always were after bedtime, and the soft illumination combined with the quiet soothed her. She'd been allowed, or rather required, to stay up late to finish a thorough scrub down of the walls, floors, and toilets in three rooms identical to hers at the other end of the main corridor. She'd wondered if she were playing a part in preparing them for new *participants*, but had to banish the thought. It sickened her. She didn't want to imagine someone asleep in their bed, snuggled against a lover maybe, with no idea that one day soon they'd be ripped from their lives and thrown into hell by their *loving families. I can't even help myself. How can I keep this from happening to anyone else?* She just wanted to sleep. She pulled her nightgown over her head and let it fall down around her body.

With a bang, the door slammed against the wall, and two men rushed in.

A bright light blinded Jordan.

"Get on the floor," a man yelled.

Jordan froze. *The bright light. The booming sermon. Beginning again.* She was inundated with the memory, with the terror. *No!*

"On the floor! *Now!*"

Jordan covered her face and dropped to her knees. She began to shake.

"All the way down."

On her stomach, she felt her hands yanked behind her back and her wrists cuffed. Then the light was gone.

A man knelt beside her. "What's your name?" he asked, his voice still gruff, but not as harsh.

Jordan gasped for air. She couldn't speak. She couldn't think. She cut a sidelong glance up at him and saw FBI in bold, block letters across his chest. Their meaning didn't register.

"What's your name?" he asked again.

"Jordan Webber." She choked on a sob. In seconds, the cuffs were removed, and she was being helped to the bench.

"I'm Special Agent Frank Jenkins. I'm a friend of your brother's. We're here to shut this place down."

Relief flooded her. She began to cry. Long, deep sobs of pure joy tore from her throat. She heard other shouts from somewhere down one of the corridors and knew it was finally over. She began to calm. She wiped her face on her nightgown.

"We already have the minister and his wife," Jenkins was saying, "and the security people and staff from upstairs. Can you tell us who's down here?"

Jordan shook her head to clear it. "Staff. A few others, maybe. I don't know," she said, giving up trying to make sense. Nothing about anything she said about the past seven—maybe eight, by now—months would ever make sense.

"Have any of them ever been armed?" Jenkins asked.

"No." Jordan said.

A loud shriek blasted down the hallway and echoed off the stark walls.

Jordan bolted to her feet. "*Lena!*" She raced out of the bathroom. She had no trouble following the sound. It was one long, shrill wail that seemed to have no end. She ran through a set of double doors she'd never been through, then turned into another hallway. She could hear Jenkins and the other agent behind her. She skidded into the open doorway of a room.

Lena was backed into a corner, arms flailing, clawing at the air.

A female FBI agent caught one wrist and tried to spin her around.

Lena went white. What came from her throat didn't sound human.

"*Lena!*" Jordan screamed.

Lena stared, unseeing.

"Please!" Jordan yelled to the agent. "She can't be touched! Please!"

The agent shot her a look, then saw Jenkins behind her.

In that split second, Jordan raced forward and slipped between Lena and the agent. She held up her hands. "Please, let me do this." She gave Jenkins a pleading look.

Jenkins hesitated, then nodded.

The female agent backed away.

Jordan turned to face Lena. "It's okay," she began, wholly unsure how to handle this. "It's okay, Lena. It's me, Jordan."

Lena's shrieks subsided to mere crying when the agent released her, but now she curled inward and slid down the wall.

Jordan followed, kneeling in front of her. "Shhh. It's okay," she whispered. "Everything's going to be fine. We're getting out of here."

Lena continued to cry, shaking her head frantically. "No. No. No. No dark. Please. No shocks."

Christ! How had Sister Katherine calmed her down? *The fucking bitch.* Jordan tried to remember. The song. That hymn. *What was it?* The garden. The one about the garden. Jordan didn't know the words, so she started to hum.

After a while, Lena quieted, but she still stared into space, her eyes vacant.

Jordan lay on the floor, as close to Lena as she could get without touching her, and repeated the melody over and over again. She closed her eyes and listened to the sounds from outside the room—crying, praying, an occasional *Praise the Lord. They're all so fucking crazy.* If not for her rage, she might have felt a little sorry for them. After all, they were probably as damaged as she and Lena in their own way.

"Jordan," Lena whispered.

Jordan opened her eyes to find Lena focused on her. She smiled. "Hey, you're back," she said softly.

"What's happening?"

"We're being rescued," Jordan said with a grin. When Lena didn't seem to understand, she added. "We're getting out of here."

Lena tensed. "We're leaving Father's?"

"Yes." Jordan's anger surged at the reminder of Palmer.

Lena's eyes widened. "I can't. I'll be all alone. I don't have—"

"No, no." Jordan had to catch herself to keep from taking Lena's hand. "You'll be with me."

Lena studied her. "Promise?"

"I promise." Jordan drew an ex over her heart. She knew it would probably be the first promise in her life she'd ever kept.

Lena started to smile, then lifted her gaze over Jordan's shoulder. Jordan glanced behind her.

Across the hall, hands cuffed behind her back, Sister Katherine stood, watching them, her expression so conflicted it was unreadable.

Jordan flipped her off and then turned back to Lena. "Ready?"

Lena nodded.

After they'd changed into the FBI sweat suits Jenkins gave them, they climbed a double flight of stairs and stepped outside into the brisk air. A night sky more beautiful than Jordan remembered ever seeing stretched above them. She reached for it and inhaled a deep breath. *I am free!* Tears of gratitude streamed down her face. She turned in a slow circle.

She stopped at the sight of the huge mansion that loomed against the deep purple sky, its landscaping lush and thick. In the lit windows, she could see FBI agents combing every room, but she realized without that, the house would look perfectly normal. The part of the facility in which she'd been held must have been underground, the gardens tucked discreetly behind it, camouflaged by the landscaping at this level. She remembered what Lena had said about the place being surrounded by acres of undeveloped property. She blanched and felt queasy. She squeezed her eyes shut. *No one ever would have found us here.*

She had so much to be grateful for. She didn't know what to expect next. She didn't know how screwed up she really was. She didn't know how long she and Lena might have to be in therapy or perhaps even under more intensive treatment. All those were things she'd find out. What she did know was that she had changes to make, amends to offer, a proverbial new leaf to turn over. This was her second chance, the one she'd asked for, the opportunity to do and be better. And she knew exactly where to start.

David had already said, and proven, he didn't hold the past against her, but *this*, what he'd done to get her out, couldn't have been easy for him. In order to turn in Palmer and Loraine, to bring the FBI down on this program, he would also have had to turn in his own parents. While Jordan had made her break from them years ago, David still had some kind of tie there. She literally owed him her life for what he'd done.

And Hannah and Nikki... She had no idea if either one of them would ever forgive her for her lies and betrayals, and she wouldn't blame them if they didn't. She *would* face them, though. She'd face them and acknowledge who she'd been and apologize. And if they could forgive her, she'd show them she could be better.

Someone stepped up beside her. She turned to find Lena gazing up at her, the way she had when she was a child.

And Lena... She owed Lena so very much. Jordan would have either cracked or ended up dead from her outbursts and punishments way before David ever got there had it not been for Lena's steady presence and reminders. And later, for the solace of her quiet company. Now, Lena needed *her* to be strong, needed her to be a better person than she'd ever been before. And, she would be.

She grinned. "You ready to blow this Popsicle stand?" she asked with a wink.

Lena smiled. "I never want to see this Popsicle stand again."

The spark in her eyes warmed Jordan's heart. They'd both heal, eventually. For now, it was enough to see the stars above her and know her life was her own again.

CHAPTER TWENTY-TWO

Nikki topped off everyone's wine glass and settled back in her chair.

"But everybody's dead at the end," Kate said, arguing her point about the movie they'd watched that afternoon. "How can they say it's a true story when there wasn't anyone left to tell it? How do they know what happened?"

Nikki smiled in pure contentment at the scene. Some days she couldn't stop smiling. She watched Hannah—her girlfriend, her lover, her partner—from across the table, took in her laughter, her enjoyment of the conversation, her happiness. Some days, she still couldn't believe it. She and Hannah were together. They lived together. They made love almost daily. They fell asleep in each other's arms. Hannah loved her. Hannah was hers, and it was everything Nikki had dreamed it would be.

Kate continued her end of the animated discussion with Robin defending the position for the component of suspended disbelief. Nikki and Hannah were both still reeling from *that* turn of events— Kate with a woman—but Kate seemed happier and more at peace than she'd ever been. In the two months since Nikki and Hannah had moved into their new apartment, Kate and Robin had been over for dinners, for movie nights, for simply hanging out at least once a week, and Delia, Marti, and Ringo had been over a few times as well. Life was good.

But Nikki missed her friend. Even with everything that'd been revealed in the investigation, even with the eight months of silence, she still missed Jordan and wondered what the hell had become of her.

At times, she still felt guilty they'd given up on looking for her, even though there hadn't been anywhere else to turn.

But then, if Jordan hadn't left, nothing about this scene that made Nikki so incredibly happy would have happened. There'd be no new apartment with its big windows and cheery décor. Kate and Robin never would have met. And Hannah... Well, simply, Hannah certainly wouldn't have woken Nikki that morning with her warm mouth and deliciously talented fingers. Hannah wouldn't be hers if Jordan hadn't left. Or would she? Nikki remembered *Sliding Doors*, that first movie she and Hannah had watched together, and considered the parallel depictions of two vastly different possibilities, the one outcome. Would everyone still be sitting at this table tonight, happy and in love, only via an entirely different set of circumstances, had Jordan *not* disappeared that Saturday morning?

The doorbell rang, pulling her from her reverie.

"I'll get it," Nikki said, chuckling at Kate's declaration to quit her teaching job and become a movie reviewer to put an end to the travesty of perspective in the film industry. She opened the door and blinked in surprise. "Dana. Hi." Dana had been part of the friend crew that'd helped on moving day, but she didn't socialize with them in general. The weight of Jordan's disappearance was always there between them, and although they liked her, it seemed like something they couldn't overcome.

"Hello, Nikki," Dana said in her typically brisk and businesslike tone. "I'm sorry to barge in like this, but do you and Hannah have a little bit of time?" She paused. "It's important."

Nikki glanced at the man behind Dana who stood partially shadowed outside the pool of the porch light.

"Sure, come on in." Nikki stepped back, making way.

"It's about Jordan," Dana said as she passed.

"What about Jordan?" Hannah asked.

Dana looked at Hannah, then halted at the sight of Kate and Robin. "I'm sorry. I didn't know you had company."

"It's okay," Nikki said, knowing Hannah would want Kate there, and Kate would want to be there. And Robin was quickly becoming family. Besides, she'd known more of the real Jordan before any of them. "Whatever it is, you can say it in front of them."

"What about Jordan?" Hannah asked again. Her gaze went to the man, and her brow furrowed.

Nikki looked at him for the first time. He was a male version of Jordan—a few inches taller, a husky masculine build instead of Jordan's slender, femininely muscular physique, but eerily similar gray eyes and an identical crook to his smile. And, like Jordan's smile sometimes, it didn't touch his eyes.

"You're David," Hannah said. "Aren't you?"

"Yes," he said. "And you're Hannah?" He shook her hand.

"I'm sorry," Dana said. "It's been quite an afternoon. My head's still spinning." She made the rest of the introductions. "This is going to take a little while. May we sit down?"

Hannah looked wary. "Of course. I'm so sorry."

When they were all settled, all eyes went to David expectantly.

He rubbed the back of his neck and let out a sigh.

Nikki noticed the dark smudges under his eyes and his weary demeanor.

"There's no easy way to say this, so I'm just going to say it." He sounded reluctant despite the directness of his words. "We found Jordan. She was kidnapped by our father and has been forcibly undergoing some experimental conversion program the minister of our family's church made up. Our father's always hated that she was gay. She's alive and physically okay, but emotionally and psychologically, some damage has been done. We won't know how much until she's done some therapy."

Hannah gasped and covered her mouth with her hand.

Nikki's stomach clenched. *We should have kept looking. We shouldn't have given up.*

"Oh my God," Kate said, obviously the only one who hadn't lost the ability to speak. "Where is she?"

"Right now, she's up in San Francisco," David said, seeming more comfortable now that the initial news had been broken.

Nikki could tell there was more, though. There had to be, for Dana to be shaken.

"She's in an inpatient facility," David said. "She decided to check herself in because we found a doctor there that specializes in psychological deprogramming for this kind of *treatment*." He spoke the last word with a note of derision.

"Her *father* did this?" Nikki asked in astonishment.

A deep fatigue shaped David's expression. "According to Jordan, he wanted her to pay for the financial damage as well as the damage to his professional and personal reputation caused by that case Jordan won against the firm and her statements in the interview she did. He thought it was the best way to get back at her. *He* hasn't said a word about any of it since his arrest."

"He was arrested?" Hannah's voice was weak.

David nodded. "Along with our mother, the minister and his wife, and everyone else involved. Kidnapping, conspiracy, assault. A whole list of charges have been filed."

Hannah gripped Nikki's hand, her color ashen.

"How did you find her?" Nikki asked. "The police got nowhere. Neither did the private investigator we hired."

"Yeah, I read the police report," David said. "My father did a great job making it look like Jordan just ran off, even ensuring the airline tickets were used." He shook his head. "Part of the plan was to get Jordan under control enough to bring her back into the family, have her make a public statement denouncing everything about that case and her accusations, her life, and being gay. Partly to repair my father's reputation, but mostly to humiliate Jordan and get even with her by ruining the life she'd made. I'd started asking questions after your phone call."

He looked at Hannah. "And there was something a little too satisfied about my father's reaction when I told him you'd contacted me, but it wasn't anything I could put my finger on. Then, when he told me that *she'd* asked Reverend Palmer to help her change her sexuality, every red flag in my head went up. She hated him. Even if she did want to change, she'd never go to him. The first time I saw her, though, she seemed so *in* with it all. So compliant. But I had to go back and check, talk to her alone. It was a while before they let me have a private visit. Fortunately, Jordan had been smart enough to fake a lot of the psychological changes so she appeared to be further along in her program than she really was. So when the time came to bring the rest of the family in, she still had the ability to think." He released a heavy breath. "She says she has Lena to thank for that."

"Who's Lena?" Nikki asked.

"The minister's own daughter. Apparently, she went through even worse than Jordan and has been held captive for years."

"This is all too crazy," Kate whispered.

"That's the word for it," David said. "Dr. Selby, the doctor who'll be working with Jordan and Lena now, has looked through the case notes that were kept on them, and he's already said what was done to them doesn't fit even the most outlandish of the customary conversion programs he's seen. He said it may take longer to reverse the effects, if he can do it at all."

Nikki felt sick with the thought of how damaged Jordan must be and with her own guilt. She pushed the latter aside. "How'd you get her out?"

"I have a friend from college who's with the FBI. I went to him. I don't know how he did it, but he's high enough up, he pulled some strings and they raided the place. They're still putting together the complete case, but kidnapping across state lines, conspiracy charges, and the illegal use of drugs was enough for the initial warrant."

A weight settled in the room.

"I can give you more details if you want, but I just wanted to talk to you before you saw something on the news or had someone ask you about it. With my father as influential as he is, his arrest for Jordan's kidnapping will be a top story in the next few days." David looked from Nikki to Hannah. "Plus, Jordan has asked to see you both."

Nikki's guilt swamped her. How could she face Jordan? She glanced at Hannah. She saw the same question on Hannah's face.

"She told me to tell you she already knows you two are together. Apparently, our father continued having you watched so he could torture her with what was happening in her life without her," he said with obvious disgust. "She said to tell you she understands. She just needs to see you both."

Nikki realized she was nodding. *I owe her that.* Jordan was her best friend, and she was going to need any support she could get. Even with everything that'd happened, Jordan was still her best friend.

When David and Dana had gone, Nikki and Hannah sat in stunned silence while Kate and Robin quietly did the dinner dishes.

"You didn't answer," Nikki said finally. "About going to see Jordan."

Hannah continued to stare at some far-off picture in her mind. "I don't think I can."

"What do you mean?" Nikki asked. She couldn't believe she'd heard correctly.

"How can I face her?" Hannah turned to Nikki. "How can you? With everything she was going through, and I didn't even have Lantz keep looking for her. I just believed what the police said about her running off with someone else. We both did. And then we just forgot about her when we started having feelings for each other. How can I explain that?"

Nikki wanted to defend herself, her love for Hannah, but the same questions were already racing through her mind. "We didn't know," was all she could come up with. It sounded lame, even to her.

Tears glistened in Hannah's eyes, and she bit her lip. "Should we have waited longer?" She searched Nikki's face for—what? Confirmation? Reassurance? Absolution?

Nikki couldn't give her any of those things, and the uncertainty in Hannah's voice made Nikki's heart ache. She'd never wanted to be something Hannah doubted or regretted. "I don't know."

"Wait a minute," Kate said, returning to the room, the sharpness of her voice cutting through the intensity of the moment. "Don't lose perspective just because Jordan went through a horrible ordeal. I mean, yes, it sucks what she's been through. I wouldn't wish it on anyone, and from her own father.... God. But none of that changes the fact that she cheated on both of you in some way. Hannah, for the entire time you were with her, and Nikki, at least the ones you know of. Who knows how many other times? She betrayed both of you."

Nikki's anger flared. "That doesn't mean she deserved something like *this*."

"I didn't say that." Kate cocked an eyebrow. "I'm only saying there are two different situations here. The first is that Jordan has been through something terrible and is going to need the support of her friends. The second is that Jordan did some things previously that, Hannah, you yourself said you couldn't forgive. You've said several times since you found out that even if she came back you could never be with her again. You would have ended the relationship, regardless. And your relationship with her was over *before* you started anything with Nikki." Kate took a breath. "And, Nikki, you've been in love with Hannah forever. That's nothing to feel guilty about. Besides, you stayed *far* away from her as long as she was with Jordan. You were a good friend, and you're amazing for Hannah. Besides, David said Jordan knows you two are together, and she understands."

Hannah touched Nikki's hand and gave her a small smile.

Nikki let Kate's words flow through her. She felt some of the guilt being washed away. It made sense. Who knew Kate, of all people, would turn out to be their voice of reason and such a champion of their love? She felt like her feet were more beneath her again. "What do you think?" she asked Hannah.

Hannah flashed an annoyed look at Kate, but caressed Nikki's fingers. "She has always been impossible to argue with."

Kate grinned.

Hannah returned her attention to Nikki. "I think we should go." She paused. "No. I *want* to go. Like Kate said, she's going to need some friends. Maybe we can still find a way to be there for her."

Nikki brought Hannah's hand to her lips and kissed her palm. "I'll call and see if we can get seats on the flight with David in the morning."

❖

Hannah paced the visitors' lounge of the Bethany Wood Psychiatric Hospital and checked her watch for the ninth time in seven minutes. She didn't know if she was anxious to get in to see Jordan or hoping that hours would pass, staving off that first moment of coming face-to-face with her again. She hadn't slept much the night before, haunted by things she had read about conversion therapy and how torturous and detrimental the aversion tactics could be, and her guilt and doubt about if she could have done more to find Jordan. Now, she didn't have a clear thought available, and all she felt was nervous.

She glanced at Nikki—strong and dependable, arms folded, staring out a window—and felt the comfort and strength she always got from her. She remembered that first night Jordan hadn't come home, how lost she had felt, and how Nikki had taken charge and called the gym. Then the next morning, how Nikki had gently coaxed her through her reluctance to call the police because it would mean Jordan was truly missing. She thought of all the nights Nikki had slept on the couch so Hannah wouldn't be alone, all the meals she had made for her, all the moments she had held her.

As if feeling Hannah, as she often did, Nikki turned.

As much of a rock as Nikki was for others, Hannah could see the worry and apprehension etched into the lines of her face. She offered what she hoped would be a reassuring smile.

They both turned at the sound of the opening door.

David came in. "She's ready."

They followed him down a hallway.

"Just a couple of things," he said as they walked. "Lena's with her. She was pretty traumatized when the FBI took over the facility and started rounding everyone up. She hasn't been able to leave Jordan since they got here. Jordan will introduce you, but don't try to shake her hand or anything. She can't stand to be touched."

Hannah listened in horror. *What did they do to the poor woman?* "Is Jordan that way, too?"

"No. Jordan's had some of her own reactions to things, but hers aren't as severe as Lena's," David said.

"You said a couple of things. What else?" Nikki asked.

David stopped outside a door. He leaned in close to them. "Jordan isn't going to be the person you remember, in a number of ways," he whispered. "Just keep that in mind as you talk to her."

Hannah and Nikki exchanged glances, then nodded.

David knocked lightly on the door.

"Come in." There was no mistaking Jordan's voice, but it wasn't nearly as strong as it had been.

When Hannah saw her, she had to fight to hide her shock.

Jordan stood beside one of the beds, looking as though it had taken hours to choose that specific spot. Her beautiful, long, thick hair was gone, now cropped close to her head, not even touching her collar. Her cheeks were hollow, her skin pale. Her once-toned arms were thin, the muscles now stringy and loose. Hannah assumed her legs were the same beneath the plaid pajama pants she wore. *She looks so...small.* The confident expression Hannah was used to seeing on Jordan's face was replaced by one of pure fear.

Hannah couldn't speak.

"Jordan," Nikki said as she crossed the institutional carpet. She opened her arms.

Relief washed over Jordan's face like a gentle current. She all but fell into Nikki's embrace. Something else Hannah had never seen—Jordan showing a need for someone.

"It's good to see you," Nikki said quietly.

How does she do that? How was Nikki always so strong for everyone, no matter what her own feelings? Hannah knew she had to be just as stunned and horrified at Jordan's appearance as she was, and yet, there she was, acting as though nothing was different. Hannah took her cue from Nikki. She walked to Jordan's side and touched her arm.

Jordan lifted her head from Nikki's shoulder, tears streaming down her face. "Hannah, I'm so sorry."

If Hannah thought she had been shocked before, now she was stupefied. Of all the things she thought might have come from this day, this meeting, an apology from Jordan, didn't even make the list. Excuses, maybe. An explanation, at best. Hannah blinked back her own tears. "Shhh." She wrapped her arms around Jordan and Nikki together and held them.

The three of them stood like that for a long time, until eventually Jordan's shaking subsided. They eased apart, all of them wiping at wet cheeks. Then they stared at one another, apparently no one knowing quite what to say.

Hannah looked past Jordan to a woman seated in a chair by the window. Her brown hair, several inches longer than Jordan's, was tied back with a blue ribbon, revealing several red scars along her neck. She gazed outside, her lips moving silently. She was obviously oblivious to the emotional display that had taken place.

"Oh," Jordan said, moving toward her. "This is Lena." She knelt in front of her, but didn't touch her. "Lena?" she said softly.

Lena's lips continued to move.

"Lena," she said again.

Lena blinked. Her mouth stilled. Finally, she focused on Jordan and smiled.

Jordan smiled back. "I want you to meet some people. Is that okay?"

Lena nodded.

Jordan moved back. "These are my friends, Hannah and Nikki. This is my friend, Lena," Jordan said to them. "I owe her a lot."

"It's nice to meet you," Hannah said, touched by Jordan's tenderness.

"Thank you for taking care of our friend, Lena," Nikki said. "And it's very nice to meet you."

Lena smiled again, then turned back to the window.

Hannah had to look away and regain her composure at the realization of how much worse Jordan could have ended up.

"Thank you both for coming," Jordan said. She sat on one of the beds and motioned to the other in invitation for them to sit. "Lena can't leave the room yet. And I won't leave her." She gave a small shrug.

Hannah and Nikki sat beside one another across from her.

"Buddy, I don't know what to say." The sincerity in Nikki's voice almost broke Hannah open again.

What was there to say, really?

"I know," Jordan said. "It's pretty screwed up. But *I* need to say some things, and you're the only two people important enough to me to say them to. The way I've lived my life hasn't particularly built many bridges." She gave a weak laugh.

Hannah appreciated her attempt to lighten the moment.

"I know you know what I did to both of you, and I wanted to say I'm sorry, face-to-face. I don't expect you to say it's okay, or forgive me, or anything. It's just that I realized in there how I've lived my life, how selfish I've been. And I might have never gotten out of there, or I'd have come out way worse off than I am, if it weren't for David. He could have walked away, the same way I walked away from him, but he didn't. He saved my life. And now, I want to live differently. This is my chance, my wake-up call, if you will, to be a completely different person. And I also want you to know that I've known all along you two belong together, and I'm glad you found that out once I was out of the way. I'm sorry I didn't..." Jordan picked at the bedspread.

Nikki took Hannah's hand. "You introduced us to Lena as your friends," she said without acknowledging either apology. "Did you mean that?"

Jordan jerked her head up, surprise in her eyes. "You'd still want to be friends, after everything I—"

"I was just thinking we could *all* make a fresh start," Nikki said.

Hannah squeezed Nikki's hand, unable to speak through the lump in her throat.

Jordan looked at her in question.

She nodded with a smile.

Jordan began to cry again.

This new Jordan might take some getting used to. With all this newness, Hannah realized there were some things *she* needed to say, too. They were for only her and Jordan, to give them some closure and make way for the fresh start they were all talking about. She turned to Nikki. "Baby, could Jordan and I have a few minutes alone to talk?"

Nikki arched an eyebrow, but asked nothing. "Sure. I'll wait in the lounge." As Hannah waited for Nikki and Jordan to say their good-byes, she watched Lena.

Her lips were moving again, her eyes closed.

"What's she doing?" Hannah asked when Jordan stepped up beside her.

Jordan frowned. "Praying." Her tone was flat. "She did it all the time when we were being held. I thought she did it to pretend she was doing what was expected because that's what she told me to do. But she's continued it since we've been out." Concern moved over Jordan's face. "Dr. Selby says that since she was in there so long, being thrust into a strange place might have made her retreat into something familiar. He said she might come out of it, but we won't know for a while."

Hannah heard the affection in Jordan's voice. "Are you two..."

"No." Jordan gave a humorless laugh. "I'm not sure she'll ever be able to have a normal relationship again. I won't leave her, though. I wouldn't have survived in there without her. I know we both have a lot of work to do, and we're going to do it together. Maybe normal for us will just mean being able to sleep without the lights on."

"I'm so sorry." Hannah ran her hand down Jordan's arm, then intertwined their fingers.

"We'll see," Jordan said, tightening her grip. "Selby's supposed to be the best." She met Hannah's gaze. "What did you want to talk about?"

Hannah sighed. "I wanted to tell you that I had some realizations of my own throughout all this, and that I think I owe you an apology, too."

Jordan cocked her head.

"I was selfish, too. In a different way. I used you."

"How?"

Hannah studied her. "Can I ask you something?"

"Anything. A new start, remember?"

"Did you ever love me?"

Jordan looked at the floor. "I don't know how to love, Hannah. That's something I learned in all this." She shook her head. "So, no, I don't think I did."

"I didn't think so, but it took finding all those emails from those other women for me to face it. And now that I'm with Nikki, I realize I wasn't in love with you either. I used you for a sense of security without having to give anything. You made me feel safe and didn't demand anything from me, so I never gave you anything in return. It was all a lie, though—the safety and security, the love, the whole relationship. But it wasn't just your lie or just mine. It was both of us from the beginning. We searched for you, even after the emails. But everything made it look like you'd simply walked away. I'm so sorry. But I'm not sorry Nikki and I ended up together."

"You're happy with Nikki. I can see that," Jordan said.

"I am." Hannah smiled.

They sat together in the honesty, the only sound in the room the slightest whisper from Lena's lips.

"I should go," Hannah said. "David said you have an appointment with Dr. Selby."

"Every day," Jordan said, her slightly crooked smile reminding Hannah of the best parts of the old Jordan.

"Would you like some company later? Our flight doesn't leave until this evening," Hannah said, rising. "We could bring some takeout for an early dinner."

Jordan grinned. "Oooh, real food? Can it be junk food?"

Hannah laughed. "You name it, and it's yours."

Hannah found Nikki perusing the vending machine in the lounge and slipped her arms around her from behind. "Don't spoil your appetite. We're dining with Jack tonight."

Nikki covered Hannah's hands with her own and leaned back into her embrace. "Jack?"

"Jordan wants monster tacos from Jack in the Box."

"We're coming back?"

"I didn't think you'd mind."

"Not at all. I'd like some more time with her." Nikki turned in Hannah's arms to face her. "Did you two get everything worked out?"

"We did," Hannah said, considering Nikki. "You were wonderful in there, by the way. I couldn't have done this without you."

"Done what?" Nikki looped an arm around Hannah and began walking them toward the door.

"Faced her. Kept it together when I first saw her. Put my own stuff aside long enough to see how much she needs us. Any of it. You make me a better person."

"Oh, I don't know. I think you're a pretty amazing person all on your own." Nikki snuggled her close. "Especially now that you've made making *me* happy such a high priority in your life."

Hannah grinned up at her. "A *high* priority? It's my *top* priority." Hannah turned serious and moved into Nikki's embrace. "I know, even more now, just how lucky I am to be loved by you. You've opened my heart and shown me what love is. I want us to spend the rest of our lives together."

"We've already started," Nikki said and kissed her.

About the Author

Jeannie Levig is an award-winning author of lesbian fiction and a proud and happy member of the Bold Strokes family. Her debut novel, *Threads of the Heart*, won the 2016 Golden Crown Literary Society Award in the Debut Author category and was a finalist in the 2015 Rainbow Awards. Her second novel, *Embracing the Dawn*, a contemporary romance, was released in June of 2016.

Raised by an English teacher, Jeannie has always been surrounded by literature and novels and learned to love reading at an early age. She tried her hand at writing fiction for the first time under the loving encouragement of her eighth grade English teacher. She graduated from college with a bachelor's degree in English. She is deeply committed to her spiritual path and community, her family, her four-legged best friend, Dexter, and to writing the best stories possible to share with her readers.

Visit Jeannie at her website, www.JeannieLevig.com, or send her a note to say hi at Jeannie@jeannielevig.com. She'd love to hear from you.

Books Available from Bold Strokes Books

A Quiet Death by Cari Hunter. When the body of a young Pakistani girl is found out on the moors, the investigation leaves Detective Sanne Jensen facing an ordeal she may not survive. (978-1-62639-815-3)

Buried Heart by Laydin Michaels. When Drew Chambliss meets Cicely Jones, her buried past finds its way to the surface—will they survive its discovery or will their chance at love turn to dust? (978-1-62639-801-6)

Escape: Exodus Book Three by Gun Brooke. Aboard the Exodus ship *Pathfinder*, President Thea Tylio still holds Caya Lindemay, a clairvoyant changer, in protective custody, which has devastating consequences endangering their relationship and the entire Exodus mission. (978-1-62639-635-7)

Genuine Gold by Ann Aptaker. New York, 1952. Outlaw Cantor Gold is thrown back into her honky-tonk Coney Island past, where crime and passion simmer in a neon glare. (978-1-62639-730-9)

Into Thin Air by Jeannie Levig. When her girlfriend disappears, Hannah Lewis discovers her world isn't as orderly as she thought it was. (978-1-62639-722-4)

Night Voice by CF Frizzell. When talk show host Sable finally acknowledges her risqué radio relationship with a mysterious caller, she welcomes a *real* relationship with local tradeswoman Riley Burke. (978-1-62639-813-9)

Raging at the Stars by Lesley Davis. When the unbelievable theories start revealing themselves as truths, can you trust in the ones who have conspired against you from the start? (978-1-62639-720-0)

She Wolf by Sheri Lewis Wohl. When the hunter becomes the hunted, more than love might be lost. (978-1-62639-741-5)

Smothered and Covered by Missouri Vaun. The last person Nash Wiley expects to bump into over a two a.m. breakfast at Waffle House is her college crush, decked out in a curve-hugging law enforcement uniform. (978-1-62639-704-0)

The Butterfly Whisperer by Lisa Moreau. Reunited after ten years, can Jordan and Sophie heal the past and rediscover love or will differing desires keep them apart? (978-1-62639-791-0)

The Devil's Due by Ali Vali. Cain and Emma Casey are awaiting the birth of their third child, but as always in Cain's world, there are new and old enemies to face in post Katrina-ravaged New Orleans. (978-1-62639-591-6)

Widows of the Sun-Moon by Barbara Ann Wright. With immortality now out of their grasp, the gods of Calamity fight amongst themselves, egged on by the mad goddess they thought they'd left behind. (978-1-62639-777-4)

18 Months by Samantha Boyette. Alissa Reeves has only had two girlfriends and they've both gone missing. Now it's up to her to find out why. (978-1-62639-804-7)

Arrested Hearts by Holly Stratimore. A reckless cop with a secret death wish and a health nut who is afraid to die might be a perfect combination for love. (978-1-62639-809-2)

Capturing Jessica by Jane Hardee. Hyperrealist sculptor Michael tries desperately to conceal the love she holds for best friend, Jess, unaware Jess's feelings for her are changing. (978-1-62639-836-8)

Counting to Zero by AJ Quinn. NSA agent Emma Thorpe and computer hacker Paxton James must learn to trust each other as they work to stop a threat clock that's rapidly counting down to zero. (978-1-62639-783-5)

Courageous Love by KC Richardson. Two women fight a devastating disease, and their own demons, while trying to fall in love. (978-1-62639-797-2)

One More Reason to Leave Orlando by Missouri Vaun. Nash Wiley thought a threesome sounded exotic and exciting, but as it turns out the reality of sleeping with two women at the same time is just really complicated. (978-1-62639-703-3E)

Pathogen by Jessica L. Webb. Can Dr. Kate Morrison navigate a deadly virus and the threat of bioterrorism, as well as her new relationship with Sergeant Andy Wyles and her own troubled past? (978-1-62639-833-7)

Rainbow Gap by Lee Lynch. Jaudon Vickers and Berry Garland, polar opposites, dream and love in this tale of lesbian lives set in Central Florida against the tapestry of societal change and the Vietnam War. (978-1-62639-799-6)

Steel and Promise by Alexa Black. Lady Nivrai's cruel desires and modified body make most of the galaxy fear her, but courtesan Cailyn Derys soon discovers the real monsters are the ones without the claws. (978-1-62639-805-4)

Swelter by D. Jackson Leigh. Teal Giovanni's mistake shines an unwanted spotlight on a small Texas ranch where August Reese is secluded until she can testify against a powerful drug kingpin. (978-1-62639-795-8)

Without Justice by Carsen Taite. Cade Kelly and Emily Sinclair must battle each other in the pursuit of justice, but can they fight their undeniable attraction outside the walls of the courtroom? (978-1-62639-560-2)

21 Questions by Mason Dixon. To find love, start by asking the right questions. (978-1-62639-724-8)

A Palette for Love by Charlotte Greene. When newly minted Ph.D. Chloé Devereaux returns to New Orleans, she doesn't expect her new job, and her powerful employer—Amelia Winters—to be so appealing. (978-1-62639-758-3)

By the Dark of Her Eyes by Cameron MacElvee. When Brenna Taylor inherits a decrepit property haunted by tormented ghosts, Alejandra Santana must not only restore Brenna's house and property but also save her soul. (978-1-62639-834-4)

Cash Braddock by Ashley Bartlett. Cash Braddock just wants to hang with her cat, fall in love, and deal drugs. What's the problem with that? (978-1-62639-706-4)

Death by Cocktail Straw by Missouri Vaun. She just wanted to meet girls, but an outing at the local lesbian bar goes comically off the rails, landing Nash Wiley and her best pal in the ER. (978-1-62639-702-6)

Gravity by Juliann Rich. How can Ellie Engebretsen, Olympic ski jumping hopeful with her eye on the gold, soar through the air when all she feels like doing is falling hard for Kate Moreau, her greatest competitor and the girl of her dreams? (978-1-62639-483-4)

Lone Ranger by VK Powell. Reporter Emma Ferguson stirs up a thirty-year-old mystery that threatens Park Ranger Carter West's family and jeopardizes any hope for a relationship between the two women. (978-1-62639-767-5)

Love on Call by Radclyffe. Ex-Army medic Glenn Archer and recent LA transplant Mariana Mateo fight their mutual desire in the face of past losses as they work together in the Rivers Community Hospital ER. (978-1-62639-843-6)

Never Enough by Robyn Nyx. Can two women put aside their pasts to find love before it's too late? (978-1-62639-629-6)

Two Souls by Kathleen Knowles. Can love blossom in the wake of tragedy? (978-1-62639-641-8)